THE GREAT WESTERN RAILWAY GIRLS

JANE LARK

Boldwood

First published in Great Britain in 2025 by Boldwood Books Ltd.

Copyright © Jane Lark, 2025

Cover Design by Colin Thomas

Cover Images: Colin Thomas

Interior Images: Boldwood Books, Alamy and Shutterstock

The moral right of Jane Lark to be identified as the author of this work has been asserted in accordance with the Copyright, Designs and Patents Act 1988.

Every effort has been made to obtain the necessary permissions with reference to copyright material, both illustrative and quoted. We apologise for any omissions in this respect and will be pleased to make the appropriate acknowledgements in any future edition.

A CIP catalogue record for this book is available from the British Library.

Paperback ISBN 978-1-83656-558-1

Large Print ISBN 978-1-83656-557-4

Hardback ISBN 978-1-83656-556-7

Ebook ISBN 978-1-83656-559-8

Kindle ISBN 978-1-83656-560-4

Audio CD ISBN 978-1-83656-551-2

MP3 CD ISBN 978-1-83656-552-9

Digital audio download ISBN 978-1-83656-553-6

This book is printed on certified sustainable paper. Boldwood Books is dedicated to putting sustainability at the heart of our business. For more information please visit https://www.boldwoodbooks.com/about-us/sustainability/

Boldwood Books Ltd, 23 Bowerdean Street, London, SW6 3TN

www.boldwoodbooks.com

Firstly, this is for my parents, Judy and Geoff Smith, for the love, support and family stories that have crept into and helped mould so many of these scenes.

Secondly, to recognise the wonderful volunteers and residents who take care of the Railway Village in Swindon. Thank you for preserving such a precious place and for sharing your knowledge and stories with me. I have aimed in the final acknowledgements to capture every organisation I should mention. I hope that bringing some more colour to the story of the works and the village by reimagining this world in The Great Western Railway Girls, will help the care of Swindon's amazing heritage thrive.

1

SEPTEMBER 1939

Lily Franklin

Lily watched her older brother, her arms wrapped around the work jacket he'd tossed at her a minute ago. Art pulled his shirt off over his head and threw that across her arms too, as though she were a clothes-horse.

'I aint your pack mule,' Lily grumbled. The cloth stank of oil, grease and his sweat.

'If you're gunna follow me around like a shadow, our Lily, you might as well av a use.' He smiled, the twinkle in his eyes laughing at her.

She poked her tongue out in reply, acting like they were both still children. She wanted to ask him something but she was waiting until he turned the tap on. She'd never catch him alone in the cottage. Out here in the yard she hoped the sound of the outside tap running into the tin bucket would drown out her voice so the words would not carry through the windows to her father.

Her father was asleep in his parlour chair at the minute. His stomach full of beer from the pub as well as his Sunday roast dinner. He always nodded off and snored in his chair on a Sunday evening. He was usually out for the count long before Art came home from his weekend shift in the Great Western Railway's iron workshop, covered in black coal dust from the furnaces and sweaty from working the hot iron with a hammer.

Sunday was the safest day for this conversation. Her father rarely woke up.

Art turned the handle of the tap and the water ran clear. Now stripped to the waist, his braces hanging loose at his sides, his trousers clinging low on his hips, he ducked down into the flowing water and let it run over the tight curls of his black hair. Lily reached for the bar of lye soap balanced on the windowsill and placed it in his searching hand.

He was meeting up with his sweetheart tonight, and he was in the best mood he'd been in for days. He was grinning from ear to ear. This was the right time to ask. On the wireless this morning Prime Minister Chamberlain had announced that Britain was at war. It meant Art could escape their crowded cottage and Lily had to find a job quickly.

Her father had predicted that in a few weeks, maybe even days, the army reservists, including Art, would be called to fight.

She had to get out of the cottage. Everything would be ten times worse when Art left. Art was her lifeguard, he kept her afloat. She'd drown if she stayed here without him.

'I want to ask you somethin,' she said quietly. She had to be careful of the neighbours either side of the terraced cottage over-hearing too. They might tell her father what her plan was.

'Then ask me,' he responded, rubbing the soap over his arms and chest, scrubbing away the black soot and sweat. Tonight, it was to her gain that her stepmother wouldn't let him use the kitchen sink because he was too dirty.

She took a deep breath, swallowed and spoke, using an even quieter voice that was almost a whisper. 'Ow do I sign up to work at the factory?'

He didn't answer. She knew he'd heard.

If her father found out that she wanted to work, he'd never let her go. But if she got a job, he couldn't prevent her starting it. It would look bad on him if she got a job and didn't turn up at the factory gates. But she needed Art on her side to defend her against her father's anger here in private.

'Art.' She nagged for his attention as he repeatedly cupped a hand beneath the running water and threw it across his skin, washing away the soap and dirt.

'Art.'

He straightened, lifting the linen square off the windowsill. He rubbed the cloth over his face.

'Art!' She was losing her patience.

As the flannel slid to his neck, his brown eyes looked hard at her. The expression told her, as his eyebrows rose and lowered, he didn't agree with her wanting to work.

'*They're peas in a pod, the older Franklin children,*' people said. She and Art had tan-coloured skin, coal-black, tightly curled hair and brown eyes so dark they were almost black too. So were Lily's younger brothers and sisters, with their wheat-blond hair and sky-blue eyes. '*Little angels,*' Lily often heard her younger brothers and sisters called. Of course, all of them took after their mothers. Lily and Art's mother had died two hours after giving Lily life, when Art was five. Their stepmother had joined the household one week later, because their father needed someone to look after the children so he could work.

Art's lips parted and he sighed out a breath. 'You can't, Lily.'

'I can. They'll need women to work.'

'Mam needs—'

'Mam can look after er own brats. An when you're gone, Mam will need money more than she needs me ere anyway.'

'They aint brats. None of us asked to be born, an all of us deserve some lovin. An I bet the Government will need to ration food as well fuel pretty quick. Money won't make no difference durin the war.'

'You won't be the one stuck in this ouse. Dad'll av no one else to clout when you're gone.'

'You'll av your little gardener to elp you, an one day ee'll marry you.'

'I aint marryin no one. I don't wanna wipe arses an wash nappies for the ole of my life. Not for Mam, an not for an usband either. I aint avin a pile of babies.'

His lips quirked at one side, in a cheeky half-smile. The judging look in his eyes became that twinkle that laughed at her without making a sound.

'Devilishly andsome,' that's what her stepmother called him. He was. Just as Lily was 'beautiful enough to tempt the Devil imself'. Which was not a good thing according to her stepmother, who regularly warned her against any man who flattered her but didn't mention putting a ring on her finger.

Lily never went near the doe-eyed fools who winked at her when she walked out.

'Tell me.' She lowered her voice to a whisper again. 'Where do I go? Do I walk up to the gate?'

He wiped a forearm over his face, leaned down and turned off the water. 'I'll ask in the offices tomorrow lunchtime. But you'll need to work it out with Mam. She can't manage this lot on er own.'

'It's Dad's an Mam's choice to av the children. They could act less like rabbits.'

Laughter choked from his throat and ended in a cough, then a deep breath. 'You shouldn't talk like that, Lily. If Dad eard you, you'd get a clip around the ear.'

'I'm faster than im. I can run away out ere,' she whispered back, holding his shirt and jacket out for him to take.

Another laugh escaped. 'Even so. Don't throw the news at them. If you really want to do this, pick your moment.'

'I'll tell them when I av a job, when Dad can't say no. The younger ones will av to do more for themselves, that's all, an Polly is fourteen – she can take on some of my chores. I've done it all since I was ten.'

'I suppose so.'

'Can I walk along the road with you, when you go out?' The younger ones were already in bed. The smaller ones crowded into one bed, heads at both ends and toes touching. They looked like a tin of sardines squeezed into the single bed at the foot of her father and stepmother's bed. Art shared a bunk bed with her oldest half-brothers. He had the top to himself. But she shared a single bed with her two oldest half-sisters. She was too grown up to be sharing a bed like she was still a kid. Lily wanted space. But there was no possibility of that unless she was earning a wage, or willing to marry.

'Why, where are you goin? Are you off to meet with your little gardener?' he teased, in a voice that implied meeting Lenny was romantic.

'It aint like that.' Her tone sharpened. Art teased her about Lenny at least once a day. 'I keep tellin you, Lenny an me are friends. Ow many times do I av to say it?'

'At least a million before I'd believe you. But yes, I'll put on some clean clothes an walk you along the street.'

* * *

The short walk to the Great Western Railway Village's park on Faringdon Road was eerie tonight. People had covered their windows, fulfilling the new blackout law. An official voice had crackled out from her father's little Bakelite radio on the parlour hearth reciting a long list of dos and don'ts immediately after Chamberlain had told everyone Britain was at war. Things they all had to do to protect themselves against the threat Hitler presented. There was no knowing when the Nazi aeroplanes would come. Tonight...? Tomorrow...?

While Art had dressed, Lily had helped her stepmother cut up some cardboard so they could black their windows. Lily had hammered nails into the window frames to hold it in place. They planned to slide the cardboard out from behind the nails each morning and slot it back in the evenings.

Normally at night the clouds were gilded orange on their undersides by light rising from the windows in the roofs of factory sheds, where the furnaces burned constantly to melt the metals. Tonight, not a single beam of light rose from the other side of the train tracks. Art had told her the windows in the workshops' ceilings were painted black in the lead-up to Prime Minister Chamberlain declaring war. He thought the people who ran the Great Western Railway knew Britain would join the war weeks ago. She was used to the puddles glittering with the reflection of the streetlamps too. Instead, pockets of moonlight, interrupted by the shifting shadows of clouds, made a black-and-white patchwork of the paving she walked over.

Head down, in an unbecoming posture that annoyed her stepmother, Lily watched the toes of her boots as she walked, making sure she avoided the puddles. The water would get into the hole in the sole of her left boot. She'd packed it with torn bits of an old newspaper to make it more comfortable, but the paper didn't stop water from seeping in and soaking her darned woollen stocking.

Art walked with his hands in his trouser pockets, the heels of his boots striking the paving with heavy steps. He had his Sunday-best black waistcoat and jacket on, and his clean flat cap. No overcoat. But it didn't look like it would rain again.

Lily didn't have any best clothes. She'd worn her stepmother's cast-offs since she was twelve. Then, they'd hung like a sack on her unformed frame. At least now she had a bosom and hips to fill the dresses out. The coat had a rip in the sleeve that Lily had patched up using a scrap from the rag bag. Beneath the coat she wore a dress her stepmother had burned with the iron. Anything bought from the St Mark's Church jumble or bring-and-buy sales was always for her stepmother. Only the damaged or stained clothes were passed on to Lily.

In Lily's dreams she had money to buy the clothes she chose – even if they also came from jumble sales, because she could never imagine being rich enough to buy a dress in anywhere like the McIlroy department store in Regent Street.

Art stopped at the park's iron gate. 'There you go. Go knock for im an ask im if ee's comin out to play.'

She poked her tongue out. 'Goodnight. Don't go knockin Betsy up before you leave.'

'Cheeky cow.'

He waited as she lifted the creaky iron latch and opened the gate. The chief gardener's lodge was at the edge of an acre of lawn, inside the railings. She lifted a hand, waved goodbye to Art and closed the gate behind her.

The path to the detached house Lenny's family lived in was shrouded in shadows, but her feet knew every step by rote. She'd been visiting this house since she met Lenny on the first day she attended St Mark's School. He'd made her his blood sister sitting on the bandstand steps in the park, when he'd cut the palm of her hand and the palm of his with a rusty pen knife and pressed their hands together, mixing their blood. She still had a scar on her palm. '*Spit swear,*' he'd said to her once too, '*that we'll always be best friends.*' Then he'd spat on his hand, made her spit on hers and shaken on it.

She knocked on the back door, with a firm fist.

The door opened quickly. His broad smile welcomed her. 'Hello.' Pale blue eyes shone with his smile, catching the light in the back hall, where the family stored muddy work boots and outdoor things. His hand brushed the long fair fringe of hair off his forehead as he stepped out. He flopped his flat cap on his head with his right hand as his left pulled the door closed behind him.

'Aint you meant to turn the light off inside before you open the door?'

'Lord, give a man a chance to get used to all of this, Lily.'

'They said the Nazi pilots in the aeroplanes will see.'

He glanced up at the sky. 'There are no aeroplanes. But I'll be more careful next time. I've already had a lecture from Mum. She's joined the Civil Defence Committee. She said we can't be the ones to let the side down, with Dad being chief gardener too. Shall we sit on the bench under the oak tree? I don't think it's too dark.'

'Don't you think the Nazis will come tonight, then?' She looked up at the sky as she fell into step beside him. 'My dad thinks they might.'

His shoulders shrugged up and down. 'Don't know. I imagine they have enough to do dropping bombs on Poland, don't they? They can't attack us, France and Poland all at once, can they?'

'I don't know. I don't know ow many Nazis there are.'

'Nor me.'

Lily breathed in and caught the scent of myrrh on the cool evening air. The perfumes from the hundreds of rose blooms in the flower gardens. The paths there wove through and around the flowerbeds so people could stroll around and around. 'Tell your dad the roses are lovely still. It'll be sad to lose them when the first frost comes. But then I like it when the green buds grow an tell you spring is comin soon.'

'The roses won't be here in the spring. Dad's been told to pull them all out. All the flowers. Everything. Everywhere must have a purpose now. Not a single bit of land can be wasted.' He pointed a finger towards the far end of the park. 'That area is going to be air raid shelters, and the lawn will be a practice parade for volunteer guards from the factory. The flowerbeds will be used to grow vegetables. We're planting carrots, beetroot, turnips, spinach, leeks, kale, onions, potatoes and all sorts for next year. It will keep people in the Railway Village in food, at least. The Government are handing out bags of seeds. I said I'll help Dad get them growing in the glasshouse, but the other gardeners and I are signing up at the factory, so' – one shoulder lifted in the cockeyed way he had of shrugging – 'I'll have to help him after work.'

He'd been a gardener's apprentice since they left school two years ago, when they were sixteen, walking in the footsteps of his father.

She caught hold of his arm, slowing his steps as they walked the last few paces to the wooden slatted park bench with its black cast iron sides and legs. 'Everythin is changin so quick. When was your dad asked to pull up the flowers? Art said they were paintin windows in the factory weeks ago. Weren't the Government ever tryin to agree peace?'

'I think they hoped. I don't think they had much faith Hitler would back down. Mad men don't back down. They set up the Ministry of Supply at the beginning of August, doesn't that say it all? Dad said they've been busy as bees in London, working on every detail to make sure the country was ready for war. People have been visiting the factory from London every week since, asking for this and that to be made. Dad said the council have just been waiting for the nod to get the air raid defences up. Most of the shelters and guns will be in place from tomorrow. And this war isn't going to be short, so the Ministry of Supply needs to be sure we'll have enough food for us here and to send to the troops. We won't be able to rely on imports, certainly not from Europe.'

'Guns...' *In Swindon...*

'They'll have to protect the station and factory. They'll be anti-aircraft guns to shoot the aeroplanes down.'

She let go of his arm when they reached the bench, tucked her coat beneath her bottom and sat, a little shaky with shock. It sounded like Lenny knew this was coming but he hadn't said a word before. Or perhaps he'd mentioned Hitler and she'd not listened because she had enough to worry about with the wars going on in her own home. She looked at Lenny. *How much was going to be different now?*

The wooden slats of the bench were damp and cold. Lenny sat next to her and leaned forward, his hands settling on the thighs of his trousers. He'd put his jacket on over his shirt but no coat, and Lenny never wore waistcoats.

'Can I go to the factory with you?' she asked. 'I want to work too.' It would be even more important during a war that she had her own money and could make her own choices. The crackling official voice on the radio had talked about everyone only being allowed a small, rationed amount of some things to make sure there would be enough for everyone. If that included food she'd lay a bet on her stepmother not giving her a fair share.

The rumble of engines, high in the air above them, silenced her. Lily's head tilted back as she looked skyward at the same time as Lenny, her heart pounding and her breath sticking in her throat.

'Is it the Nazis?' she asked him as she strained to see through the clouds. 'Should we run?'

'No, there's nowhere to run to, and being on the lawn or the paths in the open would be more dangerous.' Lenny reached out and held her hand. 'Anyway, I reckon they're ours. They sound like Hurricanes. One of the local squadrons must be practising flying at night.'

For minutes she sat in silence holding his hand and looking up, watching until the clouds parted, revealing three aeroplanes high above the tree's canopy. Almost immediately, they disappeared above another cloud.

No bombs dropped.

'You know, Lily' – he stared at the sky not towards her while he spoke – 'I want to fight Hitler for you.'

Her nose screwed up. 'Don't fight im for me. I don't want anyone to fight.'

He looked sideways at her and nudged her arm. 'You look like you bit into a pickled onion.'

Lily laughed.

'Seriously though, Lily, if they conquer Poland, they'll be heading into France and then they'll come for us, and the Nazis don't like coloured people. I heard the Nazis treat any one they think isn't like them badly. Really badly. Torture them, even...' He stopped speaking, letting her imagine what that might mean.

She didn't want to imagine it. Britain was an island. Even if Hitler used his favourite lightning assault tactics that she'd read about on the front page of Swindon's *Evening Advertiser*. '*Blitzkrieg*' they called it in German. A sudden attack from the air and on land, then constant bombardment. But how was an army going to cross the sea and invade Britain on the land? And anyway... 'Don't call me coloured,' she reminded him. Her father was adamant no one called her or Art that. He'd hit a man after church once, round the side in the churchyard. They'd taken off their jackets and rolled up their sleeves and had a fist fight in front of the congregation who were trickling out from the open church doors.

Her father won. The other man had walked away with blood running from his nose. Father Arnold had said he expected to see them both in the confessional.

Lily didn't know what the man had said to her father. But she was proud of the colour of her skin. It wasn't as dark as Art said their mother's had been, Lily's skin wasn't anywhere near black, but the colour came from her mother and she treasured it. She liked looking at her hand beside Polly's sometimes or against the skin of the younger ones when she held them. She liked that her skin colour was rarer, it made her more special.

'I don't think of you as—'

'My great—'

'I know your family had money.' He smiled. 'Your great grand-daddy on your mother's side, who was dual heritage, owned a sugar plantation in the Caribbean, on the island of St Kitts, and you take your colouring from him. You've told me a dozen times that your mother's family were well respected in Bristol because they still own the land on St Kitts.'

He didn't mention what else she'd told him, that Art had told her, that her three greats grandmother had been a black slave on the same plantation. Art had learned their family history from their mother and Lily had learned it like folklore never to be forgotten, reciting it along with him.

'But the Nazis won't care where your colour comes from,' Lenny continued. 'They'll see your skin and your hair and they'll judge. Didn't you read the story of that Jewish boy in the paper the other week? He's German. If they've turned against their own, they won't be kind to us. The Nazis have lumps of coal in their chests in place of hearts, and I won't let them come here. As soon as I can fight, I'll fight, but until then I'm going into the factory and I'll make whatever the troops need to fight the Nazis.'

This wasn't the conversation she'd come for. She didn't want to feel afraid when she was with Lenny. But... 'That's what I want to do too. Can I go to the factory with you in the mornin?'

'I'm walking over at eight.'

'I can be ready. I'll meet you ere.'

NOTICE
TO RAILWAY PASSENGERS

NOTICE IS HEREBY GIVEN

that, due to the National Emergency, the following alterations in Passenger Train travel, as applying to the Railways in Great Britain, will come into force on and from MONDAY, 11th SEPTEMBER, 1939:-

1. Passenger Train Services.

The Passenger Train Services will be considerably curtailed and decelerated. For details see the Company's Notices.

2. Cancellation of Reduced Fare Facilities.

Excursion and Reduced Fare facilities (except Monthly Return, Week-end, and Workmen's tickets) will be discontinued until further notice.

3. Season and Traders' Tickets.

Season and Traders' tickets will continue to be issued.

4. Reservation of Seats, Compartments, Etc.

The reservation of seats and compartments, and saloons for private parties will be discontinued.

5. Restaurant Cars and Sleeping Cars.

Restaurant Car facilities will be withdrawn, and only a very limited number of Sleeping Cars will be available.

By Order
11th September, 1939   THE RAILWAY EXECUTIVE COMMITTEE.

2

Maggie Abbot

Maggie threaded an arm through her oldest sister Dot's, connecting herself to all her sisters. The last daisy on the chain of four, that's what her father always said. Maggie's sisters had walked along Bristol Street side by side like this every workday for years, linked into a chain by their elbows. Today Maggie was with them for the first time, and today Britain had begun its second day of war.

Unusual noises followed her, sounds travelling from the GWR park. Shouts from one man to another and hammers ringing on metal as men erected rows of long, narrow, arched air raid shelters for the workers to run to.

Dot braced Maggie's arm against her side, as though she was saying 'don't worry kid, I have you'. The gesture didn't console but irritated Maggie. Sometimes she was willing to use her position as the youngest of the family to her advantage. Her sisters let her get away with lots of things. Edith had admitted to breaking their father's favourite pipe when Maggie had knocked it off the arm of the chair. Dot had said she accidentally caused the burn mark in the rug when she was putting a fresh log on the fire, when Maggie had struck a match and it had slipped from her fingers. Marjorie had said she chipped the vase that had been their mother's favourite, when Maggie had knocked it over while pirouetting around the room like a ballerina. But despite their kind gestures, at times, being treated like a child infuriated Maggie. Today was one of those times.

This was her first day joining them at work in the GWR laundry, and she was a woman not a child. She'd been working as a maid since leaving school five years ago, at sixteen, cleaning for Mr and Mrs Long, scrubbing stone floors, rubbing the brass and silver, brushing and dusting, because there were no opportunities in the GWR works.

People didn't leave the GWR company. Once the men were employed, they had a job for life. Fortunately, more opportunities were coming up for women. She'd got a position now because two women had married soldiers last month and GWR's policy was to dismiss married women. Even though their husbands had left for Poland hours later, a married woman's place was at home. So two positions had come up and, as Maggie's best friend's mother was the supervisor, Maggie and her best friend had taken their places, no interview necessary. It was better pay, with better prospects. So this job was important, and being treated like a child by her sisters might ruin her chances of earning more money and making a life for herself as Maggie, not the youngest of the Abbot girls.

She didn't mind being with her sisters; it would be nice to work together – as long as they didn't embarrass her. It would also be nice to work with her best friend, Violet. She also knew Mrs Turner would be kind compared to the old bat of a housekeeper Mrs Long employed. Work would be fun. She crossed her fingers. She hoped to be promoted quickly to somewhere outside of the laundry.

A beige three-wheeled Scammell lorry, painted with the GWR branding, was parked on the edge of the road, in their way. The flatbed was piled high with sandbags that men were throwing down to others on the pavement.

The men who caught the bags turned and laid them in a wall-like pile in front of the windows of some of GWR's workshops, at the bottom of the sixty-foot-tall embankment wall. They were using sandbags to protect the glass and stop it shattering if the Nazis dropped their bombs here.

The Nazis would never stop Swindon carrying on as normal, though. Maggie knew that. The families in the Railway Village were as hard as the iron nails the men forged in the GWR foundries.

Hundreds of men in their black or grey wool jackets, waist-coats, shirts and oily flat caps walked through the streets around her. A sea of workers heading into the factory.

The factory workers weren't issued with uniforms, unlike those working on the trains or in the stations. But they wore a uniform of sorts. Even in the sizzling heat of the iron workshop her father said the men wore their caps and waistcoats, albeit with their shirtsleeves rolled up to their elbows. It was not a flat-tering uniform. The men's clothes often stank of stale sweat, and some of them reeked of oil or soot too. It depended on where they worked. Maggie's sisters smelt of the starch used in the laundry. A perfume Maggie would be wearing from now on too.

Elbows bumped Maggie's side and back as some men forced their way past.

Everyone walked in the same direction, towards the open red gates of the subway that passed deep underneath the railway tracks and led to the 300 acres of GWR's workshops on the other side.

'Maggie! Maggie!'

Maggie's head turned, her arm unravelling from Dot's as she looked for the owner of the voice.

Maggie's best friend, Violet, waved vigorously so Maggie would spot her in the crowd. Maggie would have spotted her anyway, Violet's vivid red hair clearly stood out among the men's flat caps.

Maggie rose onto her toes and waved back. 'Vi! Mrs Turner!'

Violet and her mother lived at the opposite end of the Railway Village from Maggie's family. They joined Bristol Street from Emlyn Square. Mrs Turner walked beside Violet.

'We'll meet you in the laundry,' Dot said, leaving Maggie standing, trying to hold her place, a one-woman island in the flow of humanity heading towards the three-yard-wide tunnel.

When Violet reached her, she caught hold of Maggie's hand, making sure they wouldn't lose each other in the ever-increasing crush.

'I'm so excited,' Violet said. Violet had been working in a greengrocer's shop until today.

'Good morning, Mrs Turner,' Maggie acknowledged her friend's mother.

Ahead of Maggie, her sisters disappeared down the subway's gullet, swallowed whole like the Bible story of Jonah and the whale, that a nun made them read in their school days. In the past Maggie had said goodbye or hello to her sisters here. Today, she entered the tunnel holding Violet's hand tight in the overwhelming squeeze of people. Maggie didn't like small spaces or crowds, they made her anxious. She'd accidentally become stuck in the understairs closet once. Her sisters had been busy arguing.

It had been twenty minutes before they'd heard Maggie shouting and let her out.

The factory's hooters sounded.

The noise was a warning, people had scant minutes to reach their workstations. If they were one minute late, GWR docked half a day's pay.

Violet leaned to Maggie's ear. 'Today feels strange, doesn't it? I mean the war, not work. Mum said the GWR works made bombs in the Great War. The foundries here are the largest in Europe, they'll be a target for certain.'

The subway tunnel stretched ahead of them. Maggie couldn't even see the exit through the heads of the men in front of her. There were other entrances to the 300 acres site, but this was the quickest route from Isambard Kingdom Brunel's purpose-built 'New Swindon Town' to the laundry shed.

The sea of GWR workers flowed like tides through the narrow passage at different hours of the day. In at daybreak, out at lunchtime, back in again for the afternoon shift and out again at dusk. Her first memory was waiting for her father's familiar figure to appear from its mouth.

A line of electric light bulbs flickered above them, illuminating the passage.

The foul odours seeping from the men's clothing became more cloying the further she walked into the low-ceilinged space. Maggie's stomach turned over. She swallowed against a heaving sensation that threatened to bring up the porridge she'd eaten for breakfast and walked a little faster, pulling Violet with her by their joined hands.

Dot's laughter echoed back to them. Her sisters had not even reached the end of the tunnel yet. It went on and on. It must be a quarter of a mile long. Finally, Maggie glimpsed a line of daylight in gaps between all the heads in front of her.

When they walked out, Maggie sucked in a lungful of air as though she hadn't breathed for a week. Even though the air tasted of the smoke from the tall chimney stacks of the metal and glass furnaces, it was still a relief to breathe.

The throng of workers fanned out, walking in different directions towards different workshops. The men worked with steel, brass, tin, wood, glass and copper.

Violet's hand slipped free from Maggie's.

'This way, girls.' Mrs Turner led on.

A tall, square tower of scaffolding stood across the path.

'They've put that up quick,' a female voice said behind them.

'What is it for?' Violet asked, ducking under a horizontal steel pole and swinging around an upright one as she used to around the climbing frame in the school's playground.

'An anti-aircraft gun,' a stranger walking past her answered. 'There's a dozen of them goin up on site. One is bein erected to protect the railway station too. We'll shoot the Nazis down if they dare come ere.'

Guns? Maggie and Violet shared a look of disbelief. It was only yesterday that Chamberlain had said there was a war.

Around the corner, four GWR lorries piled high with hessian sacks filled with sand were parked beside buildings. The men on board threw bags into the waiting arms of men on the ground, who turned and stacked the bags into walls. Every window in the factory buildings must be being covered.

Maggie looked at the sky, as though she'd see a Nazi aeroplane. Violet's father had died in the Great War. In France. Aeroplanes were new then – now they were commonplace. Now war could travel everywhere.

'Tonight is the first time I am glad I don't have a son,' her father had said yesterday, when Prime Minister Chamberlain's voice had crackled through the wireless's speaker.

Violet had no brothers either, or sisters, but Mrs Turner had lodgers. Ron – Ronald – Smith and Frank Nelson rented beds in the small two-bedroom cottage Violet lived in. Unbidden, the scent of Ron soaked through Maggie's senses and tugged at her soul. Ron might be conscripted – forced to fight. Maggie's heart felt tight like it had cramp. She rubbed the heel of her palm against her left collarbone to rub away the feeling.

Ron was the only man she knew who worked in the GWR factory and smelt nice. He worked in the carriage shop, as a carpenter, and the scents of the woods he planed, chiselled and rubbed to a smooth surface with sandpaper in the day clung to him in the evenings. Whenever there was a reason to spend the evening at Mrs Turner's cottage, Maggie grasped it and would find a way to position herself beside Ron.

In the warmth of Mrs Turner's kitchen, the scent of wood carried from his skin and his sable hair. He was a storyteller. He liked to tell a good long shaggy dog story, with a silly punchline at the end. At times the story's punchline was not even funny, but she always laughed. She liked it when his forget-me-not blue eyes focused on her. She'd search her mind for something to say so he would look at her.

Maggie's home wasn't like Violet's. The Abbot house was noisy. Her sisters constantly teased one another, laughed or argued. It was frantic, and no personal possession was sacred. Everything could be borrowed. She'd look for her favourite cardigan only to see it on Dot. There was no order, no rules.

When Maggie spent an evening in Violet's cottage, Mrs Turner sat quietly reading, knitting or sewing while Maggie and Violet talked, and Ron and Frank either read, played a game of cards or walked round to The Glue Pot or The Cricketers Arms for a pint. Occasionally, Maggie and Violet persuaded the men to play a hand of cards with them. That was when she'd first noticed how clean Ron's hands were. Every other man she knew had unshiftable dirt around his cuticles and deep in the grooves of the skin of their palms. Not the carpenter.

Maggie liked the quiet. When she married and had her own home, she was going to have a quiet, ordered house like Mrs Turner's and a man who was clean, smelt nice and would look handsome beside her hearth. She wanted Ron Smith.

The factory hooters blasted for seven seconds, announcing the five-minute warning.

Maggie followed Mrs Turner along the pathways between the workshops, wondering which one Ron worked in.

The doors were marked with letters and numbers. The factory named workshops alphabetically and numerically. But when they reached the laundry, there was nothing on the door.

'It has no letter,' Maggie said.

'The laundry is too humble for a letter or a number,' Dot answered. She stood at the laundry doorway, holding the door open, waiting for them. 'We don't make things here we just wash them. Laundry is insignificant. No one else needs to know where to find the washing.'

'Clean linens and cottons are not insignificant to GWR's passengers,' Mrs Turner replied as she passed Dot. 'They expect freshly laundered hand towels in the trains' lavatories, clean covers for the headrests in the carriages and starched white table-cloths on the tables in the first class restaurants.'

Maggie walked through the door. Dot followed and let the door close behind them.

'You good, our kid?' Dot asked.

Maggie nodded. Though now she was here, inside the belly of the GWR beast, it was a bit overwhelming.

'You can use these pegs.' Mrs Turner pointed towards hooks

on the wall of the cloakroom, looking at Maggie, then Violet. 'I'll find you some pinafores.'

Maggie unbuttoned her coat. They were in good time, with a couple of minutes to spare. She slid the mustard-coloured hand-me-down coat off and hung it on the hook Mrs Turner had pointed at.

Dot stripped off her gloves and pushed them into her coat pocket, revealing red skin and cracked, sore, scabbed knuckles. The hands of a laundress.

Her father moaned that the whole house smelt of the cold cream ointment Maggie's sisters smothered over their hands after work. A concoction of caster, almond and rosemary oils.

'Let the thrills of the day begin,' Dot jested as she slid her arms into a white pinafore. 'How many Brylcreem stains will we have to scrub out of the headrest covers today?'

'It looks fine enough in a man's hair, not so grand on his pillow,' another of the women said, and laughed.

'Especially when oil an soot mix in with it, like it does in my Jack's cap.'

Maggie tied the pinafore Mrs Turner had handed to her as she thought of Ron again, or rather of the curls of his sable hair. She imagined if she touched them, they would be soft and silky. He didn't grease his hair back in the same way Frank and many other men did.

'How many of the men who work here will have to fight?' asked a woman Maggie knew from the village. Maggie often saw the woman with her sweetheart. She must be thinking about him. Many women must be thinking the same thing.

Mrs Turner opened the laundry door. The pungent smells of starch, bleach and lye struck Maggie's nostrils and stung the back of her throat, catching her breath for a moment. Her sisters had said she'd get used to it.

'Most men in the works will be in protected occupations. The Government need metal workers and carpenters.'

'Women can do that work,' Dot answered. 'We don't need the men here.'

'It takes ten years to train a man from an apprentice to a skilled worker,' a woman Maggie didn't know replied.

'I bet it would take a woman ten weeks to learn the same work,' Dot jested.

A lot of the women laughed.

Dot had a reputation for playing the fool, and her jovial nature had given her a reputation for playing fast and loose with lads too.

Maggie had always thought Dot was the prettiest of her sisters. Dot had the largest eyes, longest eyelashes and the widest smile. These days, Maggie watched Dot lure men like fish to a fly on a hook with her looks and her sharp wit. Dot caught a man's attention, let him buy her a drink and share his cigarettes, then at the end of the evening she would decline his offer to walk her home and throw him back in the sea with a smile and a little wave that was like a ripple across her fingertips.

'Here.' Mrs Turner lifted two small brass circles off a board of hooks. They had numbers carved in them. 'This is how you check in, girls. Remove your token and keep it in a pocket while you're here, then hang it on the corresponding numbered hook when you leave.'

All the women were taking brass tokens off the hooks.

'Then the checky can easily see if you've arrived on time,' Mrs Turner added, nodding towards a youngish man who stood beside the board. 'Brian is the checky. If you need any advice, he knows everything. He's a mine of GWR information.'

'Hello, ladies, pleased to meet you.'

'And you,' Maggie answered.

'Hello,' Violet said.

Maggie glanced up and saw the foreman, standing at the top of a staircase watching the women remove their tokens.

'If you remove a token for someone else, to pretend they're here,' Mrs Turner said more quietly. 'You'll lose your job.'

The railway works' hooters sounded for the last and final twelve-second announcement. 7.30 a.m.

'Good morning, ladies,' the foreman called from his domineering position at the top of the stairs.

'Good morning, Mr Armstrong,' the other women answered.

Maggie was struck dumb by the atmosphere. This was nothing like working for Mr and Mrs Long.

She stared, probably inappropriately, as Mr Armstrong turned his back, opened the door of his office and disappeared inside. The office was perched on stilts in the corner of the long building. She saw him walk to his desk because there were no walls on the front and side of the office. It was made from windows. He must sit up there and watch the women all day.

During dinner last night Dot had warned Maggie that Mr Armstrong would come out of his office and shout from the top of the stairs if Maggie talked too much, and he usually found a reason to shout at new girls even if there wasn't one, 'Just to put you in your place from the start,' Dot had said.

'And if he speaks directly to you, don't look him in the eye,' Edith had warned, 'That man has a real mean streak.'

'And never speak to him anywhere other than on the laundry floor or in his office where everyone can see because he'll put his hands in inappropriate places,' Marjorie had added in a voice that said she knew from experience.

The butler at the Longs' house had done that once when Maggie had been bending over scrubbing a hearth. He'd earned himself a good slap that had left an obvious red mark in the pattern of her hand on his cheek and he'd never done it again.

The threat of the foreman's appearance did not stop the other women's conversation. Their chatter flowed across the room as they unpacked the large sacks of items to be laundered.

'If you're out at the pub, best keep your legs crossed for the next few weeks, Dot Abbot. If the men are signing up to fight, they'll be looking for a bit of comfort before they board the trains.'

Dot laughed. 'I'm not going to let any man that near me.'

Dot was a flirt, not a slut. Maggie had seen her push their hands away if men got overly friendly.

Maggie often watched Dot in the lounge bar of The Cricketers Arms. Watching was a habit of hers, something she had learned to do as a child. Away from her sisters, she was better known for talking too much. She'd been told she dominated conversations sometimes. That meant no one noticed when she played chameleon and blended in. She was the youngest of four loud sisters. She could sit in a room as quiet as a mouse when she wanted to. She'd learned that people would forget she was even there.

She'd become known for being loud when she was separated from her sisters, because it was only when she was away from them that her voice could be heard. That meant everyone outside her home expected her to be loud. They didn't see her choose which of her selves to be. She could sit in the pub all night, nursing a glass of shandy, watching and not talking to anyone. Trying to learn how to lure a man.

She wanted one particular man, and she wanted to lure him into putting a ring on her finger, not buying her a drink. But getting him to buy her a drink would be a start. Ron often stood at the public bar in The Glue Pot, on the other side from the lounge. Or he'd tuck himself into a booth talking to other men in the Cricketers. His voice always carried to Maggie's ears; it had a musical quality in her head.

'That's enough of that sort of chatter!' Mrs Turner called, glancing up at the office. 'You'll have the younger lasses blushing.'

Maggie helped throw the laundry from the sacks into the copper boiling pans. The pans must have been made by the copper-smiths somewhere on the site. Everything other than the very specialist machinery was made by the men here. Her father was always proud to share that fact. The iron handles and wooden rollers on the mangles would have been made here. Maybe Ron had made one or more of the rollers. But probably not. Thousands of people worked for GWR because they made so many things, not just trains. The firm owned a huge transport system. Their trains, lorries and ships carried all sorts of goods and passengers around the world. In Britain, the company would pick up a package in a van, carry it across the country on a train, and deliver it at the other end.

Maggie's father was lucky to have a GWR cottage in the Railway Village that he rented from the firm. The workforce had outgrown GWR's purpose-built terraced housing beside the railway tracks, decades ago.

When her father had become a foreman they'd been lucky again because one of the larger cottages was free, an end-terraced property with a third bedroom. Aunt Alice, his sister, had moved into the third room after Maggie's mother passed and Maggie and her sisters had slept top to tail in two narrow iron beds in the second room. Aunt Alice had married when Dot was thirteen and left them to fend for themselves. Now Maggie and Dot shared one room and Edith and Marjorie shared the other. Maggie's middle sisters were closest in age and closest in friendship. Dot was seven years older than Maggie.

Dot told everyone she was the matriarch and she hadn't settled down with a husband or her own family because she could only handle one lot of silly girls at a time. None of them were children any more, but Dot was still the bossy one.

'Ladies!' the foreman shouted over their chatter, drawing all eyes to the top of the stairs.

He wore a bowler hat, like Maggie's father, not a flat cap. The hat showed his status no matter where he was on the site or in the town. The tradesmen wore flat caps, the middle-management bowler hats, and the senior managers, the chiefs, wore tall top hats.

'The Great Western Railway are asking for female volunteers to take on roles in the metal works!' he shouted through the steam from the boiling pans, as his gaze passed across the women, the angle of his nose suggesting that the lot them smelt like rotten eggs.

'To do what?' Dot called out.

His gaze levelled on Dot. 'I've not been told. I believe there will be a variety of opportunities.'

'Didn't we make bombshells ere during the Great War?' someone called.

'We did. But I am not sure what is required now.' He raised his bowler hat off his forehead for an instant and repositioned it. It looked like a nervous habit.

Maggie breathed in. Maybe this was the opportunity she was looking for. A chance to break away from being an Abbot girl and be Maggie, full stop. So what if she'd only worked here for one day? Opportunities were to be grasped with both hands, and if it was men's work it might mean better wages.

'I'll volunteer.' She raised her hand.

Dot looked at Maggie with surprise in her eyes.

'Me too.' Violet raised her hand.

Mrs Turner spun around, looking at Violet with disbelief.

Maggie looked at Edith and Marjorie. They hadn't lifted their hands. Edith and Marjorie always followed Dot's lead. Dot had crossed her arms over her chest. That was just like Dot – she'd wait to hear exactly what she was volunteering for before she committed herself, even though she'd bragged she could do the men's work.

Maggie was the impulsive one.

Dot looked at her sister, rolled her eyes and smiled.

Maggie smiled back.

'Everyone who has volunteered come up to my office.'

Maggie was the first to climb the stairs, with Violet behind her. The foreman couldn't do anything inappropriate with so many women entering his office.

He'd left the door open and seated himself behind a desk, with a leather-bound book open in front of him. He had a fountain pen in his hand. 'Your name, girl?'

'Maggie Abbot.'

When she said her surname he glanced up and looked harder at her face. Then nodded, looked down and wrote her name.

'Next.'

'Go back to work,' he added, when Maggie hadn't moved away fast enough.

Maggie's heartbeat thumped like a hammer in her chest as she walked down the stairs. She didn't know what she'd volunteered for.

After the last woman walked down the stairs, Maggie saw the foreman pick up a phone receiver and talk to someone.

'I'll talk to you later,' Mrs Turner told Violet, lifting her eyebrows in an expression that implied she wasn't happy with Violet's decision to volunteer.

Maggie shared a nervous smile with her friend.

Maybe they'd volunteered to go into the blistering heat of the ironworks her father described as hell on earth.

3

Catherine Pearce

Catherine formed one final tick with the stroke of her fountain pen. Her hand ached horribly from the couple of thousand ticks her pen had created in the past few days. The identical girls, obviously twins, who stood in front of her were the very last children on her list of London evacuees.

The GWR trains had been filled with children at London's Paddington Station. Then the children were deposited at various stations along the southwest line, from Swindon to Penzance. Catherine's responsibility was to ensure the right children disembarked at Swindon Station and the rest remained in the carriages. She had prowled the platform, calling out names until her voice was hoarse, then ticked them all off on her list.

She'd begun working for GWR in July solely to organise the company's part in Operation Pied Piper. When her fiancé, Charles, had been posted to Europe, she'd become a stray end, searching for tasks to fill her hands and her mind rather than think about what was happening abroad. When her father had said, at the dinner table one evening, he needed more clerks and asked for her help because the Government were planning to evacuate every child from England's largest cities if war broke out, Catherine had immediately volunteered.

She had dotted all the GWR *i*'s and crossed the *t*'s, writing a formal application, but of course with a father high up in the firm, the job was hers.

She slipped the lid of the pen over the nib as she smiled at the twins. They were short for ten years old, but very neat in appearance, their mahogany-brown hair recently trimmed into jaw-length bobs, and they were wearing identical brown winter coats. Two pairs of brown eyes looked at her for guidance and reassurance.

Their religion was listed as Jewish. A rare enough belief in England that these were the first children of that faith she'd met amongst the evacuees.

'Miss, our mother said I should give you this.' One of the girls pulled a white paper envelope from her pocket and held it out.

Catherine slipped her pen into her coat pocket and accepted the shivering piece of folded paper. 'Thank you.'

These girls had been allotted a place on the charabanc that would take them to a remote farm near Corsham. An older couple had offered to provide a home for both girls.

Catherine's manicured thumbnail slipped into a gap in the envelope where the lip was not fully sealed and tore it open. She smiled at the girls before her gaze dropped to read the short note. It had been untidily, quickly, written. A sudden change of mind, perhaps, or a response to a last-minute fear.

Please, I beg you, find my girls a good Jewish home.

The foster home the billet officer had planned for these twins was a Christian household.

This task had made Catherine feel wholly fulfilled. She'd had responsibility. She had no idea what she would do with herself next. However, for now it may include finding a different house for these girls.

'Miss Pearce, are these young ladies ready to board?'

Catherine's thoughts were interrupted by the scoutmaster's sharp tone. He raised his eyebrows expectantly. Keen to board the last of their charges.

A scout troop were steering the children from rail carriage to charabanc, ensuring no children were lost between ticks on lists. She had taken pity on a few of the youths dressed in their khaki shorts and short-sleeved shirts, they were shivering. She'd sent them for breaks in the passengers' waiting room to warm up. Though the scoutmaster kept insisting they were a hardy bunch. Some were, those standing in the sunshine were warm enough. The teenagers on the platform, standing in the shadow of its roof, with nowhere to hide from the strong breeze that swept along the track, were cold.

'I'm not sure these girls should board,' Catherine replied, her mind running through possibilities. She looked at the girls and smiled, an idea germinating. 'I think there's a better home up the hill in the Old Town.' She showed him the note. 'There was a story about a Jewish family in the Evening Advertiser a few weeks ago. Did you see? They took in a child who'd fled from Germany in the Kindertransport. I will approach them. If they say no, I can take the girls to their original billet.'

He cleared his throat and lowered his voice. 'Their parents sent them out of London to avoid bombs. You know Swindon is on Hitler's list of targets.'

'This area of the town is, because of the works. Not the old part of town. They will definitely be safer there than in London, and their mother has particularly asked for them to be placed with a Jewish family.'

'I am not sure. Old Town is not far awa—'

'To be clear' – her voice grew in depth, becoming more assertive – 'the decision is not yours. Your role here is to help. Mine is to administer. These girls will come with me. I will write a note for the driver of the charabanc so he can let their original foster family know why the girls have not arrived.' She looked at the twins and ironed out the irritation from her tone. 'I have a wonderful home for you to go to. We will see the other children on their way, then you are going to come along with me.'

The girls nodded in unison. Each a carbon copy of the other.

Catherine turned back to the station master's desk she'd borrowed for the last few days, wrote the note and handed it to the scoutmaster. 'There.'

As he left, she picked up her scarf and wrapped it about her neck. As the door thumped shut, she slipped her navy beret on her head, then tugged on her leather gloves, hung her handbag on her forearm and picked up the ledger containing all the names and all her ticks.

'Follow me,' she directed, and smiled towards the girls. She led the way down the steps from the platform to wave the other children off.

She'd been supporting the evacuation of London since the day Prime Minister Chamberlain threw his ultimatum down at Hitler's feet – withdraw from Poland or you will be at war with Great Britain. No one in the Government had expected Hitler to actually withdraw from Poland, so the obvious outcome would be that Britain joined the battle. Within an hour of being notified of the ultimatum, the trains had begun moving children from many of the major cities. She knew GWR had moved precisely 112,994 children, she'd seen the lists. It had taken 163 trains in four days. Quite frankly, Catherine felt as though she could fall asleep on her feet, she was so exhausted. At least now the last of the children she was responsible for had arrived.

She'd played a part in finding homes that would billet the children too, visiting numerous parish councils across Wiltshire. She'd also hired the charabancs to take the children there. This, she knew from working in the chief clerk's offices, was just one project the Departments of Transport and Supply had commissioned to prepare for Hitler's attacks. GWR had been asked to do many things. The minister of transport had issued the Emergency (Railway Control) Order on 1 September. The factory, the trains and tracks were all operating in the hands of public service now. The chief clerk's offices were a flurry, with everyone dashing here and there, scribbling letters and memos to go off to the typing pools to change equipment orders, identify engineers who could design some of the Government orders and have patterns in place as quickly as possible.

One of the girls touched Catherine's coat sleeve as Catherine led them out from the station entrance. 'Are the other children going to the same place as us, miss?' The girls could see the charabanc, where the other children filled the seats, in the company of some of the scouts.

'No, the families taking them in are spread across Wiltshire. It is unlikely most of you will see each other again, I'm afraid. But you will make friends where you are going. Shall we wave them off before we go?'

Catherine stood beside the girls and, balancing the ledger in her left hand, her handbag hanging from her left arm, waved vigorously with her right as the charabanc pulled away. Some of the children waved back through the windows, others looked nervous. When she looked down at the girls, they had the same nervous expression.

Catherine decided it would be best to borrow her father's car and drive the girls. Then she could drop the ledger off too. His car was outside the main office block in the works, which was a bit of a walk away. Of course, she could catch a bus from the rail station, but if she borrowed the car, if the Isaacs did not want to take them in she could drive on to Corsham, to the farm where the girls were supposed to be staying.

It was quite a walk from the station to the railway works for shorter legs, so Catherine moderated the length of her stride. The path followed the foot of the high railway embankment, passing the first cottages of the Railway Village.

'Through here.' Catherine raised a hand, directing the girls into the long subway that served as one of the factory's gates. A man sitting in a narrow wooden box, monitoring those who entered, raised his cap. 'Good day, miss?'

'Evacuees,' she explained simply. 'We are collecting a car from the works so I can take them to their new home.'

'No bother, Miss Pearce.'

She was about to ask how he knew her name, then realised she was still wearing a name badge.

The sound of their footsteps echoed through the empty red-brick tunnel. It was a good hundred yards long and not a walk for the faint-hearted.

As they exited the tunnel the girls looked everywhere. Catherine was certain they had never seen anything quite like Swindon's railway works before.

'This way.' She led them on with a bright voice. 'Are you hungry, or thirsty? Is there anything you need before we find you your temporary home?'

'The lavatory, miss,' one of the girls said.

She should have asked them at the station. There were no female lavatories even in the clerks' offices. It was the first thing one of the other female clerks had told her. That illustrious Isambard 'Kingdom' Brunel had never considered women might work in his offices was an annoyance for all the women there, and the men who managed the site had never cared to resolve the issue.

'It seems women won the vote but not toilets,' she'd growled at her father on the evening of her first day at work.

'There is no need to be crude, Catherine,' he'd answered, and no more was said about the lack of toilets.

The girls followed Catherine into the office where she worked. She handed the ledger to another clerk, removed her name badge, then took the girls out to the gentlemen's facilities.

While the girls were inside, Catherine stood outside the door, whistling 'Frère Jacques' so the girls would know she was there, and that they were safe to manage themselves as they wished.

Afterwards, the girls energetically climbed the stairs ahead of Catherine, gas mask boxes swinging from their hands and backpacks bouncing on their shoulders. When they reached the upper floor Catherine opened a door and encouraged the girls to enter. She nodded towards Miss Bollingbrook but did not speak as the secretary was busy typing. Miss Bollingbrook's fingers raced across the typewriter keys, slapping alphabetic imprints onto the paper. In the typing halls, where up to a hundred women typed at this pace, the noise was as intense as the foundries, though in a different pitch.

Catherine strode across the room, walking straight to the door beyond Miss Bollingbrook. The gold painted letters declared who worked in the office.

GWR Chief Clerk, Mr. P. Pearce

She tapped the glass pane and called, 'Mr Pearce?' She never called him Papa or father at work.

'Come in, Catherine.' The acknowledgement came through the glass.

'I need to borrow the car,' she began as she turned the brass handle, pushed the door wide and ushered the children inside. 'Oh.' She stopped still. 'I'm sorry, I did not mean to interrupt.'

Three men were standing this side of the desk. On the opposite side, her father rose to his feet. Catherine glanced at the open register in front of him. It contained a list of names.

'You are not interrupting anything that cannot wait a few moments.' Her father walked around the desk. 'Who have we here?' he addressed the twins.

'Two of our evacuees. I am taking them to a family in Old Town. If I may borrow the car?'

He nodded, not questioning her, his hand slipping into the pocket of his pinstriped trousers, reaching for the key of his Austin 7. 'There you are.' He held it out. 'You can help us afterwards. There's another task to fulfil. We need to be ready to replace the military reservists. I have a list of female volunteers. I would be grateful if you could take the list and allocate these women roles in the workshops.'

She glanced at the large GWR-made clock on the wall. It ticked away the minutes of the working day. 11.41 a.m. The lunchtime hooter would sound soon. 'I'll look at the list this afternoon.'

He nodded. 'Thank you, darling.'

You see, here was the problem – no other clerk was called darling in his office. How could she expect people to accept her as an equal.

She glanced at the other men in the room before turning away. She remembered one of them; he'd disembarked from a train earlier. Come to that, the other men may have disembarked with him. They had been wearing top hats, so they were not GWR clerks.

With a hand on their shoulders, she steered the girls out of the room.

'Do Mummy and Daddy have a car?' she asked the girls as they walked downstairs.

'Father drives a Rolls Royce.'

Well, that told Catherine! War did not discriminate by wealth or status. They would all be levelled up by this, shaken up like sand until every grain of society lay flat. Rich and poor children alike needed to be moved, not only for their safety, but to reduce the pressure on those who might be managing the bodies of the wounded and dead within days. GWR trains were also ready to move the wounded, if necessary. Many of the GWR carriages and ships were being converted into mobile hospitals, and some of the vans were being refitted to be used as ambulances in London. She knew the plans because, rightly or wrongly, her father discussed the amount of work the factory had to deliver over dinner in the evenings.

When Catherine opened the car door the girls climbed in and settled on the cream leather of the back seat, rucksacks and gas masks between them. Catherine closed the door, took the driver's seat and started the engine.

There were three main roads that climbed the steep hill to the oldest part of Swindon. People called the area at the top of the hill the 'Old Town'. Old Town was a nickname coined long ago by Swindonians who wanted to separate themselves from the working-classes in Brunel's new town. Her home stood in Bath Road, on the crest of the hill at the top of the Kingshill Road. The house was so high up she could see for miles through the windows of the attic rooms, looking over Swindon's rooftops to the first hills of the Cotswolds on one side and the chalk downs, where ancient tribes of people had carved white horses into the hills, on the other.

Usually, Catherine left the GWR site through the Rodbourne Road gate. Today, she decided to drive across the site to use the Drove Road gate. She drove more cautiously than usual; the war preparations meant there were lorries in unexpected places and newly erected platforms to hold anti-aircraft guns, as well as numerous significantly dented sheets of metal left outside workshops, haphazardly discarded – for the moment, anyway. She knew some of the men were testing the thickness and construction of metals to identify the density that would survive bullets and bombs.

As she drove through the open gates the hooters sounded, announcing the lunch break.

She took the fastest but steepest route, turning onto Victoria Road.

Her mind returned to her own home as the car climbed.

Most evenings she retreated to the attic rooms, sitting in a chair close to a window, where she watched the sun set and wrote letters to Charles. At the top of the house, she imagined she could see all the way to France. Sometimes she imagined she was a bird and would fly across the English Channel to be with him. Or she'd pretend the attic rooms were their home, as no one else used the upper floor of the house. She'd imagine he was sitting beside her, smoking a cigarette and reading the paper, a glass of whisky in his hand, balanced on the arm of the chair, and the paper open wide across his lap.

The attic rooms had been empty for years. The last live-in servant was the nanny who'd cared for her and her four brothers. Now the only help her mother employed was Mrs Fletcher, who came daily to handle the house and kitchen work.

From the attic windows, if the Luftwaffe attacked Swindon, Catherine would have a horrible bird's-eye view. She could see from those windows how the houses and shops had spread from the hubs of the old and new towns and flowed like streams of lava around the hill and out into the fields, consuming the surrounding hamlets and villages.

GWR alone employed over fourteen thousand people, and other companies had come to Swindon to poach their skilled workers. The town was a hive of industrial works and workers. It would be a target, with its crucial train links as well as the factories, but they were preparing.

Watching from the attic windows on the other side of the house, looking away from the town, she'd seen people build great domes on the flat tops of the chalk downs beyond Wroughton. Aircraft hangers. They could be creating an airfield up there to protect Swindon, but surely that would mean aeroplanes might shoot at each other in the sky above the town.

Perhaps the scoutmaster was right. She should not have kept the girls here. But wasn't faith the most important thing at times like this?

The Isaacs lived in Albert Street. The family had stood out in her memory because of their kindness towards the Jewish boy and also because, within a few days of the newspaper article being published, Catherine had seen the name Isaacs on a salary card. Naomi Isaacs of Albert Street had been appointed to a position in the carriage workshops. The year of birth on the card – 1918, the same as Catherine's – implied Naomi was a daughter of the family.

The car reached the crown of the hill, she changed gear, turned into Albert Street, stopped against the kerb, pulled on the handbrake and turned the engine off.

'Wait here, girls. I will only be a moment.' She opened the door and slipped out, not waiting for their reply.

No one else was in the street. She walked along the narrow, uneven pavement, walking down the hill and looking at the numbers on the doors of the slender terraced houses. She did not remember the house number but recognised an unusual arched lintel above a basement window and three very steep steps to a front door. This was the house the family had stood in front of in the paper's image. She climbed the steps and knocked on the door, her heartbeat pounding.

There was no sound of life. She knocked again. There was no way of knowing if anyone was inside: with the house being on a steep section of the hill, the pavement sloped so significantly that even if she stood only a few feet away from the steps to the front door the front window would be too high for her to look through. She knocked one last time.

At last footsteps sounded on the other side of the door. A bolt was released.

Catherine swallowed, realising her mouth had become dry. This might be a dreadfully rude assumption.

The door opened cautiously. The German boy held it. He was taller than she'd assumed from the picture, five foot and a few inches, with a long fringe of black hair and brown eyes that asked warily, *Who are you? Why are you here?*

'Is Mrs Isaacs at home?' Catherine asked, using the friendly tone she'd deployed to reassure the children at the station for the past few days.

He opened the door further, revealing a woman walking along the hall, the woman Catherine had seen beside the boy in the paper. The woman dried her hands on a tea towel. The apron she wore over her dress was dusted with flour.

'Thank you, Dietrich. Would you take this?' She handed the boy the tea towel. He walked away.

Catherine took a deep breath and began explaining herself. 'Good afternoon, Mrs Isaacs. I am Miss Catherine Pearce...' She had a terrible habit of stopping after she gave her name these days, as though everyone in Swindon should know the daughter of GWR's chief clerk. Working in the factory offices, where everyone knew she was Catherine PEARCE, had given her narcissistic characteristics.

Catherine held out her hand. She still wore her leather gloves.

A slightly floury hand accepted Catherine's.

She held the hand of this generous woman with firm respect as they shook, while Mrs Isaacs' handshake was more tentative.

'I saw your story in the paper,' Catherine said as they released hands. 'It was a wonderful thing to do, to take in the boy. I know it must seem very odd of me just to turn up at your door, but I have been administrating the dispersal of the evacuees from London, and, well, I have two girls, you see. Sisters. Twins. They were to be billeted on a farm outside the town, but they gave me a note from their mother. They are Jewish, that is the thing, and their mother particularly asked for them to be found a home with a Jewish family. The farmer and his wife are not Jewish. So, I wondered...' Catherine ran out of words, as her throat dried entirely.

Mrs Isaacs did not reply.

Catherine took a breath, swallowed, and began again. 'I know this is a terrible presumption, but you are the only Jewish family I know of, and you are obviously willing to take in children. I know I can trust you... If you agree... Or perhaps you know another family... The girls are in the car.' She pointed back along the street. 'They are ten, so they will be able to help around the house. They need not be a burden.' Now she was begging and babbling.

'Sorry.' The tempo of Catherine's speech dropped away. 'All of this is so strange, isn't it? I think I'm in shock. One minute we are all going about our own business like every other day and now...' She swallowed again, fighting back unexpected tears. 'I should not have put this pressure on you.' She brushed the silly tears aside. She was not one to blub normally. She was made of tougher stuff. But the tears expressed her concern for Charles, not herself. His last letter had said his regiment was heading into Poland, where the Nazis' bombs were raining down.

'No.' Mrs Isaacs spoke at last. 'Of course you should have asked. If I was their mother sending them off to who-knew-where, I would want to know that at least I had the comfort they would be with a Jewish family. Bring them inside. They will have to share a room with my daughter, and they might be on a mattress on the floor, but they will be welcome, and they will be treated like family and made to feel at home.'

'Thank you.' Relief flooded through Catherine's chest.

She walked up to the car, opened the back door and beckoned the girls out. 'Come along. This will be your home. This is Mrs Isaacs.'

'Hello, girls!' Mrs Isaacs called, walking down the front steps to welcome the girls as they scrambled out, backpacks pulling on their shoulders and gas mask boxes dragging across the seat.

'My name is Abigail,' Mrs Isaacs said, holding out a hand for them to shake in turn. 'You'll be staying with me.'

'This is Golda and Esther.' Catherine introduced them both as she was not sure which was which.

The girls climbed the front steps ahead of Mrs Isaacs, who continued to address them. 'My daughter is Naomi. She'll be home for her lunch in a moment, and we have a young man, Dietrich, living with us too, as well as my sons, Nathaniel and Samuel. They'll be home later, as will Mr Isaacs, but they usually eat their lunch at work. Are you hungry? Dietrich and I were just about to eat. We were waiting for Naomi.'

Dietrich reappeared at a door further along the hall as one girl's stomach rumbled so loudly it made them all laugh.

'I suppose that's a yes then.' Mrs Isaacs smiled. 'Come in and sit by the fire. Will you stay for lunch, Miss...? I am sorry, I have forgotten your name.'

'Catherine. There's no need for formality.' It would be inconsiderate to drop the children and run. 'Yes, thank you. That's kind of you. If there's enough...?'

'There's plenty. I have just finished the week's baking, and I am sure we can stretch what's in the larder among us.'

Catherine stopped to wipe her feet on the mat as Mrs Isaacs helped the girls remove their backpacks and coats and took their gas mask boxes. Catherine released the buttons of her coat, took off her scarf and gloves and pressed them into a pocket.

'Let me take your coat,' Dietrich offered, the syllables in the English words deepened by a German accent.

The walls in the terraced cottage were a little wonky and the floor sloped in places and creaked. The house was older than it looked on the outside, and though it was narrow it was also long. It was, though, still a humble size compared to the Palladian terraced property Catherine's father owned. She followed Mrs Isaacs past a front room, which contained a long dining table, to a back parlour. The delicious scent of freshly baked bread came from what must be the kitchen beyond that, and the smell of something sweet. Biscuits perhaps.

'Please, take a seat.' Mrs Isaacs raised a hand and directed Catherine and the girls into the warm room.

Catherine entered the room and perched on a narrow wooden settle beside the girls.

Flames licked about glowing coals in the fire grate. The warmth was welcome. Catherine held her palms towards the fire, suddenly realising how cold she'd become, standing on the station platform.

'You must have a cup of sweet tea while we eat.' Mrs Isaacs' gaze met Catherine's. 'You're as white as a ghost. Dietrich, will you warm the kettle while I finish preparing the lunch?'

Left alone in the room with the girls, Catherine's gaze shamelessly circulated, exploring the space as avidly as the girls did.

A sewing basket stood open beside the fireplace, where the chair's cushion had a deep dent. Late blooming roses, probably cut from a garden, stood in a vase on a crocheted mat on a side table. Beside the vase was a cigarette box and a book with a strand of ribbon marking a page. Across the room there was a chessboard with pieces seemingly left mid game. But most telling was the short branch of wood with some of the bark carved away, left on a wooden chair. The curls of wood that had been shaved off the branch to create whatever was in progress were still in the trug that had caught them on the floor. She assumed it was Dietrich's work.

Nostalgia threaded through Catherine's thoughts. The room reminded her of her grandparents' home. They were born in the Railway Village, as was her father. She had visited them there even when he thought himself too grand and no longer would.

Mrs Isaacs and Dietrich walked back into the room carrying full trays.

The sound of the front door opening drew Catherine's attention beyond the room.

'Ima! Dietrich!' a woman's voice called. The bump of the closing door followed.

'Here, darling. We have some unexpected guests I need to introduce you to.' Mrs Isaacs smiled at the twins, who were watching and listening to everything, wide-eyed.

Footsteps, a woman's low-heeled shoes, walked along the floorboards in the hall.

Catherine rose from the seat.

'Do sit down,' Mrs Isaacs told Catherine as she set the tray down on a low table. 'No need for ceremony. It's my daughter, Naomi. She works in the GWR factory now and comes home, if she can, for lunch.' Mrs Isaacs turned to greet her daughter as Dietrich lifted the teapot to pour.

'We have two more guests in our home, Naomi, for a little while at least. Meet Golda and Esther. They arrived on the train from London today and were looking for a Jewish family.'

'Hello.' Naomi's gaze and smile welcomed the twins, hiding any surprise admirably.

'And this is Catherine, who brought the girls to us.' Mrs Isaacs looked at Catherine. 'I'm sorry, I have forgotten your surname...'

'Just Catherine is fine.'

'Hello.' Naomi held out a hand, stepping forward.

'Hello. I...' Catherine repeated her reasons for bringing the girls here as everyone began to eat.

The fresh bread was warm and as delicious as it smelt. The butter melted as Catherine spread it with a knife; such small novelties were to be relished today. If the war was long, simple pleasures like butter and flour might become rare luxuries. Petrol rationing had begun even before Britain declared war, which meant the transport of products and produce from country to town would be more difficult. The GWR carpenters were building carts to return to the use of horse-drawn vehicles.

Following Catherine's explanation, Naomi and her mother

calmly pried the twins' tongues loose with careful questions. Catherine watched the girls' shoulders relax as they became more animated, rapidly describing their parents and their home.

When the clock chimed the half-hour, Naomi stood hurriedly, as though she'd forgotten time passing. 'I must get back to work.'

Catherine put her plate on the tray left on a low table. 'I can drive you back. I am returning to the GWR works myself. I'm a clerk there.'

'I couldn't ask—'

'You are not asking. I offered.'

'We'd best be on our way, then. I'll fetch our coats.' Naomi left the room.

'Goodbye girls.' Catherine smiled towards them, then looked at Mrs Isaacs. 'May I visit occasionally?'

'Of course.'

'Thank you, and thank you for taking them in. It was nice to have met you, Dietrich.' Catherine left the room. In the hall, she accepted her coat from Naomi.

Once more wrapped up against the autumn cold, Catherine led the way to the car. She climbed in and reached over to open the front passenger door. She started the engine as Naomi slid into the seat and pulled the door closed.

The first warning call from the factory hooters travelled up the hill as Catherine drove out of Albert Street.

'This is a long way to come in the time you have to eat lunch,' Catherine said.

Naomi sat with her hands in her lap, looking apologetic for her presence in the car.

Catherine drew in a breath and made a decision that was utterly unlike her – she would lie. 'I was lucky. I borrowed the chief clerk's car so I could return quickly.' She told herself it was out of kindness to make Naomi feel more comfortable and that it was not really a lie, she had only omitted to say the chief clerk was her father.

'My mother appreciates my company,' Naomi replied. 'She keeps herself busy, but poor Dietrich isn't very talkative. My visits break up their day.'

'Keeping busy is sensible.' Catherine kept her eyes on the road.

'I used to sew in my father's shop on Wood Street. He's a tailor. But in July, when I heard GWR were asking for people to sew stretchers and bunks, I applied. The carpenters have stripped out compartments and seating and made many trains ready to carry the wounded.'

'I began work in the summer too. I could not sit at home doing nothing while peace slipped through our fingers. I helped plan the evacuation of children from London, but now we are at war I am not sure administration is the best way for me to help.' She took her eyes off the road for a moment and glanced at Naomi. 'I hope you don't mind that I brought the girls to your mother.'

'Of course not. Helping the children is one more way to fight.'

Catherine nodded. Then found herself confiding, in a voice that expressed her fear... 'I have a fiancé, and brothers, in the British Army. Their regiments are in Europe.' Perhaps it was because Naomi sat beside her, not facing her, that drew emotions from Catherine.

'My brothers said they will sign up to fight. I wish I could. I would sign up in a heartbeat, if the army would take women.'

'I would too. I would much rather be alongside Charles – my fiancé – than administering ledgers here. I am sure I could stop the Nazis in their tracks as successfully as any man if I had a weapon in my hands.'

A note of humour choked from Naomi's throat and the sound brought a smile to Catherine's lips. She needed the medicine of laughter. Evacuating the children had meant the last few days had been mentally exhausting. She would much rather feel a physical fatigue. At least if she was working with her hands she might sleep, rather than questioning herself a hundred times in bed at night about what she might have forgotten, and then worrying over where Charles was.

She really would rather have a gun in her hands in Poland.

'Sewing is too easily done. My thoughts wander to dark places even though my hands are busy. I... I think of holding guns and shooting men who do bad things,' Naomi admitted, as though she had read Catherine's mind. 'The Nazis are inhuman. The things they are doing... I don't even want to imagine it.'

Catherine glanced at Naomi. Naomi's colour was rosy. She had admitted a very dark thought.

'Me too, I mean I would happily shoot them,' Catherine confessed, then redirected her attention to the road. The streets at the bottom of the hill were crowded with workers hurrying back to the factory. 'Did you volunteer to transfer today?' she asked.

'Transfer?'

'The company has gathered a list of women who are willing to move to men's roles. I am looking at the list this afternoon. Is your name there?'

'No. I didn't hear anyone asking the women in the carriage works. But I only recently started and they need me to sew.'

'There will be very little sewing to do once the hospital carriages are complete. There will be no new passenger carriages for a while. Would you like to add your name to the list? I am not sure where you would be working, though. The factory will be making all sorts of wartime equipment. If you volunteer, I will too. I think it will be better than managing lists. I can place us somewhere together.'

'I would like that.'

Catherine glanced sideways and met Naomi's gaze, her spirits rising with a renewed sense of purpose.

'Sign me up,' Naomi confirmed.

4

Catherine Pearce

Catherine parked the car in the space allocated for the chief clerk's use. She had dropped Naomi off closer to the carriage works.

She joined the other clerks returning to the rows of desks in the long hall below her father's office.

Catherine sat in the chair in front of her empty desk. Which was odd to face when the desk had been filled with the ledgers of children's names and the corresponding billets she'd been juggling for weeks. She hid a yawn behind her hand, wishing she could go home and sleep. But now she had to be the one to manage the list of female volunteers or she would not be able to add her own and Naomi's names. Should she run upstairs and collect the list from Miss Bollingbrook?

A man placed a black leather-bound ledger on the desk in front of her just as she was about to rise.

'Mr Pearce said, rather particular like, that you would manage the register of the women who have volunteered to fill the vacancies.' His snooty tone reminded her she was not welcome in the central clerks' offices.

The men made sure she knew they did not accept her as a true employee. They spoke in tones and used words that made her feel unfairly favoured and under-qualified. Their attitude was unsurprising considering her father called her darling and asked her *rather particular like* to manage tasks, singling her out in a hall of forty-five clerks when she was an unqualified apprentice.

She'd said nothing to her father about the men's behaviour. She preferred to fight her own battles.

She opened the register and looked at the women's names. It occurred to her that no one would know if she did not write Catherine Pearce but recorded herself by another name. Naomi did not know her surname. Then, also, no one would know she was the chief clerk's daughter. She reached for a fountain pen, turned the pages until she reached the end of the list, then quickly wrote.

Catherine Clifford
  Naomi Isaacs

She slipped the pen back into its holder.

The first thing to do would be to find the women's record cards. She could check their ages and capabilities. But she also needed a list of the positions to appoint them to. Where was that?

'Good afternoon, gentlemen, and ladies!'

Catherine looked up, her gaze turning to the door. 'Hello, Joe.'

'Good afternoon.'

Many of the clerks also greeted Joe Marsh, one of the carpentry foremen. His visits always brought a welcome change of atmosphere. Joe was a good-humoured man and he treated Catherine as he treated every other clerk. Consequently, she had a habit of glancing at the door in the afternoons waiting for his appearance, even though his visits were brief. The checkies managed the daily attendance registers so that the payroll clerks could note non-attendance. Joe was the only foreman who brought the register across to the offices.

He walked with a limp. He had one stiffer leg. She'd told him, when she'd first joined GWR, the register could be collected. The other clerks in the room had broken into laughter. Of course, having worked for GWR for years, Joe knew what was possible. He had not laughed and added to her humiliation but thanked her kindly for the offer. *'I like the exercise,'* he'd said. *'It's good for me to move around in the day.'*

Catherine had favoured his company ever since.

'Is everybody enjoying the day?' he asked the room in general. 'The sun's come out.' He shuffled across the room with his uneven gait.

'I can't see the sun through the sandbags,' a man at the far end of the hall responded.

'Enjoying? Didn't you hear Chamberlain announce a war,' another man said.

'There was a dark cloud over there at lunchtime.' An apprentice clerk pointed to the north wall.

A woman close to Catherine bit back. 'It's great you can enjoy the day, Joe. I have a stack of work, thanks to the Ministry of Supply.'

'Righty-ho,' Joe answered with a smile, as jolly as ever. 'Nice to know you have it all in hand.'

Catherine had an urge to laugh. He always brought a smile to her lips. He was never mindful of the miserable mood of the clerks' hall.

Joe was younger than most of the foremen. The foremen, in general, had joined the company as apprentices, worked hard and, after about thirty years of gathered knowledge and skilled experience, with a handful of determination too, progressed to their senior positions. This slow rise, and the personality required to stand out among a crowd of skilled men all trying to make the same move, meant most of the foremen had also developed an over-inflated ego and a stubborn belief that everything they said was the only right answer. Her father grumbled over dinner about the stubbornness of foremen and their refusal to listen to directions. Her mother would sit opposite, nodding as though she was not thinking about pots calling kettles black – Catherine's father had his own stubborn streak. But when Catherine complained about her father's rigid opinions, her mother often pointed out that Catherine had the same flaw.

Catherine didn't know the history behind Joe's appointment, but he did not have the air of a stubborn man suffering with over-inflated self-worth and he was, she would guess, in his late thirties or early forties. One clear sign of his difference was that he trusted the men to continue working while he left the workshop to walk here. In other workshops she'd collected or taken information to or from, the foremen rarely took their eyes off those working on the shop floor, even while they spoke to her.

He handed his register to another clerk, whose name she could not recall, and walked across the room towards Catherine.

She met his gaze and they shared a smile. Through their conversations in the few minutes he spent here each day, she knew Joe better than any of the clerks she spent the whole day with.

'I have not seen you for a few days, Miss Pearce. How are you?' His smiling hazel eyes were different from Charles's green-tinted ones. The different shades in Joe's hazel irises created the colour of copper beech leaves – she'd always likened Charles's eyes to moss.

Every day Joe picked her out for a longer conversation. It probably provided another reason for the other clerks to gossip, but she didn't care. The GWR way of life flowed in her blood and she liked spending time with Joe. He smelt of the wood that was worked in the areas he managed.

Her father had joined GWR as a boy, and his father and grandfather, and great-grandfather before him, and every generation had told their stories to hand down. So Catherine felt as though she understood the lives of the people in GWR and the operation of the firm as thoroughly as the mechanics understood the steam engines they built in the sheds. She knew how a steam train operated and every aspect of the carriages from third to first class. Joe felt like her peer more than the stuffy men in this room who had no idea how men made things in the workshops.

'I've been working at the rail station, welcoming the evacuated children and making sure they reach the right homes.'

Joe rested a hip on the side of her desk, as he always did, she presumed to rest the leg that gave him a limp. His auburn eyebrows kicked up. 'I didn't realise you were helping the young ones. I've seen them flowing out from the station.'

She breathed in his pleasant scent. He knew who her father was, but she didn't think his kindness was related to that. 'How are you all in the carpentry workshops?'

'Busy.' His smile drooped at the edges. 'Very busy. I'm interviewing for new apprentices tomorrow. There's been a few lads turning up at the gates and asking for work. They want to get involved in the war effort, they're too young to sign up for the forces and there's plenty of work for them here.'

She looked down at the names in the open register. He looked down too. She closed it. Her father had instilled in her the need for everything to be secret, even things that had no need to be secret because *'there will be spies in Swindon and if they discover anything, even simple unsensitive information, they may work out where or by whom the secret work is being undertaken.'* She did not think Joe was a spy, but he might mention a name, thinking it was harmless, and it was better not to take any risks.

'What is it you have there?' He nodded towards the ledger she'd shut.

She drew in a breath. He'd know they were recruiting women, and she needed to ask someone about the work they wanted the women to do. The other clerks would deliberately be awkward. They did not like helping *'the favoured child'.* She'd heard someone call her that when they didn't know she was listening.

She lowered her voice, hoping the others wouldn't hear and so he knew to keep it private. 'Can I ask you something?'

'Of course.' His palm pressed on the desk and he leaned forward slightly.

She rested a hand on the leather cover of the ledger. 'This is a list of women who are happy to take on the roles the reservists will leave vacant. Have the foremen met? Or the chiefs perhaps? To agree the priorities of the positions to be filled. Or should I walk around the workshops to ask? Mr Pearce asked me to match the women to the jobs, but with no list of jobs, I can't.'

'There's no meeting that I've been made aware of,' he whispered back. 'But I was asked to contribute to a list.' He straightened up, shifting his hip off the desk, stood tall, turned and looked across the desks. He was tall when he stood to full height, over six foot. He must be able to see what was on top of everyone's desks. That had not occurred to her before today.

He smiled suddenly. He'd noticed something. He walked across to one of the apprentices, who knelt on the floor, slotting Manila cardboard files into a drawer. Every worker had a file, there were rows of drawers with alphabetical labels. Catherine had never been asked to do the filing, even though she was also an apprentice – probably because her father had said something.

'Harry, are the lists of the current vacancies on Mr Quince's desk?'

The young man pushed the drawer shut and rose to his feet. 'Yes, sir.'

Catherine rose to respond, but Joe was already moving, his uneven gait a little more pronounced than usual. 'Mr Quince!' he called.

Mr Quince must have heard Joe, but his head did not rise to acknowledge the use of his name. Catherine had noticed he suffered with selective hearing, particularly when she spoke. He was the most senior clerk in the office and her direct manager. Catherine decided to play the same game, sitting down and opening the ledger containing the women's names, trying to appear as though Joe was not acting on her behalf.

'Mr Quince' – Joe was right in front of him now, and the other clerks in the room had fallen so quiet she could hear every word – 'I believe Miss Pearce needs this ledger.' Through the cloak of her fringe, with her head tilted low, she watched Joe point towards it. 'Shall I hand it over for you?' Joe had kept his voice light, making it sound as though he thought it was an oversight. The whole room knew it was not.

'Oh, I did not realise I had this still. Yes, please do,' Mr Quince replied in the calmest, most pleasant, voice.

Catherine gritted her teeth to hold back the anger pressing on the back of her tongue, urging her to shout a rude accusation. Mr Quince was a petty-minded man, risking the delay of supply when there was a war at stake only to ensure she'd fail. What good would that do GWR or Britain, or Charles for that matter?

Joe picked up the ledger and brought it to her.

'Thank you,' she said as she accepted it, knowing her skin must be pink, not with embarrassment but with rage.

He winked. 'There's so much to think of now, isn't there? Things are easily forgotten,' he said loudly. 'Keep a sensible head. Sensible is as sensible does, my old mum used to tell me.'

The ridiculous statement sprung a laugh from Catherine's throat. 'That makes no sense.'

'I know.' A comic expression mocked his own words. 'I never knew what she was on about either. Mad as a box of frogs, that woman was, God rest her soul. But it made you laugh anyways. Good luck with those registers. I need to get back to the workshop. You won't see any positions in carpentry; I'll fill the roles with the young lads. It can be heavy work.'

'Thank you, Joe,' she repeated, before he left the room.

* * *

It was not a simple task,

Catherine wrote in a letter to Charles later.

As it turned out the task was not one for a favoured daughter as everyone else assumed. It involved searching through the drawers marked with an a to z of surnames, thumbing through the dusty little cards to find the women's information. Papa asked me because he knows I would be thorough. In the end, I employed a couple of the other apprentices to help, and between us we allocated all the roles.

She did not mention any more details in case the letter was intercepted, even though the women were only being given simple tasks, like polishing the metal in T shop or pressing buttons to operate machines in V shop, or making hooded lamps for the railway workers.

'I made a new friend today. The daughter of a family who have housed evacuees. We are like-minded in our desire to act. I added her name and mine on the list to take on men's work. When I start this new role on the shop floor, I am going to use your surname and not tell anyone who I am, so no one will treat me differently.'

Differently – it felt like an odd word now that everything was different.

A single oil lamp had burned in the centre of the dining table as they'd eaten tonight. The room had been darker than normal due to the black fabric someone from the factory had nailed across the windows during the day. Papa planned to leave the fabric in place in the front of the house, rather than take it down each day, and just leave the curtains drawn to hide it.

Her bedroom window was covered too. Only the attic windows remained clear.

The writing paper rested on a closed book on her lap, and she tapped the non-business end of the fountain pen on her lower lip – a bad habit that had annoyed her teachers. The sky was cloudless. Catherine could see all of Swindon's rooftops, no matter that no light rose from the town.

It was such a clear night she waited to hear engines and see the Luftwaffe's aeroplanes appear on the horizon. But the night sky remained quiet.

She had a strange sense of being suspended in time. As though the war, the blacked-out houses, could not be reality but a dream. Charles must know it was not a dream. There had not been a letter since he had been sent to Poland. She imagined the fighting was fierce if Hitler was deploying one of his lightning assaults, constantly bombarding the Polish from air and land. The threat of such an attack here was why everywhere was black and silent. It was why the British Government had evacuated the children from cities and prepared train carriages for the movement of thousands of wounded civilians. It was not happening here tonight, but in Poland it was.

Was Charles somewhere warm? Did he have a roof over his head? Or was he lying in a tent somewhere, cold? Hiding in a ditch, in woods or a field, wet? He never told her where he was when he wrote.

She closed her eyes and tried to imagine, to feel what he might be feeling, to see and hear... Aeroplanes overhead. Bombs falling. Tanks approaching. Guns firing. She could not really visualise it. Such things were beyond her sheltered comprehension. Yet she could visualise herself with the weight of a rifle in her hands and see herself standing in front of him, protecting him as she stared into the eyes of a Nazi soldier.

A smile touched her lips as she opened her eyes. Yes, she was as stubborn as her father and happy about it. Perhaps because she'd inherited his personality. Or because growing up with four older brothers meant she'd had to grow up to be *'as tough as nails'*, as her grandfather used to say about the people in the village. But either way the Nazis would have to shoot her or run her down with a tank before she'd willingly give up and move out of their way. She hoped when she started the men's work she'd be making things that would stop them. Perhaps Charles or one of her brothers might even use a weapon she'd made to stop a tank.

Her attention returned to the letter she was writing.

I confess, I am far more excited than I should be about the idea that I might be doing something like...

She could not write 'making weapons'. If the letter was intercepted in the Channel or travelling across France and read by a Nazi... It might be something so simple that brought the bombs to Swindon.

> *... cooking up the spicy cakes you are all desperate for in our little home furnace. I very much hope that is what I shall be doing. I will have to pray for forgiveness for some evil thoughts this Sunday, because if I can do anything to help rid this earth of THAT man and his cronies, I am quite happy to soil my soul with a hand in their deaths if it is in the defence of others. You men should not bear all the weight of this war. I will play my part.*
>
> *I love you. God bless you. I pray for you every night.*
>
> *Write soon, dearest, it is days since I saw your writing and I long to see it.*
>
> *Your adoring,*
> *Catherine*
> *xxx*

She set down the pen, closed her eyes again and pressed her palms together in prayer. 'Please, God, protect Charles, Harold, Alfred, Roger and Graham, and all the men who must fight. Bring peace in Europe and comfort to all those who are caught up in this war, and help me to help those who are innocent and good as best I can. And Lord, forgive us if to defend ourselves we must take the lives of those who are murdering others.'

5

Lily Franklin

Lily's gaze travelled around. She looked up and down, left and right, taking in every detail of the iron workshop. It was just as Art had described. As hot as she imagined hell would be. Heat radiated from the huge furnaces and the glowing molten metal that men poured out of great pans into moulds of the products they were making. Other men struck glowing pieces of metal with thick iron mallets, sending orange sparks flying. Giant machines thumped down and cranes swung heavy-looking parts from chains overhead. The sounds were like a hundred church bells chiming out of time.

'Come along, ladies! No dawdling!' Mr Abbot shouted over the noise, beckoning with his hand before coughing into the white handkerchief he held. He'd coughed lots, and he kept the handkerchief in his fist to hide it as best he could, but she'd seen the red blood on the white cotton. Mr Abbot obviously had a lung disease. He coughed again, holding his fist to his mouth as he walked ahead of them.

Lily trailed at the rear of the line of women. The skin of her left foot burned from the heat creeping up through the hole in the sole of her boot. The wooden cobble-like blocks on the floor had absorbed heat from the furnaces. Art had told her if they used stone on the floors, the whole room became like an oven, and the stone was slippery if the tar or oil spilled, whereas wood absorbed it. So the men laid wood and replaced it once a year. When they changed it, Art brought blocks home for burning on the fire. The soaked in tar and oil meant they burned better than coal.

Lily might be given some wood to burn this year. The idea of being the one to supply the wood for the hearth made her smile. It made her feel important rather than feeling like the family skivvy.

Lenny had started work today too. She'd knocked at his house and they'd walked to the Rodbourne Road entrance together. They'd had to separate at the gate because he'd gone to work with the carpenters. All the buildings only had letters or numbers on the doors, she had no idea what was being done where. She'd been taken in through the door of J shop, and they were moving into other buildings. She was very confused but at least she knew Mr Abbot, the foreman who was showing her around, and his daughter, Maggie, who was in the line of women ahead of her. Everyone knew the Abbot sisters. Lily used to watch them through her bedroom window while they played in the street, feeling jealous of the way they laughed and messed around.

She knew Violet Turner too. Violet had worked in the grocers. She'd given Lily a discount on some of the vegetables that were past their best a number of times. Lily's stepmother always sent her to buy things at the end of the day when the bargains could be had.

She didn't know the other women. There was one who

sounded posh – too posh to be working in the foundries.
Catherine Clifford, she was called.

The woman in front of Lily looked around as much as Lily
did. Her name was Naomi Isaacs.

'Ladies!' Mr Abbot shouted again over the noise and
beckoned with a raised hand. Lily realised how far she and
Naomi had dropped behind. She hurried forward feeling guilty
for causing the coughing fit that rocked his tall frame.

'Dad.' Maggie Abbot stepped forward, but he waved her back
as the coughing eased.

'Follow me.' He led them through a door and out of the Iron
Workshop. It was a lot cooler on the other side. The walls were
painted white. It was much less like hell. The last to pass through,
Lily closed the door behind her.

'You'll be distributed among the fitters, turners and machine
men, across W, V2 and P2, and will help to work the machines to
fit the engines' boilers in P1,' Mr Abbot explained. 'There are a
few rules to remember...'

Lily concentrated hard.

'You are not to tell a soul what work you're doing even if you
are *not* doing something for the war effort. If the Nazis find out
which workshops are not making items for the Ministries of
Supply or Transport, they'll slowly work out which ones *are*.'

Lily's shoulders slid back as she stood taller. She didn't just
feel important, she *was* important if she had to keep secrets to
help win the war.

'Loose lips sink ships, ladies. So no gossiping to your sweethearts and no chatter if you meet outside the works.'

Lily nodded.

'Black sheets of tarpaulin will be hung between some areas,
so you will not see what others are working on, and you are not to
ask them...' Mr Abbot continued listing his warnings. They were

not to talk to the men about anything other than work, there was to be no flirting, and no fraternising in working hours. They must ask to use the toilets and go in pairs, and they would only be given five minutes – the checky would be counting.

Something touched Lily's left hand. She jumped and looked sideways. Naomi's hand closed around hers and squeezed Lily's hand gently in a silent communication of solidarity as she leaned close. 'It's a little terrifying, isn't it?' she whispered.

Lily nodded and accepted the offer of friendship by holding the hand that had taken hers. She appreciated the feeling of companionship. Only her youngest half-siblings and sometimes Lenny held her hand, she had no female friends to hold hands with.

'I was sewing in the carriage shop,' Naomi confided. 'This looks very different. But if the men can do this, so can we.'

'Of course we can.' Lily's voice came out croaky from a throat she hadn't realised was so dry. She tried to swallow but her tongue stuck on the roof of her mouth.

'This way,' Mr Abbot called them on again.

Naomi released Lily's hand.

What was Lenny doing? Was he being shown places like this, with machines and men everywhere?

Lily trailed through rooms where, one by one, the women were told what they would do and introduced to the men they'd work with. The group reduced until there were five women left following Mr Abbot: Lily, the posh-sounding woman – Catherine – Naomi, Maggie and Violet.

In the next room, the women were introduced to men who were working on large machinery. Lily was the very last to be taken to a machine to meet two middle-aged men, neither of whom she recognised from the Railway Village.

'Gud-day, lass. Come ere then an we'll show you what you'll be about.'

Bill and Don, the men were called.

All Lily had to do was press a big red button that switched on a lifting machine the men used to manoeuvre large, heavy parts. The men steered the parts into position and secured them into place; she just had to press the button to stop and start the machine when they called out.

'This is easy,' she said after half an hour.

'That's cause you're doin alf a job, lass,' Bill snapped. 'Bernard could lower the arm on top of a packet of fags an not make a single crease in the pack. It takes a good long time to be that skilled an operator. You just keep pressin the button when we say, love.'

Bill made it sound as though he didn't think she'd ever be able to do more than press the button when he said so.

'Press it.'

'A little longer.'

'Just a count of one.'

'Stop.'

'Stop!'

Bill and Don talked and chuckled as they worked. Standing at the other end of the ten-foot wide and tall machinery connected to iron runners above them, Lily was too far away to hear them properly. What Lenny would call her persistent paranoia had her imagining their conversation and wondering if the chuckles were about her.

She glanced at the clock every few minutes. She needed the privy. Mr Abbot had not told her when there was a break, and she didn't like to mention it to the men. She gritted her teeth and tightened her muscles. It was probably only a nervous need for a pee.

'Press it!'

'Stop!'

She grew sick of those words as the clock ticked towards lunchtime. But she told herself, at the end of the week, she was going to work out how much money she'd earned for every time they'd said start or stop.

A bell rang. A hand bell, though she couldn't see who rang it. In response, the men straightened and backed away from their task. 'Stop it there, lass. We're eddin ome for lunch. I don't know about you.'

Every day of her life had been timed by the sound of the GWR hooters, and for the first time they'd been silent today. Her father had read the news out loud from the paper this morning – and Art said they told him at work – that the hooters would only be used to call out an air raid warning from now on.

Lily walked away from the machinery. Naomi was already at the exit door, pulling her coat on. She obviously had somewhere to go. Lily had agreed to meet Lenny at the Rodbourne Road gate, but she didn't know how to find her way back there. She hadn't realised the factory was so big. She reached to hang up her brass token and lifted her coat off a hook near the checking board.

'How are you?' Violet asked. 'How did you get along?'

Lily looked over her shoulder, imaging that Violet was talking to someone else, but she stood there, sliding her arms into the sleeves of her coat, looking at Lily. She was talking to Lily.

'Fine. I think.' Lily's throat was still dry. She was dying for a pee and a drink and her stomach growled with hunger.

'The men don't say much, do they?' Violet's lips parted in a broad smile.

'No.'

'Oh my Lord, that was the longest morning I've ever spent.' Maggie Abbot joined them.

'What are you all doing for your lunch?' Catherine asked as she opened the door.

Lily followed Maggie and Violet through the exit. Catherine came out last and let the door close behind her.

'I said I'd meet my friend Lenny at the Rodbourne Road gate, but I aint sure ow to get back there.'

'Is he your boyfriend?' Violet asked.

'No just a friend.'

'I'll point you in the right direction when we reach the corner of this block,' Catherine said. She wore a pale face powder, blue-grey eyeshadow and vivid red lipstick. Lily thought wearing make-up was an odd thing to do when she'd come to work. But Catherine seemed nice enough, despite looking and sounding as though she'd stepped out from a picture in the pages of a *Vogue* magazine.

'Do you know where the outhouses are?'

'Oh, yes. I can show you that too.'

'Maggie and I are going to my home for lunch. You can come with us, Catherine, if you'd like.' Violet made the offer. 'You too, Lily.'

'No, thank you. I can't leave Lenny waitin at the gate.'

Lily hadn't told anyone other than Lenny she was starting work. Not even Art. She'd decided just to leave the house and let her stepmother get on with it. She wasn't going back to the house in the day in case she saw her father and he didn't let her return. But she would have to go home for dinner and face him then.

'The gate is that way.' Catherine pointed around the corner at the end of the building they'd been working in. 'Straight ahead of you. The conveniences are here. We'll wait while you use them.'

'Thanks.' Lily nodded.

Catherine sang while Lily hurriedly used the men's toilets.

When she came out, she thanked the other girls again and then ran all the way to the gate.

Her back pressed against the cold bars of the cast-iron as she tried to keep out of people's way and rose onto her toes, looking all around, trying to see Lenny through the hoard of men leaving the site.

'Lily!' His shout travelled across the heads of taller men, searching for her. 'Lily!'

'Lenny! Lenny! I'm ere.' She raised a hand high, waving in the hope he would see.

'Lily?'

'Ere!' she yelled again.

She saw him a few feet away. He smiled as he forced his way across the stream, like the pike she'd seen swimming hard against the current in the River Ray.

'Lily.' He said her name with relief when he reached her, and one side of his mouth quirked up in an apologetic half-smile. 'Sorry I was late. I thought you might have given up on me and gone. I'm working near the subway. Let's get home quick, otherwise we won't have any time to eat lunch.'

She knew she wasn't supposed to tell people what she was doing. She did know there were enemies here. The papers were printing stories daily about the people arrested because they were fascists, for publicly commending Hitler or just because they were foreigners from enemy countries, whether they approved of Hitler or not. Last week a man who was renting a room in Swindon had been caught talking German into the handset of a radio device. With all these enemies hidden among the English, people were now looking sideways at each other even in the Railway Village. The Nazi aeroplanes hadn't come yet, but everyone still looked at the skies every day, especially when

they heard the British aircraft. Nervously waiting for the Luftwaffe to have found out what Swindon was up to.

But she'd known Lenny most of her life; he wasn't a Nazi spy.
There had to be one person she could say anything to. So she
glanced around – no one was listening to them – and she told
him, 'I'm pressin a button on an off, on an off. That's all I do.' She
laughed.

'I've been hauling logs around. Loading them onto a huge saw
and slicing them into planks for the carpenters to use. I suppose
we have to start with the easier tasks.'

Walking beside Lenny felt so normal, she relaxed more with
every step. 'The men spent most of the morning laughin at me,
but the women are nice. I'm in the same place as Maggie Abbot
an Violet Turner. What are the people you work with like?'

'That's nice that you know people. I don't really know anyone
in the sawmill. The carpenters from the Railway Village are all in
the workshops. But I took a delivery over and saw Ron Smith. Do
you know him?'

Lily nodded. 'Ee's the Turners' lodger, isn't ee?'

'Yes. There's a German boy in the sawmill. He's young. Dietrich. He's a Jew. We've all been told by Mr Marsh, one of the foremen, to treat him well. He's no threat. He's a refugee.'

'I thought they were lockin up all the Germans.'

'He was locked up. He told me. In a prisoner of war camp up
north somewhere, but they let him out. A family in Swindon
convinced the authorities he wouldn't harm anyone. I think the
only people he'd harm are the Nazis. His family are missing and
they're German. Like I told you the Nazis have lumps of coal for
hearts.'

Lily wrapped her hand around his arm. 'Don't let's talk about
the war. Talk about somethin else. Were you good at slicin the
wood? I think I'm gunna be very good at pressin a button.'

Lenny laughed, and his laughter triggered a feeling of warmth in her chest. Every moment she spent with him the world was peaceful. If she shut her eyes and didn't look at the air raid shelters and gun platforms and bare flowerbeds in the park, when she was with Lenny they weren't in a war.

NATIONAL  REGISTER.

NATIONAL REGISTRATION DAY IS FRIDAY, 29th SEPTEMBER, 1939.

SEE INSTRUCTIONS IN SCHEDULE AS TO "PERSONS TO BE INCLUDED."

RATIONING.—The return on the schedule herewith will be used not only for National Registration but also for Food Rationing purposes. It is to your interest, therefore, as well as your public duty, to fill up the return carefully, fully and accurately.

Help the Enumerator to collect the schedule promptly by arranging for him to receive it when he calls. Do not make it necessary for him to call a number of times before he can obtain it.

When the Enumerator collects the schedule, he must write and deliver an Identity Card for every person included in the return. Help him to write them properly for you by letting him write at a table.

If the whole household moves before the schedule is collected, take it with you and hand it to the Enumerator calling at your new residence or to the National Registration Office for your new address. The address of this office can be ascertained at a local police station.

6

Violet Turner

Violet ran down the narrow, twisting, cottage stairs as the enumerator walked up the short path of the front garden. For the last hour, as dusk had turned to night, she'd watched him moving from one house to another through the window of the bedroom she shared with her mother.

The house still smelt of the steak and kidney suet pudding they'd eaten for dinner before she'd disappeared upstairs. Her mother had put the muslin-wrapped pudding on to steam slowly in a pot on the old iron stove before they left for work and checked it at lunchtime, adding more water to the pot. The coals in the oven were burned to ash when they'd come home after work, but the pudding had cooked and the house was warm.

Frank bought the steak and kidney. He'd said he was going to have as many solid meals of meat as he could if the Government were going to ration food.

Violet had relished every mouthful, eating slowly to savour it.

She reached the door before the enumerator knocked.

Ron and Frank were in the parlour, occupying the two comfortable armchairs, reading magazines and smoking cigarettes. Violet had taken a cigarette from Ron before dinner and smoked it in the back yard, too quickly. It burned her lips and she ended up coughing and wasting half of it. Maggie would have laughed. But Maggie had nothing to worry about when the enumerator walked through her front door.

A firm knock had every muscle in Violet's body jumping, even though she knew he was out there.

She glanced across her shoulder. 'He's here!' she shouted towards the back of the house where her mother was washing off the dinner things in the sink. Her heartbeat felt as loud as the hammers in the workshop as she opened the door. 'Good evening. Come in.' She brightened the tone of her voice and stepped back, making space for him to enter.

'Good evening. Are you ready for me?'

'We are. Everything is in the kitchen.'

As Violet shut the front door, the parlour door opened. Her teeth gritted. She was trying so hard to control this. She didn't want Frank and Ron there when the man looked at her mother's information. But, as always, Ron and Frank refused to be managed.

'Hello. You'll be wanting to talk to us too.'

Ron stood there, framed in the parlour entrance, his hands in his trouser pockets. He had taken off his suit jacket, but still wore the figure-hugging waistcoat, securely buttoned, over his shirt. That wonderful scent of wood sap lingered in an aura around him even though he wasn't wearing workday clothes.

Frank walked up behind Ron. 'Good evening.' He'd also removed his jacket, and the buttons of his waistcoat were freed so it hung open.

The hall was too narrow for them all. The men were held back in the parlour.

'Come on through.' Violet lifted a hand urging the enumerator to follow her.

'Are you all set up in there, Mrs Turner?' called Frank.

Her mother was standing beside the kitchen table, her skin much paler than normal. She'd complained of a headache during dinner. 'The kettle has just boiled if you would like a drink?' she asked the enumerator, her words carrying hard ends. Expressing a forced calm.

'Thank you for the offer, but I'd look like a teapot if I accepted every cup I've been offered tonight.' He lay his briefcase on the kitchen table, lifted off his trilby hat and put that on the table too.

Mrs Turner looked at Ron and Frank. 'You two sit down and get yourselves sorted first.' That would get the men out of the way.

Violet saw a nervous pulse beating at the base of her mother's neck.

Ron and Frank withdrew chairs at the same time as the enumerator and sat around the small square table.

Violet leaned back against the wooden draining board, beside the stained ceramic sink, tucking her hands behind her bottom, restraining them so no one would see how much they shook. Her gaze caught on her mother's, who responded with a trembling smile.

The enumerator sat beside Ron, looking through the information Ron had completed on their household form. He asked him to confirm the date of birth he'd written.

What should I say? How will I explain?' her mother had whispered to Violet three nights ago as they'd lain in bed, as though Violet were the older and wiser one.

Violet had stood in the kitchen this morning, feeling her

mother's pain and fear as though it was hers, and she'd made the tea and put the porridge on so her mother wouldn't have to.

'Tell him you reverted to your maiden name when my father died. Say the certificate was with him when he died. You have me, why wouldn't he believe you were married?'

It was common for marriage certificates to be lost. Marriages were recorded in churches, where fires happened and records were burned or lost. Surely the man was not going to insist on seeing certificates. He just wanted to make sure they weren't going to claim rations they shouldn't, and that they weren't potential enemies of the British Empire. This would become the official register of everyone living in the country. If her mother was recorded as 'Mrs Turner', she would be Mrs Turner for the rest of her life.

Violet watched her mother's hands clasp together in front of her, so firmly Violet saw the muscles tighten in her forearms and her knuckles pale.

She'd told Violet the truth about her birth on Violet's eleventh birthday. *'You are old enough to keep our secret now.'* It was not a gift to know. It was a burden Violet carried every day. She'd not even told Maggie. No one knew. No one else could know.

'That's me done.' Ron stood, holding the precious identity card he'd been given. 'Do you want this chair, Vi?'

She stepped forward and accepted the seat, while Frank began reeling off the information he'd written and the enumerator checked the form.

The chair's feet scraped on the flagstone floor as Ron tucked the seat up against the back of Violet's knees and slid it underneath her.

'Mrs Turner.' Ron pulled the spare chair back, encouraging her mother to sit too.

Her mother did sit.

Frank stood a moment later and the two men left the room, their heads down, reading the information on their cards, Ron's soft curls gently shadowing his eyes, Frank's Brylcreem-greased hair flopping forward in a clump.

'Do you want to check my information first?' Violet opened, unsure whether the delay would extend her mother's torment or ease it.

'Miss Violet May Turner?' The enumerator read the words she'd written on the document.

'Yes,' she confirmed.

'Where were you born?'

'Here. In this cottage. I mean, in Swindon.'

The questioning progressed, repeating those on the schedule, double checking that she was the woman listed there and not trying to defraud the Government.

When he was satisfied with her answers, he withdrew an identity card from the battered tan briefcase, wrote her name on it in black ink and added a unique number. A Citizen of Britain number that would mean everyone knew she was a friendly party in this war and entitled to her British rations.

Her mother's card might pronounce her a liar every time she showed it. She would be shamed on a daily basis. Everyone thought she was a widow. No one knew she was an unmarried mother. Not *Mrs* Turner but *Miss*. Even GWR did not know. If the officials in the firm found out she'd lied, they might take away her job and the cottage with it.

The man looked up from the schedule. 'Rose Turner?'

'Yes. *Mrs* Rose Turner,' her mother said, too eagerly.

'Born on...'

Her mother's date of birth rolled off her tongue, but there was a nervous tremor in her voice. 'My occupation is—'

'Hold on a moment. No need to rush, let's not get ahead of ourselves. Where were you born?'

Violet watched her mother take a deep breath, then she told him about the town on the coast of Cornwall, where she was born. 'In Bude.' All this information was the truth.

'Who are your parents?'

Did he think something was wrong? He had not asked Violet or the others this question. But then they had shown certificates. But there was very little information for anyone to prove who they said they were. That was why the Government were undertaking this National Day of Registration.

Her mother cleared her throat with a cough.

'Would you like a cup of water?' Violet offered.

'Oh yes please, love.'

As Violet rose from the chair, her mother replied, 'Ernest and Maud Turner.'

Violet's mother had used her real name and only illegally changed her title. *It is just a small white lie,* she'd told Violet. Today, it felt like a dark, dangerous, gloomy, black lie.

The man's grey eyebrows lifted and he nodded. 'Where are they now?'

'Still in Bude. I imagine they are in the same house they lived in when I was born, but we are estranged. They did not approve of my marriage.'

'Yet you use your maiden name?'

'When my husband was shot in the Great War, we had only been married for a month. We'd kept our wedding a secret. I was used to Turner and everyone still knew me as Turner. No one knew me by the Bishopstone name.'

'Bishopstone.' His grey eyebrows rose. 'It is a little odd to shun your married name so promptly. I understand in the case of a divorce, but to be widowed...' He shook his head, apparently battling with a thought. 'Do you have a marriage certificate?'

Violet's heart sunk to the soles of her feet.

Her mother took a sip from the cup Violet had put down on the table. She had to tell a big, fat lie now. 'My husband had the certificate. He took it with him. He was so proud that we were wed, and we were going to tell our families later. The next time he returned. Truthfully, the main reason I never used his name is because his family never welcomed me. That's why we kept our wedding day for us.' She took another sip of water. 'It was also the day I conceived Violet. He never came back and so neither did the marriage certificate.'

Violet watched the man watching her mother, his facial expression a solid clerk's mask.

The light from the single wall lamp in the kitchen caught on the sheen of tears in her mother's eyes. 'My husband was from a very good family. My family are from a lower class than his. Neither were happy when they discovered what we'd done.' She sighed. 'Oh well, there is no point in me wasting your time with painful and unnecessary memories. It is all history. Water under the bridge, as they say.'

The man's expression softened. His closed lips lifted into a smile. 'To lose your husband before you even had your daughter must have been, and still be, very difficult to bear.'

'Yes,' her mother agreed, her shoulders relaxing.

'You gave your daughter your maiden name too? Is that for the same reason?'

Damn it. It was even odder for Violet to be given her mother's maiden name.

Her mother sat taller in the seat, growing an inch in height. 'I did so because Eric was not here to sign his name, and I had no certificate to prove we were married.' The tempo of her voice had changed as she defended Violet's name. Violet knew how much her mother had done, how many times she'd lied, to protect Violet from scorn.

Violet was proud of her mother. She was proud her mother worked. That she'd navigated life alone and had achieved so much. She was a supervisor at the factory. Respected in her community.

'Well,' the man said, making his judgement. 'I can see you are both here in the house. Two women – one elder, one younger – marriage certificate or no.' He smiled again. 'I'll fill in your card.' He withdrew another blank card from his briefcase.

Violet leaned a little forward, watching him write.

MRS

Her heart leapt.

ROSE TURNER

He completed, with careful strokes of the tip of his fountain pen.

Violet was unsure whether he believed the story but, for whatever reason, he allocated a Citizen of Britain number to 'Mrs Rose Turner' and now no one could say her mother was an unmarried woman.

Her mother drew in a shaky breath as she accepted the card from the man's hand. 'Thank you.'

He pushed their house schedule into his briefcase and stood, picking up his hat. He'd not taken off his coat. It had all taken hardly any time, really.

Violet rose quickly. 'I'll show you out.'

'Mrs Turner.' He bowed his head towards Violet's mother before putting his trilby on.

'Are you sure you wouldn't like some refreshment?' she asked.

'No, thank you. There are still quite a few houses on my route, and I'd like to be home before midnight.'

Violet breathed away her former fears as her mother slid her identity card into the pocket of her skirt. She led the enumerator through the hall, as she had led him in, opened the front door and closed it firmly behind him.

When he'd gone, Violet sat down at the kitchen table, her limbs still shaky like a newborn lamb's, and looked at the small booklet he'd handed her. The document that would now identify her.

1. **Always carry your Identity Card**. You must produce it on demand by a Police Officer in uniform or a member of H.M Armed Forces in uniform on duty.

2. **You are responsible for this Card**, and must not part with it to any other person. You must report at once to the local National Registration Office if it is lost, destroyed, damaged or defaced.

3. If you find a lost Identity Card or have in your possession a Card not belonging to yourself or anyone in your charge you must hand it in at once at a Police Station or National Registration Office.

4. Any breach of these requirements is an offence punishable by a fine or imprisonment or both.

'I am going to bed, darling.'

Violet looked at her mother. She did look tired. Wan.

'I'll stay up a little longer,' Violet said.

They shared a bed so that they could rent beds in the other room.

'Vi!' Ron called from the living room. 'If you're staying up come and sit in the parlour with us.' Violet's gaze was drawn to the closed parlour door.

If Ron had heard what Violet had just said, he'd heard every other part of the conversation in the kitchen. That was the problem with having lodgers in the house, there was never a moment of privacy.

'I'll be there in a minute!' Violet called back.

Her mother's eyes were glossed with tears again. Violet switched off the kitchen light, leaving the hall dark.

'Goodnight, Mum,' she said in a quiet voice, then wrapped her arms around her mother and kissed her cheek.

'Goodnight, love.'

Her mother opened the door to the stairs as Violet turned to the parlour door.

The parlour was the lightest room in the cottage, with three wall lamps. It was supposed to be a room just for Sundays, but it was the best room for reading and sewing and they all used it most evenings.

'You have this chair, Vi' – Ron stood – 'you look ashen.'

'I'm fine. It's just a bit overwhelming, all of this war stuff, isn't it?' She may have claimed to be fine, but her legs were still wobbling. She was glad of the comfortable seat his backside had warmed.

'It is that,' Frank agreed, not looking up from the paper he had spread over his crossed thighs.

Ron pulled over one of the plain wooden chairs and sat near Violet.

'Would you like a cigarette?' He tapped his open packet so one slid up, then held the packet towards her. She shouldn't accept. Her mother hated her smoking. But Violet needed one now to calm her nerves.

'Thanks.' She pulled the cigarette out and held it to her lips.

Ron put a cigarette between his lips, too, and reached into his pocket for a box of matches. Striking a match on the side of the box, he held it out for her to light her cigarette first. Then lit his.

Violet breathed in and the smoke filled her lungs.

She exhaled upwards, so as not to blow smoke into Ron's face.

'Will you stay here?' she asked. Asking them both, but really asking Ron. 'Or will you fight?'

Ron had lived as a lodger in the second bedroom for almost four years, and Frank three. She was attached to them. If Frank volunteered it would feel like saying goodbye to a brother. She'd worry for him. If Ron volunteered it might break her heart.

'The Ministry of Transport need carpenters here,' Ron said.

Frank wasn't a carpenter.

'They'll need the engineers too,' Frank said, and looked up. He met her gaze and smiled. 'We'll be filling up the chairs in your parlour a good while longer, Vi.'

Her mother needed the money they paid. If they left, she'd have to find other lodgers. It would be a struggle to pay the rent on the cottage on a woman's salary, even with two women working. She'd seen the salary figures in the GWR magazine, the men earned a quarter more than her and her mother's 5 shillings 3 pence a week.

The floorboards creaked upstairs. Violet glanced upwards as she sucked on the cigarette. Above was the bedroom she shared with her mother.

'Vi.' Ron drew her attention. 'We'll be here to help. Tell Rose not to fret over things.'

He must have seen the tears in her mother's eyes.

Violet met his gaze, nodding, accepting his assurances. His

smile creased the skin at the corners of his eyes, forming thin lines in the shape of crows' feet.

Ron was handsome. He had a charm about him too. He was very likeable. Probably because he was always thoughtful. Kind. Polite.

She'd liked Ron for a long time. Too much. Her friend Maggie fancied Ron. Even though Maggie had never spoken about it to Violet, she made it obvious. Too obvious sometimes. Whenever she came for dinner, she'd rush to the chair beside Ron's, and when he told his stories she'd laugh like a little kid, even if it wasn't funny. It was embarrassing. Violet didn't think Ron fancied Maggie. He'd never treated Maggie differently from anyone else. But because Maggie liked him, Violet had never flirted with him.

Violet drew another lungful of smoke from the cigarette. It sent the blood rushing to her head, and the room spun.

Violet would describe her feelings for Ron as a soft spot. Maggie was obsessed. But what woman wouldn't like a kind man? She doubted any young woman with a heartbeat could know Ron and not be a little bit sweet on him. Sometimes he'd do her chores if she was too tired, and he often asked her to join him and Frank for a game of cards, and he'd change the game to gin rummy because she liked that game.

There was something magnetic about Ron's blue eyes too; when Violet looked into them it was hard to look away, the colour was so pure. She didn't know anyone else with eyes as blue as his. Especially when he wore his blue shirt on a Sunday.

Maggie was awful. She'd shamelessly rest an elbow on the kitchen table, her chin on her hand, and stare at him in a way that annoyed Violet's mother. *'Has that girl no shame?'*

Ron never looked Maggie's way when she was being so obviously adoring. He would smile at Violet instead and sometimes raise his eyebrows and make her laugh. Which was a bit mean of her because it meant she was laughing at her best friend.

He finished his cigarette and threw the stub into the empty hearth. Since the Government had said gas and electric supplies may need to be turned off at certain hours of the day, they'd all agreed the coal should be saved for heating water and drying laundry in the kitchen on wet days.

Violet sucked in one last breath of smoke, blew it out more slowly, then tossed her stub into the hearth too.

'I should go upstairs and check on Mum.' Now her legs felt steady enough to get her up the stairs. 'Thanks for the cigarette, Ron. Goodnight.' She stood and her stomach tumbled over, turning topsy-turvy with all the emotions of the last hour or so. She might just vomit into the chamber pot when she got upstairs.

'Goodnight,' Frank said, as she left the room.

'I know it's hard.' Ron's voice caught up with her in the hall.

She turned. She hadn't realised he'd followed.

He closed the parlour door behind him, shutting them off from Frank, and the shrewd look she saw in Ron's eyes before he closed off the light said he had done so for a reason. Sometimes she wondered if he fancied her. But he treated her more like a sister. She didn't even know if he thought she was pretty.

Broad-shouldered, and taller than her by a good few inches, he crowded the narrow space at the foot of the stairs, and in the dark his close presence sent shivers of a different sort of emotion racing up her spine.

'For those who remember the last war with such brutal clarity, this is difficult.' His voice was quiet, which made the conversation seem secretive and intimate.

She hesitated. There was something in the unusual tone of the comment that made her think it was about more than the loss of her father. For a moment she thought he'd guessed her mother's secret. But it wasn't that. He had been personally impacted by the last war too. Her eyes had begun adjusting to the gloom. The kitchen door was ajar and there was some light from the coals and embers left burning in the kitchen hearth. 'I... Who did you lose?'

'My father was severely wounded,' he answered in a whisper. 'He can't walk and can barely talk at times. My mother's life is very different. That's why I left home. Sometimes I felt as though my presence only reminded them of who he once was. I look like he did when he was young and healthy. Anyway, my mother needs someone earning a good wage more than a son hanging on her apron strings. I send most of my earnings home; it means she can pay someone to help with Dad.'

'I'm sorry, I didn't know.'

'You didn't know because I don't talk about it. It's private. But... Well... Tell Rose I am sorry she's upset. It must have been hard losing your father. If she needs me to do anything to help, she only has to ask.'

'Thank you. Are you going up to bed too?'

'No. I'll sit up with Frank and play a hand or two of cards. I don't think I could sleep if I tried.'

His hand lifted and his warm palm rested over the sleeve of her cardigan. 'Don't fret, Vi.' The silence in the house meant the tick of the clock on the wooden mantel in the parlour was clear as day, and those ticks timed the seconds his hand remained on her arm. One. Two. Three. His hand lifted and dropped to his side.

Her head bobbed. 'Thanks Ron.' She turned and hurried upstairs.

He was being kind. He was just being kind, she told her beating heart.

'Mum?' she called quietly, before turning the door handle.

'Come in,' her mother answered, confirming she was still awake.

The room was light enough to see in because they'd not blacked out the windows, so the moonlight could come in. It seeped through the thin cotton curtains. Her mother was a dark statuette sitting on the bed, facing the window, her head bent, looking at something in her hand. Violet walked closer, to see what she was holding. It was a picture frame. She knew which picture it would be. It always stood on the chest on her mother's side of the bed. It was the one picture they had of the man who'd fathered Violet.

She sat down beside her mother, the old horsehair mattress sinking and the rusty bedsprings creaking.

Her mother looked at Violet. 'Why must men like Hitler wage war?'

Violet hitched up and dropped her shoulders, expressing her own bewilderment. 'The man's mad. Even Prime Minister Chamberlain says that.'

Violet stared at the picture in her mother's hands. She only knew her father from this image and her mother's memories. He was killed by a bullet in the head. They had not married before he left. He'd said they'd marry the next time he had leave. It was true he'd died the same month that Violet was conceived.

As soon as Rose's family found out that Violet was on the way, she was tossed out of her childhood home like a bag of old rags. She'd travelled until she found work here in the GWR factory. She'd lied – said there was a dead husband so that they'd take pity on her and let her work even as she grew big with Violet inside her. She'd lived in one room when Violet was born and worked with her baby swaddled to her chest. Then the woman who had rented her the room offered to look after Violet. Rose was lucky when a cottage in the Railway Village became available, along with better paid work in the factory. Being a widow had given her priority over others and given her the respectability to become a supervisor. If anyone knew it was not true... Violet could not even imagine the consequences.

Violet wrapped her arms around her mother's shoulders, enfolding her in a hug.

'I love you, Mum,' she said. 'Whatever this war brings, we'll survive it. You're not alone this time.'

7

Naomi Isaacs

Naomi pulled the front door open. The man on the other side of it lifted a bowler hat off his head an inch and set it down again, his moustache twitching as he smiled quickly. 'Good evening, I am your enumerator. May I come in?'

'Good evening. Yes, come through.' Naomi led him to the dining room at the front of the house. The electric lamp shone on the sideboard.

'Is everyone who lives in the household at home? I need to see everyone before I issue their cards.'

'Yes. I'll round them up. Please take a seat.'

He rested his black briefcase on the white tablecloth. The Sabbath candlesticks and candles still stood on the table, the candle flames flickering in the breeze from the front door being opened and closed.

Naomi left him there, walked back into the hall and called out, 'Dietrich! Golda! Esther!' They were all in their rooms, Dietrich in the basement and Golda and Esther in Naomi's room upstairs. 'Ima! Abba! Nathaniel! Samuel!' she shouted towards the kitchen.

When Naomi returned to the dining room, the enumerator had piled eight blank identity cards beside his elbow, and the household schedule lay open in front of him. Her father's neat writing filled the boxes.

Dietrich was the first to reach the room, then her mother and father came, the twins and her brothers. They sat around the table in the same chairs they'd used to welcome the Sabbath at sunset.

As Dietrich sat down first, the enumerator began by looking at his details. Naomi's mother handed him Dietrich's passport. He looked at every page, then returned to the page where Dietrich's face looked out from a black-and-white picture. He looked at the boy. 'Why is your middle name not on the schedule, young man?'

'Because it is not my name,' Dietrich answered. His pronunciation of English words always sounded sharp, almost irritable, due to his German accent.

'This passport clearly says—'

'It is not my name,' Dietrich snapped. 'The Nazis made my father and me and all the other Jews change our names to add Israel as our middle name, it was one of their ways of knowing us and belittling us. My mother and my sisters all had to use the middle name Sarah. Israel is not my name. I do not want it in my English papers.'

'It would be wrong to force that name on Dietrich here,' Naomi's mother said.

The man did not reply. 'You were born in Berlin? You are German?' His questions sounded like accusations.

When Naomi and her mother had brought Dietrich home,

they had experienced a lot of judgement. People did not like hearing a German accent. It was why her father had invited a local reporter into their home, so that most people would know Dietrich was not their enemy but a refugee fleeing the Nazis' violence.

'Yes, I am German...' Dietrich's tone asked why that was relevant.

Naomi knew being German meant nothing other than pain to him. He had been betrayed in Germany. His whole family had been betrayed. He had no idea where his parents and his sisters were. Naomi could not even begin to imagine how horrible he felt. But she had heard him screaming and shouting for his parents in his sleep.

The man tapped a fingertip on the passport. 'And this, this 'J' that is stamped on your passport here. What is this?'

'I was born in Germany, but the Nazis do not consider me to be German. To them, now, I am only Jewish, not German at all. The 'J' is for Jew.'

Naomi sighed out a breath in the same moment as her mother and father. She was fed up on Dietrich's behalf with this man's questions. In Germany Dietrich was not welcome because he was a Jew. In England he was not welcome because he was German.

'You are a carpenter's apprentice here, and you are fifteen?' the man queried.

'Yes. I began an apprenticeship in the Great Western Railway works recently. I volunteered when war was declared. I must do something to fight the Nazis. Schooling will not help. My father was a clever man, a lawyer. Learning did not help him, or any of the Jews in Germany.'

The man's grey eyebrows lifted, expressing his surprise to

hear Dietrich speak so vehemently against Germany. He put Dietrich's passport down and reached for an identity card, picked up his pen, took the lid off and filled in Dietrich's name in black ink – without writing Israel – and he allocated Dietrich a Citizen of Britain number.

8

OCTOBER

Lily Franklin

Art walked into the kitchen, dressed in his reserves uniform and carrying the large backpack containing his possessions over his shoulder. 'That's me packed. I'm on my way.'

Lily's heart sank, as if it were sucked into wet sand, like her feet, when she'd stood on the muddy beach in Weston-Super-Mare.

His sweetheart, Betsy Lloyd, stepped forward and took possession of his hand.

Lily was going to walk to the station with them, putting off saying goodbye until the last moment. Her father was walking to the station too, despite a foul mood that he made sure Lily knew she was responsible for.

She'd made *'is life ell'* – his words. Since she'd begun working for GWR she'd been called a traitor, a deserter and ungrateful. *'Your mam can't do without you. You selfish girl.'*

Lily had learned long ago that nothing she said would help, so it was best to keep quiet when her father was angry. She'd sat at the table every evening and eaten the dinner she'd hurriedly cooked, or got up early to put on the stove to stew, in absolute silence.

She didn't even speak when he'd told her she'd have to hand over the whole of her wage. She knew Art had been allowed to keep half of his, so she was never going to hand over all of hers.

She had not even spoken, or flinched a muscle, when her father's hand had lifted to slap her. Art had caught his arm and pulled it down.

But if her father dared tell her she couldn't walk to the station with Art to say goodbye, she'd tell him to do something rude with himself.

Her stepmother had threatened to lock Lily in the room she shared with her sisters to stop her going to work. Art had argued, '*What good's that, if then she can't work in the ouse either?*'

'*She'll get the sack an then she'll av to stay ere!*' her stepmother had screamed back.

'*Then Dad will be blamed for is daughter not turnin up, an ee'll get a bad name!*' Art had shouted.

When her stepmother had let Lily leave she'd run at full pelt to meet Lenny on the corner by the park. They walked into the GWR site together every morning. He'd held her hand through the subway the first time because she didn't like so many men pushing all around her when she was shaken up. It had become a habit after that. She held his hand most days because it made her feel happy.

'Come on, Lily, cheer up,' Art told her. 'I'd rather remember you smilin when I leave.'

She hadn't realised her expression was so obviously glum. She forced a smile for his sake.

Art led the way along the narrow hall, Betsy behind him holding the hand he'd let hang behind his back. Her father walked behind them. Lily followed. She closed the door behind them all.

A group of boys played cricket in the middle of the road with an old packing box in the place of stumps. Crack. A boy struck the heavy leather ball with the bat. Lily ducked as it flew past, only missing her by inches.

'Ey!' Art shouted. 'Mind out!'

He'd been her guardian angel since she was a baby. Her earliest memory was of Art stopping her from eating a snail. He'd told her he stopped her from falling into a bed of nettles once when she could hardly walk, and he'd pulled her hand away from the fire lots of times. It was always Art who saved her.

He waited then, looking at Lily, holding Betsy back by their joined hands when Betsy would have walked on. Lily caught up so she could walk beside them. Their father walked on in front.

'Thanks,' she said, not for what he'd just done, but for everything he'd ever done.

A few other men in the reserves uniform walked along the pavements. All walking towards the rail station. Art spoke to some of them.

Lily noticed Betsy clasped Art's hand tight, like he was a rope above a pit of snakes. Her tensed fingers were bleach white with the pressure of her grip.

Her father walked with his hands in his pockets, and his head down, the brim of his flat cap shadowing his eyes.

Lily curled her hands into fists in her coat pockets, pressing her fingernails into her palms, fighting the desire to cry.

By the time they reached the station there were dozens of men climbing the stairs up to Platform 2, with their wives, girlfriends and families around them.

The clock on the platform showed there were five minutes to wait before the train to Reading was due. Lily bit her lower lip hard and blinked away tears as Art gave Betsy a hug and they shared a long kiss. All the men in uniform were hugging and kissing people, saying their farewells. Lily wasn't sure where to look.

She chose to watch the seconds tick away on the clock. The seconds became one minute, and then another.

A train whistle captured everyone's attention. Then the noisy rhythm of its pistons announced how close the train was. It was early. The smell of coal smoke drifted ahead of it, as the steam and smoke spewed from the engine's chimney, rising into the air in a column that was caught on the wind.

The cloud of steam and smoke smothered the engine as it slowed and rolled past. When it came to a halt, the steam hovered in a mist beneath the carriages and drifted up over the platform.

'Lily.' Art had let go of Betsy and stood in front of her.

Lily's heart exploded with the pain of saying goodbye. She wrapped her arms around Art's neck – what if he never came back?

Everyone moved to the edge of the platform as the men got ready to board.

The platform was such a crush, it was like saying goodbye to Art in a cattle truck.

'Don't do anythin stupid,' she said into Art's ear. 'Don't step forward. If they're after volunteers, step back.'

She felt his body shake with his chuckle of amusement at the same time she heard it.

'You know me, Lily. I won't be able to old my feet back. But if the worst appens, you'll know I died doin my best to make sure those bastards don't get this far.'

She breathed in and out. Tears wouldn't help him, but they ran down her cheeks anyway.

'Lily, let go of me,' he spoke into her ear.

'I love you.'

'I know. I av a deep affection for you too.'

A laugh choked its way out of her throat. She let him go, slapped his arm and then rubbed her tears away with her sleeve. He never used the word *love* to her. His avoidance of it was a joke between them. *'Would the word give you pox or somethin?'* she'd joked long ago.

'Betsy.' He looked past Lily, smiling towards his girlfriend. 'One last cutch, ay? Then I better board.'

Selfishly, Lily wanted his last hug, but it was right it was given to Betsy.

Her father had positioned himself a couple of steps back, as though he were hiding. As if he weren't here to say goodbye to Art. Lily wasn't even sure why he was here.

Betsy embraced Art harder than Lily had, and even though they whispered, Lily heard them making promises that they'd stay true to each other. They shared another kiss. Lily didn't look away this time, capturing every last second she had with her brother.

The train driver blew a long blast of the engine's whistle to chase the stragglers, like Art, aboard.

Art broke free from Betsy. 'I need to get on. I can't be in trouble on my first day.' He looked over Betsy's and Lily's heads. 'Goodbye, Dad.'

Several of the carriage doors slammed shut.

Art turned, stepped aboard and pulled the carriage door shut behind him. Lily watched him throw his bag down and immediately turn back. He pushed down the window, leaned out and reached out as Betsy stepped forward. His hand touched Betsy's cheek.

Lily had no idea what she was going to do when the train pulled away. She'd stayed on her knees in church this morning, when the others rose from their prayers, begging God to keep Art safe. Begging God to stop Hitler somehow and end all of this. Lily didn't understand why, if God was so great, he didn't just strike Hitler down dead. The church was setting up prayer evenings and dozens of candles burned near the altar, lit by people also praying for the war to end as quickly as it had begun.

Art reached beyond Betsy, holding his hand out towards Lily. She captured it and squeezed his fingers for a tenth of a second before the conductor blew his whistle and the train began to move. The train driver blew the engine's whistle. Smoke and steam swept along the platform as the carriage rolled forward. Art's hand was pulled away. They shared a smile, then his gaze reached to Betsy.

Betsy ran beside the carriage and caught his hand for a moment until the carriage moved too fast for her to hold on.

Lily waved.

Art waved to them all.

Her father lifted his cap off his head and waved that. 'Good luck, son!' he shouted, finally deciding to show he cared.

Lily's hand lifted higher and she waved as hard as she could until she could no longer see the train, let alone see Art.

Long black streaks of running mascara marked the powder on Betsy's cheeks.

Lily's eyes were dry now, her innards had hollowed out. Her heart was broken into as many pieces as the best china plate her little brother Jimmy had knocked off the table last night – he'd got a clout for that. She didn't want to go home without Art.

She stared into the distance at where the train had disappeared.

'You an I need to speak about this job now, girl.' Her father's hand surrounded the back of her neck, his thumb and forefinger pressing hard at either side, turning and steering her towards the station exit. To anyone watching, the embrace might look endearing, but it controlled and it hurt. Her father sometimes had this way of being silently angry. Those were his worst days, because then she didn't know she needed to avoid him or at least be mindful of what she said and did.

Betsy walked on the other side of Lily's father as they left the station among a crowd of sobbing relatives.

Lily's stepmother had sulked yesterday. 'I can't manage the kids an the ouse on my own.'

'It's a war,' Art had thrust the words at their stepmother. 'They need women in the factory. Lily's right, the others can do more chores. Polly can look after the baby. Lily's volunteered to elp on the ome front, an I say good for er.'

Art had told Lily beforehand to say she was doing it for the war effort, not herself.

Lily's father was volunteering too, as an air raid precautions officer. So he should be happy he could tell people his daughter had volunteered to work. But he'd probably volunteered because he thought it would help him earn a promotion to supervisor, or because the Government were talking about rationing everything and he thought he'd be entitled to more.

When the crowd funnelled out from the station, Lily ducked her head and twisted her neck, breaking free from his grip. She could feel the bruises his finger and thumb left. He grabbed her upper arm before she could run. The press of his fingers hurt even through the layers of her coat, cardigan and blouse.

Lily stared defiantly at him. She'd started her job now; he couldn't stop her doing it.

'I aint gunna stop workin, Dad,' she said. 'I'll elp pay the rent, like Art did. But I am gunna work.' She tried to pull her arm free, making it obvious to everyone in the street around them that he was restraining her. Art had gone, so she had to stick up for herself now no one else would.

When she jerked her arm away, she caught him, and herself, off balance. His hand released her, but she stumbled backwards. She would have stayed on her feet but he lashed out, pushing her back. She landed on her bottom in a puddle on the pavement in front of the dozen or so people still in the street and the boys playing cricket. Lily's gaze caught Betsy's.

Yes, this is what our family is like, Betsy.

Lily's skin tone hid blushes. People rarely noticed when she was embarrassed. But sitting in a puddle, with the dirty water slowly soaking through the layers of her coat, skirt and knickers, made her embarrassment unmistakeable. The boys had stopped playing their game of cricket, and watched her get to her feet.

'I'll say goodbye, then.' Betsy nodded towards them both, turned away and scurried across the road as fast as a fleeing mouse.

You can't run from the truth, Lily shouted in her head.

'Bowl, Enry!' one of the boys shouted out, to get their game going again.

Lily's father stood stiff and straight in front of her, the anger ticking in the muscle near his ear.

People walked around them. Some glanced her way but said nothing. Everyone knew everyone else's business in the village, and everyone knew whose business to keep out of.

'Get inside,' her father ordered.

The mid-terrace cottage was a few yards away. When the door shut there would be no way out and no one to help her.

She shook her head as terror throbbed from her heart all the way to her fingertips. She felt like stone. She couldn't move if she tried.

'You'll do what I say. I'm your father.' The threat was spoken in a deep, quiet voice. 'If I say you'll go ome, you go ome, an you'll stay there if your mam needs you.' His right hand lifted. For a moment she thought he'd strike her, but he lifted the brim of his flat cap and repositioned it on his head. She knew him well enough to know his hand had itched to lash out.

Her chin rose and her back stiffened. Everything had changed today and if she went into the house it would be more of a hell than working in the iron shop. 'I'm goin, Dad,' she told him. 'I aint stayin with you. I'll take my wages elsewhere.' He wouldn't hit the others; her stepmother wouldn't let him hit her children.

The first slap burned. Her cheek caught into flame. The second, as she turned away to avoid it, caught her eye and ear hard, and it bruised.

The third never came. He leaned right up into her face and snarled instead, like a rabid dog, baring his teeth, perhaps remembering they were in the street and being watched. He turned away but he didn't walk towards the house, he walked in the direction of The Glue Pot. He'd be worse later when he was drunk.

Lily moved quickly, running back to the house.

'Did Art cry?' Polly shouted from the kitchen as soon as Lily had opened the door.

Lily didn't stop to answer. She raced up the steep stairs, her head throbbing with pain from her father's slaps. All she wanted to do was get out of the house. She had no bag, no box or suitcase, so she stripped the flannel pillowcase off a pillow, opened a drawer and shoved the few clothes she owned inside it.

'What are you doin?' Polly stood in the doorway.

'Leavin.' Lily didn't look at her as she pressed the hairbrush and comb she'd inherited from her own mother into her makeshift sack.

'You can't leave!' Polly declared.

'I can't stay.' Lily pulled out a handful of the rags they shared to manage their monthlies and shoved them in with everything else. 'I aint stayin with them any longer. I'm sorry Pol, but Mam's a bitch to me an Dad will murder me one day if I don't get out of ere.'

Polly stepped out of the way, letting Lily pass. She followed her downstairs, the soles of her boots hitting the stairs heavily as she rushed. 'But what about us?' In the hall, she pushed past Lily and blocked her path to the front door.

All her half brothers and sisters looked up to Lily as if she were their mother, even Polly who wasn't that much younger. 'You'll manage. They won't be mean to you. I'll see you at church next Sunday anyway. Let me go, Pol.'

'Aint you even sayin goodbye?'

'I'll tell them I'm goin, then I'm gone.'

'Lily's goin!' Polly shouted out.

Lily's young siblings appeared from the other rooms, gathering like wasps on a jar of jam, encircling her, pulling on Lily's coat sleeves, begging her to stay.

'Your dad will kill you.' Her stepmother stood in the kitchen doorway.

Lily didn't mind the threat. She was never coming back to this house – he wouldn't have the chance.

She hugged Polly, kissed her other sisters' cheeks, and kissed the cheeks and heads of the younger ones, lifting the babe from little Pen's arms and holding him for a moment, smelling his sweet head before kissing his forehead and handing him back. She didn't like being responsible for his nappies but she did love him. She loved them all, she just didn't want to be chained to them.

'I'll see you in church on Sunday,' she told them. Then she walked out of the door wearing the only boots and coat she owned and carrying a pillowcase of everything else that was hers. She only had one place to go. Lenny's. She hoped his family would take her in. She was not too proud to throw herself on their mercy.

* * *

Lenny put a cup of sweet tea on a little table beside where Lily was sitting on the end of the sofa. 'That's coming up a real shiner,' he said, looking at the bruise around her eye. 'You'll have everyone's sympathy in work tomorrow.'

'Hush, Leonard,' his mother told him. 'I want to listen to Churchill.'

In the corner of the parlour, Churchill's serious voice vibrated through a large wireless speaker set into a shiny polished wooden frame. An upright piano stood against another wall. They were in the Sunday parlour. The chief gardener's lodge had two parlours – one for every day and this best parlour they used on Sundays and when they had visitors. There was a separate dining room too. It was a very grand house. A modern chilling machine, called a refrigerator, stood in the kitchen. Lily had not seen one before.

'Churchill is in charge of the Royal Navy,' Mr Faraday had said when the speech began.

'There are no entertainment programmes now. The BBC Home Service has become a Government voice since war was announced,' Mrs Faraday had explained, as though Lily had never listened to a wireless before.

Lily's father listened to the Bakelite wireless in the parlour sometimes. No one else was allowed to turn it on. No one was allowed in the parlour unless her father or stepmother were in there, but it wasn't kept for use on Sundays. They only had two rooms downstairs in their house, and there were too many of them to only use the kitchen during the week.

'...*Hitler and all that Hitler stands for have been and are being warned off the east and the southeast of Europe,*' Churchill said. '*The U-boat attack upon the life of the British Isles has not so far proved successful. It is true that when they sprang out upon us and we were going about our ordinary business, with 2,000 ships in constant movement every day upon the seas, they managed to do some serious damage. But the Royal Navy has immediately attacked the U-boats and is hunting them night and day. And it looks tonight very much as if it is the U-boats who are feeling the weather...*'

Lily sipped the tea. It tasted nicer than the tea her stepmother had at home, and Lenny had stirred two teaspoons of sugar into it. She wasn't allowed to use the sugar at home.

'So there,' Mr Faraday said. 'The Government thought the Nazis would attack from the air, instead they're under the water. They're using their full force on lightning attacks in Poland and in the meantime taking down our supply ships from below. The clever devils are trying to starve us into submission and stop us getting equipment to our forces so our men can't fight them.'

'Do you think that means the Luftwaffe won't ever drop bombs on Britain?' Lenny asked. 'Some of the men in the factory are saying there isn't really a war, it's just the Government trying to control people. It's so quiet, we don't see or hear anything from the Germans. The only aeroplanes in the sky are ours. Yet the military are locking people away left, right and centre, and the Ministry of Supply are talking about rations.'

'These stupid people with their conspiracy theories.' Mr Faraday shook his head. 'Who knows what Hitler will do, son. All I know is we need to keep on our guard and use what we have responsibly for the very reason that none of us can be sure what will happen next.'

Upstairs, Lily's pillowcase of clothes rested on a single bed in a spare room. She'd never had a whole bed to herself, let alone a whole room.

'I now wish to speak about what is happening in our own island...' Churchill continued on the wireless.

Lenny's father slid forward on the seat of his chair, as though he hadn't been able to hear well enough. He was still wearing his tie and three-piece Sunday suit, with his waistcoat buttoned up.

Lenny dropped onto the cushion at the other end of the sofa to Lily. His shirt collar was loose and he had no waistcoat. He looked at her and smiled.

'Too right,' Lenny's father said, in response to something Churchill had said.

Lily had never gone beyond the Faradays' kitchen before. It might as well be Buckingham Palace compared to the London Road terraced cottage she'd come from.

Lily had knocked on the back door as she always did and stood on the step, scared and shaking. Lenny's mother had opened the door and as soon as she saw Lily, Mrs Faraday had opened her arms. Lily had stepped into the embrace, tears streaming.

'Oh dear, Lily, love. What on earth has happened to you?' Her embrace had been tight, holding Lily in the way Art might have. No one else had held her like that.

Mrs Faraday had sat Lily down in front of the kitchen fire and poured her a little of the cooking sherry to bring some colour into her cheeks. Then she'd said, 'I'll pop upstairs and let Leonard know you are here.'

Lenny had been in his room, so he hadn't known she'd arrived. His mouth had dropped open when he walked into the kitchen. 'Oh my,' he'd said, his eyes popping wide open too, making a good impression of a fish on a fishmonger's marble slab. 'Was that your father?'

Lily had answered with a nod, unable to speak as a lump swelled in her throat.

He'd come to her, just like his mother, arms wide, and held her just as tight, as she'd blubbed like a baby on his shoulder. She'd cried in an ugly way, sniffing and hiccupping.

Mrs Faraday had run a flannel under cold water, wrung it out and handed it to Lily to hold against her sore eye and cheek to bring down the swelling. Lenny had made her swallow some aspirin he'd dissolved in a glass of water.

'She's in shock, poor dear,' Mrs Faraday said to her husband, later. 'She's going to stay with us,' she'd added before Lily had even asked.

'Thank you,' Lily had said. 'I don't want to impose on—'

'You are not. Leonard has already taken your things upstairs. You will stay for as long as you need to.'

A dark cloud of shock still hovered in a headache behind Lily's left eye. In one minute she'd said goodbye to Art and in the next she'd run away from home.

'Prepare for a war of at least a year...' Churchill prophesied through the wireless speaker.

Lily's shoulders shook as though someone had walked across her grave.

'*...Patriotic men and women, and those who understood the high causes in human fortune which are at stake, must not only rise above fear, they must also rise above inconvenience and boredom...'*

'And that's right too.' Lenny's mother took a turn to punctuate Churchill's speech. 'The number of people coming to complain to the Civil Defence Committee about the cinemas, theatres and dancehalls being shut. It's the first time I have realised what a self-centred nation we are. Complaining about boredom...'

The chance to be bored would be a fine thing. That was a luxury she'd never had in her life.

'That's it then, Hitler's army and air force have their hands full fighting on the continent. We should be thanking God for sparing us from a storm of bombs.' Lenny's father reached forward and turned the knob on the wireless, switching it off with a sharp movement. 'Instead, the British claim conspiracy. With no thought for the lives lost at sea and ships being sunk, they bewail the chance to dance or watch a film. May the Lord above help us if these are the same young men we'll have to rely on if we lose the fight on the continent and the Nazis do come here.'

'Let's hope they won't be tested,' Lenny responded.

'Indeed, let us hope so.' He looked at Mrs Faraday. 'If the U-boats are sinking the merchant ships and sending our food supplies to the bottom of the sea, we need to make sure every single person knows how to grow their own vegetables. The railway workers will not starve on account of any lackadaisical nonsense on my part. I will write to the author of the gardening article in the GWR magazine.'

'I'll raise it at the committee meeting in the morning. We can communicate the impacts of the battle in the English Channel, that people seem to be ignoring, and promote the importance of self-reliance wherever possible. Raising awareness and giving people some sort of personal purpose may silence this nonsense about boredom and a phoney war.'

Lily sipped her tea. Her fat lip throbbed and her eye and ear ached. Here was Lenny, adored by his parents, and here was she, beaten by her father.

When she'd drunk the tea, she asked, 'Would you mind if I go to bed?' Not only because her head hurt but because she didn't want to envy Lenny his parents' love. That was a mean feeling.

'Of course you can,' Mrs Faraday answered. 'Go on up, dear,

there's a towel and flannel on the bed, and fresh water in the jug and a bowl in your room, and feel free to use the bath, if you would like to.'

'Goodnight,' Lily said to the whole family as she stood up.

'Goodnight,' Lenny replied.

The bathroom and toilet were at the top of the stairs. She'd never used an indoor lavatory until today, and the bath at home was a tin tub that Art carried into the kitchen on a Sunday evening. She'd boil the water on the hearth stove to fill it, and the whole family shared it, taking turns to bathe, one after the other. Oldest to youngest. The water was filthy by the time the youngest got into it. The Faradays' bath had its own room and taps that ran right into it, one for cold water and one for hot. The hot water came from a little tank, a gas water heater. There was another water heater in the kitchen, above the sink, so Mrs Faraday didn't have to boil any water on the stove.

Lily slid her stockings off and walked around her bedroom, barefoot. Her toes curled into the soft carpet as she poured the water from the jug into a bowl, cleaned her teeth and washed her face, under her arms and the back of her neck. Then she put on her nightdress and got into bed. The cotton sheets released the scent of lavender. She was more used to the smell of her little sister Pen's piss. The soft mattress embraced Lily, not a single broken spring sticking into her back.

The narrow hearth in the chimney didn't contain any coal, but no one was lighting fires upstairs since the war began because who knew if there would be more coal, and if the electric and gas were cut off, they'd need it. She tucked her arms under the covers. The room was cold but the bed wasn't. There were two blankets and a satin eiderdown on top of the sheet, and a hot water bottle made of rubber had already warmed the bed. Art would be teasing her something rotten if he saw her here, mollycoddled and snuggled up in Lenny's home. It was odd, though, not having Polly's and Pen's dirty, cheesy, stinking feet in her face.

Despite the luxuries, she lay awake, her face throbbing with pain.

'Goodnight,' Lenny said, in the hall below, then his footsteps sounded on the stairs. A minute later, the door of the bedroom on the right of the one she was using opened and shut.

She concentrated on the creaks, bumps and taps that told her he was undressing, and she heard him pour water into a bowl and use it to wash with.

She liked the sounds. Her home was constantly noisy. It had been too quiet before.

More footsteps climbed the stairs. Mr and Mrs Faraday.

The sounds were like a lullaby to her...

9

Catherine Pearce

Catherine stretched out her legs on the grass and crossed her ankles as she leaned back on one hand and bit into an apple held in the other. She was eating her lunch beside her fellow GWR workers, sitting in a circle on the lawn in the GWR park. She tilted back her head, closed her eyes and let the sun catch her face, uncaring that it might form freckles, bathing in the warmth of the lovely day. The girls had walked down to the park for lunch to make the most of this last burst of warm weather. An Indian summer, they called it, when days like these persisted into late October.

In the sky above, Spitfires circled – turning sharply, rocking their wings and rolling over. Her father had told her that pilots were being trained over Swindon. It was a fake dogfight between pilots. Lily's friend Lenny watched them, his hand pressed to his forehead masking the sunlight so he could see better.

Catherine constantly heard the aeroplanes. Sometimes they

flew low over the town, almost touching the rooftops. Sometimes she saw them high over the hills behind her parents' house, gliding like buzzards, circling in the thermal updrifts. The constant sound of aircraft, like the dozen steel and concrete air raid shelters in the park and the tall towers of the gun mountings outside the workshops, had become normal.

Just as, in scarcely more than a month, this small group of women had become the best friends she'd ever had. Excluding Charles, of course. But he was more than just a friend. She was one of them. They treated her exactly the same as they treated each other. Just as she'd hoped. Their families and friends had accepted her without question too. She fitted in like a jigsaw puzzle piece in the workshop, even though they could see her curvy edges that were not a neat fit – like her accent, her clothes and make-up that were obviously too good a quality for a poorer household and gave the game away to some degree.

Together they were like a... She tried to think of a collective noun for their group. A determination of factory girls? A melee of machine girls? No, she had it – a rally of Great Western Railway girls.

A flush glowed like hot coals under Catherine's skin. It was not the weather, nor the thick denim of the dungarees she was wearing, nor the heat from the furnaces in the factory that made her feel too warm half the time. She was sure she was as rosy as the ripe Cox apple she'd just taken a bite out of. Here she was, even lying to herself. She was not treated as the odd one out because no one here knew her father organised production across the whole factory. She was defrauding these women she'd started calling her closest friends.

No. She was not hiding anything about herself. She had only omitted to tell them some things. She had not told them anything false. They just didn't know who her father was. But they had not asked, so, she had not lied.

'Hey, sister.' Maggie tossed something that hit Catherine's shoulder and fell into her lap. A flat cap. 'Dietrich says you should use his cap, your skin is too nice to ruin. I say, cover your face or you'll look like a leopard with your fair skin.'

Catherine smiled.

Maggie had begun saying 'sister' a few days ago. She'd said she spent as much time with them as her sisters and liked them more. It made Catherine feel even guiltier, not only deceiving new friends but deceiving new friends who thought of her as closely as their family.

Catherine extended her smile to Dietrich. He was such a serious young man, with those ghostly memories in his dark eyes. 'Thank you.' She placed the cap over the scarf she'd tied around her head to stop her hair from being caught up in the machines and pulled the brim low so it shaded her eyes.

The smell of wood clung to the fabric of his cap, a smell that brought Joe to mind. She'd not seen him since she'd changed jobs. But both Dietrich and Lenny spoke about Joe during their brief lunchtime encounters. He was not their foreman, but he was well known among those who worked with wood in any capacity, for taking the time to at least say hello and ask them how they were getting on.

'We should call ourselves the railway sisters of the machine shop,' Maggie declared, obviously having had similar thoughts to Catherine.

'I was just thinking our collective noun should be a "rally" of Great Western Railway girls,' she said.

'Ahem.' Lenny performed a fake cough into a fisted hand and made a frowny face. 'I don't think I can be a sister.'

'You don't work in the machine shop.' Maggie rolled her eyes at him.

A one-shouldered shrug responded.

Lily laughed at Lenny's comical expression.

With her eyes shaded by the brim of Dietrich's cap, Catherine watched Lily speaking to Lenny.

At the beginning of October, Lily had turned up at work one morning with an awful bruise around her eye that she had not wanted to explain. She'd moved into Lenny's parents' house then. There was still a yellowish shadow encircling Lily's left eye, where the bruise had begun as a vivid red and slowly faded over the last fortnight. At least now, though, Catherine had not seen Lily wince after laughing. The bruise might still be visible but the pain had gone. Or, rather, the pain from the injury...

'It was her father,' Violet had whispered to Catherine. 'She's left home for good.'

Violence like that, inflicted by someone who should love you, was a thing Catherine could not imagine. She had endured bullying at school, but she'd had a safe home to go to. She thanked God for people like the Isaacs and the Faradays who were willing to take others in. But that was her biggest bugbear these days, that her father and mother had their huge house and were not helping anyone.

Catherine crept out of the house every morning, checking the street for anyone she might know. Beginning her working day feeling guilty. But at least what followed was a day with these women. She understood what Maggie meant. She joined them on the shop floor not long after dawn, and even as they worked they shouted a conversation across the sound of the machines, which annoyed some of the men. The thought made her smile as she remembered the deathly quiet clerks' hall. *Deathly* – the word made her shoulders shiver. Such a phrase would have meant nothing before the war – now it brought thoughts, fears, about what Charles was experiencing to mind.

She used the men's lavatory beside these women, shared tea from a flask with them, ate meals beside them, and as dusk came, walked back up the hill in the company of Naomi and Dietrich. Since Catherine was small she had dreamed of having a sister to be her friend. Now she had four friends and four sisters, and she felt more at home here in these difficult days than she did in the house on Bath Road.

She hadn't had many friends in her life. She'd attended a girls' school, and none of the girls liked her. Because, despite her father's success and wealth and how hard he had studied and worked to leave behind her grandparents' rented GWR cottage at the bottom of the hill, the mentality of school girls was that they still saw Catherine as a working-class girl from the New Town. Or maybe it was only that one of the girls chose this as a reason for cruelty. For whatever reason, it meant her childhood self had never felt as though she fitted into either half of Swindon. Until now.

Lily laughed over something Lenny had said, drawing Catherine's attention back to them. Lily was very pretty, her tan colouring and the tight black curls of her short hair made her looks stand out among other women. When she laughed there was a little spark in her brown eyes. She'd been quieter than normal on the shop floor after her father had hit her. But Lenny's company at lunchtimes always brought Lily back to life.

Catherine remembered laughing with Charles when they were younger. She had known him but never spoken to him until they had both sung in the Christ Church choir. Charles used to stand on the opposite side of the church nave. Their interactions began with smiles. Then he'd winked and she'd winked back. Then he'd made faces at her, trying to make her laugh while she was meant to be singing. He used to have some solo pieces and she would relentlessly return the favour, contorting her face. He'd look up at the rafters. After a while their non-verbal communications became notes. He drew little cartoons and hid them in her hymn book. There were opportunities to speak during evening practices and before and after church services, but he didn't approach her to talk for months.

She smiled at the memory of Charles telling her, *'I felt too intimidated by your pretty smile. The words would stick in my throat. It was easier to write.'*

She was the first to admit she had a particular feeling for him. She'd written a reply on one of his cartoons, telling him he was a silly fool but she liked him anyway. She'd pressed the note into his open palm as they'd left the church. The written messages had still passed between them for a few weeks before he'd plucked up the courage to walk across the room and say, *'Hello, I'm Charles Clifford.'*

'I know,' she'd answered, and laughed.

He'd said his sister was going to the cinema with her boyfriend and would she like to go with him, because he didn't want to sit with them on his own – that was how their relationship began.

Catherine could not remember laughing as much as Lily and Lenny for a very long time.

She tried to see Charles beside her, legs stretched out on the grass, but she could not imagine him sitting here with her, not while she was with people who lived in the railway cottages and ate sandwiches from tin boxes.

The movement of Lenny's hand caught her eye, pulling her attention away from thoughts of Charles. He'd lifted his hand to look at his wristwatch. 'Nearly time to get back. We'd better head off.'

For a short while life had felt idyllic, though, sitting here in the sun with friends.

The others got up, brushing grass and debris off their clothes.

Catherine took a last bite from her apple and dropped the core into her empty tin. The apple had been a little soft, but edible. The apple harvest from the two trees in her parents' garden was spread evenly on trays and layered with hessian sacks to keep them in the dark, cool and separated from one another, so they'd not rot for a good while. Catherine had been learning a lot about preserving things this year, skills her grandparents probably knew and that her parents had forgotten. Mrs Fletcher was a wizard at pickling all sorts of things.

'Come along, Cath. You're a cloth-head today. You were away with the fairies over there,' Maggie teased as Catherine dallied.

'I was thinking about Charles,' she said. 'Your cap.' She lifted it off her head and tossed it to Dietrich, who caught it cleanly.

As they walked back to the factory, Maggie threaded her arm through Catherine's, linking their elbows. 'Lily,' Maggie called her closer, and wrapped her other arm around Lily's. Violet joined on the other side of Lily with a broad smile.

Catherine looked at Naomi on her other side and raised her arm for Naomi to join the chain. 'Come along, I can't leave you hanging off the end.'

Catherine walked with her arms linked to the other girls all the way back to the factory gate. It aggravated some of the men, who tried to walk through the middle of them, pushing and trying to break the link between Catherine's and Maggie's arms. With a shared glance and a smile, they'd braced their muscles, strengthening the connection. No one was pushing through and dividing Catherine's railway sisters. They were solid. Solidity was the best description for this rally of Great Western Railway girls.

When the man gave up, walked all the way around their chain

and hurried off, red-faced, Catherine laughed along with Maggie and Naomi. It was a story she'd remember for her letter to Charles this evening.

When they stopped to say goodbye to the boys, before parting to follow different routes in the factory grounds, Lenny glanced around them all. 'Mum said if you want to come to dinner one night, you'd all be welcome.'

'I couldn't,' Naomi said, her arm pulling free from Catherine's. 'I wouldn't want to walk home in the dark.'

'I'd be with you,' Dietrich said. 'We could walk back together.'

'I know, but even so, if it is a very dark night, I don't think we should.'

Catherine could offer to drive but Naomi didn't know the car she'd driven on that first day was her father's, and she was also nervous of meeting the Faradays in case they knew who she was. She didn't think she'd ever met them, and she wasn't using the name Pearce, but even so, perhaps she'd met them at a GWR event when she was with her father and forgotten.

'I'm sorry, I agree with Naomi,' she said. One of the few real things her friends knew about her was that she lived in Old Town. 'And I do not have a Dietrich to walk me back to my door.'

That brought a rare smile to Dietrich's lips.

'We better walk on,' Violet said. 'But I would love to come.'

'Me too,' Maggie agreed.

Catherine saw Lenny look towards Lily and smile. 'I'll meet you by the subway entrance later.'

Lily nodded. 'Yes.'

When Maggie teased her, Lily had regularly denied anything other than a sisterly affection for Lenny, which may well be true, but Catherine had watched Lenny's expressions, and his face often shared a different tale about their relationship.

Catherine released her arm from Maggie's and held a hand to

her stomach, guilt playing games with her gut. She wished she'd been honest in the beginning, because every day the truths she had not told became more uncomfortable to hold in.

She'd begun working for GWR with such good intentions, feeling so righteous. Now she was ashamed of herself. Every night she sat in the dining room with her mother and father around a table with ten chairs. In a house with five bedrooms, not including the attic rooms. Three of those bedrooms were empty every night. They should do what the Isaacs had done and take in refugees.

Her father's excuse was that *'up on the hill, we are sitting ducks; we would not be offering anyone a refuge.'*

But why would the Nazis target their bombs on the houses at the top of the hill when there was an expanse of factory buildings at the bottom?

'It is only the three of you here?' the enumerator had clarified on National Registration Day, in a voice that implied he thought it very odd.

Only – the word had made Catherine's skin burn with shame.

'Yes. Just the three of us,' her mother had replied with no concern.

Just and *only* were not words to be used in wartime when on the continent people were being tormented, tortured and killed. *Try. Give. Help.* Those were the words for wartime. Words the Isaacs knew. Words poor Dietrich knew. Although she would never use the word poor to his face, she always felt sorry for him.

'Our sons are abroad, in the army,' her father had advised the enumerator, as though he felt the guilt too and needed to provide an explanation for their half empty four-storey house. 'They are all married now, and their wives live independently.'

Then her mother had added, 'Our maid comes in daily. So she is registering at her own home.' The innocent comment had made the situation more embarrassing. Here was only – just – the three of them, and not only were they keeping this whole house to themselves but they had a maid to help them achieve it.

Catherine had swallowed against a dry throat, embarrassment in full flood as she'd opened the front door and let the enumerator out of the house.

How could she admit her truth to these friends who shared even small homes and welcomed strangers into their lives so willingly?

* * *

Catherine gathered up the used cutlery and crockery and followed her mother out of the room with a tray, carrying the items to be washed into the kitchen. They would leave them in there for Mrs Fletcher to wash in the morning. Catherine stacked the things she'd brought through in the sink, her fingers itching to turn on the tap and just wash them.

'You have not got away with this, young lady.'

The accusation in her father's voice had her spinning around. 'Pardon, Papa? Got away with what?'

He walked into the kitchen, a deep frown marring his forehead as he waved a sheet of paper. He must have just opened his post. He dropped the letter on the kitchen table. She recognised the handwriting.

'I received a letter from Charles.'

She'd received two letters from Charles this morning. They were the first she'd received for a couple of weeks, and they'd been sent two weeks apart even though they'd arrived together. She had not realised there was a third letter addressed to her father.

He waved his 'angry finger', as her brothers had named it as children. His forefinger always came out when he was on his high horse about something, and it pointed like a pistol.

Charles's letters to her had conveyed his feelings about her employment in the GWR workshops. He did not agree with her working on the shop floor.

We will marry soon, and then you will not be able to work, so why take this risk? Resign, Catherine. Please.

'I cannot believe you are calling yourself Catherine Clifford.' Her father spoke quietly despite deploying the 'angry finger'.

Charles must have told him everything she had written to him in confidence.

'You told me you volunteered to assemble the brass lamps the Ministry of Transport commissioned.'

If her father knew she was not doing that then he must have looked for her GWR file, or asked one of his clerks to, because she had not told Charles what she was doing.

'I knew you would grumble if I told you I was going into the machine shops. But I want to do something valuable and I am learning so much. I can work the metal lathes now.' She kept her tone low too, she would not shout.

There were some advantages to being the youngest in a family – she had watched and learned from her brothers' mistakes and their victories. Keep calm, do not express your emotions, and if not initially, eventually her father would calm down too and consider the request from a more logical viewpoint.

'You need women to fulfil the men's roles. The Government will not let women fight. But there are not enough men to win this war unless we help. More men will leave the factory. You know they will have to. They must. The country needs sailors, pilots and soldiers, but we also need the weaponry and supply items to sustain the army, air force and navy. I am healthy, strong and intelligent. I could fight too, but as I am considered too weak for that, I will do more here. I am able—'

'I did not say you are unable. Remember, I asked you to work as a clerk. You can do your part as a clerk!' As his temper broke, his angry finger folded into an angry fist that thumped down on the kitchen table, marking the point where he expected the conversation to end.

She gritted her teeth. She was not going to give in. Sometimes their stubborn natures clashed as firmly as if they were stags with broad antlers that locked, tangled and held with equal strength. Facing each other, head to head, neither giving in and backing away.

Charles had said that about her – that when she held an opinion, she was like *'a right royal stag'*. He'd had to explain that term to her. Apparently, red deer stags were graded by the number of points on their antlers. More than twelve and they were known as royal, fourteen and they were imperial, and with sixteen they were known as a monarch. *'My very own monarch of Swindon Town,'* he'd teased often after that. Everyone else thought he was saying she was queenlike – only the two of them knew he meant she was the head of the herd when it came to defiance. The term was always followed by a shared smile that kept their secret.

She stiffened her backbone, ready to face this standoff. Sometimes there was a need for defiance.

Her mother began running the kitchen tap to wash off the dishes. Catherine knew she was trying to drown out the argument. She did not normally wash up and she hated family conflicts.

The thumping fist was the moment her brothers had raised their voices, which meant her father's voice boomed. As a child, that was the moment she'd retreated to her bedroom.

In the weeks Catherine supported Operation Pied Piper, she'd heard his angry finger and fist at work in his office too, and seen clerks backing out blushing, having been told bluntly to do or not do something.

She was not his employee here, she was twenty-one, and she would make her own decisions.

'I do not want to be a clerk. The other clerks saw me as your daughter and that was it. I did enjoy helping the evacuated children, but in the workshop, I am not the mollycoddled chief's daughter and I feel of more value.'

'Listen to your father, Catherine.' Her mother's voice was as firm as her father's.

She acted as though everything he said became law in this house, and that was the real reason this huge house was empty. Because his immovable opinions had chased her brothers out the door. They could have joined GWR, not the army, but they had not wanted to work with him and his angry finger and thumping fist.

Catherine looked at her mother. 'No.' Then she looked at her father and broke her own rule, letting the emotions inside her swell and anger flare. 'This is not about what you want, Papa! Britain is fighting a bloody war!'

'Don't swear, it is not becoming,' her father snapped.

'I wasn't. I meant bloody literally. Charles, Harold, Alfred, Roger and Graham risk their lives every day. I want to stop the Nazis too. I wish I were in Poland. They think women are too weak to fight, but I don't see why. I can do everything men do. I have arms and legs and a mind to move my limbs just like them. I stood up to the boys when we fought as children. I am strong...' She stopped and took a deep breath. Ranting was not going to get her anywhere. Papa could not enable her desire to join the servicemen abroad. But... 'I can't speak about the things I am doing in front of Mama, but you know I can make a practical difference and help our forces where I am working. In the workshop, I feel that I am taking part in the battle.'

His fist opened and he raised his palm, holding it upright, telling her to stop.

'Those workshops are too dangerous. People are frequently injured. Men lose their lives. I am proud of you for wanting to help but I will not let you take that risk. You will resign tomorrow or I will have the foreman fire you. There is no argument. While you live under my roof, you will do as I say. That is the end of this, Catherine.'

She stared at him. Unsure how to respond, not because of his words, but because the man who faced her was not the father she clashed horns with. This man, who expressed his opinion in a calm voice with swimming eyes, was a stranger. His eyes did not say he was laying down a new law in his home – they said *I love you too much to let you do this.*

'Catherine...' Her mother's voice urged her to stop arguing.

Her father withdrew a handkerchief from his pocket and blew his nose.

She could not stop what she was doing, it was too important. Even though he was asking her because he loved her, she would not back down. Men were risking their lives fighting. Women and children were dying in Europe. Not only in Poland, even in Germany. Look at poor Dietrich who still had no idea if his family were alive. She was willing and proud to take the same risks as the working men here. She lifted her chin higher and swallowed against a dry mouth. Her heartbeat pulsed so fast she felt the rhythm beating in the artery in her throat.

She took another breath, then said, 'I am leaving home.'

'Leaving...?' Her mother's voice became a high squeak.

'I will leave,' she confirmed. 'If I am not under your roof, then

I can choose to live how I please. And if you dare ask the foreman to fire me, Papa, I will tell the *Evening Advertiser*, and how embarrassing would that be for GWR?'

'Where will you go?' her father challenged, his voice and his expression saying he thought she was calling his bluff.

'To a friend's house in the Railway Village.' Her chin tilted up another defiant notch. 'I'll leave in the morning. It will be easier for me to walk to and from work if I live in the village anyway.'

'Stay,' her father said. It was a simple one-word command, as though she was his dog not his daughter.

'No. You are right. If I am not under your roof, then you needn't be concerned about what I am doing.'

'I will be concerned, whether you are here or there,' he snapped back. 'Wherever you live will not reduce the risks of working with the machinery. If you disobey my request and leave this house, Catherine, do not think I shall welcome you back with open arms if, God forbid, the worst happens.'

Catherine heard his last statement as the dominant stag's final bellow at the challenger who retreated. But it was not really retreat. She may have withdrawn from the fight with him, but she had not backed down. It felt better than it should to know she was taking complete control of her life when the reason behind it was a war.

She looked at her mother.

A tear rolled down her mother's cheek.

'I will only be at the bottom of the hill,' Catherine reassured her.

Her mother turned to the sink, hiding her feelings.

Catherine loved her father and mother, and all of her brothers, but when it came to expressing emotions, they were a malfunctioning bunch. She longed for Charles – to have him here to embrace.

'I am going upstairs.'

Catherine left her mother to hide her distress in washing crockery and her father to shut himself away in his study with his paperwork and cigars. Usually, he would closet himself away and behave smugly whether he had won the argument or not. Though possibly not this evening. She believed he was genuinely afraid for her. But fear would not win this war.

She wiped tears from her cheeks as she climbed the stairs. She did not really want to leave, but she had to if she wanted to carry on living the life of Catherine Clifford. If she stayed here, their stubborn natures would clash constantly on this subject and in the end he would just enforce his threat to have her dismissed.

She did not go to her bedroom but climbed the stairs to the attic. She'd left her paper and pen in the room there. It was cloudy outside tonight, and the room was pitch black. Her eyes began to adjust, but it was too dark to write. She sat on the chair by the window, her arms folded over her chest. She could not write physically, but in her thoughts she drafted the first angry letter she'd written to Charles.

If I write a private letter to you, I do not expect Papa to talk to me about the contents of it. He is not my keeper, Charles, and nor will you be when we are married. I am telling you what I told him; I am going to continue working with the machines whether you like it or not.

Her folded arms released their grip of anger, and she looked into the dark clouds as her fingers twisted her engagement ring around and around. She would not tell Charles where she hoped to live. How could she trust him not to tell her father now?

The sound of engines drew her closer to the window. Aircraft. Her gaze scanned the undersides of the dark clouds, but the aeroplanes must be above them, which meant they were British and flying towards Europe. They might be carrying supplies to the troops, or perhaps flying across to fight a real air battle over there.

She closed her eyes, pressed her palms together and began her nightly prayer, firstly for peace, and if God could not bring about peace, then for the safekeeping of everyone she loved. Lastly, she prayed for the Lord to protect every other good person that she didn't know.

10

Catherine Pearce

It was 6 a.m. and still dark when Catherine tapped her knuckles on the front door of the chief gardener's lodge. Her other hand clutched a small suitcase that she'd quickly filled with clothes and a few personal items. She didn't want to appear as though she expected to move in permanently – she only intended to ask for a bolthole – but she had to go somewhere and she knew the Faradays still had one spare bedroom. She was taking a risk that they might know her as Catherine Pearce, but she'd weighed up her choices and decided it was worth it. There would not be space in anyone else's home and she wanted to stay here in the village with her railway family.

Her hand lowered from the door and both hands held the worn leather handle of the case she'd used for as long as she could remember.

She waited.

She did not want to knock again as the Faradays might still be in bed. They had an hour yet to rise and for Lenny and Lily to get themselves into the workshops.

Sounds stirred on the other side of the door. A bolt slid back and the lock turned.

It was Lenny who opened the door. 'Cath. What on earth are you doing here?' He was wearing his shirt and trousers, but his feet were bare and his braces hung down from his waist. He opened the door wider and at the same time looked over his shoulder, shouting up the stairs. 'Lily! Cath's here!'

When he turned back, he reached out and took the case from her hands. 'Come in. Don't stand there in the cold. The fire's burning in the kitchen and there's porridge on the stove if you want something to eat. Lily will be downstairs in a minute.'

He talked at the pace of a train's pistons, his words running at full steam.

Catherine had a soft spot for Lenny. He was eighteen, like Lily, and a lovely young man. She was not that much older than them but she still felt motherly instincts for the younger members of her railway family.

'Are your mother and father home?' she asked as he reached past her to close the door.

'Yes.'

'Can you tell them I'd like to talk to them?' She had not moved from the doormat. She didn't like to step in any further in case they wanted her to leave.

His blond eyebrows lifted, lines forming on his freckled forehead. He looked upstairs again. 'Mum! Dad! Cath Clifford is here. She'd like to talk to you!' He was still holding the suitcase.

The thump of her heartbeat throbbed in her temples. How did she go about asking to stay in another person's home? Charles used to tease her and say she was a presumptuous child. This was a very rash, overconfident and impolite thing to do.

A sound at the top of the stairs drew her gaze. Mr Faraday stood there, clothed in a similar fashion to any other GWR employee in a three-piece working suit with corduroy trousers and patches on the elbows of his jacket. She had never seen a GWR chief who was not clothed in black tails and a top hat. Now she knew she had never met the chief gardener before.

'*He enjoys getting his hands dirty,*' Lenny had told Catherine once when they'd been talking about the rose bushes that had been pulled up. '*He'll love growing the vegetables.*'

She could see that was true within a few seconds of meeting Mr Faraday. He descended the stairs quickly, glancing towards the suitcase in Lenny's hand. 'Miss Clifford, how can we help?'

'Cath. Good morning.' Lily appeared on the stairs too. 'What's happened?'

Lily had had a good reason to seek a new home. Catherine had run from a perfectly good home to impose unnecessarily on this kind couple.

The grandfather clock in the hall chimed the quarter hour.

'May I talk to you privately?' she asked Mr Faraday.

Mrs Faraday passed Lily and hurried down the stairs, smiling in a welcoming way that also expressed her concern. 'Hello. Leonard has spoken of you, Miss Clifford. It is a pleasure to meet you. Leonard, make a pot of tea please, and we'll join you and Lily in the kitchen in a minute.' Her gaze returned to Catherine. 'Shall we go into the parlour?' She raised a hand as Mr Faraday stepped from the bottom stair.

Catherine entered the room ahead of them, telling herself she was only going to ask for a room she might rent for a couple of nights until she found somewhere to stay for longer.

'Sit down, Miss Clifford,' Mr Faraday said. 'You look as though you might faint, you're quite pallid, lass.'

She did sit, dropping into a cushioned armchair, wearing her coat, beret, scarf and gloves, with dungarees underneath it all. She braced her handbag and the gas mask box, which hung from her forearm, on her lap. She was probably the most eccentric-looking runaway anyone had ever seen.

Mr and Mrs Faraday stood in front of her, awaiting some sort of explanation for this stranger turning up on their doorstep like a stray cat.

'May I stay with you?' She forced the words out. 'I will pay for my board. I do not expect you to keep me.' Her throat dried. She swallowed. 'I am sorry. This is very rude, to just turn up. But it need not be for long if you do not want another lodger, only until I find somewhere else. I came here because I know you have a spare room, and I had to leave my parents in a hurry.' Had to? She did not have to – that was another untruth to be ashamed of. She could have stayed at home and lived with the arguments or conceded and stopped working in the factory. She had chosen to come here. She was not in Lily's situation – she did not need to be here.

'Why?' Mrs Faraday sat in a chair facing Catherine. 'I mean is there something we should be aware of?'

Such a simple question and such a complex answer, and for no clear reason the room blurred as Catherine's eyes filled with tears.

'Oh, lass, there's no need for tears,' Mr Faraday said. 'You're right. We have a spare room you're very welcome to use, and all we will ask in return is a contribution towards the running of the house. I will ask Lenny to take your suitcase up now.' He left the room, closing the door behind him.

'Is there anything I should know? Anything you want to talk about?' Mrs Faraday asked.

Catherine shook her head. 'No. I did not have to leave home. I am not in Lily's situation. It was just a silly argument, really. My father does not want me to work in the factory and I refused to give up work.'

Mrs Faraday smiled, her expression kind. 'Miss Clifford, you do not need to explain. Whatever your reasons, you are more than welcome to stay with us.'

'I would rather you know. I will feel easier if you understand. I just do not think it is right that more is expected of men than women. My fiancé and my brothers are fighting in Poland at this very minute, at risk of being hit by bullets and bombs. I cannot sit down and do lighter work without it playing on my conscience.'

Catherine was very aware that Mrs Faraday was a home-maker, like her mother – a phrase her mother insisted on Catherine using. She did not want to insult Mrs Faraday, so she picked her words with care.

'As I told my father, if I could fight with them I would, but I cannot, so here I am taking much smaller risks to do whatever I can to help the men fight, and I will not back away from danger here any more than they would in Poland. If we all did that, Hitler's Nazis will be walking around England within a month! So I told him if he wouldn't let me do what I wanted to do while I lived under his roof, I would leave, and I did.'

Mrs Faraday gently clapped her hands together a couple of times.

Catherine's mouth dropped open in what Charles called her 'unbecoming fish-like expression'. She was unsure if she'd said something upsetting.

'There is no need to look so forlorn or fearful, Miss Clifford. I approve wholeheartedly of your choice, and your little speech was very inspiring. Quite deserving of a standing ovation. I applaud your desires. I shall invite you to come along to our committee meetings. You can help us rally the troops, as it were.' She laughed, briefly, stopping herself, perhaps realising laughter was not an appropriate response. 'You may have a room here for as long as you like. For as long as the war lasts, if necessary. And a contribution towards the household bills and food will be very welcome.'

Catherine had no idea what Lenny had told them about her, but it must have been nice things, and they did not know her real name. A desire to tell Mrs Faraday the whole truth, every little detail she'd been hiding, twitched on Catherine's tongue. But she did not speak.

'Do you have a handkerchief, my dear?' Mrs Faraday asked.

'Oh yes.' Catherine undid the clasp of her handbag and withdrew a lace-edged square of cotton, with the initials CP embroidered in pale blue silk thread in one corner. She wiped her eyes, blew her nose and tucked the handkerchief away again.

When she left the parlour, she faced Lily waiting for her in the hall, dressed in her blue overalls, a headscarf tied around her dark curls. She looked at Cath with a concerned expression. 'Are you stayin?' she asked.

'Yes, Miss Clifford will be living with us for a while,' Mrs Faraday answered. 'Can you take her up to the spare room, Leonard?'

'I'll come too,' Lily said.

Lily walked upstairs beside Catherine, and Lenny followed with her suitcase. The room they showed her to was spacious, the bed looked comfortable and there was a dressing table, a tall bevelled mirror, wardrobe and chest of drawers. Catherine put her handbag and gas mask on the bed and took off her beret.

Lily raised her arms, offering an embrace, and once more tears rolled from Catherine's eyes and a sob escaped as she held Lily. Catherine had become such a pathetic watering pot she annoyed herself. She sniffed back the tears and let go of Lily.

'I'm sorry,' she said.

'You don't need to apologise for being upset,' Lenny told her. 'Do you want some time on your own, or would you like to come downstairs for a cup of tea and some porridge?'

Catherine smiled, looking at him and then Lily. 'Thank you, I think I need your company and a bowl of porridge would be lovely.'

She'd crept downstairs this morning and snuck out of the house before her father and mother woke. She had left a note saying she loved them.

Catherine wiped the tears from her cheeks with her sleeve. There were smears of mascara. She would have to sort her make-up out before she left for work.

'I'll tidy myself up and be with you.'

Lily and Lenny nodded and left the room together.

When she joined them in the kitchen a few minutes later, Catherine realised she had run from the guilt of living in a large house and the frustration of being asked to apply too little of herself to the war effort, but she had not escaped her shame. She was still uncomfortable. These people who encouraged her to join them at their table and filled a bowl with porridge for her didn't know who they had taken into their home. If she stayed, she would have to add hiding her British Citizen card to her deceptive way of life, and she would not be able to hand over her ration book to Mrs Faraday. Nor could she tell Charles her new address, because his letters would arrive addressed to Miss Pearce. This deceitful web she'd spun was thickening into a cocoon around her.

She must come clean. She could not keep up this pretence. But she would have to work her way up to the revelation.

She only hoped her father was not stubborn enough to seek her out and tell Mr and Mrs Faraday who she was before she told them. What would Mr Faraday think when he discovered the father she had fought with was his superior in GWR? She stared at her porridge and the drizzle of honey that melted into it, certain she was red-faced. But Mrs Faraday had been so supportive of her protestations, Catherine didn't think the Faradays were classist. What difference did it make who had given birth to her, really? It made as much difference as her gender when it came to the war effort. The only thing that mattered now was that they stopped the Nazis in their tracks.

11

Lily Franklin

Lily sat opposite Catherine at the Faradays' kitchen table, a cup of tea held between her hands, as Catherine held hers by the thin handle and sipped from its lip. Lenny and his parents were upstairs.

'Did your father clout you?' Lily asked. She couldn't see any bruises, but that didn't mean there weren't any, and Catherine was shaking.

'Heavens, no. No. It was nothing like that.' Catherine's expression shifted into what Art called a *'bitter lemon face'* and her cheeks burned as red as a punnet of strawberries. 'No. We had a verbal disagreement not a physical one. My father does not want me to work in the machine shops. He thinks it is too dangerous. My fiancé does not want me to work at all and he would probably agree that it is too dangerous if he knew exactly where I worked. But he and my brothers are being shot at. I would say *that* is dangerous. And can anyone avoid danger during a war? Some people think everything should remain the same even though we are at war. It can't be the same and I am not a coward.' Catherine shook her head, in a way that disapproved of something she hadn't said aloud.

Lily nodded, but she hadn't seen much that was different in Swindon, apart from the Government beginning to ration things and destroy places, like Mr Faraday's beautiful park. The only other thing she knew that was different was the flipping aeroplanes that disturbed her sleep. The pilots were flying low last night, probably practising manoeuvres over the dark town. She'd woken up to the sound of an engine heading towards the house. They'd scared the hell out of her. But the factory horns never sounded, shouting out a warning that the Luftwaffe were coming.

Some of the men she worked with were saying the Government were the villains and lying about everything. She did know that wasn't true. Art had said he was exhausted, and every bone ached from their effort to stop Hitler's army progressing. Bill, who she still worked some shifts with, had said, 'There aint no war. It's a load of nonsense.' When she'd asked him who 'they' were, he'd stuttered and mumbled and pulled at the brim of his mucky flat cap, unable to tell her who was saying that there wasn't a war.

'I'd be careful if I were you,' Lily had said. 'If you spout nonsense about the Government these days, you'll get yourself arrested an thrown in a jail.' He'd not said any more about phoney wars after that.

'I feel very embarrassed, forcing my presence on Mr and Mrs Faraday, but I couldn't think of anywhere else I would feel comfortable.'

'They won't mind,' Lily said. 'They av the space. It'll be nice avin you ere with us. We'll be like real sisters, an I miss my sisters.' Lily smiled.

It would be fun to have Catherine staying here. Catherine was the most different to Lily in their group of friends, but in the workshops their lives outside those spaces didn't make a difference, and Lily did miss her family. Art was right, they weren't brats. She'd always called them that in her head, but she did love every one of her brothers and sisters, and she missed the younger children tugging on her skirt for her attention as much as she missed Polly and Pen.

The truth was she didn't like their dirty nappies and all the washing it meant, but she loved holding the babies in her arms and she missed the young ones excited voices calling for her to look at something. She didn't miss her sisters' stinky feet in her face in bed at night, but she missed their warmth. A hot water bottle was not the same.

She missed the things they laughed about when she was tying rags into Polly's and Pen's hair, to make their silky blonde hair as curly as Lily's was naturally. She couldn't go home, but she could ask Polly and the others to visit her here. She should do that.

'I don't have sisters, or I didn't until I began working in the workshop.' Catherine's lipstick-painted lips parted in a shallow smile. 'I have four brothers.'

'Older or younger?' Lily realised she didn't know very much about Catherine's life. Probably because she knew it was so different from her own, she hadn't ever thought about asking. But family was family.

'Older. All of them.'

'I only av one older brother; the rest of my sisters an brothers are younger. My dad married again. They're ers. Art, my older brother, is a soldier now.'

Catherine smiled again. 'It's hard isn't it? Not knowing where they are or if they're safe?'

Lily nodded, realising she had more in common with Catherine than working on the shop floor. She could get to know Catherine better now.

'What does your father do?' Catherine asked.

'Ee works in the factory.'

'Mine too.'

Lily would never have guessed that Catherine's father worked there. Catherine had a plum-in-her-mouth accent – that's what Lily's stepmother would call it – and a way of carrying herself: she never hunched her shoulders. Catherine's father must be wealthy, or at least have been wealthy. Maybe he'd gambled it all away or something.

Lily stared into what was left of her tea, where loose tea leaves floated in the dregs at the bottom of the cup. She'd turn them out and try to read them when she was done. She looked up at Catherine. 'I'm good at readin tea leaves. Would you like me to read yours when you're done?' She nodded towards Catherine's hand that contained the teacup and noticed the lipstick stain on the rim.

'Can I use your lipstick?' she asked. She'd always thought the scarlet colour Catherine wore on her lips was pretty, and Lily had never had money for make-up. The make-up Catherine wore had always fascinated her, but the pale powder wouldn't match her skin.

'Yes, of course. I've never had anyone read my tea leaves. I had my palm read once...'

When the kitchen door opened a few minutes later, Lily was staring at Catherine's tea leaves, which she'd tipped out onto the saucer, trying to decipher all the different clusters and single specks. Catherine looked up in the same moment Lily glanced over her shoulder. Lenny. Lily looked back at the leaves.

'Are you ready, ladies?' he asked.

'Lily is just about to tell me my fortune,' Catherine answered.

'I can do that for you,' he responded. 'If we don't leave in ten minutes you'll be late and docked half a day's pay.'

Catherine laughed.

Lily didn't like what she thought she saw in the leaves. It showed a separation, and she didn't think it was about Catherine leaving home – that was not in the future.

'What do they say?' Catherine prodded.

'It's got a lot colder today an you'll need a warm jumper on,' Lily answered, making it up. Catherine didn't need to worry about any other possible separations when she'd just had to leave her home.

'I need to run upstairs an fetch my boots.' Lily rose from the chair.

'Shall I fetch one of my warm jumpers for you, Lily?' Lenny asked, as though Lily was really concerned about the change in the weather. 'I have plenty, you can keep it then.'

She'd never had a warm jumper in her life. She was used to being cold. She heard her dad's voice. *Don't be a baby, child. Toughen up. A bit of cold is good for you.*

'Yes, please,' she answered. It was nice that Lenny must have remembered never seeing her wear one and thought she might want one. 'Thank you.' It would be nice to be warm when winter came.

'Shall I come upstairs with you? If you want to try my lipstick,' Catherine offered.

Lily nodded. 'Yes, please.' Life was so different with Lenny – better, happier – and now she had Catherine's company too, everything was 'coming up roses'. That was a phrase Lenny had taught her long ago. She felt like she had roses blooming in her heart, even though all the ones in the park's parterre gardens had gone.

In the bedroom she used, Lily slid her feet into her boots quickly. Catherine had gone to the other room to fetch her lipstick. Lily sat on the chair to tie her laces, doubling over, keeping the soles flat on the carpet. She kept her boots in the bedroom to hide the hole in the sole. She cleaned and polished them every night herself, even though Lenny offered, and took them upstairs. She was saving up to have them resoled, or if they were too bad to be repaired, to buy a pair at the Staff Association bazaar.

Catherine knocked on the door. 'It's me.'

'Come in.'

As Catherine crossed the room she turned the lipstick so the tip rose from its cylindrical container.

'Look up at me,' she commanded. 'And open your lips like this. No, not like a fish. Smile, but pull your lips taut.'

Lily broke into laugher.

'Don't laugh, or I won't be able to do it.' But Catherine was laughing too. 'Seriously, don't laugh, Lily, or we'll be late for work.' Catherine bit her lip to stop herself laughing.

Lily stretched her lips as Catherine had shown her, her hands pressed on the knees of the boiler suit Lenny's father had given her, as Catherine carefully drew the tip of the lipstick across her upper then her lower lip.

Lily's father would call her a slut if he saw her in lipstick.

'Press your lips together, like this. Don't move them too much, otherwise it will smudge. Now kiss the side of your hand to remove the excess, then you can wash it off your hand.'

'Thank you.' Lily did as Catherine advised and washed her hands quickly.

On the other side of the door Lenny waited with a jumper in hand.

'Thank you.' Lily accepted it. She slid her arms into the sleeves and pulled it over her head as she walked downstairs, letting the neck linger near her nose for just a minute as she smelt Lenny in the wool.

When she put on her coat, she saw Lenny looking at her lips.

They left through the kitchen door. As soon as the door had shut Lenny reached out for Lily's hand. They didn't normally hold hands when they were with the others, even though it was a usual thing for him to do when they walked together now. She pulled her hand free because she didn't want Catherine thinking anything of it.

As they walked on, Lenny lifted his hand higher, tilted the brim of his cap, as though that was what he'd intended to do in the first place, and afterwards slid it into his trouser pocket.

Maggie was waiting at the end of the path outside the Abbots' cottage. When Maggie saw Catherine her mouth dropped open. 'What are you doing here?' she asked before she'd even said good morning.

At least Lily had not had to explain her bruises time and again, because most people could guess why. Catherine was going to be asked by everyone.

'And good morning to you, Maggie Abbot,' Lenny said, playfully, as they walked closer.

'I'm living with the Faradays now,' Catherine said. 'To make life easier.'

Maggie's face screwed up into a good impression of a boiled prune.

Violet joined them at the corner of Emlyn Square.

Violet looked past the rest of them to the unusual face in their group. 'What are you doing here, Cath?'

Lily braced an arm around Catherine's. She was pretty certain Catherine wouldn't want to tell everyone she'd left home because of an argument with her dad. Catherine blushed a lot. She was easily embarrassed. 'She's livin with us at the Faradays'. Now it's dark in the mornins an evenins it's not very nice for er to walk up an down the ill every day. So, she's lodgin there.'

'And I knew the Faradays had a spare room,' Catherine added as they walked on.

Maggie wrapped her arm around Catherine's. Violet threaded an arm through Maggie's other.

Lily had a feeling they all knew that was not the reason Catherine had moved in.

In that moment – as they supported Catherine, accepting that she didn't want to tell them the real reason – Lily knew these women would always be a part of her life.

The mouth of the subway entrance swallowed them.

When they reached the other end of the tunnel, Lenny took his hand out of his pocket and raised it in a farewell gesture. 'Have a good morning. See you at lunchtime.'

'Yes, see you later,' Lily replied, and sent him a smile.

'Goodbye, Lenny.' Violet waved.

'Have a good morning!' Catherine called.

'Say hello to Ron from me!' Maggie shouted, as Lenny walked away.

Maggie shouted the same words to Lenny every morning. Lily looked at Violet and caught the moment her eyes rolled up.

Behind Maggie's back, Violet made the same expression every day. She hid the look every day too. Not looking at anyone else as she made the mocking expression. She probably hoped no one saw it. Lily had noticed days ago. It made Lily smile every time. Sometimes she wondered if Violet was carrying a torch for Ron too. Every time Maggie started talking about Ron, Violet slipped into silence, as if she was biting her lip and saying nothing rather than saying what she'd like to say and saying something wrong. But it was only a suspicion, and Lily wasn't the sort to say something to Violet about it if Violet really was smitten with Ron and trying to keep it a secret. It was up to Violet what she did and said.

'Good morning to you, ladies! And you, Lily!' The voice separated her out from the use of the word *lady* in a rude tone.

Lily looked up to the very top of the scaffolding tower they'd just walked past. John Finch was standing on the top deck, beside the anti-aircraft gun. She hated him. He'd been a horrible boy and now he'd grown up into a horrible man. Art had punched him once when he was being mean. In The Glue Pot. Art had got a ban for a month for fighting in the bar. She raised two fingers in his direction, in the shape of a *V*, telling him to get lost. Someone had told her the two-finger salute was centuries old. Archers used to taunt their enemies from castle battlements by holding up their fore and middle fingers, to say – *Missed me! I can still hold a string and shoot my arrows at you.*

The others just ignored him.

The first time she'd seen him up there, she'd wondered which idiot had put John Finch in charge of a gun? She'd guessed he'd volunteered. Not because he was patriotic, but to have bragging rights. He was a bully. The last time she'd walked past when he was up there, he'd made a pistol shape with his fingers, pointed it at her and laughed. No one else had seen and she hadn't told anyone. She'd had a lifetime to learn how to handle bullies, and one important thing was to not draw attention to them, because that's what they usually wanted most.

Naomi was waiting outside the workshop door, having walked into the site from the Drove Road entrance with Dietrich. She completed their little machine shop gang.

The noise in the furnace room next door was deafening. It sounded as if the men in there were smashing the place to pieces. They must have worked through the night. The women had been told the men were lowering the floor to fit taller machinery so they could make larger, longer munition shells. The women were learning to use the machines, so when the munitions came out of the furnaces they could finish them and ensure they were safe and ready to be used. They'd be packed with explosives somewhere else in England. Gunpowder and furnaces on one site was not sensible.

They were told yesterday, when the munitions foundry was in operation, they would need to work through the night at times.

Naomi pushed the workshop door wide as Catherine released Lily's arm. Maggie and Violet separated too.

Catherine smiled towards Lily as they walked across the room. A thank-you smile.

12

NOVEMBER

Lily Franklin

Every single muscle in Lily's body screamed no as she climbed the stairs after dinner. She was going straight to bed. She was sore all over. She'd swear the men she worked alongside were having fun at her expense, asking her to lift heavy things. She'd seen a coin passing from one man's hand to another's after she'd hauled a great lump of iron up on the chain today, not with the machine but with a pulley. She had a feeling they'd bet on whether she could do it or not.

'Just pick that up an move it over for us, love.'

'Pull on this chain. It'll be ard but it'll move if you give it a good tug. One and over the other, that's it.'

She'd told Lenny she wished they would bugger off to fight in the war. That was something she wouldn't say to Catherine or any of the others. Lenny was still her best friend. She'd developed bulges of muscle in her forearms as well as her upper arms and shoulders. Lenny had challenged her to an arm wrestle at the kitchen table, and even though he'd become more muscular too, she'd won.

The bedroom was quite dark tonight, there were clouds covering the moon. She closed the door, walked to the bed and fell on her belly on top of the covers, arms wide like a cross. She lay still. She'd undress in a minute...

Tap. Tap. Tap.

Tap. Tap.

Lily was lying on the sand of Weston-Super-Mare beach. Her father was sitting in a deckchair next to her, with knots tied into the corners of his handkerchief to turn it into a sun hat. He was snoring, fast asleep. Art was sitting on the sand on her other side, licking ice cream from a cone. Her father and Art had saved up from their wages to bring the whole family away on the GWR annual trip. It was the best day of her life, lying flat on the sand with her skirt pulled up, and her bare feet and toes playing with the grains of sand.

Tap. Tap.

She woke, not on a beach but on top of a fancy satin eiderdown, lying on her belly in the dark. Where was she?

Tap. Tap. Tap.

She rolled to her back, sat up and climbed off the bed, feeling guilty, as though she wasn't allowed in this room, even though she had remembered where she was.

'Lily.' Lenny whispered her name through the door. He must have heard her moving. The bed springs had creaked.

'What?' she answered, as she walked across to the door. There was no bolt, he could have just come in.

She opened the door, her other hand rubbing the tiredness from her eyes.

The room was dark, as was the landing, but her eyes had adjusted and she could see him well enough.

'Can I come in?' he asked.

'Why? I'm tired. I was sleepin.'

'You'd sleep better in your nightdress. But I need to tell you something. I haven't had chance to talk to you all day with Cath here.'

She stepped back and opened the door wider. 'Come in.' She shut the door behind him so his parents wouldn't see him in the room. They wouldn't be happy if they knew he was in her room. She didn't want to be asked to leave because they thought she was flirting with Lenny and luring him into her bed.

'Shall we sit on the bed?' he suggested, as casually as though he were asking her if she'd sit beside him on one of the park benches.

'If you want.' She was too tired to care where he sat. Too tired to talk either, really.

She thought he'd sit on the edge of the bed, but he sat down and shuffled back to sit upright against the headboard. She crawled onto the bed and lay flat on the cover beside him.

'Lift your head.' He slid the pillow beneath her head.

She rolled to her side, facing his hip, her cheek on the soft pillow. 'What is it?' she asked. He had always willingly given her a chance to talk when she wanted to, and listened. She should keep her eyes open and do the same.

'Nothing bad. There's just so much going on, isn't there? So much changing, but there's no fighting. My mind feels like a raging ball of flames sometimes. Thinking about work, and being able to feed and defend ourselves, and do something more than eat, work and sleep.'

Her eyelids slid closed. 'There is fightin, on the other side of the Channel. Cath keeps remindin me an Art tells me about it, when I get a letter from im.'

'I know.' He sighed.

Her eyelids lifted. She'd never heard Lenny moan about things, not ever. He didn't complain. He joked and played around.

She lifted her head a bit and rested her head on her palm, looking up at his dark silhouette. He was looking out through the window, not down at her. The way the shadows fell on his face she could see the growth of stubble on his jawline. His jaw, all his bone structure, seemed more prominent these days. His shoulders were broader and his waist narrower. He'd grown up more in appearance in the weeks they'd been working in the GWR factory than he had in the year before that. She probably had too.

She didn't see the boy she'd played with for years – she saw a man. For a brief moment she felt as though she didn't know him. But of course she did.

'I would rather be abroad than sawing up wood to build carts here. I feel powerless.'

'You're not meant to talk about what you do,' she reminded him. But he'd told her weeks ago.

'I don't do anything decent, and I know you're not a spy. I've known you since you were six.' He looked down at her and his teeth flashed white in the darkness as he smiled. His smile made him the Lenny she knew again. 'Is it mean...' he whispered, '... that I don't like Cath staying here?'

Her head lifted off her hand, expressing her surprise. Not because it was unlike him to be honest but because it was unlike him to be mean. He didn't moan and he wasn't mean. 'Why?'

'Because you talk to her, not me. You didn't even look at me during dinner.'

'I'm knackered. I struggled to lift my knife an fork. I feel like ten men right now, an one of them is dead an the other nine are on the critical list.'

He laughed as she repeated one of his favourite nonsense

jokes, then bit his lip, probably realising his laughter was too loud.

'I'm sorry. I didn't know I was ignorin you.' She smiled, the exchange slipping into a normal moment of comradeship. 'Are you jealous of er?' she teased.

He lifted a hand and showed her a gap he left between his thumb and forefinger, the silhouette of his hand captured in a shaft of moonlight that snuck through the clouds. 'Maybe a little bit.'

She smacked his thigh and tumbled onto her back, laughing, though she closed her mouth trying to hold in the sound. Catherine was upstairs in her bedroom, writing a letter to her fiancé.

'Sh.' He pressed a finger to his lips.

'Where are your mam an dad?' she whispered.

'Downstairs. She's working on something for the Civil Defence Committee and Dad's reading.'

'Well, anyway, I'm sorry if you think I ignored you. I didn't. You're still my best friend.'

A childish grin lifted his lips, and his hand knocked against her arm. 'You're mine, too.'

They carried on talking in hushed tones, whispering to and fro until sleep crept up and shut Lily's eyes.

When she woke, the room was lightening. It was dawn. She was still wearing the dress she'd worn to eat dinner last night and she was cold because she was on top of the bed and not under the covers. Her hand reached across the bed, stroking over the satin counterpane. There was a dip and it was wrinkled where Lenny had sat last night. He must have crept out of the room after she fell asleep.

A smile lifted her lips and she didn't rush to get up but lay there, her palm resting on the place where he'd sat. He'd said he thought she spoke to Catherine more than him. But no one made her feel like Lenny did. He only had to smile, or wink, or give her that wonky shrug of his and she felt happier. Her smile perked up a little higher. She only had to touch the place where he'd sat and talked to her and she felt calmer.

A familiar roar outside stole the moment. The sound of the aircraft came closer and closer.

She sat upright and rigid, waiting for the factory hooters to wail or for someone to shout 'Nazis!' The aeroplane noise drew so close she thought the aircraft would hit the house. It passed above. Followed by two more. No warning of danger followed. No bombs fell.

Lenny had learned the different sounds of the engines. He could tell if they were British, and say which type of aeroplanes they were, without even seeing them. She couldn't. She didn't really want to know. She'd rather they'd just stop using the sky above Swindon as a playground. It was a terrifying threat. Even though Mr Faraday said that if Hitler thought they were heavily defended, his Luftwaffe would stay away.

'Lily! Are you getting up? I boiled some eggs for you!' Lenny shouted from somewhere downstairs.

His voice freed her from her stupefied trance. 'Thank you! I'm comin'!' She climbed off the bed, rushing to wash and dress for the factory, her stomach growling longingly at the thought of food.

13

Maggie Abbot

Maggie walked along Regent Street in the company of her sisters, her father, Violet, Mrs Turner, and a few hundred other people heading to the cenotaph. The memorial cross. An empty tomb which commemorated the Swindon men who had lost their lives in the Great War. Their names were inscribed around the sides of the monument which stood in the middle of the road in Regent Circus, between the town hall and the Baptist Tabernacle. Also, halfway between the old and new towns, in the heart of Swindon.

The people around her were far more sombre than normal, even for a Remembrance Day. It must be harder this year, though, for people who'd lost men then – with the soldiers, sailors and pilots fighting again. She thought about Mrs Turner, who'd lost her husband. Maggie had seen tears in Mrs Turner's eyes every year for as long as she could remember. Maybe she hadn't seen the level of other people's grief before because she didn't know their stories. But she'd looked at Mrs Turner and wondered what she was thinking, because she knew about Violet's dad dying in the war.

It was absurd that Hitler wanted to take them all back to brutal bloody battles. It was only twenty-one years since Armistice Day had assured them of the end of the last war, and here they were involved in another. She might not have anyone particular to remember who lost their life in the last war, but she was still feeling sombre because of what might happen in this one. Not a single aeroplane had passed over Swindon today. It was a bit eerie that they couldn't be heard. She'd become so used to the sound of the pilots learning how to fly that she found the silence scarier.

Maggie glanced at Dot, who walked on one side of her, with her head down and her hands in her coat pockets. Dot was not herself. She'd been in an odd mood all week. Dot was the happiest, bubbliest, noisiest one in their house and she'd been quiet and distracted all the time lately. It was like she'd folded herself up and hidden inside, like the origami boxes they'd folded and folded again and again as girls, the ones where they had to pick a colour and then a number to reveal a truth about themselves.

Even Maggie's father had said, '*What's up with you, girl?*' to Dot during dinner last evening.

Dot normally held her head high and smiled at passers-by. She knew lots of people in Swindon because she liked to go dancing. Maybe she was tired. They were all working around the clock these days and walking around droopy-eyed. Dot, Edith and Marjorie were working on the shop floors now too, in different places, and everyone was working shifts to keep the factory running day and night.

'Production is paramount for success' was the latest phrase in all the management propaganda. It was the GWR workforce's responsibility to supply the military and the country with a raft of items people needed to fight and survive. Production was so important the Government had moved this year's Remembrance Day service from the 11th of the month to Sunday the 12th. The service today was replacing Morning Mass. They didn't want people putting down their tools to attend services on the Saturday as well as Sunday.

Maggie's cold hands rested in the patch pockets of her hand-me-down coat.

A woman near Maggie had her hands hidden in a fox fur muff. Maggie had looked at the muffs in the McIlroy department store. They were lined with smooth satin. She'd stood there and stroked the lining of one for a minute or two. Then lifted it off the shelf and tried it out. The woman's hands must be lovely and warm. If she had one, Maggie would sit at home with her hands inside it in the evenings too. But McIlroy's fur muffs, stoles and coats were far beyond Maggie's budget. She hoped, though, that one day she'd have a fur muff – and a fur coat too.

'*Only if someone donates one to a bring-and-buy sale,'* Violet had teased as they'd walked along the coat rail in McIlroy's, stroking all the furs on the hangers.

Now there was another person who was not herself. Violet was as full of life as a wet rag today. But that was a mean thought. She was comforting her mother. Holding her arm rather than Maggie's.

Maggie spotted a familiar head among the people walking in front of her. She lifted her hand from her pocket. 'Ron!' she shouted and waved.

Other people looked her way. Ron didn't.

'Ron Smith!' she called, louder.

His head turned, his gaze met hers, then moved to Violet, and he stopped walking, letting others pass him, waiting so they could reach him. He wasn't with Frank, but another man had stopped beside him.

Maggie had hoped he'd be at the house when she called for Violet. She'd hoped he'd walk up to the cenotaph with them, but he'd left before Maggie arrived. It would be rude of him to walk on without them now she'd called his name, though, and Ron was never rude.

'Good day, Maggie,' he said. 'Mrs Turner. Vi.' His smile rose as he said her friend's name and Violet's cheeks became a little rosier. Why was she blushing? They must have seen each other less than half an hour ago, so there wasn't any reason for him to be so happy about meeting her.

'This is Asher Cohen, a friend from the factory.' He introduced the man beside him, looking only at Violet.

Maggie's gaze turned to the olive-skinned, brown-eyed man. Asher raised his flat cap in a gesture that said pleased to meet you. He had a dark look in his brown eyes. A hollowness. The look reminded her of Dietrich's eyes. It was like you could see into his soul and all that was there was sadness. She guessed he was Jewish – Asher was a common Jewish name.

'Nice to meet you,' Violet said.

'Good morning.' Mrs Turner smiled.

'Ye... es. Hell... o.' Maggie stuttered out the words, her mind circulating through the possibilities of where this man came from, and what he'd experienced.

The man's eyebrows lifted, the darkness in his eyes softening.

'Shall we walk on together?' Ron asked, raising an elbow towards Violet, implying she should hold it.

Maggie stepped across Violet. 'Yes, we'd love to.' Violet was holding her mother's arm, she wouldn't want to take Ron's. As Maggie wrapped her fingers around his arm, holding onto the thick wool sleeve of his long overcoat, Ron did not look at her but sent a look over her head towards Violet and Mrs Turner. Maggie glanced back. Violet was smiling for the first time today. The look Ron had sent her was some sort of confidential comment that had amused her.

'How are you today, Ron? This is harder this year, isn't it?' Maggie drew him into motion.

Her father, Dot, Edith and Marjorie were a few yards ahead now. They hadn't stopped to say hello. Maggie pulled Ron through a space in the crowd and left Violet, her mother and his friend to follow.

While Maggie held on to Ron's arm with one hand, as they spoke, she pressed her other hand against his arm at times with tactile punctuations. She heard herself babbling and knew she was too talkative for the events of the day, but it was a rare moment when she had Ron's attention to herself. If he minded, he didn't say – though people around them glanced across at her.

When they reached the cenotaph, they'd been divided from Violet, her mother and Asher by the crowd. Maggie saw Lily, Lenny, Catherine, Naomi and Dietrich. They'd stood right at the top of the Baptist Tabernacle's wide steps so they could see and be seen. Lenny spotted Maggie and Ron, waved and beckoned them over, then turned, tapped Lily on the shoulder and pointed them out. It looked like they'd saved room for Maggie and Violet to join them. There wasn't space for Ron and Asher as well.

'Lily! Cath! Naomi!' Violet called.

Maggie looked back and saw her waving.

Maggie hung on to Ron's arm. Now she had him she was keeping him. She stood in front of the iron railings, holding Ron in place. Asher stood on his other side. Violet climbed the steps with Mrs Turner and filled up the space that Catherine and Lily had saved between them.

Maggie lifted onto her tiptoes. She wasn't tall enough to see anything from her position at pavement level as senior towns-people laid wreaths. All she could see was the stone cross right at the top of the cenotaph's obelisk.

The GWR hooters normally sounded the start of the two-minute silence. Today, eleven chimes from the town hall clock announced the moment for the crowd to keep quiet.

In the otherwise silent space, she heard faint sobs.

Maggie's hand released Ron's arm and she looked over her shoulder, towards Violet. Violet's eyes glittered. But when she caught Maggie looking she smiled. Maggie smiled back, reassuringly, wishing she had made the effort to stand with Violet and hold her friend's hand. This day *was* more distressing than the other Armistice Days.

Maggie's father would be somewhere in this crowd, thinking about the friends he'd lost in the Great War. Armistice Day was the one day a year he had too much to drink. He'd need a hand to get upstairs to bed tonight.

She realised Ron was looking down at a pocket watch he'd withdrawn from his waistcoat, watching the two minutes tick through time in seconds.

Did he know someone who had died? His expression was very serious.

After the service, as the crowd dispersed, Maggie waited for Violet to walk down the steps, and together they walked over to the cenotaph. They looked at the wreaths that had been laid, bowed their heads and said their own prayers.

'Is your usband's name on ere, Mrs Turner?' Lily asked. She and Lenny had climbed the monument steps and were reading names.

'I can't see a Turner,' Lenny said, as he leaned to one side reading the lists.

Maggie looked at Violet. She was looking at her mother, who was very pale, even though it wasn't terribly cold.

'No. You won't see my dad's name there,' Violet answered. 'Mum moved to Swindon after he died.' There was something about Violet's tone of voice that was off, like the smell of rotten eggs, the stink of something wrong drifted in the air. None of the others seemed to notice and Maggie wouldn't embarrass Violet by asking questions. But she had known Violet longer. When Violet lied, or tried to act, her voice had a wooden quality, her tone didn't fluctuate. But why would she lie about a name on the cenotaph cross?

'I am going to head home,' Mrs Turner said, nodding towards Violet, saying something without saying it.

'I'll stay with my friends, Mum, if you'll be all right on your own?'

'I'll be fine, love. I shan't be good company today anyway.'

'See you in a while, Mrs Turner,' Ron said.

'Goodbye,' Maggie said.

'It was nice to meet you,' Dietrich said.

'Yes, it was,' Naomi agreed.

'I'm sorry about your usband.' Lily was the last to speak.

Mrs Turner didn't answer any of them, she walked away.

'I don't know about you but I need a pint,' Ron declared to no one in particular.

'I could do with a sherry,' Maggie answered. 'Can I come?'

'Sure.' Ron looked at Violet. 'Vi, I take it you'll come too?'

'I suppose so.'

In the end they all walked up the hill to The Goddard Arms because Ron said it would be less busy up there.

The booths in the hotel bar were cosier than anywhere Maggie had been before, as smart as the GWR first class carriages. In the public bars in The Glue Pot and The Cricketers

Arms, the benches were bare wood because the men went there in their sooty and oily work clothes. The Railway Village public house was called The Glue Pot because the men had to bring the glue from the works with them at lunchtimes, to stop the glue hardening. They put the pots on a stove and stirred it to make sure it didn't set. The Goddard Arms was not a working man's place. It was the sort of place where Maggie aspired to spend her evenings.

With so many of them squeezing into a booth, Maggie had to shuffle along until her thigh pressed snuggly against Ron's. Violet was sitting opposite, squashed up by the window, like Ron. Catherine was next to her, and beside her, Naomi. Naomi spoke mostly across the table, talking to Asher and Dietrich, who were beside Maggie. Lily and Lenny had pulled chairs up to the end of the booth and were wrapped up in their own conversation, as often happened.

Lily constantly claimed she did not have any romantic feelings for Lenny, but Maggie would not put down even a ha'penny to back her in a bet. Lenny was always looking at her, and Lily would catch him looking and they'd share this *I know you so well you don't even need to speak* smile.

'Vi, what happened...?' Ron leaned forward, joining Catherine and Violet's conversation on the other side of the table.

'Hey, Joe!'

The splintered conversations around the table stopped abruptly, and everyone followed Asher's gaze.

He beckoned to a man who stood alone at the bar, with a tankard in hand.

'Joe!' Lenny called his name too.

'Who is Joe?' Maggie asked Ron quietly, as the man they'd called to walked over.

'A foreman in the carpentry workshops.' Ron's deep breathy whisper sent a tingle running through her nerves.

This foreman, Joe, had a limp. Maggie looked at him, smiling a welcome, while in the corner of her eye she noticed Catherine did the opposite. Catherine's eyes focused on her glass, and her perfect complexion was visibly scarlet through her face powder.

Dietrich stood and offered Joe his seat, then reached for another chair.

Joe sat down, his gaze passing around the booth. It stopped on Catherine.

'Oh. Hello, Miss—'

'Catherine,' Catherine jumped in, interrupting him. She was even redder. 'Everyone here calls me Catherine, or Cath, there's no need for formalities.'

She knew him.

Maggie frowned, realising she did not know very much about Catherine's life outside work, other than that she had a fiancé. The diamond in her obviously expensive solitaire engagement ring often winked in the factory lights while she was working, never letting them forget about the fiancé in Poland.

'Hello, Catherine. It's nice to see you. I haven't seen you for a long time. I heard you'd moved to the workshops.'

'I have yes.' Her response closed down the conversation.

As everyone began talking again, Maggie watched Catherine and the foreman.

There was something unusual about the way this Joe's attention focused on Catherine. He looked at her quite often, while everyone else drank and conversed and probably didn't notice anything.

Maggie's belly started growling after her second sherry. The sweet drink was going straight to her head because her stomach was empty. She wouldn't be able to afford the food this hotel offered, though. Through the window she could see into Wood Street. All the shops were shut on a Sunday, so there was nowhere to buy anything. Except... 'Is anyone else hungry? There's a man selling roast chestnuts in the street. I really fancy some.'

'I'm ungry,' Lily agreed.

'Me too,' Lenny said. 'We could buy a paper bag of chestnuts each and walk along to the Town Gardens.'

'That's a good idea,' Naomi smiled. 'I could do with a walk.'

'May I join you?' Asher asked, his eyes on Naomi.

'Of course,' Lenny agreed.

'And, Joe, you'll join us...' Ron offered.

'My leg could do with a stretch. Yes, I'll come along.'

Because she'd walked up the hill holding Ron's arm, Maggie didn't see a reason not to do the same when they stepped out of the hotel door. She wrapped her fingers around his coat sleeve. He glanced down and the skin crinkled at the corners of his eyes as he smiled. When they reached the chestnut seller, Ron delved into his pocket to pay for his and Maggie's bags. Then he looked at Violet. 'Would you like some, Vi?'

'Yes, please.'

Violet still sounded off, even now her mum had gone.

Maggie watched her as Ron paid for her chestnuts too. Violet looked at Ron but as though she was looking through him into the middle of nowhere, her thoughts obviously off with the fairies somewhere. Maggie had never told Violet how much she fancied Ron. She probably should tell her. She was hoping after today she'd convince him to walk out with her, so, if Violet had a soft spot for him too, it was better to have everything out in the open.

Lenny paid for his and Lily's bags. Joe bought the rest.

Violet didn't hang around Maggie when they walked through the residential streets of the old town. She walked ahead with

Dietrich, Lily and Lenny. Maggie walked beside Ron, with Naomi and Asher on the other side of him. The bag of chestnuts warmed one palm as she picked the shells off the soft flesh so she could eat them. The struggle to pick off the shells one-handed gave her a reason to slow her pace, in the hope Ron would too and they'd fall behind the others. He did. But Asher and Naomi also hung back. It felt nice all the same, like being one of two couples out courting.

Catherine trailed even further back than them, walking with Joe.

Naomi bombarded Asher with questions, finding out everything about him. He was Jewish. He came from Austria. He was lodging above The Cricketers Arms public house. He was also a skilled carpenter. He'd made the outer cases for clocks in Austria. He'd come to England, and to Swindon, a year ago, to escape the Nazis.

'...the tension has been building for a long time. From the beginning, Hitler encouraged people to be cruel to Jews. Every bad thing is our fault, so everyone should hate us.' Asher sneered as he said this. 'I couldn't stay.' Anger – because he had obviously not wanted to make the decision – sounded in his voice.

Ron rested a hand on Asher's shoulder and Naomi saw the shoulder of Asher's coat crease briefly as Ron gripped him firmly for a moment. Then Ron's hand released Asher and dropped quickly.

Ron leaned forward, looking around Maggie. 'He left his family there,' he said to Naomi. 'They wouldn't leave their property. All he knows is that they've been forced to leave their house now, with hardly any possessions. Like Dietrich's family, they have disappeared...'

The last word hung in the air for a minute or two. Maggie

couldn't imagine what it would be like to lose her family. 'I'm sorry,' she said to Asher.

'I'm sorry too,' Naomi added.

He didn't answer.

It was Maggie's worst trait not to notice when others were suffering, but it wasn't because she didn't care. When she chose to notice things she did, but she didn't always take the time to look at the right moments. She had been called self-centred at times.

'You're too impulsive,' her dad had said. When she'd asked him what he meant, he'd said, 'An idea comes into your head and everything and everyone else is forgotten. And you may be passionate about whatever little plan it is you've conjured up, but you have to remember how some of these ideas of yours impact others.'

The day he'd said that was when she'd made half the clothes pegs into dolls and sold them at the bring-and-buy sale. She'd earned herself enough money for a whole bar of chocolate. But they couldn't hang the laundry on the line to dry and all her sisters had been angry.

'If I hear any of the men at work saying that this war isn't real again,' Maggie said to Asher, 'I'll give them a bloody nose.'

Naomi burst out laughing and covered her mouth with her hand.

Asher grinned.

'Too right,' Ron said, and nodded with a crooked smile. 'Every Jew in Europe will thank you for it.'

'Were they cruel to Jews during the Great War?' Maggie asked. She didn't understand why one human would be cruel to another.

Asher's shoulders lifted and dropped in a shrug that expressed helplessness, not lack of concern. 'Some people did not like Jews. We were not targeted and slaughtered like animals though. I believe that is all Herr Hitler's fault.'

Maggie closed her hand around what was left inside the paper bag she carried, the paper crumpling in her fist. She couldn't stomach eating any more chestnuts.

Slaughtered... What a word to use. But she had read in the papers about people being lined up and shot. She'd wondered earlier, why Hitler wanted to go back to bloody battles. But this war sounded worse than the last. The Nazis were killing civilians in cold blood in the towns and cities, even women and children.

14

Catherine Pearce

As Catherine neared the entrance to the Town Gardens park, she and Joe were at least twenty yards behind Maggie and Naomi, who walked with Violet's lodger and his friend. Catherine glanced around for about the hundredth time. She'd put on a hat with a broad brim in the hope she could tilt her head or turn her back and hide from anyone who knew her as Catherine Pearce, and she'd succeeded. Even her mother and father had not seen her in the crowd. Or, rather, she had succeeded until the men had seen Joe in the public bar of The Goddard Arms.

Fortunately, Joe had accepted her invitation to use her first name and not asked why she was with this group of workers from the Railway Village.

'Joe,' she began, silencing the story he was telling her about his mother setting up a church jumble sale to raise money for the refugees Swindon was welcoming.

He looked sideways, towards her. 'Yes.'

She thought his leg must be hurting him, because his eyes were shadowed with tiredness. But then, for all she knew, he'd just finished a night shift at the factory before they met at the bar.

'Catherine.' He said her name with a smile, his voice playfully mimicking how she had spoken his name. Mocking her serious, I should tell you something, tone.

She crushed the packet of chestnuts in her hand and slid the almost empty packet into her pocket. 'No one knows me as Miss Pearce any more. I mean, to my friends here and in the workshops I am Catherine Clifford.'

'You're married?' His voice rose in pitch, expressing surprise.

'No. Not yet. Though it is Charles's name, but I didn't want everyone to think of me only as the daughter of the chief clerk and behave differently. So, I changed my name, and I am living in the Railway Village with the Faradays.'

'With the chief gardener? Lenny's parents?' Joe's russet eyebrows lifted. 'I didn't hear young Lenny change his name.'

She tapped his arm with the back of her hand. 'Oh, don't say it like that. You know that Mr Faraday is not anywhere near as high in the instep as Papa—Sorry. Mr Pearce. My father almost runs the whole place. He organises everything. Lenny's father looks after the park.'

Joe smiled, in that way he had of letting his eyes laugh at her while he remained absolutely silent.

'You are a secret rogue, Joe,' she told him, and it was the most natural thing for her to wrap her hand around his upper arm. It was hardly a close contact; she was wearing leather gloves and he a thick overcoat. She had often held Charles's arm, and she noted the difference in the sensation of Joe's uneven gait. If it made it more difficult to walk, he didn't say, and now she'd held his arm she didn't like to let go and leave him thinking she'd regretted it and it meant anything particular.

'Were you born with a limp?' she asked. 'Oh, I'm sorry, you don't have to answer that, that's a very rude question.'

'No. I mean no, it's not rude. You are allowed to be curious, it's natural. I fought in the Great War. I was wounded.'

'I'm so sorry. I didn't know.' She released his arm and pressed her hand to her chest. She felt a little sick at the thought. She didn't know anyone who had fought in the trenches – well, no one who had survived. She knew of extended family members, and some of Charles's family, and other people who had lost sons, brothers or cousins. 'I'm sorry,' she said again. 'Today must have been more poignant for you, and there were we chatting carelessly in the hotel.'

'There's no reason you should know and, like now, we fought so that life could carry on as normal, not so that everyone else would spend their lives mourning those lost.'

'Was it awful? Sorry, that's another stupid question, you were obviously severely injured and I know how many men died.'

'It was.' He swallowed, as though something had stuck in his throat, and she saw moisture gathering in his eyes. 'Most days I try not to think about it, but then that leaves me feeling guilty that I want to forget. My older brother died in the mud beside me when I was seventeen. I'd lied about my age because I wanted to go with him. That's when I got this injury. A shell landed between him and me. It took his life, and it took my leg. I have a medal for bravery but I can't wear it. I should have saved him.'

'I didn't see you among the servicemen at the cenotaph.'

'No, for the same reason. I don't deserve to be there. I didn't do anything brave. I was only at the front for four months and then I was injured.'

'I don't know what to say. That must be such an awful memory. I am sorry you lost your brother, but I am glad you survived. And just to go to war is brave.'

He blinked away the moisture. 'Thank you, that's kind of you to say so. Come on, I better hurry up or you'll lose your friends.' He held out his elbow so she would take his arm again.

15

DECEMBER

Violet Turner

Violet faced Maggie across the kitchen table. She'd not invited Maggie. Maggie had invited herself. No doubt with the hope of seeing Ron. But it was nice having her here, because they were alone and it felt like it had before the war when they had time to do things together and sit and chat.

Violet picked up a piece of newspaper. She'd cut the paper up into narrow, short strips to make paper chains to decorate the parlour for Christmas Day. She threaded the piece through the last in her chain of a dozen or so links and used the glue to close it.

Ron had told her she shouldn't make paper chains because there was a shortage of paper. There had been a shortage of everything since war was declared.

'It's only using bits of old newspaper,' she'd complained.

'That could be pulped and reused,' he'd answered. 'They might make the paper in this country but the components for it come from Scandinavia and North Africa. Sailors risk their lives for that paper.'

He was right. The newspapers reported the number of merchant ships that were sunk by Nazi U-boats on a daily basis. Everything imported was struggling to get through. Even the GWR and St Mark's Church magazines had reduced their pages due to paper rationing. They had to apply for a quota these days.

'Scrooge! You can pack them up for pulping after Christmas. After I've hung them on the walls for a week!' she'd shouted at him. 'Just because you don't like Christmas...' He was always miserable at Christmas. Her mother said it was because he missed his family. Violet didn't see why he didn't just go home to them, then '...you want us all to be miserable. Even the GWR Company are making sure people can decorate their houses – they're shipping hundreds of thousands of Christmas trees! So, if you can't cheer up and be festive, go away.'

He had gone, either to The Glue Pot with Frank or to meet Asher in The Cricketers Arms. That was why she'd been alone when Maggie arrived.

She had stubbornly progressed with cutting up the paper, even though she knew that the clerks in the factory were busy emptying out filing cabinets and ripping unused pages from old ledgers to pack the sheets and send them off for pulping. Maggie had arrived just after Violet had finished cutting. She'd immediately agreed to help make the strips into a chain.

'Where's your mum?' Maggie asked as she picked up a strip of paper to add another link.

'She's sewing shirts for soldiers at the Mechanics Institute hall with the Sister Susies group. She sews every hour she doesn't work these days. Since they reopened many of the restaurant carriages, she's working harder too, because, like us, most of the laundresses have left to work on war production lines.'

'Everyone I know is working hard for the war effort, but the men on the wireless keep reproaching people for complaining about being bored of the restrictions. And they tirelessly remind us of the importance of the rules—'

'Like not wasting paper.' Violet laughed. 'Don't you start. I've had an argument with Ron about these paper chains.'

When Ron had walked out of the door, he'd left her blushing. Violet had poked her tongue out at his back. He'd glanced over his shoulder and seen her do it, as though he'd sensed that she was being mean. He'd shaken his head, as if telling her he was not going to react to her childishness.

'Do you think Ron likes me?' Maggie asked, not looking up from her task. Her head hanging down, the unusual double crown of her black hair visible. She'd taken her headscarf off, and it looked like she'd curled her hair with rags last night, perhaps because she'd hoped to see Ron today.

'I don't know,' Violet answered, watching for Maggie's reaction. It was the first time Maggie had dared to admit her interest to Violet. 'He wouldn't tell me.' Violet's heart lurched, and more words stuck in her throat. She should admit her feelings... She couldn't. She really didn't know what Ron thought and she didn't want to be embarrassed if he did like Maggie and not her. After all, he'd spent most of Armistice Day in Maggie's company.

Maggie looked up and met Violet's gaze. 'But you hear the way he speaks to me. What do you think? Is it different to the way he speaks to other women?'

Violet stared into Maggie's eyes, trying to remember how Ron spoke to her. Was it different to the way he spoke to Maggie? 'Is that why you came here?' she asked, her eyes narrowing with suspicion. 'Maggie, you are so transparent. I know you like Ron. Did you come here to grill me because you saw him leave?'

Maggie shrugged her answer, admitting Violet was right.

Really it was a wonder they'd become best friends. Maggie was forward. She liked to show off. Violet preferred to retire into the background. Maggie was loud, her voice could be heard over most people's and she talked a lot when she wasn't drowned out by her sisters.

Violet was quiet. Perhaps because she was an only child and had never had to compete to be heard. She mostly kept her opinions to herself.

But she and Maggie fitted. They complemented each other. Two sides of a coin. At least it would mean that if Ron liked Maggie, Violet would know she'd never stood a chance, because his preference would be for the opposite of what she was.

'I don't know,' Violet answered. 'I don't know how he'd be any different if he liked a woman. I know he likes Asher. He always smiles and laughs more when Asher spends the evening here. He doesn't speak to any women like that.'

Violet liked Asher too. Her mother had asked him to join them for Christmas lunch, but he'd told her he didn't recognise Christmas. He'd celebrated Hanukkah with Naomi's family, and he'd said he was spending the Christian holiday days with them too.

'And he hasn't said anything to you about me, or asked about me?'

'He's Mum's lodger, not my friend.' The words came out too snappy. Violet swallowed back the annoyance that would give her away.

'But you live with him. You must know if he walks out with women. Have you seen him with anyone?'

'No.' Violet shook her head as she finished off another link with glue.

He had said things about Maggie.

'Lord your friend is a bit over the top, isn't she?'

'Does that lass ever stop talking to take a breath?'

'I can stretch my legs now there's no risk of Maggie trying to play footsie with me under the table.' Violet had heard the last statement through the kitchen door. It had been spoken to Frank after Violet had left the kitchen, and choked a laugh out of Frank's throat.

But that was before Armistice Day – maybe his feelings had changed.

Selfishly, Violet hoped he didn't ever like Maggie like that. It would be too awkward if they started courting.

'He speaks to you differently,' Maggie said. 'I thought it was brotherly. But is it? Do you like him?'

Violet felt a blush rise in her skin. She should say yes. She didn't. She shook her head. 'It is brotherly.' If nothing happened there was no need to admit anything. She had no clue what Ron thought.

'I wish I could join you on Christmas Day,' Maggie said, as if she had not asked the previous question.

Violet rolled her eyes. This was the fourth time Maggie had tried to invite herself. 'We're eating a chicken. There'll scarcely be enough for the four of us. I bet, as your dad's a foreman, you'll have a better lunch than us.'

'We have a fruit cake. We had the dried fruit in the cupboard. Dad said there might not be any fruit for next year – he said save it but we voted to treat ourselves this year. I'll save you some.'

'Do you think we'll be fighting next Christmas?' Violet changed the subject.

'Even Churchill said it would be a year.'

'Churchill isn't running the country. People think the war will be over soon,' Violet said. 'The papers say Chamberlain's working on a peace agreement now, as the air raids haven't happened. I heard trains full of the parents of the evacuated children arrived on Sunday, and half of them took their children back.'

'I know. Naomi said the Jewish twins her family took in went home. There were hundreds of Londoners piling off the train to visit the children. Edith saw them. She said it was like a human stampede as they hurried off the platform to get a seat on the charabancs. Cath said the clerks put three trains together to bring them out of London, and they only asked them to pay a cheap day return. I don't think they were meant to take the children back. But Dad said he wondered if that had been the Government's plan all along. It saves the civil servants having to organise their return, if the parents pick them up. There'll be more trains for the parents on Sundays in January.'

The conversation became more like their normal banter after that, while they finished the paper chain.

'Come on, let's get it hung now,' Maggie said, smiling. 'Let's decorate the room before your mum comes home and surprise her. I know she's been miserable since this war started. She could do with cheering up.'

'We could all do with cheering up.' Violet smiled too.

That was the thing about Maggie – she was such a self-focused force of nature most of the time Violet didn't expect her to notice things about other people. Then she'd suddenly surprise Violet by recognising something others hadn't seen. This was why they were friends. Because Maggie had noticed Violet sitting alone in the school playground and asked her to join a game.

'Thanks for helping, Maggie.'

Violet's mother had been suffering even more since Lenny had pointed out there was no Turner on the war memorial. Of course, he didn't know there was no Mr Eric Turner, husband of Mrs May Turner, on any memorial. Eric Bishopstone's name must be on a plaque in Bude. Violet had told her that no one would know. But the fear of being found out was hovering. For the last few weeks, when they had been in bed at night, even over the sound of Frank's snoring rattling through the wall from the other room, she had heard her mother quietly crying.

Violet held one end of the chain and a couple of yards of it, Maggie the other end and the yards on that side, and together they carried it through to the parlour. They climbed on the chairs and pushed drawing pins through the paper into the plaster of the ceiling to hold the chain in place, letting it drape in pretty swoops about the room.

'Have you got any holly sprigs?' Maggie asked.

'They're in a bucket in the yard outside.' They'd all had permission from Mr Faraday to cut boughs off the holly tree in the park.

Maggie fetched the holly and they worked together decorating the hearth and the picture frames.

The parlour did look festive by the time they'd finished.

When Violet's mother opened the door, Violet leapt up from the parlour chair. 'Stay there and close your eyes,' she called. 'I want to show you something.'

Maggie waited in the parlour as Violet fetched her mother and led her into the room by the hand. 'Now you can open your eyes.'

'Oh!' Her mother's hand covered her mouth, and tears moistened her eyes. 'It's lovely. Did you do this together?'

'We did,' Maggie confirmed.

'It's beautiful. Thank you, girls. Now it will feel like a proper Christmas Day, and for one day at least we can forget this blasted war.'

But as her mother spoke the growl of a Spitfire engine made

them all jump. The aircraft flew so low over the roof, the windows rattled in their frames.

'Do you think they'll take Christmas Day off?' Maggie grumbled.

Violet and her mother laughed. It was the way Maggie had said it, rather than what she'd said, and perhaps because they were all under so much pressure they just needed to laugh.

'Bloody aeroplanes,' Maggie said, and laughed too.

16

Catherine Pearce

Catherine walked through the front door of her parents' Bath Road house into a dark hall. The grandfather clock standing against the wall began its Westminster chime. She closed the door and set down her suitcase. The clock's short hand pointed towards the roman numeral *V*. Five. No emotional tug pulled at her as she took off her gloves, no home-coming feelings. Perhaps because of the darkness. The house itself was not the same as it had been before the war. She remembered it illuminated not only by light and warmth but with the noise of four rambunctious boys and one rebellious girl. She smiled at that thought.

This Christmas stay had come about due to a great deal of negotiation on her mother's part. Catherine had given in easily. Her father had taken longer to accept the idea of her brief return without any agreement by her to compromise on her choice to work on the factory floor. She'd agreed because staying here over Christmas meant she could see Charles easily, and he was only home for three nights. He was coming back today. He had leave but could only stay for Christmas and Boxing Day. He had to return to his regiment the day after.

'Catherine! Is that you?' Her mother's voice sounded through the house, reaching for her.

'Yes!'

The door at the far end of the hall opened, and her mother appeared, bringing light and warmth into the hall as she left the kitchen door wide open. A lovely smell followed her along the hall too.

'Are you making sage and onion stuffing?' Catherine's mouth watered shamelessly at the thought of the roast goose they would have for Christmas dinner tomorrow.

'Mrs Fletcher made it. I am stuffing the goose. And do not give me that look already, Catherine, you are barely inside the house. Yes, we still employ help, and Mrs Fletcher is very glad of the employment. I suggest you run up to your room and change out of your work clothes before your father comes home. Is Charles coming here this evening?'

'He is going to his mother's. I'll see him tomorrow.'

'Very well. Well, I am glad to see you anyway.' She walked forward, her arms rising, and her hands beckoning. 'Let me hold you for a moment.' Physical expressions of affection were rare for Catherine's parents. She'd always assumed it was because she had four older brothers who did not want to be fussed and hugged. But Catherine wanted it. She held her mother with all her strength and her mother returned the embrace as solidly. Now Catherine felt that sense of being home: it was in the smell of her mother's perfume, her hairspray and face powder.

'I love you,' Catherine whispered in her mother's ear.

'I love you too, darling.' She released Catherine. 'Now run upstairs and take off those dirty overalls and that awful headscarf.'

Catherine probably smelt of grease. She would have a bath too and borrow some of Mama's lavender bath salts. It was Christmas Eve, it would not harm to spoil herself for a brief time.

When she walked back downstairs, she wore a dress she hadn't put on for weeks. A dress she'd left in her wardrobe here, and she'd opened a packet of silk stockings that were in a drawer, untouched. She'd even put on a pair of shoes with heels. She had not worn heels for an age. Now she was in her childhood home, with all her family's things, it felt as though for weeks she'd been living in a dream.

Catherine hadn't come back to the house since she'd argued with her father. She had seen her parents at Sunday services, though, because she walked up the hill to attend Christ Church. The Faradays and Lily attended St Mark's Church, which practised the bells-and-smells style of Catholic worship that was not to Catherine's taste.

She had not sat with her parents, but her mother sought her out every Sunday, and they talked while her father stood stoically stubborn and silent somewhere nearby. He wanted Catherine to concede. She would not yield. She liked her job more every day, so their stand-off had continued until a truce had been arranged by her mother for Christmas.

The agreement was, she and Papa would not mention the subject of where Catherine worked for the period of the Christmas holiday. 'So we can spend the holy day as a family should,' Catherine's mother had declared, and relayed that he'd agreed for her sake, 'not yours, I'm afraid, Catherine.'

Her mother had been passing Charles's letters on to Catherine on Sundays and invited him to eat lunch with them tomorrow. Catherine could not have spent the day with him in the Railway Village without risking the lives of Catherine Pearce and Catherine Clifford colliding. She'd been lucky so far. Other than on Armistice Day when they'd met Joe there had not been any risks, and he'd promised not to mention who her father was.

The only problem was she really should pluck up the courage and tell people. The more time that passed, the harder it felt to own up to who she was connected to. It had become a spiral of fibs descending into mayhem because she continued to put the moment off. She was afraid of losing her valued friends.

Catherine and her mother worked together in the kitchen. Catherine peeled and prepared the vegetables for tomorrow's dinner while her mother made a chicken thigh casserole for tonight's meal. Catherine had not known her mother knew how to cook. She had never cooked in Catherine's company before. But she had a recipe book open on the table and was reading through the steps as she worked.

Charles was meeting Catherine at the church service in the morning. He was staying with his parents tonight because he was with Catherine tomorrow. Two of her brothers' wives and Catherine's nephews and nieces were coming here for Christmas lunch too. It would be lovely for the house to be full.

'We will use the dining room tomorrow,' her mother said. 'But we normally eat dinner in here these days, so we'll eat in the kitchen tonight.'

The Faradays were doing the same; to preserve the scarce amount of coal they lit the one fire in the kitchen and spent their evenings in there. Mr Faraday had even moved the wireless into the room. The doors to the parlour and dining room had been shut so no heat was wasted on warming empty rooms.

The room Catherine slept in had been as cold as a refrigerator this morning. The window had been covered with a thick layer of condensation that had turned to ice, and the rubber bottle that had been filled with hot water the night before had lain like a cold wet fish by her feet. Fortunately, Lenny had taught her and Lily the trick of tucking their clothes under the covers, so she had warmed her clothes while she slept. She scrambled out of bed in the mornings and dressed as quickly as she could.

A click – the front door handle. Then the sweeping sound of the door opening in the hall.

Her mother looked across at the closed kitchen door at the same time as Catherine. 'That will be your father.'

It was almost nine. He was very late. But she'd worked in his offices, she knew he must be in constant meetings with the Government ministries, discussing what was needed, where things slowed the delivery down and how to unstick supply problems. It was easy to say they'd need metal to make bombshells, but the metal ore had to come from somewhere in the first place.

Catherine dropped the peeler on the table and hurried to say hello. To help the truce begin she was willing to take the first step.

Her father was lifting off his top hat.

'Papa.' She rushed into arms that opened wide to receive her, and he wrapped his arms around her as tightly as her mother had. The embrace expressed what he'd said before she left – that he loved her. That he only disagreed with her risking her life working with the machines because he loved her.

She could feel that he'd lost weight. His overcoat hung loose where it used to be tight across his portly stomach. Her mother had told her he rarely slept these days, with the weight of supplying the troops, protecting civilians and GWR workers alike on his shoulders.

When she let him go, she raised her hands to lift his overcoat from his shoulders. He freed his arms, a tired sigh escaping. She hung his coat on a hook while he stripped off his gloves.

'They are calling up more men on the 1st of January,' he said, to explain his sigh. 'I have been speaking to the Ministry of

Supply about how we will keep up production to meet the Government's needs with no staff. We cannot slow the pace.'

'Aren't the factory's men in protected roles?'

'They are, but even so, women can fulfil the unskilled roles and many men will want to go, and the services need them.' He pressed his gloves into the coat pocket and unravelled the soft angora wool scarf from around his neck.

'How many men are being called up?'

'All those between nineteen and twenty-seven. Two million men across the country.' He sighed again, his expression down-turned. He had more grey hairs and wrinkles. 'I admit it. You were right, Catherine. I need women working in every workshop. You cannot avoid the heavy machinery. There will not be enough men left here. However, I do not have to like it or be happy that you are one of the women risking their lives. But that is enough said of that for the next couple of days. Let's not talk about work or war for twenty-four hours.' He sounded so depleted. He did not sound like the same man.

'Come into the kitchen,' she encouraged. 'We're cooking. I'll warm up some mulled wine. Mama and I agreed we will make the most of the store cupboard this year as we have no idea what next year will bring.'

'I hope you kept some spices. Rationing increases in a fort-night and the food we can have may be rather bland.' He smiled, but it had been a weak effort of a joke.

Catherine spent the rest of the evening listening out for Charles's first knock on the front door. The knock never came. But he had not said he would call this evening. It was only that she had hoped that if he'd missed her as much as she'd missed him, he wouldn't be able to stay away.

At eleven o'clock, Catherine walked upstairs to her childhood room and changed into her nightdress. The bed was cold and a little damp, having not been used for months and because the fire had not been lit for all that time.

Her heartbeat hammered as she lay down. Every nerve in her body felt eager to see Charles, excited and terrified in equal measures. She had no reason to be scared of seeing him. But it had been so long. Yes, they had written constantly, even if the letters didn't arrive that regularly. But somehow she had lost the physical memory of him.

After a while Catherine gave up trying to sleep, reached for her dressing gown and slippers, wrapped herself up warmly, and quietly made her way up another flight of stairs to the attic room where she used to sit. The blanket she'd used then had been folded and lain over the back of the armchair. Someone had been up here, seen where Catherine's presence once was and wanted to preserve it.

She lifted the blanket off the back, sat, curled up her legs on the cushion of the chair, then lay the blanket across her lap. She tucked her hands beneath it too, holding the blanket up to her chin. It was different sitting here today, because when she looked across the moonlit roofs of the houses, all the way to the factory, her mind's eye could see the people she knew living in the cottages at the bottom of the hill. Her friends. Her sisters – the word brought a smile to her lips.

She'd wanted Charles to meet them, but his letters had made it clear he would not lie about who she was. So she could not take him to meet her friends unless she was happy to say goodbye to who she was in the village. She liked Cath more than Catherine. Cath had purpose.

* * *

A sharp strike of the brass knocker on the front door had Catherine's heart leaping. She had laid the dining table ready for Christmas lunch, taken down the blackout fabric, lit a fire to warm the room and then resorted to dusting – keeping herself busy to waste the time before she could walk to the church and meet Charles.

She walked to the window and leaned to look out at the front steps and see who was knocking on a Christmas morning. 'Charles!'

She ran with childlike eagerness, pulled the front door wide open, threw herself into his arms and kissed his lips.

He'd grown a tickly moustache, and his body felt harder, stiffer, beneath his clothes, his shoulders broader, but it was her Charles. A solid whole human being, not the small black-and-white image of him that she kissed every night before she fell asleep.

She drew away, smiling into hazel, almost green eyes. 'I cannot believe you are actually here. I thought we were meeting at the church.'

His smile, familiar despite the moustache, parted his lips. 'I couldn't wait any longer to see you. I thought we could walk there together.'

'I'll put on my coat.' She turned away from him, reaching to the coat stand. 'Papa! Mama! Charles is here! We are going to walk on to church! We will see you there!'

She did not wait for their answer. She did not want to give them chance to say wait for us. She wanted Charles to herself for at least this one small part of the day.

'Happy Christmas,' she said to him as she joined him on the doorstep and pulled the door closed behind her. She slid her arms into her coat sleeves as they walked down the steps. 'I cannot believe you are real.' She laughed. It had the same awkward tentative sound of a laugh she might have shared when they'd begun courting.

'It feels very much the same to me. Believe me, I am glad to be here. Lucky to be here, in fact. Not many have been allowed home.'

'I am so glad you were.' She secured the buttons at the front of her coat. She'd forgotten her gloves and scarf.

He did not offer his elbow but reached out for her hand. It felt so much more intimate when she did not have a glove on. She was glad she'd left her gloves indoors, his hand would keep hers warm.

'Was the journey difficult. I mean, from Poland? What is it like there?'

'I'd rather not talk about Poland, Catherine. I have seen things I can never unsee, and even done things... Well... Needless to say, you do not have to share that hell with me, so I shall not torment your mind with it. For the few days I have here, I want to pretend there is no war and put all those memories and thoughts aside. What are we having for lunch?'

'Goose, with stuffing, roast vegetables and sprouts.'

His hold on her hand firmed, bracing her close to his side as they walked and talked, and it was like slipping into comfortable clothes, slipping back into their comfortable pre-war life. She need not have worried that she wouldn't know him, or that she wouldn't feel the same as she had – her heart pattered with a flickering pulse every time she looked into his familiar eyes.

In the church they sat together, his parents on his side of them, her parents on her side, and he retained her hand, his fingers constantly playing games with hers. She knew his fidgeting was absentminded, not conscious, yet it was endearing the way he would not let go of her. During the vicar's sermon, about the peace Christ offered, he nudged her knee with his, and when she looked at him, he smiled. Even as she knelt to take communion at the altar rail, she felt the warmth from his body close beside hers.

This was love, she thought, as she watched him in profile, speaking with others, his hand still clinging onto hers, not letting her part from him for one minute. Yes he had changed, in physical appearance and emotional experience, and she had changed too, grown up emotionally, but she need not have worried, she was still desperately in love with him. It was going to be hard to say goodbye at the end of his leave.

There were other men in uniform talking outside the church, and other women holding onto their hands and arms. She would not be alone in her sadness when the time came to say goodbye.

'I am hungry,' he said to her mother as they began the walk home. 'It's been a long time since I had a home-cooked meal.'

17

Naomi Isaacs

Naomi slid the needle into the fabric of the torn seam in her dungarees and drew the thread through. It was almost dusk, her mother and father had fallen asleep in the hearth chairs, and Dietrich had gone to his room to read. Dietrich had a softer mattress and warmer room now he'd moved into Nathaniel's bedroom and consequently he spent more time there. Nathaniel had said he would share with Samuel or sleep in the basement on visits home.

Naomi prayed nightly that her brothers would come home to sleep in their beds.

Christmas Day was quiet every year. Britain not only did not work but, come the lunchtime hour, everyone shut themselves in their homes and, unless you wanted to celebrate Christmas, there was nowhere to go.

This year, though, her home was miserably quiet, with no twin girls giggling, nudging one another and whispering confidences, and no older brothers conversing in deep teasing tones.

Then there was poor Dietrich, who had found Hanukkah particularly hard without his family here and barely spoke a word to anyone.

Nathaniel and Samuel had signed up and left in November. Golda and Esther had left the Sunday before last with their mother because she did not believe Hitler was planning to attack London after all. The general departure of the evacuated children had saddened Dietrich, too, because he had no home and no parents to go back to – which was all he longed to do.

Naomi had waved the twins off at the train station. They'd boarded the carriage with their mother, wearing and carrying the same small number of possessions they'd arrived with.

Then, having lost so many people from the house, there was the person who had somehow managed to join the family and made everything feel odd too. Asher Cohen.

Since Naomi had met Asher on Armistice Day, he'd visited their home at least twice a week, if not three times. Her parents adored him. A son to replace their sons. Dietrich treated him like an older brother, to replace his missing family. Her father had invited Asher to join them for Hanukkah, and Asher shared their Sabbath meal most Friday evenings. He was a regular presence in her home, and she was not sure how she looked at him – certainly not as a brother.

He was watching her sew now, as he smoked a cigarette, sitting in a chair beside her sleeping father. She hadn't spoken. She did not want to wake her parents.

He always made her feel as though she had thumbs for fingers – clumsy and nervous. If she looked at him, she would end up stabbing the needle into her finger. He unnerved her. Flutters trembled through her stomach when he was in the house, and she never knew what to say to him.

On the first Friday she had opened the door and discovered him outside, she'd been surprised.

His cap had been crushed between his hands, and he'd looked sheepish, his eyes holding the hollow look of trauma he sometimes had. He'd asked, 'May I come in and join you for the Sabbath meal? I have not had the chance to be with a Jewish family for so long.'

The words had touched her mother's and father's generous hearts, and from that day forward he came again and again, as though he were a member of their family. She could not think of him like that – she was too aware of how handsome he was. She had even imagined what it might feel like to kiss his lips... But here they were in the parlour acting like family.

'I could do with a walk. I need to stretch my legs,' he said suddenly, in a quiet voice that would not disturb her parents as he tossed the butt of his cigarette in among the glowing coals in the hearth.

Naomi looked up from her sewing.

'Will you come with me?' he asked.

He had brought a cloth bag with him, containing what he needed to spend the night in the house. He was going to stay in Samuel's room.

'Just for the night,' her mother had said when Naomi asked her why. 'It would be cruel to leave him to spend a lonely night in his room in the lodgings when the public house is closed.'

'He can cook himself a meal,' she had answered.

'Don't you like Asher?' her mother had asked, sounding shocked by Naomi's response.

Naomi had spoken too sharply and responded too quickly. It was not because she did not like Asher, it was because she liked him too much. She could not relax and feel free to be herself when he was here. She was self-conscious. Fearful of saying or doing anything she might normally do without thought. Too concerned about what he would think of things she did and said.

'Will you walk with me?' he asked again. 'It would be nice to have your company.'

She put aside her sewing. 'I would like a walk.' She'd spent very little time outdoors since they'd begun shifts in the workshop, other than to travel to and from work, and she'd had no time to talk with Asher alone since the day they met. 'I'll fetch my outdoor things.' Perhaps if she spent time talking to him alone, she would recover from her bewildering, and embarrassing, infatuation.

She left him putting on his overcoat in the hall, climbed the stairs and tapped on the door of Nathaniel's room first. 'Dietrich?'

'Yes?' he replied through the door.

'I am going for a walk with Asher, would you like to join us?' It was only fair that she offered.

'No. Thank you.'

'Ima and Abba are asleep in the parlour. If they wake, will you tell them where we are? We will not be long.'

'Yes. Enjoy your walk.'

'Thank you.'

She put on her coat and scarf in her room and pressed the long hat pin through her felt hat to secure it to her hair as she descended the stairs.

Asher looked up as she came down, his brown eyes seemingly absorbing everything about her appearance, and then finally he smiled, not broadly, but it was a warm smile. 'You look very pretty in that hat.'

She returned his smile as she stepped from the bottom stair. No doubt blushing a vivid red. 'Thank you.'

'In which direction shall we walk?' he asked as he opened the door.

'We could walk through the Christ Church graveyard and across The Lawns meadows,' she answered, passing him. She waited at the bottom of the front steps as he shut the door.

'The Lawns...?'

'It's the old park belonging to the Goddard family estate. On this side now it's just grassland.'

'Which way?' he asked. 'Left or right? I don't know old Swindon, other than where your house is. Take my arm,' he offered, lifting it a little. 'The pavement is frosty, it's slippery.'

She accepted the offer. 'Right,' she answered as her fingers tightened about his arm. She had not held any man's arm other than her brothers' and father's. The feel of Asher's strength and warmth, even through his coat sleeve and her glove, inspired another blush.

The streets were entirely empty of people. The town was utterly still and quiet.

Normally on a Christmas Day she would at least see families through their front windows, sitting together, eating in warmly lit dining rooms or playing games in parlours. This year, because the blackout hours approached, they had covered their windows so all signs of life would be hidden if the Luftwaffe did come. She looked up at the twilight-blue sky. It was also empty and quiet. She'd become so used to the aircraft passing overhead, on the days when they didn't, that was oddly eerie too.

As they walked, the climbing moon painted Swindon black and white – day transitioning to night.

Naomi led Asher across the road, through the gate into the graveyard and along the path that ran between the tall standing gravestones and tombs.

'Have you heard about the sabotage in the sawmill?' he asked, with the sound of a smile in his voice.

She looked towards him. She liked looking at his eyes.

Studying the variance in the colour of his brown irises. Especially when he noticed her looking at him and smiled. His smiles made his eyes grow in depth and melt into a pool of glittering bronze. It had become too dark to see the colour in his eyes this evening.

'No. What happened?' Her heart pounded at the thought of a Nazi spy in the factory, or a fascist trying to interfere with production. She held his arm a little tighter.

'Don't worry, they found the culprit.'

'Who?'

His eyebrows lifted and he nodded towards her, then smiled. 'Just listen and let me tell you. Every morning a man goes down to the basement beneath the sawmill to oil the machinery that sucks away the sawdust when the saws are running. There is a huge system of pipework down there, apparently, and no one goes down there other than this one man once a day. But one day, the machines weren't working. He opened the casing to find out why and found shredded confidential documents. More than that, documents marked as "Secret".'

'No.' There really had been a spy?

'Yes.' His voice sounded playfully dramatic.

'What did he do?'

'Removed the paper and gave the bits to his superior. Then the next day there was another torn up document.'

'No.' Her protestation was higher pitched.

'Again, he removed it, and the foreman was advised. Then a third night and third small pile of shredded documents. His chain of superiors agreed to keep this quiet, telling only the people who needed to know—'

'Then how do you know?'

'Quiet. Let me tell you the story. So it was agreed they would set up a watch, and that night a man sat in the cellar all night in the dark watching the door. He didn't see anyone, and he claimed he was awake the whole time. Though the pipes are wide enough for a man to wriggle through, there is no other entrance point. But again there were torn pieces of secret documents in the pipe.'

'How?'

'Be patient,' he grinned. 'They set up a watch for a second night, and still the watchman saw no one. Then a supervisor had a suspicion and laid a trap inside the pipe, and for a third night the watchman hid himself in a dark corner of the room.'

She realised she was pressing against him, listening hard, both hands now holding his arm as her heart raced, but he didn't seem to mind.

'Again,' he said, 'no one came, but when they opened the access point in the pipe in the morning the culprit had been caught red-handed.'

'Who?'

'A mouse. There was an access to the pipe the engineer was unaware of and the mouse had been stealing documents from an office and pulling them through the pipes to build her nest.'

She laughed and smacked his arm. 'I thought there was a spy.'

'So did the management. Of course, once the culprit was found it did not take long for the story to spread. I'm surprised Dietrich didn't tell you as he works in the sawmills.'

'No. Dietrich is very tight-lipped, he is too afraid of the Nazis to risk anyone finding out anything that might mean they come as far as here.'

Asher's body stiffened.

She had said the wrong thing. He must have similar fears to Dietrich. 'I'm sorry. I am sure you are just as mindful of what that would mean. Tell me about your family... I would like to know more about your life before you came here.'

The stories he told about his family, three younger sisters, two older brothers, his parents and grandparents on his father's side, were flavoured with a sad tone full of longing. They had all lived in his grandparents' house. Like Dietrich's, his family home had been confiscated and reallocated to Nazi officers. He had received one letter from his father since he'd arrived in England, then nothing more.

'They could be anywhere,' he concluded. 'Or dead. Though I can't let myself think that. I left, you see... I should not have left them.'

'But you left before the Nazis invaded. You were not to know what they would do. How could you imagine such cruelty?'

'Regardless, I will feel guilty every minute of the day until I know they are safe and well.'

Now silent, the conversation no longer easy, Naomi climbed over the stile into the sloping meadow in the grounds of Lawn House. The expanse of unmanaged grass rolled from the crown of the hill, with its grand old house, all the way to the streets below leaving a clear view for dozens of miles, all the way to the outlines of the Cotswolds hills.

'No one lives in Lawn House these days.' She pointed towards its lonely dark outline on the brow of the hill. The windows and doors were boarded up. 'The last owner passed away without an heir. It is only ever occupied by inquisitive children snooping around and playing in the empty rooms. No one is here to chase trespassers away and no one mows the meadows or keeps the pathways clear of nettles and brambles around the lakes on the far side. I think it is still a nice place to come, though.

'When I sit up here, looking at the view,' she confided, 'I feel on top of the world. Like Noah in his ark. Safe above the currents of life trying to pull and push me. Sometimes life makes me feel as if I will drown.'

'Yes. People expect me to be like them. To do this or that as they would. I just want to be me. Shall we sit down for a while? We can spot the stars as they appear,' he suggested.

'You wanted to go for a walk. Do not stop here just for my sake.'

'The night sky and the view are too beautiful not to stop and admire them.'

'Yes, then. Thank you.'

She held her coat beneath her bottom so it would not rise up when she sat on the damp grass and cause her best dress to become damp or muddy.

'No.' He caught her arm. 'Let me take off my coat.'

'You'll be cold.'

'I am wearing a waistcoat, a jumper and a jacket. I'll survive.'

He stripped off his overcoat and lay it on the floor like a blanket for them to sit on side by side. For a moment, they sat in silence, looking at the view of Swindon. She lifted her gaze to the sky. 'Where do you think Yahweh is?'

'That is not a thing you should ask.'

She looked at him. 'But you know what I mean. Why? Why does God let people treat others so violently?'

'He must have His reasons.' The tone of Asher's voice said he did not know God's reasons and did not want to be asked to explain them.

'Do you know which star is which?' she asked instead.

'Some.' He lifted his hand and pointed out the stars he knew, one by one.

As it became darker, it also grew colder. She shivered.

'Are you cold?' He wrapped his arm around her shoulders, even though he was the one who wore no coat, and drew her to his side.

She rested her head on his shoulder. He smelt nice. All the carpenters smelt nice.

He turned his head, and she lifted hers from his shoulder, and then he pressed his lips against hers.

She rose in a fast, fluid movement of escape. She should not kiss him, it didn't matter how much she wanted to, it was wrong. 'I should go home.'

'Forgive me,' he said immediately, as he rose from the ground and picked up the coat.

He put it on as she waited, with her arms folded across her chest, her hands clasping her elbows.

'Naomi,' he said, as they started to walk. 'I am sorry. It is only that you looked so pretty in the moonlight and I like you. It felt like the right thing to do.'

She did not answer, and nor did she take his arm, even though he held his elbow at an angle that offered his support. She pressed her hands into her coat pockets. She did not say a single word to him all the way back to the house, walking a foot or two apart from him. Thoughts spinning in her head and emotions writhing in her stomach.

He did like her, in the same way that she liked him. But this had nowhere to go. There was the war... And her family... Jewish women were expected to marry a man their parents chose. Jewish women should not kiss men until they were married, and she could not marry while she was working. She would lose her job. Married women could not work.

'I am truly sorry,' he said again, as they walked the last few yards to the house. 'Will you forgive me for being too forward?'

She glanced his way before climbing the front steps. 'You are forgiven.' She did not want him to think she disliked him. She liked him, and she had liked his kiss, far too much.

'Naomi.' His hand caught her wrist and held her still when she would have turned to climb the steps. 'Please. I want you to know. I did not kiss you without care. I have feelings for you that are deeper than simply appreciating your beauty. I will talk to your father and ask for his permission to court you, if you agree? Will you allow me to court you? I would like to marry you.'

Her head bobbed a nod before she'd even thought about how she should respond. It was too soon to explain her feelings and fears to him. But even though she could not marry now, she would like to spend more time with him and get to know him better.

She pulled her arm free, climbed the steps and, inside the house, climbed the stairs, leaving him below.

18

Lily Franklin

Ten minutes after Lily had heard Mr and Mrs Faraday say goodnight to Lenny, her bedroom door opened quietly, as it did every evening at this hour. There was no need for him to come this evening. Catherine was staying at her parents, so she could see her fiancé, and Lily had talked to Lenny alone in the day. These night-time conversations, on her bed, in the dark, had become their new habit, though. It felt no different from the days they'd sat on top of walls, legs dangling, or on the park benches or the bandstand steps, talking for hours as children.

'Hello,' he whispered across the room.

'Ello,' she replied.

He walked quietly to the bed. She shuffled over to make space for him. She'd stood a pillow up beside her for him to lean back against.

The mattress dipped as he sat and rocked as he shuffled back against the pillow.

'It's been a nice day, hasn't it? I'm still full from lunch.'

'Me too. I've never ad a Christmas like this one. Your parents put so much on the table, an your mam was so sweet to buy me a new scarf. I've never ad a silk scarf. An thank you for my boots, Lenny, they fit perfectly. I tried to find some in the jumble sale but there weren't any.'

'You're welcome. I saw you looking and didn't like to embarrass you, but I knew you'd been walking around with a hole in your old ones. I had to save up, though.'

She reached up and thumped his arm playfully. 'Well now you av embarrassed me. But I will be very glad of dry feet. Thank you.'

He rubbed his arm. She had probably hurt him more than she'd intended, now that she was stronger.

'I like the shirt you sewed for me, Lily. I'll keep it for best. I came in to talk, though, because I want you to know something.'

She rolled to her side, looking up at him. His voice sounded more serious than normal. 'What's wrong?'

'Nothing is wrong. But I'll be nineteen on New Year's Eve—'

'I know,' she interrupted, sitting up and folding her legs to sit cross-legged facing him. He was talking in a strange way. 'Do you want me to bake you a cake for your birthday? It might be the last one befo—'

'Lily.' The pitch of his voice rose. 'Listen to me.'

She knew, before he spoke, what he was going to say.

'I'm going to sign up on the 2nd of January.'

Her heart dropped through her chest, as heavy as a lump of lead, and the breath stuck at the back of her throat.

'I have to go. I can't stay here sawing up wood when the Nazis are spreading across Europe like rats.'

Her lips parted, and she stared at this black-and-white moonlit version of Lenny. A grown man. Not the boy she'd talked to on the bandstand steps in the park. Not the boy who'd cut her palm with the knife his father used for pruning hothouse plants in the park's greenhouses. She looked down at the scar on the hand that rested in her lap.

She'd always had Lenny. What would she do without him?

'I want to tell you something else...' he said.

She looked up and met his gaze. He looked directly into her eyes.

'I love you.' It was said with a note of simple truth.

He'd said it before – they'd said it before. They were blood brother and sister. Best friends for life.

'I love you too,' she answered.

'No.' He turned to the side, crossing his legs in a lithe movement, and faced her. He lifted his hand and held her chin with his finger and thumb. 'I *love* you.' His voice forced the meaning towards her. He loved her as a man, not a child. Not a friend.

She swallowed, her throat was so dry. But the words were on her tongue and in her mouth. 'I love you too.'

He leaned forward and kissed her, and she kissed him back, lifting her arms and wrapping them around his neck as a thousand butterflies took flight in her stomach. She wouldn't beg him not to go to war – she knew he had to go, as Art had – but she was going to miss him so much.

19

JANUARY 1940

Maggie Abbot

'For auld lang syne, my dear. For auld lang syne. We'll drink a cup of kindness yet. For the sake of...' Maggie's sisters sang loudly, along with Violet and Mrs Turner, standing in a round, lifting their crossed arms and joined hands up and down to the rhythm.

Violet smiled across the circle at Maggie. Maggie smiled back. Everyone in the circle was smiling; they'd all had a glass or two of Maggie's father's homemade blackberry gin before midnight to ensure it. Her family's front parlour was full to the brim with life and laughter. It had not been like this for weeks, with her father and sisters working different shifts in the factory and Dot still not being her normal bright self.

Mr and Mrs Faraday had invited everyone and their families to their cottage, but Maggie had insisted Violet came here instead, to let Lily and Lenny have some privacy. Poor Lily had finally realised Lenny was more than a friend when he'd decided to up off and fight in the war. They didn't have much time until he left to learn what it was to be a couple.

Maggie was having trouble feeling in a party mood anyway. Her smiles were fake. Nothing felt good lately. Not because of the war. Or perhaps it was because of the war... Her father was coughing more and always tired. She worried about him. They all did, of course. But to watch him struggling caused a physical pain in her own chest. Then there was Ron – who since Armistice Day had taken to either ignoring her when she visited Violet or disappearing out the door, behaving as though Maggie had upset him in some way. Lastly, there was Dot, who had been Maggie's sister, mother and friend, and now barely said a word to her or anyone.

War had changed everything, and yet come to nothing. People in the pub were now calling it a government conspiracy. If the Nazis were so brutal, so dangerous and strong, where were they? Maggie prayed nightly for things to go back to how they were before.

Where was Dot anyway? She'd disappeared half an hour before midnight.

'We'll drink a cup of kindness yet for the sake of auld lang syne.' The singing ended with everyone releasing arms and applauding. Maggie glanced around the room as the circle broke apart.

'Someone needs to go outside with a lump of coal,' her father called from his chair in the corner, before coughing, his lungs heaving. He'd lost so much weight recently, and yet he ate his dinners.

'First foot! First foot!' Marjorie clapped to the pace of her chant. Her cheeks were rosy from the blackberry gin.

It was a north England tradition, the first person to walk through the door in the new year had to be black haired and bring in a lump of coal. Dad's northern relations were long gone, and Maggie wasn't even sure if they fulfilled the ritual in the right way, but nevertheless, Edith volunteered to take a lump of coal and go outside so she could be let in again.

Maggie went in search of Dot. Something must be wrong if Dot wasn't joining in with new year celebrations. It was about time Maggie made her talk about it. Dot would not have left it this long to find out what was upsetting Maggie. It had not occurred to Maggie before. Because Dot was the oldest, she'd always looked out for the rest of them, but who looked out for her?

As everyone squeezed into the hall to cheer Edith out and back in again, Maggie opened the door at the bottom of the stairs and rushed up to the room she shared with her oldest sister.

Dot wasn't in there.

Maggie checked the other rooms. Dot wasn't anywhere upstairs.

A frown pinched at Maggie's forehead as she rushed downstairs.

The others were welcoming Edith back in from the cold.

Maggie snaked around them and walked through the kitchen to the back door. If Dot wasn't in her room, she might be in the outhouse.

Maggie walked through the blacked-out kitchen, her hands stretched out, searching the darkness to make sure she didn't bump into any of the furniture, but it was a straight path to the back door.

As she opened the door, the cold night air rushed into the cottage.

'Dot,' she called quietly as she stepped outside. 'Dot, are you out here?'

The door dropped closed behind her. When it wasn't cloudy, it was lighter outside than inside these days, with the blackout screening in place.

A sob drew Maggie's attention to the outhouse.

'Dot?'

Another sob, and sniffing.

Maggie walked over and leaned close to the old door, her palm resting on the chipped paint. 'Is something wrong? It's me. It's Maggie.'

More sniffs. A cough. 'It's all right. But I don't think I can leave the privy if you need it.'

'I don't need it, but you've been out here for ages. I was worried.'

'Don't worry.'

Maggie was more worried. Dot's voice did not sound like Dot. There was no strength or confidence in it.

'Are you in pain? Or sick?' Maggie whispered in case anyone was in the kitchen. She wouldn't know if they were, not with the windows blacked out.

'No,' Dot answered.

'I don't believe you.' Maggie tried the door, pushing down the latch, but Dot had bolted it on the other side. 'You need to open the door,' she urged.

Another sob. 'I'm in so much pain, Maggie.' The sob became a whimper.

'What's wrong?' Now Maggie was really worried. Dot was unbreakable. She pulled on the handle and shook the door. 'Open the door.'

Maggie heard the bolt slide back. The blackout rules were so annoying. The small space was cloaked in dark shadows. Dot was sitting on the toilet, curled over, head down, her hands holding onto her shins.

Maggie turned, closed the door and slid the bolt back into place, shutting them both inside, then squatted down as Dot lifted her head. In what little light there was, Maggie saw the silver trails where tears must have been rolling down Dot's cheeks for ages. How long had she been in here alone?

Maggie held Dot's hands. She was really cold, she must have been here a long time. 'What's going on?'

'I'm in so much pain, Maggie, and it won't stop bleeding. He must have cut me. He must have.'

'Who? What are you talking about?' Dot's skin was as white as bleach.

Fresh tears rolled down Dot's cheeks and she sniffed a few times. 'I got pregnant. But I couldn't have the child and with no father. So I paid a man to get rid of it. I had to.'

She sounded like her heart was in as much pain as her body. The way she'd said *had to* made it sound as though the decision had tormented her – this was why she'd been so sad for weeks.

'Do you need me to find a doctor?' Maggie rubbed her thumbs across the edge of the cold hands that hung on to her.

'No. He'll know what I did. I'll be in trouble. They'll make me say who did it.'

'Who did do it?'

'Don't be daft, Maggie. If I tell you, that'll put you under pressure to keep it a secret too. Ah.' Her hand pulled out of Maggie's and pressed to her stomach. 'I feel sick.'

'Come inside. I'll help you get upstairs without Dad noticing. I'll lay towels over the bed if you're bleeding. But you'll be better indoors.'

'There's a lot of blood, Maggie. Loads of it.'

'Then maybe I should take you to the GWR hospital. Someone in there would help. If not the doctor, one of the nurses. You pay your subs, so they are there to help you.'

'They'll still tell on me. They have to tell on me by law.'

'Why didn't you talk to me about this before you did it. I'd have at least come with you.'

'I didn't want anyone to know I'd been so stupid—Ah!'

Maggie rose from her squat, releasing Dot's hand.

Dot's hand joined the other holding her stomach.

'I'll put some towels on the bed and bring some monthly rags so you can shove them in your panties and stem the flow as we walk upstairs. Bolt the door again when I've gone, just in case anyone else comes out. It's past midnight, so they'll be finishing up soon.'

Maggie hurried through the dark kitchen, catching her toe on a chair leg and her hip on the dresser before she reached the door. She cursed herself for making too much noise, but no one came out from the parlour. The door was slightly ajar, so she could see Violet, Mrs Turner and Marjorie watching Edith performing something – perhaps it was a game of charades. They would be busy for a while if they were playing party games. Dot would be safely hidden as long as no one needed the privy.

Maggie climbed the stairs, mindful of the creaky steps, and in their room pulled open the top drawer and gathered up some of the rags she and Dot used for their monthlies. With four women in the house, they had a large store of them because they all had the same cycle. She laid four folded towelling rectangles down on the middle of the bed, hoping they would be absorbent enough. If not, she'd have to find a way to scrub the mattress clean. But at least Dot would be more comfortable in bed.

The people in the parlour still faced Edith, not looking towards the door as Maggie crept past.

She was more careful to be quiet in the kitchen and left the back door not quite closed so she could open it easily while supporting Dot.

'Dot,' she whispered as she neared the outhouse. 'It's me. Open the door.'

The bolt slid back.

'Here.' Maggie thrust the handful of rags towards Dot. 'Shove these in your knickers so you won't get blood on the floor in the house.'

Dot rose from the seat and did as Maggie said. She looked so pale Maggie thought she would fall straight back on her arse, but she managed to stay on her feet, pressing a hand on the door. Her cotton knickers had a dark stain where the blood must have soaked through before she'd reached the toilet. She pulled them up and packed the crotch with the rags.

Maggie reached around Dot, glancing down in the moment before her fingers caught the hoop on the end of the chain. With no light, the water in the toilet's bowl was black with blood. Maggie flushed it away and, as the cistern refilled, helped Dot walk out.

Dot's legs were shaking from weakness; Maggie's shook from fear. How much blood could a woman lose? How much blood was even in a body? What if Dot died?

They made a lot of noise as Maggie helped Dot through the kitchen, at her side, bumping into the table, then bumping into the dresser.

'Dot and I are going up to bed!' she shouted towards the parlour. 'She's got a dodgy stomach. Too much of your home-brewed gin, Dad! And I'm tired!'

'Happy New Year!'

'Goodnight!'

'Happy New Year, again!' Violet shouted.

'God bless you!' Mrs Turner called.

'Goodnight girls! Sleep tight!' her father shouted last, the effort of shouting bringing on another cough.

'Goodnight.' Dot's weak voice gave away how poorly she must be feeling.

'Goodnight!' Maggie shouted in a bright voice to cover for Dot's less hearty call.

No one came out into the hall – *thank God*. Maggie pulled the narrow stairs' door wide. There was not a hope in hell that Maggie could walk beside Dot on the stairs. She was going to have to do more to help herself.

'You pull on the rope, I'll hold you from behind in case you fall.'

Dot wrapped her hand around the rope on the far side of the stairs that acted as a handrail, and Maggie watched her grip tighten as she climbed the first steep step, her other hand pressed to her stomach.

It took a few minutes for Dot to get upstairs, but she did. When she reached their room Dot collapsed on her bed, rolled to her side and curled into a ball, wrapping her arms across her stomach. Tears rolled from her eyes.

Dark marks told Maggie that the blood had stained the back of Dot's skirt and run down her stockings. Maggie would have to soak Dot's clothes in a bucket of brine to get the blood out.

'I'll help you change into your nightdress,' she said.

'I'm going to be sick!' Dot called out as she sat up to undress. 'Get the piss pot!'

There was one pot in the room, in case they needed to use it in the night, so they didn't have to go to the outside lavatory. Maggie held it while Dot threw up bile and nothing else, as fresh blood ran between her thighs.

'Don't worry, love.' Maggie stroked Dot's hair. 'It will all be all right,' she said over and over, even though she wasn't sure it would be. When was the right time to just insist Dot went to the hospital? Surely it was better to be alive even if they discovered what she'd done.

Dot's hand clasped Maggie's wrist. 'Stay with me.'

'I'm not going anywhere. I won't leave you.'

20

Lily Franklin

For the second time in a few months, Lily's heart was ready to burst with the pain of saying goodbye. It was only days ago that she'd persuaded the steward to let her into the Mechanics Institute hall with Lenny and watched him sign his name in a thick register to say he wanted to join the army. Along with hundreds of other men. Men had flowed through the hall door in a steady stream, forming lines in front of officers with open books. Lenny had written his name in capital letters and signed beside that, given his address and shown his identity card, then he'd had to go for a medical assessment and she'd been asked to leave him. She'd waited outside the hall, leaning her back against the embankment wall, her arms folded across her chest, as her heartbeat had pounded.

Lenny had chosen to sign up, but the newspapers said men between nineteen and twenty-seven had to fight anyway, unless they had a good reason not to – either a protected occupation or an illness, perhaps. It meant the train station platform was even fuller than it had been on the day she'd said goodbye to Art. But this time the men weren't wearing uniforms – like Lenny, who stood beside her in his Sunday suit and the shirt she'd sewn for him, holding a small suitcase, all dressed up to go to war. He'd been told not to pack much. He wouldn't be able to keep personal things. What he owned he'd have to carry in a rucksack on his back.

She'd sat on his bed, cross-legged, and watched him pack his underclothes, a couple of books, photographs, two spare shirts, his toiletries, paper and pencils. 'They'll give us our kit and clothes when I get to the barracks,' he'd said.

He had not been told which barracks he was being sent to, but he was boarding a train heading towards Bristol, not London.

'I'll write,' he'd said. 'Every day.'

She'd nodded, her cheek brushing against the bare skin of his chest as she'd lain in the embrace of his arms last night.

Every night since he'd told her he was leaving, Lenny had come into her room, undressed and snuck between the sheets, joining her in the bed. On the very first night he'd said, 'Marry me,' in the moment before he'd pressed into her body. 'You have to marry me before I leave.'

'I can't,' she'd had to say. 'My dad'll never agree to it.' He'd refuse, to spite her.

Her father hadn't talked to her since she'd left home and he'd not let her in the house to see the others when she'd tried to visit.

She'd said to Lenny, 'But I will. When I can. When I'm twenty-one an old enough for im not to av a say in it. Yes. As soon as we can.'

He'd slid a thin gold band on her ring finger yesterday, with a single small diamond. 'It's an engagement ring, Lily. So you know I mean it. So you know I want to marry you and everyone else will know it too.' She was still unused to the feel of it, but the ring expressed their commitment in more than words and she was glad and proud to wear it.

The blast of a train's whistle made Lily turn, as Lenny and his parents did too. The train was rushing along the track towards them.

'Lily.'

She turned to look at Lenny. He'd put his case down on the floor and opened his arms asking to hold her one last time before he left.

She wrapped her arms around his neck and kissed him, no matter that his parents watched. She'd wasted too many years just being his friend when they could have been... this. She'd been afraid of having children, but Art hadn't told her a man could prevent it. Apart from the first time, when they hadn't expected the sex to happen, Lenny had used rubber condoms. He'd said, 'I don't care if you never want children. I just want you, Lily, just as you are. I've loved you for years.'

'I love you,' she said across his lips as the train drew to a standstill beside the platform.

'I love you too.'

He let go of her. She never wanted to let go of him. But she had to.

He kissed his mother's cheek, then shook hands with his father. Then he looked back at Lily. 'I'm going to miss you.'

'I'll miss you more.' She wiped the back of her hand across her soaked cheeks, smearing the tears rather than wiping them away. She'd been crying since he left her bed at dawn.

He leaned and kissed her lips quickly as the train driver sounded the whistle.

Doors slammed shut all the way along the train. Steam swirled around them.

Lenny turned, picked up his case, opened a carriage door,

stepped up onto the train and pulled the door shut behind him. He immediately pushed down the narrow window in the carriage door and leaned out.

'Goodbye, Leonard. Eat properly won't you?' his mother said.

'Goodbye, son. Be careful,' his father said.

Lenny reached for Lily's hand. 'I love you, Lily Franklin. Never forget it.' The train rolled forwards. His hand pulled on hers, not letting her go. She started walking, trying to keep up with the train, then ran, but a moment later his hand was wrenched free from hers.

'Write to me!' he shouted as the carriage drew further and further away.

'I will! I promise!'

The last view she had of him, he'd taken off his flat cap and was waving with that, still leaning through the carriage window until he was swallowed up by a drift of smoke and steam, and then he was gone, out of sight.

A lump of sadness stuck in the back of Lily's throat. It was hard to swallow, and hard to breathe as a painful sense of loss struck her in the chest with the strength of a punch. It had been difficult to say goodbye to Art, but to lose Lenny... She couldn't talk.

Mr Faraday wrapped an arm around her shoulders. 'Come on, lass. Let's get home. I think a strong cup of tea would do us all good.'

Mrs Faraday was sniffing back tears too.

Lily thought of Catherine, who'd they'd left sitting at the kitchen table, scribbling another letter to her Charles. At least Lily would have Catherine to talk to. Catherine would understand how awful she felt.

21

FEBRUARY

Maggie Abbot

Maggie's father tossed GWR's staff magazine on top of the table in a gesture of disgust. 'What on earth are they thinking?' he grumbled. 'Much as I am happy that they notice us "Swindonians",' he said, quoting the title of an article in the magazine, 'one minute it is drummed into us no one can know what any one of us does, and the next they are telling everyone about it in a magazine that is being sent abroad to GWR men who have signed up. The Nazis might see it.' Having worked himself up into a temper, he set off a coughing fit and pulled his handkerchief from his pocket.

Since the weather had turned to blizzards and hoar frosts in January, and Swindon had put on a fairly good impression of the Arctic, his coughing fits had been a dozen times worse. Maggie, Edith and Marjorie had ignored his complaints and indulgently used their scarce supply of coal to keep the fires in the kitchen and parlour hearths burning all day and night so at least the cottage was warm for him. Even so, his lungs did not take kindly to the cold outside.

He tried to hide the red blood in the mucus in his handkerchief, but against the brilliant white of the starched cotton it was obvious. Anyway, Maggie boiled his handkerchiefs on wash day; she knew about the blood. There was always blood. She couldn't say anything. If she dared suggest he see a doctor it only irritated him and there would be more coughing. *'And what do you think a doctor can do for me, love? There's no cure.'*

Marjorie's and Edith's laughter echoed in the hall as their feet pounded down the wooden stairs. Edith was holding Marjorie's hand when they entered the kitchen and she spun her around, humming a song as they danced around Maggie and her father, who was still coughing.

Maggie covered her ears. She felt like screaming. Their good mood put Maggie in a worse one. She knew they were ignorant of the reason for Dot's distress, but they did not have to be so jolly while upstairs Dot laid in her bed, curled in a ball, not interested in anything. Dot didn't even care that GWR were threatening to sack her because she'd missed so many shifts.

Maggie was trying to help her recover, and these childish high spirits wouldn't help. 'Be quiet,' she ordered, as she lowered her hands.

'Misery,' Marjorie accused. 'I thought you liked dancing.'

'I do.' Just not now.

'Be nice, girls,' Maggie's father said, his coughing easing.

Edith laughed. 'It's not me.' She picked up a piece of cold toast and took a bite from it.

'That's it. I can't take any more of your nonsense. I'm going to work. See you later on, Dad.' Maggie walked across and kissed his cheek. 'Goodbye.'

She left them all in the kitchen, shutting them and the warmth in. The parlour door was ajar and the door of the staircase too, so that some warmth would reach Dot upstairs. Not that she seemed to care about the cold.

Maggie pulled her coat on. She'd layered two cardigans over her dungarees and blouse and had two pairs of woollen socks on inside her boots. She circled the scarf twice about her neck and tucked it into her coat, pulled on her woolly hat, the pompom on the top wobbling, and slid her mittens on. Then she left the house on a tide of anger and with a pressure in her eyes that threatened tears. She sniffed the tears back as she walked towards the park. The sun was rising, the light was grey, but with two feet of snow on the ground and on the rooftops, reflecting what little light made it through the layer of cloud, it was clear enough to see. The snow had been scraped off the path again yesterday, but the cleared channel had frosted over in the night.

Because it was slippery, she had to concentrate to walk safely.

Lily and Cath usually knocked on Maggie's door on their way to work now, so, today she walked towards the park to meet them.

Everyone else in Maggie's family thought that Dot had had a tummy bug of some sort. But Dot had been curled up in bed refusing to eat for weeks and Maggie knew the real sickness was in Dot's head, not because of the damage that man had done to her innards.

Maggie's father had sent for the GWR doctor, who'd declared he couldn't find anything wrong. Of course, Dot had not confessed to the abortion, and the doctor had gone away, telling her she should go back to work.

Their father kept saying he wanted to ask the doctor back, especially because Dot wasn't interested in eating, let alone working. But she'd point blank told him no. 'I just need time, Dad. Please let me be.'

When the Government announced people were allowed to gather together for fun again, even during blackout hours, Edith and Marjorie had been so pleased they'd talked about nothing else all week. The cinemas, theatres and dancehalls had opened again. The old Dot would have led the conversation to decide where they would go first. But the Dot who lay in bed upstairs wasn't interested. Not even when Edith had brought home the news that the Mechanics Institute was going to open the doors of its hall for a dance.

The factory's band were playing there to raise money for the Helping Hand Fund. GWR's staff charity were raising money to make up comfort boxes to send to the staff who had joined the services. Most of the younger people in the Railway Village had bought a ticket. Maggie had bought one because her friends were going. She did not feel like dancing any more than Dot did.

'Maggie!' Catherine called, waving, directing Maggie to stop and wait for them. The vigorous waving caused Catherine to lose balance and slip. She caught hold of Lily's arm and Lily held her up until she found her feet again.

The sun was higher and the light had found a way through the clouds, sparkling back from the crisp icy layer hardening the top of the snow and glittering from the icicles decorating every bare branch of the trees and the guttering on the roofs.

'Good morning,' Catherine said, when they were closer.

'Morning.' There was nothing good about it in Maggie's opinion.

'Ello,' Lily said, the sorrowful sound in her voice expressing that she felt as miserable as Maggie.

'Come on.' Catherine led them on more tentatively than she'd been walking before.

When they reached Emlyn Square the paths were clearer, with large numbers of people walking towards the factory and disturbing the snow. Though in some areas, where the snow was compacted and smoothed by all the footsteps, it had become a thick, slippery sheet of ice. It was easier to skate than walk.

Violet waited for them on the far corner, beside the Mechanics Institute, looking through gaps in the tide of men. Maggie caught Violet's eye and lifted a hand, waving in the same moment Violet did.

When Maggie reached her best friend, she hugged her in a physical hello. Violet held Maggie in return but it was a brief embrace that did not provide much comfort because they had to get to work.

'You look down in the dumps,' Violet said quietly as they all walked on. 'Cheer up, we're going dancing tonight.' Her voice teased, trying to lift Maggie's mood with humour. 'No one will dance with you when you have a face like a smacked arse.'

The crude phrase succeeded in dragging a choked laugh from Maggie's throat.

Violet threaded her arm around Maggie's elbow. 'You do know Ron is going to the dance. He said he'll dance with me, and I'm sure he'll dance with you too.' Violet's breath carried as mist in the cold air, the words a vapour lingering behind them as they walked on. 'You told me you liked him at Christmas, but you haven't said a word about him since. If you don't like him any longer, I might fancy my own chances...' She tossed the last words in on a teasing lilt, but there was a hint of brittleness too. Perhaps because she was losing patience with Maggie's melancholy mood.

'Ron won't want to dance with me. He's made it perfectly clear what he thinks of me,' she grumbled. 'He doesn't like me. So, if you do like him, you can have him.'

'Lord, you are out of sorts. Who are you? What did you do with my friend Maggie?'

Maggie didn't answer. Since Armistice Day, whenever he

couldn't avoid her he was curt. The first occasion she'd realised his actions were deliberate was when he'd been talking to Asher in the street. She'd called Ron's name and he'd turned his back.

One day in her company, Armistice Day, had left him with a dislike of her. Her ego was dented.

She wasn't in the mood to dance. She was only going because her friends would think it odd if she didn't. But she was torn because her heart urged her to stay at home with Dot. 'There's no reason both our lives should be ruined,' Dot had complained when Maggie had said she'd stay. But Maggie couldn't walk around all happy and smiling while her sister felt so bad.

It was hard – heartbreaking – to see Dot's vibrancy snuffed out. She was pale and listless, and often in tears. Maggie had spent her life looking up to Dot for guidance, and now she'd been knocked down like a felled tree, to a point where she was no longer able to even look after herself.

Maggie grieved for Dot, while Dot grieved for the baby.

Every night in the dark, Maggie listened to Dot crying and whispering prayers for forgiveness. She'd wanted to keep the baby but she hadn't seen how she could. What ailed Dot was guilt and grief. What ailed Maggie was anger. Dot would not tell Maggie who the father was or whether she'd been willing in the moment of conception or forced into it.

Despite Dot not going out of the house for weeks, no man had asked Maggie or any of the others, 'Where's Dot, is she all right?' No man cared if Dot was well or not. Maybe that man knew he'd got her with child and didn't care. Or maybe that man had had his way with her and not cared from that minute on.

She sighed heavily. Chances were it was a man who worked in the factory. Chances were it was someone from the Railway Village.

Maggie scanned the bobbing heads of the throng of men walking towards the factory, wondering, *Which one...?*

Lily walked ahead of them by a few paces, gazing at her feet as they navigated icy puddles. There was another sad soul. Poor Lily. She was another reason for Maggie to fret. Their little gang of railway sisters, with their men, their GWR family, had barely formed and now they were being broken to pieces. Lily's brother and Lenny had gone, and Violet's lodger, Frank, had joined the navy, and the men who were left here spent half their time talking about fighting. Even Dietrich, who was far too young, talked constantly about wanting to fight.

Maggie had complained about the strength of Dietrich's desire to fight one day when Ron happened to be in hearing distance. She hadn't known he was there. They'd been walking home for lunch and he'd snapped, from behind her, 'You would be thinking of nothing else too, if your family had been dragged from their home and disappeared to who-knew-where.' His voice had sounded like the crocodile puppet in a Punch and Judy show, so judging and so snappy that the response had hung in her thoughts. He'd made it sound as though she was unaware of how awful Dietrich's experience had been. But that was why she was worried by his obsession with joining the fighting.

'It's none of your business what young Dietrich wants to do, Maggie.'

These sharp responses were typical of the way Ron spoke to her these days. He seemed... mean. That was the only word she could use for his swings between avoiding her or criticising whatever she had chosen to add to a conversation.

Kind, polite Ron had gone, in the same way Dot had gone, and smiling Lily had gone.

Maggie's little world felt as though it had spun completely off kilter. Nothing was the same. As if to mark that thought, just as they were swallowed inside the long tunnel beneath the railway tracks, six aircraft roared overhead. British aeroplanes, of course. It was just more training and practising. There were no sirens wailing. The air raid sirens had only ever sounded during the practices last October, no one carried gas masks any more and the domed shelters that stood in regimental rows in the Faringdon Road park were redundant and sad-looking.

People used a past tense when they talked about the threat of invasion these days. That fear was last year's. The Government opening the dancehalls, cinemas and theatres felt like Chamberlain had confirmed the risk was over. Even the GWR magazine wrote about the potential invasion and assault on Britain in the past tense, as something that everyone was concerned about last summer.

So now she lived in an odd sort of limbo in which her whole way of life had changed, with food rationing and the men gradually filtering away into the services to fight a war that wasn't really a war involving Britain and leaving their families mourning behind them. Had the man who got Dot pregnant gone to war?

All these thoughts – worrying about Dot, and knowing Ron didn't want her there – had meant Maggie spent less time at Violet's. She couldn't picture Ron beside the hearth in her future home any more either, not now she knew he could be cruel. But it did not stop her from grieving over the Ron she fell for. She missed that man like she missed cheerful Dot. And Violet was right, Maggie had changed too. Sadness had buried itself inside her like a maggot in an apple. All the joy had dropped out of life. What were the men fighting for if life here was miserable?

'Lily! Cath!' Violet called forward.

Violet seemed the only one with any enthusiasm left.

Lily and Catherine stopped and waited for Maggie and Violet to catch up.

When Maggie caught up, she saw her sadness reflected in Lily's eyes.

'You and I should dance together tonight, Lily,' she said.

Lily replied with a half-hearted smile.

Maggie would make Lily dance with her. Perhaps dancing would cheer them both up, and Maggie had no desire to dance with a man. Any man in the hall tonight might be the one who had got Dot pregnant.

22

Maggie Abbot

When the checky rang the hand bell, announcing the beginning of the lunch break, Maggie rushed to pull on her outdoor things, readying herself to face the cold. She waved goodbye to the other girls and ran out onto the pathways some of the men had cleared in the snow.

Since the beginning of January, she'd not eaten lunch with the others. She went home instead, to see how Dot was.

'I'm home!' she shouted towards the ceiling as she stripped off her coat, scarf and mittens in the hall. The first thing she did was check the fires, stirring up the glowing embers with a poker and putting fresh coal on to keep them burning in the afternoon. Then she made two rounds of cheese sandwiches, one for her and one for Dot, and carried them and an enamel mug of milk upstairs.

'Hello,' Maggie said as she pushed their bedroom door wider with the toe of her boot. Dot rose, shifting from beneath the covers to sit upright, making space for Maggie to sit on the end of the bed.

Dot was wearing a jumper over her nightdress. The condensation on the inside of their bedroom window had become a thick layer of ice days ago.

Dot pressed her pillow into an upright position behind her and accepted the plate and the milk. 'Thanks.'

Dot ate precisely three bites of her cheese sandwich. Maggie was hungry, she ate all of hers.

'Your nightdress is hanging on your shoulders,' Maggie complained when she picked up Dot's plate to take it downstairs. Dot's eyes were sunken into her skull, not pretty at all. 'You'll look like a coat stand if you don't eat.'

She had at least drunk the milk. 'I'll make you a cup of hot Bovril before I leave,' Maggie said, 'and you need to drink it. You need to look after yourself. Dad is worried about you. All of us are worried. You need to try to get better.'

When Maggie sifted through all the reasons for Dot to have an abortion, with no man on the horizon, the only one that made sense was if the father had forced himself on her. It had to be that, or he was married, and that was why Dot was keeping her lips sealed.

'Why not dress yourself this afternoon?' Maggie urged. 'And come downstairs for dinner tonight. You could sit with Dad by the fire when the rest of us go out dancing. He'd like that.'

'Perhaps,' Dot answered, but then she lay down again, pulling the covers up over her shoulders and turning to look at the wall.

'I'll put the kettle on.' Maggie loved Dot too much to see her in this pain.

When she returned with the enamel mug filled with steaming, beefy-smelling Bovril, she said, 'Promise me you'll drink it all.' She put the mug down beside the bed.

'I'll drink it,' Dot confirmed, but she didn't roll over to look at Maggie.

'Dot—'

'I said I'll drink it. Don't nag me.' Dot's voice, usually so jovial, was as flat as a Shrove Tuesday pancake.

'You can't keep moping around this way,' Maggie complained. 'I know you didn't want to do it. I know if you could, you'd have kept the baby. But you can't change things and I won't let you wither away in your bed.'

Dot took a deep breath, then sighed it out as she rolled onto her back and looked up at Maggie. 'I'll get up this evening. All right? You can stop the tongue lashing.'

Maggie hurried downstairs taking Dot's promise with her. It made her feel a little brighter. Maybe pancakes would be a good thing to eat more often, Maggie thought, as she pulled the front door of the cottage closed behind her. There was flour in the cupboard, and milk and eggs were still easy to buy. Maybe she should suggest that they buy some chickens to keep in the yard so they would have more eggs.

Maggie hurried to join the stream of workers heading towards the subway tunnel, mindful of where she put her feet on the ice. It should be warmer in the middle of the day, but it felt colder. At least it was warm in the workshop.

She spotted Ron in Emlyn Square, a good couple of inches taller than most men in the crowd. Then she saw Violet's red hair. Maggie didn't feel the swell of happiness she should at the sight of her best friend and the man she'd had designs on. Instead she felt... lonely. Alone in this vast crowd.

Earlier, Violet had said Maggie had changed. She had. She had excluded herself because she held Dot's secret. She and Violet had grown apart because Maggie was guarded and miserable. Meanwhile, Catherine and Lily were closer than ever since Lenny had left.

Life wasn't fair.

At the dance tonight, Maggie was going to have to muster all her acting skills to pin a smile on her face. She didn't want to do it yet, though. She was not in the mood to smile, and certainly not for Ron. Instead of shouting and waving to catch Violet's attention, Maggie pulled up her scarf, hid her face as much as she could, quickened her pace and entered the tunnel ahead of them.

'Maggie! Maggie!' Violet's shout echoed.

Darn it. She hadn't avoided them. Maggie stopped, annoying those around her. Violet forced her way across the flow of workers, Ron in tow. Maggie's cheeks burned with embarrassment.

They walked on together, forced back into movement by the thick current of workers.

'We debated whether we should knock for you,' Violet said. 'But then we thought if Dot was asleep it wouldn't be fair to wake her.'

'How is Dot?' Ron asked. 'I didn't realise she was so ill. Vi was just telling me.'

Maggie's eyes narrowed on him. Dot was closer to his age and he'd probably talked to her a lot in The Cricketers Arms or The Glue Pot. But surely he was not the father.

But he was the first and only man who'd asked. 'Hopefully on the mend,' she answered, staring at him, looking for a reaction.

'Good,' he answered. Nothing in his expression spoke of anything other than a genuine, kind interest in another person's health. Maggie looked into blue eyes that seemed to express a sincere concern. If he knew or suspected what was wrong with Dot, he was hiding it well.

'That's good to hear,' Violet said. 'I told Ron that you're cracking at the foxtrot.'

'Why?' Maggie asked. She hoped Violet hadn't told Ron what she had said earlier.

'I enjoy dancing the foxtrot,' Ron explained. 'I told Vi, I'm looking forward to that the most, and she said I should dance it with you because you're good at the foxtrot. So will you dance the foxtrots with me, Maggie?'

Maggie's heart leapt treacherously, like it used to in his company. It was an unconscious habit. But she rarely met anyone who could dance a foxtrot.

She swallowed. Her lips were dry and cracked from going in and out of the heat of the workshops compared to the cold. She sighed, and even in the tunnel her breath turned to mist in the cold air. When she thought about the way he'd behaved towards her recently, he did not deserve her as a partner. Let him dance with a woman who would stand on his toes. 'I don't know if I'll have a free dance,' she said, her voice as cold as the arctic weather.

'Is Asher going to the dance?' Violet asked Ron, ignoring Maggie's curt reply.

'Yes. He's taking Naomi, h—'

'Taking?' Violet interrupted.

'Are they courting?' Naomi hadn't said anything to Maggie.

Ron glanced at Maggie and Violet. 'Er. Yes. He asked her father. But maybe I shouldn't have said.'

'He asked her father…'

'Has he?'

Violet and Maggie spoke at the same time.

Ron's deep chuckle echoed across the bricks of the low-ceilinged tunnel. 'He has,' he answered more quietly.

Maggie knew speaking to Naomi's father meant a lot more in a Jewish family. 'She hasn't said anything to me.' Maggie spoke more quietly too, realising anyone around them might be listening.

'Nor to me. Not a word,' Violet added.

'Then you'd better not mention I said anything and let her tell you first.'

Naomi hadn't even told Maggie she liked Asher in that way.

Violet said goodbye to Ron in the place where, for weeks, they'd said goodbye to Lenny. Maggie merely nodded her goodbye. Good riddance.

As soon as he'd turned his back, Violet wound her arm around Maggie's. 'Heavens, Maggie. There's me being nice and trying to cheer you up and make you feel better. I know you love the foxtrot, and you go and smack down his offer.'

Maggie looked at Violet and beyond her saw Ron walking away. His hands in his pockets. His head drooping a little.

He was confusing. Had he been nice just now for Violet's sake? Or had these last few weeks of his bad mood not been about her at all? Maybe she'd misread his behaviour because she felt so out of sorts herself.

But even if he did like her, what would be the point of marrying if her husband went off to fight a few weeks later? She'd end up alone anyway.

When she married she wanted to live in a quiet cottage not an empty one.

She could take Dot with her, though. She could ask her to live with her. She couldn't leave her behind now. Maggie was the only person Dot had to talk to about what had gone on. When Maggie married and had a cottage, she would ask Dot to live with her. Especially if her husband was going to be away fighting, or if he was prone to the occasional bad temper.

She'd dance with Ron tonight, she decided. There would be no harm in that. Then she'd leave whatever came next to fate.

'Maggie.' Violet tugged on Maggie's arm to capture her attention. 'You aren't listening. I said I want you to be happy. It's been horrible to see you so fed up. You've not been yourself at all lately. So, I hope you do like Ron, because I had a talk with him. I told him how nice you are. I didn't mean to upset you when I said I'd try for him. If he likes you and you like him, you can have him. I don't mind. He's just our lodger. I'm sorry I upset you.'

'Oh, Vi. You didn't. You haven't done anything wrong. It's just this bloody war.'

She had to try harder to at least pretend to be happy.

'Thanks for saying something to Ron. I might dance with him if he asks again.'

23

Maggie Abbot

Maggie opened the front door. 'Hello. Come on in. It's too cold to wait out there.' She beckoned Catherine and Lily inside and shut the door.

'Are you ready?' Catherine asked.

'Nearly. The others are. I'll just say goodbye to Dot and Dad.'

Maggie opened the parlour door. 'Cath and Lily are here.'

Edith looked up. She was sitting on the rag rug in front of the fire, beside Marjorie. They were both in their coats and scarves, but even so her hands had been outstretched towards the fire, warming her palms.

Maggie's father was in a chair beside them, his boots resting on the firedog, warming the soles of his feet. He had fallen asleep. His gentle snore followed the rhythm of the rise and fall of his chest.

Dot had kept her promise. She'd eaten dinner downstairs and now sat in the chair on the other side of the fire, a blanket over her legs.

Dot looked up from the pages of the book she was reading, looking beyond Maggie with a half-hearted smile. 'Hello, Lily. Cath.' They'd followed Maggie into the small square room, crowding the space.

Lily nodded. 'Ello.'

'Good evening,' Catherine said.

Lily was wearing Catherine's lipstick, mascara and eyeshadow. Maggie imagined Catherine applying the make-up for Lily at a dressing table in the Faradays' house. They were becoming more and more like real sisters these days.

Maggie had borrowed one of Dot's dresses. She, Edith and Marjorie had dressed together, applying each other's make-up and styling each other's hair. Edith had pinned three curls into place on Maggie's forehead and set them with a smidge of their father's Brylcreem before removing the pins.

Maggie crossed the room, passing Edith and Marjorie, who followed Catherine and Lily back into the hall. She leaned down and kissed Dot's cheek. Dot kissed hers at the same time.

'Do you need me?'

'No. You go and have fun. Dad and I will manage just fine.'

Dot's voice did not convince Maggie, but, even so, there was no point in arguing. Dot had come downstairs, so Maggie would go out.

'I love you, little sister,' Dot said. 'I don't say it often enough. Thanks for looking after me.'

'I love you too,' Maggie answered quietly.

'Enjoy the dance.'

'I will.' Maggie's voice sounded as half-hearted as Dot's smiles.

Maggie closed the parlour door quietly and joined the others in the crowded hall.

'Ready?' Edith asked everyone, before opening the door and letting the arctic blast in.

Maggie wrapped her scarf around her neck and pulled on her coat as the others walked out. She hadn't brought her mittens for the short walk to Emlyn Square, but she regretted that within a minute, Jack Frost immediately nipping at her fingertips as she tied a headscarf under her chin. It was windy and large, wet, cold snowflakes danced in the air, creating a fresh layer on the already icy ground.

Forgetting the war for a moment, she almost turned back to find a torch. Then she remembered: no torches – though no one ever saw the air raid wardens who were meant to police the blackout in the Railway Village. Lily's dad was one of them, mind, and no one would want to accuse him of not doing his job and make him angry.

Maggie had heard the Government were going to issue torches with hoods to stop the light spreading too far. Edith had said that was a joke. *'What do you think? That they'll make little coats for them...?'*

'Come along, ladies.' Edith led off, holding an umbrella over herself and Marjorie.

Maggie tucked under the umbrella Catherine and Lily were sharing. Catherine wrapped an arm around Maggie's waist and drew her closer.

For the sake of her friends, Maggie would do her best to enjoy the evening. She did not want to spoil it for everyone else, and Lily needed cheering up as much as she did.

Snowflakes landed lightly on the shoulder that couldn't squeeze beneath the umbrella's canopy and melted into the fabric of her coat, and she kept slipping on dark patches of ice. Catherine's arm braced, holding Maggie up, and she wrapped an arm around Catherine to help her when she slipped.

They were all wearing the wrong shoes for icy weather.

'Lenny wrote to me,' Lily said. 'There was a letter waitin at ome tonight. Ee told me to say ello to everyone. Ee's omesick.'

'I said he's Lily-sick,' Catherine added.

'Are you still willin to be my dance partner?' Lily asked Maggie.

Maggie hadn't really known Lily before they started working together. Of course, she'd known *of* Lily. Everyone did, because she and her older brother were the only people with brown skin in the village, and because Mr Franklin had a reputation for being a brute when he was drunk or angry. Maggie was very glad she knew Lily now. She was a good friend.

'Yes,' Maggie answered. 'I'm only looking forward to the dance because I'm dancing with you.'

'I don't know the proper dances,' Lily said. 'I never learned them.'

'We'll make up the steps then.' Maggie smiled. 'No one else will notice what we're doing. They'll be focusing on where to put their own feet and I can teach you a few easy steps. Ah!' She squealed as she stepped on an icy puddle and her heel slid.

Catherine held her up.

Marjorie glanced back. 'You'll have the Luftwaffe homing in on us with that racket.'

'Bloody puddle.' Maggie cursed at it as if the ice were human.

The others laughed.

Fortunately, it was only a couple of hundred yards to the Mechanics Institute. They were meeting Violet there as Mrs Turner's cottage was on the other side of the institute. Ron had said he'd walk with Violet, so she wasn't walking alone in the dark.

As they progressed slowly, picking their steps across the ice in inappropriate shoes, other voices travelled over the rooftops. Laughter. Conversation. The dance might be in aid of charity, but

Maggie felt like everyone in the Railway Village was a charity case today. People needed to dance to escape the drudgery of the last three months. Work, sleep, work. Life had become simply existence. Yes. Maggie would do her best to live tonight too, if only to spite Hitler and his threats.

In front of her, the tall towers of the Mechanics Institute reached up into the blizzard. *The company cathedral.* That's what her father called it. It was old. The first phase was built in 1854, and, like a cathedral, it did have spires and stained-glass windows. Childhood Maggie had thought its towers and arches were like a royal palace. It looked more like something from a Ladybird book fairy-tale with snow layered on its roofs and icicles hanging from its guttering. In reality, it was a place of learning. There were reading rooms for men and women, where you could read popular magazines and daily papers, as well as industry publications. But there was also a large, grand hall. A room where she'd enjoyed parties, and plays and pantomimes performed by The Western Players, the GWR (Swindon) Amateur Theatrical Society. The stage was one of the biggest in the country – 200 people could stand on it at once.

A sigh escaped Maggie's lips as they crossed Emlyn Square to reach the entrance.

The wind whipped up beneath Catherine's umbrella, trying to turn it inside out. Maggie caught its edge and held it down.

'Why are you sighing?' Catherine asked.

'It feels a little odd because we've not been out for a long time. I'm nervous.'

'I've never been to a dance before, an I can't dance, so if you feel nervous, I feel... petrified.' Lily added the last word in a theatrical pitch.

Maggie looked past Catherine. 'You'll be fine, Lily.'

'I don't think I've ever been to a dance without Charles,' Catherine added. 'We've been together since we were sixteen.'

'Is your stomach wobbling like a tall jelly tower too then? Like mine and Lily's? Maybe we'll dance together all night, the three of us.'

'Four,' Lily cut in. 'Violet too. She doesn't av a boyfriend.'

'Five. Naomi too,' Catherine added.

'It's a shame we're an odd number,' Lily said.

'Naomi has Asher,' Maggie cut in.

'Are they together?' Lily's voice expressed the surprise Maggie had felt.

'In Asher's opinion,' Maggie clarified. 'He told Ron, but Naomi hasn't said anything to me, so I probably should not have said it. Don't say anything to Naomi about it.'

Maybe Naomi had told someone, though – Catherine had not shown any surprise.

They joined the queue to enter, huddling close under the umbrella, all shivering. Maggie's legs felt frozen. She'd taken the last new pair of nylon stockings from the pack. There were none in the shops any more. When they laddered, they laddered and that was that, so they were a precious thing. But they weren't warm.

'Good evening, ladies.' Mr Welsh welcomed them. 'Do you have your tickets?'

Maggie searched hers out as the others did.

'Now, there's rules,' Mr Welsh began, 'or the Civil Defence Committee won't let us hold another. No touching the blackout material covering the windows, and there'll be no alcohol sneaked in and no fights.'

'Do you think we're gunna box each other's ears while we're dancin?' shouted a woman behind Maggie. She laughed at her own joke. Maggie didn't think it was funny.

'No, Miss Thorpe, but we know patience can be a bit on the short side these days. So come outside and cool your temper off if you feel the need. Any ruckus and there might be no more dancing for the rest of this war. Is everyone ready?'

'Yes!' others waiting in line shouted impatiently.

'You'll need to be careful on the stairs. It's going to be a bit dark in there, to be sure we don't let any light out. But the hall is fully lit.'

He reached out and pulled the door open. 'In you go, quick, quick.'

Maggie hurried into the reception area. The hall was upstairs. While Catherine closed her umbrella and shook off the snowflakes that had melted to drips, Maggie's eyes adjusted to the low light.

Many people were already removing their damp coats, hats and headscarves.

As they climbed the stairs of the left tower to the first floor, Maggie untied the bow holding her best headscarf in place. She slid the wet square of silk into her coat pocket. The stairs and banister were made of cold, solid iron – like many things in the railway village's public spaces that you would expect to be stone or wood.

'Here! Maggie! Lily! There's an empty hook, shall we leave our things together? We'll find them more easily at the end then.'

'Good idea.'

'Yes.'

Free of her wet things, Maggie walked into the hall, rubbing her hands together to warm them. Then she wiped her palms on the front of her yellow dress, because they'd become sweaty despite the cold. She'd been in this hall, and lived among these people her whole life, but Dot's situation had left her feeling like she didn't know anyone.

Marjorie had turned the narrow Peter Pan collar up and left the top button of the bodice undone to frame Maggie's neck. At least she felt pretty. The wide skirt swung out when she spun or swayed.

In the light in the hall, Maggie saw Lily must be in borrowed clothes too. Maggie would guess her dress was one of Catherine's. It was loose on Lily's more slender frame, but the peacock blue in the floral pattern suited her colouring perfectly.

Maggie rose onto the balls of her feet, making herself an inch or two taller so she could see more of the busy room.

She looked for Violet's red hair.

She saw Ron's sable curls bouncing. He was dancing with a blonde woman she didn't know. She was not going to run after Ron any more. If he wanted to dance with her, he could come and find her.

Her gaze travelled onwards. She spotted Violet in the middle of the hall, dancing too.

'Would you like to dance?' Catherine asked Lily.

'Oh, go on then,' Lily answered. 'But you'll av to tell me where to put my feet.'

Catherine smiled and held out her hand for Lily to take.

There were still plenty of men in Swindon, but not enough in this room for every woman to have a male partner. The number of dancing couples consisting of two women were many more than usual.

The band's rendition of Bing Crosby's 'What's New?' drew to a close, and the dancing couples separated, smiling, chests heaving as they caught their breath. Their cheeks glowed and their foreheads glistened from the exercise. Maggie lifted a hand and waved to catch Violet's attention. Violet saw and waved back.

'I bought you an apple juice.' Marjorie walked up to Maggie and held out a full glass.

'Thank you.' Maggie accepted it. 'Where's Edith?'

Marjorie rolled her eyes comically. 'Dancing with her pilot already.'

'What pilot?' Maggie hadn't heard her sister mention a pilot, and Marjorie made it sound as though, whoever this man was, he was someone Edith had favoured for a while. 'Where did she meet a pilot?'

'He's a friend of a friend. He won't say where he's stationed, but he drinks in The Glue Pot sometimes.'

Dot would love that description. She would laugh and tease Edith relentlessly... usually.

'And she likes him?'

'A bit too much. I think he takes her adoration for granted.'

'Are they courting?'

'Not officially. He hasn't asked her out anywhere. But anyway, at least tonight she'll have someone to dance with. I don't. Unless you want to dance...?'

Maggie looked over her shoulder. Violet's passage across the dance floor had been interrupted by Ron. They were talking.

The band began to play and Ron reached for Violet's hand.

Maggie looked back at Marjorie. 'Yes, let's dance.'

She and Marjorie put their glasses down on a table that stood against the wall at the same time.

'I'll be the man.' Marjorie claimed the lead as they held each other.

Because Marjorie smiled so happily, Maggie had to smile back.

As they danced around the room, Maggie turned her head one way then the other, looking for Edith, trying to spot the pilot she'd heard nothing about.

It wasn't Edith her gaze caught on, though, but Violet's red hair. Marjorie led her into a swift spin, meaning Maggie had to whip her head around to keep watching.

Violet's naturally red lips smiled warmly, her concentration all on Ron. Her eyes focused on his eyes as they talked. Ron was animated and smiling too, and looking far too handsome in his black Sunday suit. A shot of envy sparked through Maggie.

She denied the feeling instantly. *'Don't waste your feelings on an uncaring man,'* Dot had drummed into her for years.

Maggie looked up at the ceiling as Marjorie led her into another spin. Maggie had always loved this hall. The ceiling had complicated, prettily painted arches. It really was like having their own cathedral in the Railway Village.

She was so busy looking up she missed a step and stood on Marjorie's toes. Marjorie yelped and stepped back, letting go of her, and as Maggie's arm moved back she collided with someone else, bumping them with her elbow. She turned, the word sorry on her lips. 'Ron.' She faced Ron, then looked at Violet. 'Vi.'

Embarrassment gulped Maggie down whole. She hoped Ron wouldn't think she'd bumped into him deliberately. It was also embarrassing that she was dancing with her sister, not a man. It would have been much better if she might have made him jealous. Then she cursed herself in her thoughts again – she didn't care what Ron Smith thought.

'Hello,' Violet said. 'I was coming over to talk to you, but Ron asked me to dance. Hello, Marjorie.'

The four of them stood still in the middle of the floor of circling couples.

'Hello, Vi. Ron.' Marjorie looked from one to the other.

'Hey! Talk at the edge of the floor,' a man called out, as he turned his partner near Maggie's shoulder.

'I suggest we dance,' Ron said. 'You can talk later, ladies.' He caught Violet's hand and spun her away.

Again, that lurch of envy spilled through Maggie, but she refused it, smiled at Marjorie and accepted her hand.

Maggie spotted Naomi dancing with Asher. That gave her a reason to ask about Asher later. Then she saw Edith. 'Is that the pilot?' she asked Marjorie, leaning her head in their direction.

'Yes, that's him.'

'He's not in uniform.'

Marjorie shrugged.

'Don't you like him?'

'I don't know him.'

Then that was the problem. Marjorie was feeling excluded and lonely too. Maggie added Marjorie to her list of people she was concerned about.

'If she likes him that much, tell her to bring him home for tea,' Maggie suggested.

As they continued the dance, Maggie snatched a couple more looks at the pilot. He had short, light brown hair and a neat moustache. It was odd to think about the men up in the sky inside the aeroplanes that constantly passed and played over Swindon.

The band transitioned to a Glenn Miller song without pausing.

'Maggie!' Lily shouted through the dancers. 'Shall we swap partners?'

Marjorie didn't know Catherine well, but they had met a few times. 'Do you mind?'

'Of course not.'

Marjorie released Maggie and turned, smiling, towards Catherine. 'Do you want to lead, Cath, or shall I?'

'You lead,' Lily said to Maggie. 'We don't stand a chance if I try to.'

'Take my direction from the embrace of my hands. I'll squeeze your hand and press gently on your back to tell you when and where to move. I'll say it too, for now, then you'll learn what it feels like if someone is asking you to do something through hold alone.

'Step left and back,' Maggie began. 'Forward and right. In the rhythm of three. Side, forward, back. One, two, three. One, two, three.'

'One, two, three,' Lily counted along with Maggie, looking at Maggie's feet.

'Look at my face, or you'll end up dizzy.' Maggie laughed. The sound felt alien, but it had come from a true place.

They smiled and laughed quite a lot when they trod on each other's toes or when Lily moved the wrong way and they collided rather than progressed. Maggie could tell their giggles annoyed other people but she and Lily needed to laugh. It felt good to have a reason to laugh.

'I'm sweating.' Maggie swiped the side of her hand across her forehead as the third song they'd danced together came to a close.

'There will be a short interval, ladies and gentlemen. Have a drink. The good ladies who manage the Helping Hand Fund are serving apple juice or blackcurrant cordial.'

'The band are good, aren't they?' Lily said as she applauded.

Maggie heard a tone in Lily's voice that implied she'd thought they wouldn't be good. 'They practise all the time,' she answered, as she led the way to where she'd left her glass of juice. 'You can only join the band if you're good. The man my aunt married played the trumpet, until his lungs weren't up to it any more. They moved to Kent, to the coast, so he'd have fresher air.'

A trill laugh had Maggie looking over her shoulder. It was Marjorie. Her sister and Catherine were walking towards her and Lily. She heard the tail end of their conversation.

'...I know the men have gone for a good reason, but I'd like to have at least one dance with a man.'

'I can't believe ow many men av gone,' Lily declared, looking around the room. 'The Government said the industry workers an engineers could stay.'

'Most of the men I know chose to go,' Maggie said. 'Violet's lodger, Frank, told her he wouldn't fight, then in the new year he couldn't leave fast enough. It's like a virus they've all caught, this desire to bugger off and get themselves killed—' She stopped talking, realising she'd opened her big mouth and stuffed her foot into it. 'Sorry, Lily, Lenny will be fine. Sorry, Cath, I'm sure your fiancé will be fine too.'

Their smiles had fallen, and this time it was Maggie's fault. Some friend she was. 'Sorry, I didn't mean to upset you.' But she had. She gave herself a good mental kick. For being too blunt. It was typical of her. She had a feeling her bold blunt manner was why Ron wasn't a fan of hers. Like Violet, he was an only child, he probably wasn't used to noisy people.

'I'm gunna buy a drink,' Lily said.

'I'll go with you,' Catherine said. 'I need a drink too.'

'Are you having fun?' Violet appeared at Maggie's shoulder, red-cheeked and skin glistening with exertion. 'It's so nice to dance.'

'I'm going to speak to my friend.' Marjorie nodded at them both and walked away.

'It is nice to dance.' Maggie was enjoying the evening more than she'd expected to. She'd had fun with Lily. She sipped from the glass of lukewarm juice Marjorie had bought earlier. 'Don't you want a drink?' she asked Violet.

'Ron's getting me one.'

'Oh. That's nice of him.' Maggie fought back the envious stab she felt. But the emotion had probably sneaked into her voice.

'He was looking forward to tonight. He loves dancing. One of his friends is a trombone player in the band.'

From what she'd seen, what Ron loved was dancing with Violet. Maggie sipped the drink again, trying to hide a spiteful expression.

She really had to get over her feelings for Ron. What was the point of wanting someone who had no interest in her. There were other carpenters, and men who didn't even work for GWR. Maybe Edith could introduce her to a pilot. A friend of a friend of a friend.

'Are you still miserable?' Violet thrust at her. Violet had been kind earlier, she sounded annoyed now.

Maggie lowered the glass. 'Yes, and for a good reason.' She thought of Dot.

'Why? Because I danced with Ron?' Violet had plucked out every auburn hair of her eyebrows and drawn them in brown instead, so when she raised them it was annoyingly comical.

'No.' Maggie shook her head. She felt more love for Dot than Ron. Ron had been a pipe dream. 'No. There are far more upsetting things in the world right now than Ron Smith dancing with someone else.'

The look in Violet's eyes said she wanted to know what Maggie was thinking about. Maggie wouldn't tell.

Something knocked Maggie's arm.

She turned, jumping, and nearly spilled what was left of her juice over Ron.

'Ron!'

Had he heard what Violet said?

A smile opened his lips and twinkled in his eyes. He lifted his hand, offering one of two glasses to Violet. 'Cordial.'

'Thank you.'

'Lord, I'm hot,' Ron said. 'I'd take my jacket off, but it's not the done thing.' He stroked back his fringe with his free hand. His forehead glistened with sweat and he smelt a little sweaty too. He was in his Sunday suit, so there was no smell of freshly sawn wood to mask it.

Ron drank his cordial straight down, his Adam's apple rising and lowering as he swallowed.

A minute later, the band gathered back on the stage and picked up their instruments. Maggie finished her drink.

The trumpet player began the next song. The other musicians joined, the tempo leaping into a quick rhythm. The song was 'Hindustan' by Bob Crosby and the Bob Cats. A foxtrot.

Ron reached past Maggie and put down his glass. 'Will you dance with me, Maggie?' He held out his hand, his voice and movement eager.

Her emotions bristled with a need for self-preservation. She stepped back, not forward, lowering her hand to her side. 'Are you sure it's me you want to ask?'

His dark eyebrows lowered, pinching a line at the top of his nose, the expression questioning her response. 'It's you I'm asking, isn't it? Come on, Maggie. The song will be over in a minute.' He lifted the empty glass from her fingers and put it on the table.

'Come along,' he said, holding out his hand again. 'Please, dance with me.'

She stared at his work-calloused palm. Then decided. *Sod it.* Who knew when she'd be able to dance next, and it was much more fun to dance with a man.

'Oh go on then.' She laid her hand on top of his.

His strong fingers surrounded her hand and drew her into a foxtrot hold, his other hand settling on her back. Then they were stepping and skipping around a much emptier dance floor.

Not many people knew the foxtrot steps, and if you didn't, you couldn't get by via pretending. Maggie thought dancing the foxtrot with a man felt like flying, because it was such a fast dance. Her father was good too, that's why she could dance it. He'd liked the vibrant pace – she did too.

She learned quickly that Ron really was good at the foxtrot. He steered her with a press of his fingertips on her back and the turn of their joined hands, and every time those strong fingers gently pressed on her back a shiver travelled up her spine. For a tall, muscular man, he was light on his feet. She felt as though she were dancing on clouds.

A sudden dramatic note brought the music and the dance to a sharp end.

She turned to applaud the band along with the other couples on the floor. Ron clapped too, his gaze colliding with the trombone player's. Ron lifted his clapping hands a bit higher. The man winked. Then the band began another tune.

Maggie's chest heaved breathlessly, as she walked to the side of the room beside Ron. He didn't seem breathless at all. His hand touched her lower back as they approached the others. Naomi and Asher now stood with Violet, Catherine and Lily.

'Come on, let's dance.' Violet captured Lily's hand.

'Cath.'

Catherine looked over her shoulder. Mr Marsh walked towards her. He had said her name.

'This is a slower song,' he said, 'that I think even my leg might manage. Will you dance with me?'

'Oh yes, Joe, of course.' She accepted his hand.

Naomi waved a hand in front of her face. 'I can't believe how hot it is in here.'

'Would you like to go outside for some fresh air?' Asher offered. 'We could go for a short walk around the village and come back?'

Naomi glanced at Asher but didn't reply. She looked at Maggie. Maggie understood that look. '*Will you come with us?*' She nodded and hoped Ron wouldn't think she'd planned this. 'Could we go for a walk too, Ron? You said you were hot and I'd like to cool down.'

'That's a good idea.' Ron's friendly tone surprised Maggie. 'Let's go. You'd better tell Violet where you'll be, and your sisters, Maggie. We'll meet you girls in the entrance hall.'

24

Maggie Abbot

Naomi was shy. When Maggie first met her, she'd been the quietest. The way she behaved around Asher tonight reminded her of that Naomi. The Naomi Maggie knew now talked and laughed as loudly as everyone else as they worked on the lathes and other machinery, shouting across the noise. For the first time, Maggie realised that, while the others had become physically stronger in the workshop, they had also become mentally stronger. But she had not. Even Lily was stronger – she might be sad but she was more confident.

As they walked away from the Mechanics Institute, Ron lit a match to light his cigarette, then held the flame out for Asher to light his. He shook out the flame afterwards and dropped the match on the floor.

The snow had stopped falling, and moonlight broke through between the clouds so Maggie could see the ice glittering where she walked. She linked arms with Naomi, claiming her before Asher could. She wasn't sure what Naomi wanted, but Maggie knew she didn't want to have to walk along awkwardly beside Ron.

The snow may have stopped, but the wind was still bitingly cold. Maggie tucked her free hand into the pocket of her coat.

The men walked either side of Maggie and Naomi. They began a conversation, talking over the girls' heads as they smoked, the wind catching at the ends of their cigarettes and making them glow. The smoke they breathed out was swept away quickly.

Maggie's shameless imagination betrayed her better judgement and drifted into picturing Ron on one side of the fireplace in the parlour and her father on the other, talking in the same way. Her father would approve of Ron as a husband.

Ron flicked the butt of his cigarette into a tall pile of snow between the road and the path. 'Are you enjoying the dancing, Naomi?' he asked.

Maggie heard the deliberate, kind tone that sought to bring her shy friend into the men's conversation. He had not encouraged Maggie, but he knew she wouldn't need to be invited to take part.

'Yes.' Naomi smiled. 'I have never danced this much.'

'My dad used to enjoy dancing,' Maggie said. 'He taught us to dance when I was small, and he'd take us to dances whenever he could.'

'My brothers like dancing but they've never taken me.' Naomi laughed.

'I used to dance with my sisters,' Asher said, as he threw away the butt of his cigarette. 'At home. Jewish dancing is different. We did not dance in couples.' He slid his hands into his coat pockets. His flat cap was pulled low over his eyes so Maggie couldn't see his expression properly.

'My mum taught me,' Ron said. 'Because my father couldn't

dance, if she wanted to dance, she'd put a record on and pull me to my feet.' Ron looked at Maggie. 'I have her to thank for my foxtrot skills.'

'You have a resourceful mother,' Asher commented as they neared the corner of London Street. He led the way into East Street.

'Do you feel cooler?' he asked Naomi. 'You don't look as flushed.'

'I do feel cooler. Thank you.'

'Do you want to go back, then, or would you rather go home?' Asher offered.

'Let's stay. I was enjoying the dancing.' Naomi released Maggie's arm and held Asher's instead. They walked a pace ahead, splintering the conversation.

Maggie looked at Ron as they passed the arched entrance into the alley that ran between the backyards of the smallest cottages. She did not want to walk in silence. 'Why didn't your father dance with your mother?'

'He was wounded in the last war. He can't walk.'

'Oh Lord, I'm sorry.' She misplaced her foot on the ice, slipped and would have fallen but he caught her upper arm and held her up. 'Thank you. I didn't know.'

'Why would you? I don't talk about it.' He kept hold of her arm for a few paces before letting go. 'It makes no difference to anyone but me.'

'But we carry these things,' Maggie said. 'Or I do, anyway. Like a heavy backpack full of the experiences that have made up who we are. My mother loved dancing. It's the only thing I remember about her. I remember her taking my hands and dancing in the street on a warm day. I've always missed her, even though I only remember that one day. But I carry that one day with me every day.' Maggie would give anything right now to have her mother to talk to about Dot. Maybe Dot would not have aborted the child if she'd had a mother to turn to.

'I miss my dad and he's still alive,' Ron said. 'I mean, I miss what my dad could have been. Sometimes he's violent. His mind is as broken as his body. Shell shock, they call it. My mother finds it hard. I did as a boy. Now I stay away. My presence doesn't help them.'

'Where do they live?'

'On the border between England and Wales. In Shropshire.'

'Doesn't your mother miss you?'

'You would think so, but no. Not really. But that's another story, and one I won't tell you tonight.'

'My dad can't dance any more, not with his cough. I know it upsets him that he can't do the things he wants to.' Maggie's lips twisted into a wry smile, and an amused sound crept out of her throat as she saw a memory in her mind. 'He used to say he loved having four girls because it meant he'd always have a dance partner.'

'It's a shame, then, that he can't take advantage of your company any more.'

'It's sad.' The sound from Maggie's throat became a sigh, one of those that kept giving away her miserable mood. 'I worry about him on a daily basis. He's in the backpack I carry too.'

In front of them, Asher and Naomi turned the corner into Reading Street, making their walk a rectangle back to the Mechanics Institute.

Ron looked at Maggie. 'I like your father. We play dominoes in the pub sometimes and I've seen him hiding the blood he coughs up.'

'Everyone has seen the blood.' Tears leaked into Maggie's eyes. She looked straight ahead, blinking, unable to talk about her father any more.

'I wish I'd known my father before he was injured,' Ron said. 'I think it would be easier to understand who he is now, like my mother does. She's more tolerant of his outbursts than I could ever be.'

Maggie nodded, still unable to speak past the lump of emotion in her throat.

'You're good at the foxtrot.' Ron changed the subject. 'I enjoyed dancing with you.'

'You're good too.'

As Maggie's conversation with Ron fell silent, Naomi laughed over something Asher had said. She held Asher's elbow, through the sleeve of his overcoat, and she was smiling. She must like him.

As they walked past The Glue Pot, Maggie stared at the blacked-out windows, picturing the numerous men who would be behind them, and she thought about all the men in the Mechanics Institute too. Any one of them could be the man who'd gotten Dot pregnant.

'Penny for them?' Ron asked, breaking the layer of ice that had frosted over their conversation.

She looked at him and tried to smile but could not quite persuade her lips to do the job. 'I am thinking about Dot. I worry about her as much as I worry about Dad. I didn't like leaving her at home tonight. I should go home soon.'

'You just said you love dancing. Why would you leave early?'

'I love my sister more,' she answered sharply.

'Is that why you've not come to see Violet as often lately?'

At least he had noticed. 'Yes.' *That, and you've been horrible.*

He smiled, the expression saying that perhaps he knew the words Maggie had kept to herself. 'Family is important, I agree, even though I moved away from mine.' He nodded as he said it. 'But in the middle of this mess, I think having a chance to escape our worries is important too. Stay and dance to a couple more songs with me?'

The cursed sound of engines had Maggie stopping and looking up. There hadn't been so many aircraft flying because of the snow, and she couldn't see these. They were above the clouds.

'That's the Hawker Hurricanes,' Ron said, even though he couldn't see them. Even she knew the sounds of each aeroplane now. 'They sound loaded. The engines have a different tone. They're taking something over the English Channel.'

She walked on. He was right, the aircraft stayed high.

As they turned the corner and faced the Mechanics Institute, he reached for her hand. 'Stay and dance with me for just a couple more.'

Asher and Naomi crossed the road a good way ahead, also holding hands because the compacted snow on the road was one long sheet of ice.

'All right. I'll stay for a little bit.' She held his firm hand tight as they navigated the road.

In the reception hall, Ron lifted her wet coat from her shoulders. He carried it over his arm, as they climbed the stairs, and hung it on a hook with his in the cloakroom. Then held her hand as they walked into the hall.

The band were playing a waltz. He pulled her in among the dancers.

She danced the next three dances with Ron, and he led the conversation throughout, not once taking his eyes off her face. She talked about her family and the factory. She didn't think about going home to Dot until the band stopped for another interval. But as soon as they did, guilt thumped her in the chest on two counts – she'd forgotten about getting home to Dot and she'd forgotten that she'd promised to dance with Lily all night. She'd been selfishly letting Ron sweep her off her feet.

She stepped away from him. 'Thank you for dancing with me. It's made the evening far more fun. But I did say I would dance with Lily. I should check on her.' Maggie turned away without waiting for his answer.

His hand caught hold of her upper arm and stopped her. 'Maggie, could I take you to the pub next Saturday evening?'

Her mouth fell open, she was so surprised. *Why?* The question flew into her head. Until tonight he'd hardly spoken to her for weeks. 'I... I don't fancy sitting in The Glue Pot or The Cricketers Arms.' Not knowing if someone in there had hurt Dot.

'I wasn't thinking of either. I'd take you somewhere outside the village. I can collect you at six, if you want to come?'

'Okay then. Thank you, yes.' A single nod confirmed her decision.

Ron released her arm and Maggie walked to the edge of the floor to look for Lily.

Lifting onto the balls of her feet, her gaze travelled across the heads of the dancers, searching. She couldn't see Lily with a partner.

She spotted Catherine's blonde hair. Catherine was still dancing with the carpentry foreman. He didn't move very steadily with his limp, but Catherine didn't seem to care. She smiled as he spoke. Catherine was like that, though. She took an interest in everyone. She might be posh but she wasn't stuck-up like some of the people in Old Town, who walked around with their noses in the air. She made everyone feel comfortable in her company.

Maggie looked for Lily again. This time her gaze searching through the people at the edges of the room.

There. Maggie spotted her, on the far side. It was only a quick glimpse of her through the swirling dancers, but in that second Maggie saw Lily's angry expression. Another space between the couples and Maggie glimpsed a man holding Lily's wrist. He must have forced her to turn her hand and was looking down at her palm. It wasn't right. His grip looked firm, as though he was hurting her.

The beat of Maggie's heart pounded as she forced a path through the dancers, elbows bumping people out of the way. An Abbot sister on a mission. Her sisters had a reputation for being too forceful sometimes, and she'd never hidden her temper when it was called for.

'Forces to contend with, the lot of you,' her father had said once. She felt like a force as she stormed across the dance floor, ready to thump the stranger. She would not let anyone upset Lily. She was not going to stand for any hanky-panky. *Bloody men.*

'Let go of her!' she shouted when she was still a couple of yards away. His head turned and Maggie saw his face. John Finch. She knew his mother.

Lily delivered a hard slap to his smooth-shaven cheek. So hard Maggie heard the impact of it over the sound of the band.

He let go of Lily's wrist and rubbed his face instead.

'I just wanted to dance with you,' he complained.

Lily's eyes narrowed. 'Takin liberties. Or tryin to. That's what you were doin.' Lily had balled her hands into fists and she leaned right up to him as though she was going to challenge him to a fight.

Maggie stayed out of it. Lily was managing well enough on her own.

'You tried to drag me out of the room when I said I wouldn't go outside with you. I told you, I aint that sort of girl. I'm engaged to be married!' She wiggled the fingers of her left hand in front of his face.

He raised both hands, palms outwards, expressing surrender. 'Say what you like. Girls like you are only good for one thing an it aint dancin nor bein no man's wife.'

Maggie saw spittle fly from John's mouth, his words had been said with so much venom. Maggie instantly hated him.

He turned and walked away.

'Girls like what?' Lily shouted after him.

He glanced back momentarily, but didn't give her an answer.

'Like beautiful, strong, clever women,' Maggie threw at him. 'And one thing we're very good for is telling men like you to get lost.'

He turned fully back, his gaze focusing on Maggie, then he looked at Lily. 'A scrubber.' He turned again and strode away.

He'd walked too far away for Lily to hit him. Maggie was tempted to do it, she was close enough. But before she could, Lily picked up a glass full of cordial and threw the liquid from it at the back of his head. Of course, the liquid hit others too, who turned and complained at the same time as John.

'You shut your mouth, John Finch!' Maggie yelled. 'You brute!'

He walked away, wiping the back of his head and neck with his handkerchief.

'Lord, Lily. What happened?'

'He tried to force me to go outside.' Lily's eyes glittered as the lights in the hall caught the fluid of gathering tears. Her anger had become distress.

Guilt washed through Maggie. She was supposed to have looked after Lily. 'Sorry. Do you want to leave? I should be getting back to Dad and Dot anyway. You could join me for a cup of tea at home.'

'My legs feel like jelly,' Lily said. 'I'd prefer to go ome to bed.'

'What happened? Are you all right?' Naomi joined them. 'I saw you arguing with that man.'

'Lily, what happened?' Catherine arrived too, increasing the circle around their friend.

'Lily, what did that man do?' Violet joined.

Maggie's lips parted in a smile. It was probably not an appropriate time to smile, but she'd felt alone and now she knew, as deep as her bones were in her body, that these friends would never let her really be alone. All she had to do was say something and one or more of them would help. She should tell Violet about Dot being ill. She wouldn't have to say anything about the abortion, just that Dot was unhappy.

'Ee's an idiot, that's all,' Lily declared. 'But ee embarrassed me, an now I'm shakin.' Lily raised a hand, showing them the tremble.

'Can I help, ladies?' Ron's voice had Maggie turning her head.

'I'm going to walk Lily home. There was a bit of a to-do,' she told him. She looked back at Lily. 'I'll fetch our coats. You can put—'

'No. I'll come with you now.' Lily looked at the other women. 'I'll say goodnight. I don't want to stop you all dancin.'

'I'll come with you.' Ron stepped forward. 'Otherwise, after you've walked Lily home, Maggie, there'll be no one with you when you walk back. I've just seen John leave, and you don't want to bump into him.'

'I'm not coming back,' Maggie told Ron. 'I'll go home too, and it's not far between our cottage and the Faradays' lodge.'

'Even so, it's dark and I'd rather I walked with you than find out tomorrow that something happened. I'd never forgive myself.' He smiled at Lily. 'Would you be happy with that, Lily, if I walk with you?'

As far as Maggie knew, Lily didn't know Ron that well. But maybe Lenny had talked about him, and maybe Lenny had talked to Ron about Lily. If Asher had confided in him, then Ron obviously presented a good ear. But he was not a good keeper of secrets. Maggie smiled at the thought of his mistake in telling them about Naomi and Asher.

Lily nodded. 'Yes. Thanks.'

This was kind, good old Ron, back on form.

He lifted the pocket watch from his waistcoat, looked at the time and then at Violet. 'The band will be playing for a good hour and more yet. I'll walk you both home and come back for you later, Vi.'

Violet nodded.

'Cath,' Lily said, 'what about you?'

'I can look after myself. Don't worry about me.'

'We'll make sure she makes it home safe,' Violet added.

Maggie smiled at her friends. 'Goodnight. Will you tell Edith and Marjorie I've left?'

'Of course,' Catherine agreed.

Kisses were planted quickly on cheeks, and then Maggie left with Lily and Ron.

Ron held her coat while she slid her arms into the sleeves. Then, as Ron held Lily's coat for her, Maggie draped her head-scarf over her head and tied the ends at a jaunty angle beneath her chin and wrapped her scarf twice around her neck.

When they left the Mechanics Institute, large snowflakes drifted horizontally on a strong wind. Lily raised the umbrella she and Catherine had huddled under on their way here.

'I'll hold it, shall I?' Ron offered. 'If I walk in the middle, I can hold it over all of us.'

It was a good idea, but the snow was blown beneath the brolly and caught Maggie constantly anyway. It was a whiteout. The flakes were so big and the wind so strong it was hard to see where they walked.

At least it wasn't far to her cottage. 'You go in,' Ron said. 'I'll walk Lily to her door.'

'Yes, get in the warm,' Lily agreed.

Ron and Lily waited, tucked under the umbrella, watching Maggie rush along the short garden path to the front door.

She waved them off as she opened the door, calling out 'I'm home!' as she closed it.

The hall was dark apart from thin seams of light edging the parlour door.

As Maggie slid her damp coat off, the warmth in the air welcomed her. 'Dad! Dot!' she called through the wall as she unravelled her scarf.

'Hello, love,' her father called back, before coughing.

She untied her soaked headscarf and hung everything on the hook with her coat to dry.

She opened the parlour door.

Her father was coughing into his handkerchief.

Dot started, waking suddenly. The blanket that had lain across her lap slipped onto the floor. She was as white as a ghost despite the heat from the fire. She may have just woken but the dark shadows under her eyes made it obvious she hadn't slept properly for weeks.

Maggie walked across, picked up the blanket and handed it to Dot. 'Are you all right?'

'Yes.'

'Would you like a cup of hot milk and honey? I'm going to warm some up for myself.'

'Yes, please.'

Their father was still coughing.

'Do you want some milk, Dad?'

He couldn't answer as the cough shook his chest and shoulders vigorously.

'Lord, Dad.' The handkerchief he held to his mouth was suddenly soaked with scarlet blood. She pressed a hand on his shoulder. His body heaved with the coughs and blood splattered beyond his handkerchief.

Dot rose from her chair. 'Dad?'

The coughing and the blood didn't stop. He'd never been this bad.

'I'll get someone.' Maggie ran to the front door and outside into the blizzard. She didn't care about letting the light out or the cold in. 'Help! My dad's ill!' she shouted towards a tall silhouette a few yards away.

The man broke into an awkward run, his feet sliding on the fresh snow. 'Maggie?'

Ron. It was Ron, on his way back from walking Lily home.

'Dad's sick!' she shouted in a panic. 'He needs help.'

'Go back inside and stay with him. I'll get the doctor.'

25

Naomi Isaacs

The dance was over. The band were packing up their instruments. Naomi stood watching, her hands clutching either elbow. She'd had a lovely evening. At times, it had felt like nothing outside this room – the arctic night, the war – had existed. Now she had to face it all again. Beginning with a cold, difficult walk up the hill in the blizzard. Asher had gone to fetch their coats. He'd left her in the hall because the cloakroom was full of people putting layers back on to face the cold. He'd said he'd bring their outdoor things in here.

'Naomi.'

She felt a touch on her arm and turned to face Catherine.

'Ron never brought back my umbrella, so Joe's offered to drive me home. He'll be driving up to Old Town and asked if you would like a lift home. He's going to run Violet home too. The snow is awful. You can hardly see out there.'

Naomi had walked down the steep hill from the old town with Asher, but he'd had to walk up the hill to collect her. It would make more sense for Joe to drive her rather than Asher having to do the walk twice when the weather was so bad.

Asher was probably hoping to talk on the way home and repeat his offer of marriage. But they had talked while they'd danced, and she was not going to accept his proposal. She thought he would make a good husband, and every time he smiled her stomach filled with butterflies. But... she didn't want to stop working. She liked her job and her friends. If she married, GWR would insist she resigned. She didn't want to give up everything else for Asher. Being Asher's wife and losing everything else would make her life miserable. She had not admitted that to him because it sounded selfish.

'It would be easier,' she answered Catherine, making up her mind.

When Joe walked up to them it was in the company of Asher and Violet. Asher carried Naomi's coat, scarf and headscarf.

'Thank you.' She accepted her coat first. It was still damp from the walk down.

She smiled at Joe. 'Thank you for the offer of a lift, Joe. Yes please.'

Asher and Dietrich often spoke about Joe. They liked the foreman. She didn't know him well, but Dietrich did, and his trust was rare.

'You aren't walking?' Asher asked.

'No. Joe is driving my way. You go home. There's no need to for you to walk up and down the hill.' She accepted a sodden headscarf from him. Instead of putting it on she pressed it into her pocket.

Asher flopped his flat cap on his head in a way that implied he was annoyed. He only wore the black kippah over his hair on religious days. Naomi's family were not strict in their practice of the Jewish faith, but for Asher the reason was different. Before leaving Europe, he had hidden the signs of his faith because he felt he must.

Naomi instinctively reached out and touched his arm in a consoling gesture. He shrugged her touch away and put on his coat.

'I will see you at lunchtime tomorrow,' she said, very aware that Catherine, Violet and Joe observed them quietly. They were both due to work the Sunday shift. They traded their Saturdays to work on a Sunday so they could respect the Sabbath. The lunches they ate together on Sundays had given them the chance to get to know each other more.

Catherine was the only one who knew Naomi's father had agreed she could marry Asher. Naomi had not agreed yet. She'd confided in Catherine just after new year, before this beastly cold spell had begun. They'd been sitting on the cold tarmac in the dust outside the workshop door, seeking daylight and fresh air in the five minutes they were allowed to use the men's toilet.

Catherine had opened the conversation. 'I've not heard a peep from you this morning,' she had said. 'Is something wrong? I'll pay you a ha'penny for your thoughts.'

'I don't need a ha'penny. It doesn't buy much these days, not with rationing.'

'I'll pay you sixpence, then.'

That had pulled a laugh from Naomi's throat, but it had been a half-hearted one, and she was aware that she had sounded miserable when she explained.

'It is not that I do not like Asher,' she had said. 'I like him very much. But I want to work, and if I marry I don't think GWR will let me. I also want to be sure I am marrying the right man. I haven't met any other Jewish men my age here.'

'But your father agreed?'

'It is the way Jewish families do things. It is not as bad as it sounds. Traditionally, parents find a husband for their daughters, or a wife for their sons. There are not many Jewish people in Swindon, so Abba – sorry, I mean my father – has grasped at Asher's offer. He thinks that God has sent Asher to me. For him, Asher is *a good Jewish boy and that is enough.*' She'd said the last words in the tone of her father's voice.

Cath had laughed. 'Your father sounds like a wry old man.'

'He is kind, loving and old-fashioned.'

'Mine too,' Catherine had replied. 'I wonder, though, if our children will think us old-fashioned.'

'I'm sure they will,' Naomi had answered. 'I think when the war is over I will want to marry Asher. If we love one another, I will marry him. Right now it is too soon to say it is love, and I will not stop working for the war effort just because I fancy a man, or even if I love him. But my father and Asher are impatient, they do not want me to wait. My father says Asher might be called up to fight when soldiers are needed more than carpenters. Then also...' She'd stopped talking and swallowed, the fear tightening her throat. 'I don't want to fall in love with a man who might die...'

She felt herself blush even now at the thought of saying that to Catherine, who had a fiancé fighting.

'I'm sorry. I know you love your Charles, but I just... I am not sure I could be as strong as you, Cath.'

'Love isn't a choice,' Catherine had replied. 'If it is love you will fall whether you choose to or not. The emotions steal up on you; they are not made by a decision. There is nothing you can do to prevent it. If you fall for a man who needs to or wants to fight, you will support him because you have to. And I think the factory will have to change its stance on employing married women. It will become too short of workers to turn wives away.'

At that point, the checky had pushed open the door and

yelled at them both to get back to work unless they wanted their wages docked.

Now, as she stood outside the Mechanics Institute, shivering in the cold, windy night, dressed in falling snowflakes, she knew what Catherine had meant. Yes, love had crept up on her.

Asher leaned close and kissed her cheek. 'Goodnight,' he said.

'Goodnight.' Her skin flushed, because he had kissed her in front of others.

She waved awkwardly as she climbed into the front passenger seat in the car. Then she pulled the door shut.

Asher waited, watching as Catherine and Violet climbed into the back seats of Joe's car.

Joe pulled away. The headlights were cloaked and the light barely visible. All Naomi could see was white snowflakes racing towards them. The blade of the windscreen wiper swished back and forth, sweeping the snowflakes aside. Snow covered the screen before the wiper swiped back. Joe leaned forward, hunching over the wheel. Naomi thought he must be struggling to see the road.

Joe dropped Violet off outside her home first.

She climbed out quickly. 'Goodnight. Thank you, Joe.' She shut the door and ran through the snow to her front door as the car started off again.

As he drove along Faringdon Road, Naomi saw Asher talking to Ron at the back of the Mechanics Institute. Asher didn't notice the car, but he had the brim of his cap pulled low and the collar of his coat turned up.

Joe stopped the car outside the park.

Catherine opened the rear passenger door and got out quickly. 'Thank you, Joe. Goodnight. Goodnight, Naomi.' She shut the door.

Through drifting snowflakes, Naomi watched Catherine open

the park gate and run to the back door of the Faradays' lodge. The door opened a moment later and Catherine disappeared inside.

Joe started off again, turning the car to go back the way they had come.

Naomi bit the inside of her lip as the car travelled on into the blizzard. The steady rhythm of the windscreen wiper was the dominant sound, as it swiped back and forth. Her mind whisked through things she might say, as though it flicked through the pages of a magazine, looking for a topic. But her mouth was too dry to speak. She was never good at spending time with people she didn't know well. She had been shy since she was a child.

'I might have to give up driving the car soon,' Joe said, the tone of his voice implying he'd been searching for a topic of conversation too. 'The country's too short of petrol to waste it on me getting up and down the hill. I'll have to endure the wet and cold, use the buses and make the best of it.'

It would be harder for him, with his limp.

Naomi spotted a tall figure standing on the pavement not far ahead. Asher. He was waiting for the car to pass, so he must have seen them pass earlier. He raised a hand as the car approached, and waved. She waved back, even though she wasn't sure he would see. Joe sounded the horn.

'Asher is sweet on you, isn't he?' Joe said as they left Asher behind. 'He's a good man. Hardworking. He came to the factory about a year ago. I liked him from the day I met him. I'm a good judge of character.'

She looked at Joe. 'Are you providing me with a reference for him?'

A bark of laughter escaped Joe's throat, and he glanced her way. 'I may well be. He told me he wants to marry you, but you're cautious.'

He turned the car towards Victoria Road, the steepest route up the hill.

'Wouldn't you be cautious, if you had to spend the rest of your life with someone?' She'd spoken bluntly, and it was a rude thing to say. She didn't even know if he was married, but he had brought up the personal subject.

'I would be cautious too, yes.' His voice was calm and he spoke quietly. 'And I told Asher the same.'

She glanced at him, as the car reached the Victoria Road turning. He was a foreman – he might know the answer to her main concern. 'If I marry Asher, will GWR ask me to resign, even now there's a war on? I like the work I do.'

The car's wheels spun then caught on the grit that had been thrown across the ice on the steep road by the shovelful.

He glanced towards her for a very brief moment before staring through the windscreen again as the car climbed. He took a deep breath. 'I am not sure, Miss Isaacs. I can find out for you if you like, or you can ask Catherine to. No. I will find out and let you know. Now, you are going to have to direct me to your house, please?'

'Oh. Sorry.' She'd forgotten he wouldn't know. 'Turn left at the top of the hill.'

'Left again.'

'The house is there. You can stop here.'

When the car drew to a halt, she opened the door and got out. 'Thank you for driving me home, Mr Marsh. Goodnight.'

'You're welcome. Goodnight, Miss Isaa—'

She closed the door behind her, cutting off the end of her name, hurried up the steps and drew the key out of her coat pocket. She opened the door quietly, aware that everyone else might be in bed. A tiny amount of light reached from the parlour. The door stood ajar. Someone was awake.

After she'd taken off her outdoor things she walked along to the parlour and opened the door. The room was still warmish, although the coals had burned to ashes in the hearth. Dietrich was sitting in an armchair, his feet up on the seat, his knees against his chest as he hugged his legs, curled up like a dormouse in striped pyjamas.

'What is wrong?'

He didn't move, he didn't even look towards her. His face was buried in his knees.

'Dietrich?'

He was as still as stone.

'Did you have a bad dream?' Naomi rested a gentle and consoling hand on his shoulder. 'Dietrich?'

He didn't move, he seemed frozen.

She squatted on her haunches in front of him. 'Shall I make us some hot cocoa?' Like everyone else, Naomi was well aware that such things as a tin of cocoa powder were now almost as precious as gold dust, but there were occasions when these things were better used than kept. 'I'll do that. I shall be back in a moment.'

He must have had a nightmare. He often dreamt about things that had happened in Germany. She could not take his memories away. His mind needed time now, to process the dream and come back to reality. But then his reality was that his whole family were missing in Germany.

In the kitchen, she put a pan of milk on the stove to warm through and reached for the tin of cocoa on the shelf.

Asher had fled the Nazis too. Perhaps his desire to marry in haste was because he knew that life was precious, and from his point of view, too short to put off anything until later. Only God knew what tomorrow would bring these days.

She took the pan off the heat just before the milk boiled, so that it would not form a skin, and poured it into two cups, then stirred in spoonfuls of cocoa. She carried the cups into the parlour. Dietrich's head was still on his knees and he rocked back and forth as he hugged himself.

'Here.' She put the cup on the low table near him. 'Would you like to talk about your dream, or your family?'

He shook his head against his knees.

'I wish I could do something...' She felt so useless. He behaved and spoke in such a grown-up manner that sometimes she forgot he was a child still.

He lifted his head at last, showing a face that was smudged with tear stains, and he wiped the cuff of his pyjama sleeve across his face to dry his cheeks. She noticed dark hairs had sprouted unevenly across his upper lip and chin. He may not be a man yet but physically he was changing into one. His mother and father were missing this progression.

'Your parents will be missing you too, and they will be very proud of what you are doing.'

He didn't answer. He reached for the mug, his legs unravelling and his bare feet resting on the floor. He sipped the hot cocoa.

'Shall I stay with you for a while?'

'Yes please. I don't want to be alone and you are doing something.' His words were short and sharp. 'Your family have given me a safe place.'

Naomi leaned back in the chair with a sigh, embracing her mug between her hands to warm them. She felt desperately tired, but she wouldn't leave him.

26

Maggie Abbot

Maggie felt so cold, even though flames licked around fresh coals in the fire grate. It was the strangest thing to be here in the parlour with her sisters but for her father's chair to be empty. She'd left him in the hospital ward an hour ago. She and her sisters had been chased off the ward by the matron with a sharp military-style voice announcing that her patients needed to sleep. But for a short while all four of them had sat around his bed. The coughing and the bleeding had eventually stopped, but the doctor had told Maggie and her sisters that he thought their father's illness was terminal and he probably did not have much longer to live.

He'd been carried on a stretcher to a GWR ambulance, unable to walk even the couple of streets to the hospital in Faringdon Road. He'd worked for GWR since he was twelve and paid the insurance that funded the workers' hospital in the Railway Village. He'd lived in the Railway Village his whole life. GWR was his life, from the very beginning. There was a picture on the sideboard. It was taken at the annual GWR children's party in the Faringdon Road park. The photographer had captured Maggie's grandmother holding Maggie's father in her arms. He was a baby of less than a year old. Maggie had always loved looking at that picture.

Ron had fetched Edith and Marjorie from the dance. They'd arrived at the hospital shaking and pale, shocked and fearful. Afraid their father might have already passed and they were too late to say goodbye.

Before Maggie had left her father in the hospital she had said her goodbye as if it might be the last. She'd kissed his cheek and squeezed his cold clammy hand and said, 'I love you.'

Now, in front of the parlour hearth that held only cold ashes, Maggie sat among her sisters in silence, unable to believe what had happened.

She closed her eyes. A tear escaped from each eye and rolled down her cheeks. She didn't wipe them away. She wanted to cry for her father. She'd known he was seriously ill. But it did not make this any easier. She longed to feel his hand on her shoulder as she sat on the rug in front of his chair. To feel his lips kiss her cheek as he'd leaned over her bed to say, *'Sleep tight.'*

'My heart is broken beyond repair, I think.' Dot ended the silence, her voice clinical and blunt, the emotions wrung out of her – or that is how Maggie felt, and Dot sounded as though she felt the same emptiness.

'I feel like a slab of marble,' Maggie said. 'So cold and just... numb. I am too shocked to feel anything.'

'Me too,' Marjorie said.

'I don't think I'd be able to sleep if I tried,' Edith added. 'Shall I heat some milk and make some Ovaltine?'

'We probably should drink something,' Dot replied.

Maggie watched Dot. She'd heard in those words a flicker of

the old Dot, the queen of their little family. Maggie needed her to be her old self. She needed her sister to cling to. She didn't think she could hold Dot up and worry about losing her father.

Edith left the room.

'What will happen to this house?' Marjorie's voice was quiet, as though she didn't want their neighbours to hear through the walls and tell the GWR clerks their father was ill.

GWR would know on Monday. He wouldn't go back to work.

'He's given his life to the firm and we all work in the factory, surely they wouldn't take the house away?' Instinctively Maggie looked at Dot, as though she would have the answer.

Dot shook her head. 'Let's worry about that when we have to. The Helping Hands Fund will help us, if we need help, we're not going to be left homeless or destitute. For now, all I want is for Dad's last days to be as comfortable as possible, and I don't know about you but I am going to be in church on my knees tomorrow.'

Dot's gaze caught on Maggie's. Maggie sent her a shallow smile that said, *I love you*, as her heart warmed to hear some life in Dot's voice, even though there was a terrible reason for it.

When the clock on the mantel chimed twice, Dot stood. 'We need to try and sleep.'

Maggie climbed the stairs with heavy feet, not tired at all, and when she and Dot were changed and ready for bed, Maggie said, 'Can I sleep in your bed, Dot. I don't want to sleep alone.'

'Yes, come on, get in.' Dot threw back the sheet.

Maggie lay down beside her sister. Dot's fingers stroked Maggie's hair, taking Maggie back years. She'd slept in Dot's bed and Dot had stroked her hair like this when their mother had died.

* * *

The next morning, Maggie walked up the flagstone path to St Mark's Church with her hands pressed into the pockets of her coat to keep them warm. The outline of St Mark's stood proudly against a bright blue sky this morning, decorated with snow and icicles.

Maggie had always thought St Mark's was a building with an over-inflated ego. Churches were by nature a celebration of architecture, a religious offering in a way, and St Mark's was a significant offering from Sir George Scott, who had also designed St Pancras Station. It was disproportionately grand for the Railway Village. The church proudly showed itself off on the skyline of this small area of the town, far too large for the original number in the congregation.

The Railway Village's church was grandiose – she smiled as she used the word her father had taught her.

The thought of him tugged at her heart. No one was allowed to visit the ward until 2 p.m. So here she was, with Dot, Edith, Marjorie and Lily, fulfilling the rhythm of their Sunday routine – Mass, then lunch and an afternoon of chores – washing, cleaning, baking. But the day had no heart to it.

'Maggie.' Lily stepped closer and threaded their arms. Since Lenny had left, Maggie had made a habit of knocking on the Faradays' door every Sunday and asking Lily if she wanted to walk to church with them. Lily always did. Maggie's railway sisters and her actual sisters had merged into one thing these days.

'I'll pray for your dad,' Lily said, her voice reassuring.

He needed a miracle. Maggie was going to pray for that.

It was the way of things since this war had started. People left or died. Many older people had passed just because of the colder winter and lack of coal. Maggie bit her lip – she didn't want her father to die.

Immediately after they'd crossed the threshold of the large door, the pungent scent of the incense assaulted Maggie's nostrils.

The church's services were as magnificent as the building. A Church of England church with sung masses and a golden thurible swung on a golden chain, filling the church with the smoke of burning incense. A Church of England church practising in the Catholic tradition, with confessionals too.

Lily released Maggie's arm as they walked to their usual pew.

An empty feeling caught at Maggie. Every Sunday, her whole life, her father had stood in front of her with his hand out, encouraging her and her sisters to sit before he did, and for as long as she could remember Maggie would be the last to enter the pew, and the one who sat beside him. Today, she followed Lily into the pew and sat at the farthest end, well away from her normal seat.

Maggie's fingers touched the little silver cross hanging from a chain around her neck and her thumb stroked the reverse of it. In her head she prayed, over and over – *Dear God, please be kind. Be good to my dad. Save him.* She noticed that Dot did the same.

When it was time to take the sacrament, Maggie knelt between Lily and Dot at the altar rail, tears streaming down her cheeks as she prayed again. At such a significant moment, God must hear her.

'Are you all right?' Lily whispered as they walked back to the pew.

Bless her, when Maggie had first met Lily she'd been a child really, so naïve and nervous, like a lost kitten, and here she was grown into a confident young woman who was generous, even when she was suffering herself.

Maggie took Lily's hand, and they sat in the pew holding hands for the rest of the service.

27

Lily Franklin

As she did every Sunday since she'd left her home, Lily felt like furling her shoulders, curling over and hiding herself among the congregation so her father wouldn't be able to see her. She didn't. She sat tall, holding her back straight, and throughout the service she glanced at her sisters and brothers, sitting in a pew on the other side of the church aisle in a row of descending height from eldest to youngest. They glanced towards her and smiled when they could, without her father seeing.

When Lily's father fell asleep during the sermon, Polly sent Lily a broad smile. Lily didn't smile; she was too aware of Maggie's desperate praying beside her. There was little to smile about these days, with poor Mr Abbot in hospital and Lenny and Art not here.

She worried about Lenny all the time, not knowing if in that moment he was in a battle and in danger of dying. The letters she'd received from him in training had been full of his usual humour. She had heard his voice speak in the words...

I am sick of someone shouting Left... Right... Left... at me, Lily. You should hear the Drill Sergeant, Lily. He'd make you chuckle. He tells us to stick our thumbs out. I don't think Hitler or his Nazis are less likely to shoot me whether my thumb is stuck out when I march or not. The other day, he swore and told us to 'put some swank into it.' I have no idea what swank is, but it wasn't what I did, so I got a clip around the ear and told to do a hundred press-ups in the frozen mud.

It is fun to see village children grinning at us with admiration when we strut past, though. Looking at us like we'll be their saviours. Especially when we are singing. It does sound pretty impressive when a popular song is roared from the throats of a hundred or so men to the pace of our pounding boots. I would be impressed if I watched us, whether the men had their thumbs stuck out or not.

These boots are killing, though. It's like walking with buckets on my feet. I need at least another four pairs of the socks you and Mum knitted, just to fill them up. We march at least a twenty-mile route every day. That's all I do, learn to shoot guns and walk far...

The memory of his words had her heart aching. She felt as though it was hard to breathe sometimes, her chest was so tight with fear. His last letter, written at the end of his training, had a very different tone...

I am being posted to Norway. I won't be able to tell you any of this when I'm there, Lily. We've been told letters home will be monitored, and we're not to mention anything about our locations, any battles or orders. Just in case the letters get stopped by someone before they get home. I am terrified. But I know it's for a good purpose. We are to cut off the iron ore trade

*between the Germans and the Soviets, and open up a route for
our troops to support the fight against the Soviets in Finland.*

That was the last she had heard, and there had been very
little humour in that last letter, so she knew he was as scared for
himself as she was for him. She didn't know if he was in Europe
yet. He might even be on the frontline. He might be fighting Nazis
right now.

At least, because she'd escaped the role of pressing buttons
and was learning to use the lathes and other heavy machinery,
her mind was distracted while she worked. She was learning
skilled work – fascinating, enjoyable work.

Father Arnold said the final blessing over the congregation
and prayed everyone would have a good day.

Lily's mind returned from thoughts of Lenny. She should
probably confess her lack of concentration. She had admitted to
fornication in the confessional box, as had Lenny before he left to
fight. She'd told him to do it. She didn't want him to die with sins
on his shoulders.

Father Arnold's voice had sounded unsurprised when Lily
had confessed to him. Lenny had said Father Arnold had probably listened to the same confession over and over again for
weeks, because so many men were heading off to war and their
sweethearts would be taking pity on them.

'I didn't let you do it out of pity,' she'd complained. 'I chose to
do it cause I love you.'

'And I chose to do it with you because I love you.' He'd
stopped walking along the path, embraced her cheek with his
hand and kissed her firmly on the lips in the middle of the street,
in daylight.

She thanked the Lord her father hadn't seen them that day.
What a scene he'd have made.

She stood up along with Maggie and her sisters to leave the pew.

On the other side of the nave, Lily's father walked out of the pew first, then her stepmother, and then Betsy Lloyd. Lily hung back, behind Maggie, making sure her father had walked on. Betsy was wearing a coat that Lily could see had been let out at the side seams. Only a little for now. Polly had told Lily that Betsy had moved in and was now sharing the bed, top to Polly's and Pen's tails. Her parents had kicked her out of their cottage because she was expecting. She was doing her best to hide it, but it looked like it wouldn't be long before she couldn't, and Polly had said Betsy didn't know when Art was going to get any leave to come home and marry her.

She didn't judge Betsy and Art badly. After all, she and Lenny had done it once without a rubber johnny. She was lucky, and glad, that fate had kept her out of Betsy's predicament. Lily had walked around with a smile on her face all day when her period had come.

Lily had told Lenny about Betsy in a letter, and he'd replied saying that a few soldiers in his regiment had left women with a similar memory of a misspent evening or afternoon to ruin their lives. She'd asked him in her reply why the men hadn't worn condoms.

'They said because "it feels different" and "they don't like it",' he'd written back.

'Selfish pigs then, aren't they,' she'd written to him, and as she'd written it, she'd seen the reaction she knew he'd have to her words, his head thrown back and laughter escaping from deep in his throat. She tried to always write something funny to cheer him up. She never moaned about missing him in her letters, he would know she did, as much as she knew he missed her. The number of letters they had sent each other until now said that.

She had carried on writing daily, in the hope he'd receive them all when the post found him. Every evening, she and Catherine sat at the table in the warm kitchen, scribbling in tiny writing to make the most of the small amount of paper they could get hold of.

Maggie watched Polly hold back, with Pen and their brother Jimmy beside her, letting other people pass them as the congregation flowed in a procession along the central aisle of the nave, behind Father Arnold and Peter Hall, who swung the thurible, wafting the smoke from the burning incense through the air. The scent drew Lily into a peaceful state every time she walked through the door of the church. The scent of incense meant a time of safety to her.

Lily's father was a long way ahead when Maggie and her sisters walked out from the pew they'd used. Lily stepped out and stopped, pressing back against the smooth wooden end of the pew to let the tail end of the procession of people pass. She smiled at Polly through the gaps as she waited.

After the last person passed, Lily rushed towards Polly. They hugged each other firmly, quickly, knowing they had very little time.

'Lily,' Pen said.

'Lily,' Jimmy said, trying to get her attention.

Lily released Polly and hugged one then the other, kissing their cold cheeks. The taste of the week's dirt lingered on her lips as she released them. It was bath day. The dirt would be washed off in the tin bath in the parlour this afternoon.

'Ere.' Polly pulled something from her pocket. A letter. 'Art wrote to you. I id it from Mam an Dad.'

'Thanks.' Lily took it quickly and shoved it into her own pocket excitedly. He didn't write often. He wrote to Betsy mostly. 'Ow are you all?'

'Tired,' Polly answered. 'Betsy snores.'

Lily laughed and then covered her mouth quickly as the sound echoed around the church.

'We can ear er through the wall too,' Jimmy said. 'She keeps me awake. I wish you would come ome.' He wrapped his arms around Lily's middle and hugged her tight.

'I aint gunna come ome, love. I'm sorry. Dad wouldn't let me, an I like stayin where I am, an I like workin too. Dad wouldn't let me work.'

'What are you doin in the factory?' Jimmy asked.

'Usin lots of machines.' She smiled.

His eyes were wide, excited by the idea of being old enough to do the same one day. For him her father would expect it. Jimmy would be chased out of school and into the GWR factory as soon as he was old enough. Because Dad would want Jimmy earning money.

'Dad will be lookin for you. We'd better walk on.'

Lily and Polly walked towards the door side by side. Pen's sticky hand caught hold of Lily's hand on the other side. Jimmy walked on the far side of Polly, bouncing his hand along the tops of the ends of the pews.

'Stop it.' Polly knocked his hand down.

At the edge of her vision Lily saw a movement in the south aisle of the nave, which had her turning to look. It was unusual for anyone to be in that part of the church at this time. It was Dot. Maggie's eldest sister. Dot hadn't been to church since the new year. She was deathly pale and painfully thin. Her clothes hung from her. She didn't look well. She walked along the south aisle in the company of Father Arnold, towards the confessional.

Lily looked at Polly, sensing that Dot would not want anyone to have seen her. 'You're lookin thinner. Do you av enough food?'

'Enough. Not a lot. Not nice food.'

'That's the same for everyone. I just wondered if Dad is fillin is own stomach first.'

'Oh yes, but we manage, an the air raid wardens av taken to gatherin in the bakery, so they fill themselves up on the cakes that are goin out of date every night.'

Lily laughed again and covered her mouth. 'Typical.'

'I know. Ee doesn't bring any cakes ome.'

'I aint surprised.'

'The Faradays seem lovely.'

'They are.'

'When are you gunna marry Lenny?'

'When we're older. Dad would never consent, Polly. So, when I'm twenty-one.'

'Ee might, if the Faradays persuade im to. Ee respects them cause Lenny's dad is important. Ee wouldn't want to insult Mr Faraday. Imagine im avin Mr Faraday as a relative. Ee'd bite your and off for the chance of that.'

Lily hadn't thought of that. She'd tell Lenny when she wrote tonight. She'd be too embarrassed to ask his parents to say something.

When they were a few feet away from the porch door, Lily turned and wrapped her arms around Polly's neck. 'I love you,' she said into her ear. 'Be careful around Dad.'

'I will be.'

They kissed each other's cheeks.

Jimmy had run ahead of them and out into the churchyard.

Pen hugged Lily next, tears dripping down her cheeks.

'Oh, poppet, don't cry. I'm only down the road.' She would have told Pen to come and see her after school, but Lily had no idea what hours she'd be asked to work. She was home one day and working the next, the shifts dependent on when the metal deliveries came in. 'I'll see you next Sunday.'

Pen nodded and wiped the tears off her cheeks with a muddy hand. The younger ones weren't cared for as well as Lily had cared for them.

But it wasn't her fault. She confronted her guilt as they all walked out into the sunlight of a cold winter's day. They had a mother at home.

Her father stood not far from the church door. Apparently waiting for them. Everyone else was further along the path or walking home. He removed his hands from his pockets and a gut-pinching fear clasped in Lily's stomach. But he wouldn't hit her here, and he wouldn't hit Polly or the others.

'Get yourself ome,' he said to Polly.

'I was just—'

'Just nothin,' he growled. 'Get ome, you ungrateful girl.'

He didn't speak to Lily, didn't even look at her. He looked through her as though she didn't exist.

He smacked the back of Jimmy's head as they turned to walk down the path and pushed Pen ahead of him. Polly glanced back at Lily with a goodbye in her eyes.

Lily knew that next week her father would herd Polly out of the church ahead of him.

He was horrible.

She slipped her hands into her coat pockets, searching for warmth. She felt Art's latest letter there and a spur of desire to read it made her want to run all the way back to the Faradays' – or skate, as the pavements were ice. The sight of Maggie outside the churchyard stopped her. Maggie stood beside Violet, their heads pressed close while they talked, the cold air turning their breath to rising clouds of mist.

Lily didn't try to pass her father. 'Being wary is sensible, not cowardice,' Lenny had told her. She followed him to the end of the path and waited for him to walk through the gate, Polly, Pen and Jimmy ahead of him.

Violet and Maggie stopped talking and sent Lily's father evil stares when he passed them.

Lily smiled and a quiet giggle escaped her throat as he carried on walking, acting as though he didn't care what her friends thought about him. Lily knew him too well – he'd feel embarrassed.

Lily said hello to Maggie with a quick hug. 'Ow are you?' She didn't mention that she'd seen Dot with the priest, but she guessed Maggie was waiting for her oldest sister.

Maggie gave her answer with a shrug. *Awful.*

'Come an see me at the Faradays' after you've visited your dad, if you need company,' Lily said. As soon as she'd said it, though, she remembered Dot, Edith and Marjorie. Maggie already had company.

'Thanks, Lily.' Maggie's voice made it sound as though she appreciated the offer even though she had her sisters.

'Maggie!'

Lily looked over her shoulder towards the church as Maggie and Violet did. Dot hurried along the path towards them. Her cheeks bloomed with a bit more colour as she approached them, but it was probably because of the cold, as the tip of her nose was rosy too.

'Did it go as you wanted?' Maggie asked Dot as if she was speaking in some sort of code.

Dot nodded as she joined them.

Lily did not ask Dot or Maggie to explain what 'it' was. If Dot wanted Lily to know, she'd say.

'We need to get home, Maggie,' Dot said. 'We need to get the housework done before we visit Dad. He'll need the washing dry. He'll need clean nightshirts and handkerchiefs. You know Dad, he'll want to look smart even if he's in a hospital bed. He'll probably ask for his suit jacket.'

Lily laughed along with Maggie and Violet, but it was a hollow sound, not really an expression of humour, more an expression of unity and team spirit. Come to think of it, her washing was already hanging on the clothes-horse in the Faradays' kitchen, and she'd cleaned the wide hall, the upstairs landing, her room and the parlour for Mrs Faraday. She could help with the baking later. 'Shall I come ome with you both? I can elp you get through the ousework quicker, then you can visit your dad an not worry.'

Maggie shared a look with Dot. *Should I say yes? It would be a help.*

'I don't av to get ome,' Lily added. 'I don't av anythin to do, really. I'd be glad of the distraction.'

'Thank you, Lily, that would be helpful.' It was Dot who answered. 'It might keep us all in better spirits.'

'I can help too,' Violet said. 'Mum can manage alone at home for an hour or two.'

The girls threaded arms, Maggie's weaving through Dot's, Lily's through Maggie's, and Violet's through Lily's so that, in a four, they filled the width of the pavement.

Art's letter would have to wait until Lily got home. Her friends were here now and they needed her.

* * *

Dear Lily,

Sorry it takes me so long to reply to you, but when I get a chance to rest, writing isn't on my mind. I'm dead on my feet these days. It's bloody hard here. Bets said at home people moan about being bored. I'd love to be bored. I dream of putting my feet up to dry out the soles of my boots on the fire hearth and warming my hands with a mug of tea, and my stomach with some freshly toasted bread. I realise now how much you used to spoil me, doing my washing and making my dinner. I was a lucky chap.

But then I do want to stop this craziness, and it is crazy here. Even if I was allowed to explain it, I don't think I could. Not really. The sounds and the smells are the worst things. I don't think I will ever get the smell of someone dying out of my head. Or the sounds of the constant bombardment of bombs and gunfire. I have been sick a lot. I feel like a fool, but I am not the only one. It makes us feel too young to be here. But someone has to be here.

That's enough of that anyway. I didn't write to complain about things. Thanks for the new socks and the woolly hat. I wear that at night. Your knitting's getting better, but like you said, you probably need something to fill your hands now Lenny's gone.

No, I haven't seen him. The chance of me seeing him is like spotting a needle in a haystack. The frontline is across the whole of Europe and his regiment could be anywhere. I wouldn't know and I can't ask.

Can you keep an eye on Bets for me, Lil? You know what Dad's like, and I worry about her. And I can't see me getting home any time soon to marry her. (Yes, I do know about condoms, you cheeky cow!) Just make sure she has someone to go to if things don't work out in Mam and Dad's cottage.

Thanks for the prayers too. It helps knowing that I have you and others at home who are looking out for me. I pray too, that this madness will come to an end. I look forward to that day all the time, and being able to hug the people I love knowing we're all safe.

Sending you my love, Lil. Look after yourself. I do like reading your letters even though I am rubbish at replying, so keep writing. Any news from home is always welcome, and you make me laugh.

Love (yes, Lil, I used the word, not taking the mickey),
Your bossy brother Art, who misses your Sunday roasts.

The last line sparked a laugh from her throat.

'Is it a nice letter? Is everything all right?' Mrs Faraday glanced over her shoulder, smiling at Lily's laughter as she washed the dishes in the porcelain sink.

'Ee's as good as ee can be, I think.'

Lily reached out for the pen and paper to write back to him, and then she was going to continue her letter to Lenny and tell him about Polly's idea about asking his parents to ask her dad if he'd agree to their getting married.

28

MARCH

Maggie Abbot

'The Soviet Union and Finland have agreed a truce, Dad,' Maggie read from the paper. She reached out and touched his arm. But there was no response. 'It's good news isn't it?' she continued, no matter that she wasn't sure he heard her. Not even a flicker of his eyelashes acknowledged her.

He'd lain like this for twenty-four hours, his chest rising unsteadily when he breathed in, and his lungs rattling when he breathed out, even though he barely seemed to breathe at all. The matron had told them he didn't have long left.

Dot sat on the opposite side of the bed, holding his hand, her thumb stroking continuously back and forth across the back of his fingers.

'Everyone is excited. We are all hoping for peace now. Maybe it'll come much sooner than Churchill predicted. They say that Mr Chamberlain is talking to Hitler about a peace agreement too.'

Marjorie stood at the end of the bed, holding their father's toes through the layers of blankets and sheets. He was cold. But even the hospital had to be careful with fuel. Edith hadn't come. She had a horrible cold and had spent the morning sneezing. The matron would never have let her in, and it wouldn't have helped their father if he caught it. She'd gone to do her shift in the factory.

Maggie and Marjorie were missing their shifts. Dot had not returned to work yet. She was much better, although she wasn't eating properly, but she'd spent every day of the last two weeks here with their father as soon as the matron would let her through the door. She'd been warned that she'd have to go back to work or she'd lose her job, and she would have to, or they wouldn't have enough money. Things might be rationed but they still had to pay for them.

'They miss you in the factory, Dad,' Marjorie said. 'People keep stopping me in the street and saying tell Mr Abbot he's missed. He's a good man.' She smiled, as if he could see her smile. They all behaved as though he were wide awake because there was no other way to behave. Maggie had led that conversation around the breakfast table days ago. 'Let's just be normal. No crying, or sorry talk. It won't help him if we make him worry about us.'

Maggie worried in private. She didn't want to let him go. Even though she knew he'd be glad to see her mother in heaven. He'd never stopped loving her mother. He'd never considered marrying again for love of her. He was not afraid of his death. But Maggie feared it. She'd miss him too much.

He'd asked Father Arnold to visit him so he could make his final peace with God while he was well enough to speak, and he'd said, 'When I go you're not to weep over me, girls. You're to be happy for me.'

That was easy for him to say. Of course she would weep.

Maggie was falling to pieces. She would not be happy to say goodbye to him; she would be bereft. She was bereft now. At night, she and Dot talked, whispering across the narrow room as they lay in their beds, about how they would cope – or, rather, not cope – without him.

They only had the cottage because of him. He earned more money in a week than the four of them did together, and Dot had not gone back to work yet, so she wasn't earning. Thinking practically, she had no idea what to do when he'd gone and the GWR clerk knocked on the door of the cottage and told them they'd have to leave it. Four women would struggle to find rooms in the same place, and they wanted to stay together. Maggie hadn't talked to Marjorie and Edith about it. But she and Dot had heard them whispering to each other in their room as she and Dot did, so perhaps they had thought of all this too.

And physically... a hole was growing wider in Maggie's chest by the minute, a dark gaping wound. The space normally filled with her father's love.

For now, though, Maggie was here and he was here, and she was doing her best to make his last hours as happy as she could.

'Why don't we sing a hymn, Dad?' Marjorie suggested. 'You always love hearing us sing. Shall we?' She looked at Dot.

Dot's answer was to start singing. 'Morning has broken...'

Maggie joined in, '...like the first morning...'

Marjorie joined in too, '...Blackbird has spoken like the first bird.'

Maggie sang in a quiet voice, as the others did, so they wouldn't disturb the other patients too much and wouldn't incite the anger of the matron. She sang for her father's ears alone, as she'd always sung for God's ears on a Sunday in the pew beside him. Their voices mingled, merged into a more pleasant sound. A thought caught in her throat with a sharp pain – she'd never hear him sing again. She looked down, reaching for his hand. The note she was singing ended with a strangled sound. His chest had not risen. There was no rattle from his lungs.

'Dot. Dad.' She looked at Dot as if she could bring him back to life. But even if she could, he was too ill to live. It was better for him. This was better for him.

But for her... The pain she'd been suppressing for days erupted in a broken scream and tears clouded out everything.

29

Violet Turner

When she walked into the church, sandwiched between Ron and her mother, Violet felt as if she'd walked into a dream. Maggie had been her best friend for so many years, so Mr Abbot had been in her life for as long.

She'd gone to the house yesterday. His coffin had been balanced on the kitchen table, open so people could say their goodbyes, and she'd joined Maggie and her sisters for the vigil last night. Sitting with him and praying for his soul.

Maggie had insisted they didn't sit in silence all night. She'd said he'd want them to tell stories, to laugh at memories. He'd hate it if his wake was sombre. So they'd talked all night and drunk some of the blackberry gin he'd made.

Violet was tired because she hadn't slept. Aching because she'd been working so hard at the factory. Heart sore and physically exhausted.

It had snowed again last night, laying a white blanket over the world. Her boots had pressed into a crisp layer seven inches deep when she'd left Maggie's at 6 a.m., leaving the first footprints in some places.

Everyone in the pews that Violet walked past was wrapped up in overcoats, scarves, gloves and hats.

Violet's mother led the way to a space at the front of the church in the pew behind the ones Maggie and her family would use.

Maggie had a lot of relatives – uncles, aunts and cousins – but the war work meant most of them had been unable to come. Everything couldn't stop just to say goodbye to one man. But there were many working men here from the GWR factory. They were dirt-stained, in working clothes, clutching flat caps, and there were a couple of hundred of them, and four or five men in bowler hats and one wearing a top hat. GWR must have agreed to let men come – either that, or they'd walked out of the iron workshop to come.

Ron had taken off his flat cap. He'd crushed it between his hands as he followed Violet along the pew to leave room at the end for others.

People continued to enter the church until there was nowhere left to sit and people stood along the south aisle.

'Ello,' Lily whispered.

'Hello,' Catherine said.

Lily and Catherine had joined the vigil last night too. They slipped into the pew now and sat on the other side of Ron.

Violet glanced across her shoulder, sensing someone looking at her. Naomi lifted a hand. She was with Dietrich. There was just enough space for Naomi and Dietrich to squeeze into the pew too. Violet and her mother shuffled up, letting everyone squeeze along.

When the organist began to play 'Morning has Broken', Violet stood up with everyone else, in a wave of movement across the church. Tight coughs and a couple of sobs progressed forward through the congregation behind Violet. Violet looked across her shoulder and saw the men from the factory carrying Mr Abbot's coffin into the church, balanced on their shoulders. There were three men on either side.

Maggie and her sisters, who were dressed in the most sombre colours they owned, walked behind the coffin.

Violet could not imagine what this felt like for Maggie, but her mother could. She reached to hold her mother's hand as the coffin was rested on wooden stands at the front of the nave.

Violet caught Maggie's eye as she turned to walk into the pew ahead of her sisters. She walked along the pew and sat in front of Violet. Violet laid a hand on Maggie's shoulder and gently squeezed. *I am here. I always will be.*

Maggie rested her fingers over Violet's and pressed down gently – *thank you* – then moved her hand away and Violet released her shoulder.

It was probably one of the longest days of Violet's life, more emotional than the day war was declared. Like Maggie and her sisters, Violet had held a tissue in her hand all night, dabbing at her eyes, and during the service tears rolled down her cheeks.

After the service, outside the church, Violet stood in the snow, her toes going numb with cold as she watched Mr Abbot's coffin committed to the freezing ground in the churchyard. Six of his friends, factory men, let the canvas straps slide through their hands, lowering the coffin evenly.

Violet hugged Maggie firmly before leaving her at the grave-side with her sisters.

As Violet walked away from the church beside her mother, she saw children in the GWR park hurling snowballs at one another and rolling giant balls to build snowmen, enjoying a moment of escape from rations and darkness.

The thought of childhood made her think of the father she'd never known. 'Where is Dad's grave, Mum?'

Her mother looked at her with shock and widening eyes.

'Did you see him buried? Did you go to his funeral? I'd like to see his grave one day.'

'No,' her mother answered. 'And I'm sorry. I don't know where his grave is. I will speak to you later, love. Goodbye.'

Her mother, like many others, including Ron, divided and walked one way or the other to go back to the factory.

Violet had swapped her shifts to come to the funeral. Catherine, Lily and Naomi had too. They'd be working through the night tonight, when last night they'd sat up beside the coffin. At least the factory wasn't cold, though. It had been cold in Maggie's house. Maggie and her sisters had decided to save the coal, now they'd lost their father's wage.

Last night, an elephant the size of Rajah, which Violet had seen once at Bristol Zoo on a day trip on the train, had sat quietly in the room between them – a great big silent thing that was never mentioned – what would Maggie and her sisters do when the GWR stopped renting the cottage to them? They lived in a foreman's cottage, they wouldn't be allowed to stay. With all the refugees flooding into England from Europe, there were not many rooms to rent, either, definitely not for four women to stay together.

Refugees boarded trains at the ports and many travelled to Swindon, where there was a good chance of work and a lower risk of Nazi bombings.

Asher was moving into Frank's vacated bed, to make room for other refugees in his lodgings, where he'd said his room would accommodate a family, at a squeeze.

Violet's mother had also returned to the factory, so Violet walked to The Glue Pot with Catherine, Lily and Naomi, to celebrate Mr Abbot's life. Maggie and her sisters arrived half an hour after everyone else. They managed to smile and laugh with everyone sharing happy memories.

When the clock on the wall chimed three times, Violet excused herself and, eyelids drooping and feet aching, she walked home and rolled into bed, not even taking off her dress, merely kicking off her shoes and stripping off her coat. She set the alarm on the little art deco clock that her mother had bought as a small luxury because she loved the shape of the numbers on the clock-face and the little bells on top. Violet curled into a ball, her hands beneath the pillow to keep them warm and the patchwork eider-down pulled up under her chin, and fell into a place where her world hadn't changed forever.

30

Lily Franklin

Lily's eyes burned, sore and dry from the dusty, hot atmosphere of Q shop, and her eyelids were heavy with the desire to sleep. She, Violet, Naomi and Catherine were working together on the pressing machine, cutting out the four-inch-wide copper bands that would be secured around the 25 pounder quick-firing high-explosive streamlined shells. They'd learned how to use all of the machinery now and moved around the line so as not to become too used to one process and make errors through loss of concentration.

The copper press was a tall machine – more than twice as tall as Lily – and they worked in a circle around it. One woman passed the sheet of copper over, one fitted it into the machine – Lily's job today – one pressed the button to set the machine into motion and one removed the cut out band and set it aside, ready for their little production line to commence the process again.

Naomi was the only one of them who was fully awake and not yawning. She hadn't sat through the vigil with Maggie last night.

Of course, Maggie hadn't come into work. But that was why they'd raised their hands to work the press for the shift, firstly because there were four of them and they could work together, and secondly because for three of them the work was seated. Only Naomi stood, turning to lift the next sheet of copper.

They talked to help stop themselves from falling asleep in their chairs. Violet had used a supposed toilet break to nip outside and smoke a fag that she'd persuaded the crane operator to let her have, with a few flirtatious words, when he'd come to move the bands they'd cut so far. Lily had been the one elected to accompany her to the toilets, and she had one quick drag because Violet said, 'It'll keep you awake,' and felt as if she was going to cough her lungs up. It tasted horrible. Tobacco was foul stuff, she'd decided.

'Everyone thinks that at first, but then you get to like how it makes you feel and, as Maggie's sister Dot would say, how it makes you look too. Men like a woman with a cigarette in her hand, and they like it when you ask them to light it for you.'

'What a lot of nonsense,' Lily had said. 'Ow can chokin or blowin smoke out of your mouth be pretty?'

Violet had laughed. 'Dot makes it look sexy, like she's a film star.'

Lily had watched Violet finish the cigarette and tried to imagine what on earth could be seen as flirtatious about it. Nothing she and Lenny had done had been like smoking a fag. Then she thought of her father smoking, his lips tugging on the cigarette end with a desperate movement almost, and him angrily tossing the butt away, and she completely rejected the whole notion of smoking being flirtatious.

'You are silly, Vi,' had been her final judgement as they'd walked back through the door of Q shop.

Lily placed the next sheet of copper into the giant press.

Catherine pressed the button and it hammered down, pressing the metal down and outward, cutting through it in one sudden, violent movement.

The cutting press lifted automatically. Violet reached forward and removed the band that had been cut and the leftover copper, setting one aside in the basket of bands they'd cut in the past hour and putting the other into a container to go back to the furnaces for smelting into another sheet.

Naomi lifted across another gleaming sheet of copper. Lily placed it just so – the position had to be perfect.

As Lily straightened up, wiping the sleeve of her blouse across her sweating forehead, Catherine pressed the button to set the machine in motion. The press thumped down with a sound that made Lily's ears ring, and the power of it shook through her thin frame as it cut the copper.

Lily yawned. Normally, being in the warm, especially when they'd come in from a snow-draped landscape, was a relief from the general life of being constantly cold due to the lack of gas and coal. But today the warmth only made her feel more like sleeping. She was dragging herself through this shift by the collar of the blouse Mrs Faraday had handed on to her. When she got home she'd collapse on the bed and not get up again until half an hour before her next shift. She was too tired to eat or drink.

Naomi handed Lily the next sheet of copper. Lily leaned forward to lay it onto the press. She settled it just right. The men who'd taught her to do this had drummed the need for precision into her as if she were as thick as a tree trunk. As she moved to straighten up and sit back away from the press, her finger caught on the square edge of the copper – or, rather, the narrow gold ring that Lenny had given her caught and was pulled off her finger easily now she'd lost weight and it was loose.

Instinctively, she reached for it, forgetting about the machine, forgetting everything but her ring. She couldn't lose her ring.

'Lily!' Catherine screamed and at the same time reached out and smacked Lily's hand out of the way.

'My ri—'

It was too late. The press slammed down hard.

Immediately, bile lurched into Lily's throat as she watched the giant press land on Catherine's hand and pull it down.

'Get help! Help!' Violet screamed.

Naomi ran off.

Catherine turned white as the snow outside, staring as the machine rose. Lily couldn't look at what was there. She turned and picked up the jumper that she'd stripped off and lain over the back of the chair, the warm jumper Lenny loaned her months ago, and wrapped it around Catherine's hand, trying to stem the pulse of blood.

'I'm sorry. God, I'm sorry.'

'It's all right,' Catherine said in an oddly calm voice, as if she didn't feel any pain at all. As if she didn't realise what had happened. 'It was an accident, that's all.' But then her eyeballs rolled backwards in their sockets until Lily only saw the whites.

Violet caught Catherine before she fell off the seat.

'Help!' Violet screamed.

'Elp!' Lily looked around her. Everyone else in the workshop was running towards them.

'Old er arm up, wrap it tight,' one of the men said. 'I'll tie my belt around it to stop the bleedin. Stop the bleedin – that's the first thing.'

'As anyone gone for the doctor?' another man asked.

It was the few men in the room who knew what to do.

'I'll run for im now,' one of the women said.

'More rags. We need clean rags. You need to keep it clean.'

Bill. One of the men who had teased Lily and gambled on her capability in the first weeks she'd been here sent everyone scurrying, taking control.

The foreman appeared on the stairs, as though he was about to shout at them all for stopping work, but Lily saw the moment he realised what had happened. He returned to his office, and through the windows she saw him call someone on the phone.

All the men knew what to do because accidents were common here.

It took half an hour for the doctor to come because he'd been asleep in his bed in Park House, not at the hospital. He unravelled all the rags and looked at Catherine's hand. A deep frown drew creases in the skin of his forehead.

Lily leaned over to look. She couldn't even recognise the flesh, bone and skin as a hand. Bile jerked up into her throat. It was her fault. It felt as if every drop of blood in her body sank to her feet.

'You all right, love?' The man beside her, Bill, wrapped his hand around her upper arm and held her on her feet.

She took a deep breath. It was Catherine who would have to live with this.

'It'll need to come off,' the doctor said to the foreman. 'Can we get the lass on a stretcher and ring for an ambulance to get her to the hospital? I'll take the hand off tonight.'

'Yes, lass,' the doctor said to Lily. 'That hand won't be of any more use to her.'

Lily looked up and met Violet's gaze, then she looked towards Naomi... Catherine was going to lose her hand and it was her fault. Lily looked blankly at Naomi as the doctor removed a small vial, a syringe and a needle from the battered leather bag that stood on the floor beside where he knelt.

'What's that?' Lily asked as he lifted Catherine's arm.

'For the pain. It will make her feel sleepy too. It's better she sleeps at the moment.'

Catherine's beautiful face, with her red lipstick and colour-shaded eyelids, looked clown-like now her skin was colourless.

'Excuse me. Excuse me.' The stretcher bearers arrived.

'Shall I come with er?' Lily asked the doctor.

'No, lass. We'll look after her. You go and tell her family.'

Lily stared at the man, helplessness sweeping over her. She didn't know who Catherine's family were, or where they lived. Somewhere in Old Town. Though she'd said, once, her dad worked for GWR.

As the men carried Catherine away, the doctor walking beside the stretcher, Lily saw something on the floor close beside where Catherine had lain.

The ring. It must have rolled across the machine and fallen off the opposite side.

Lily bent and picked it up, guilt charging at her like a raging bull as she slipped the engagement ring back onto her finger. She stared at it. It would forever now not only be the ring Lenny gave her, but the ring that had taken Catherine's hand.

Lily turned and she couldn't run out of the workshop fast enough, shoving open the outer door. When she was outside she spewed up what little there was in her stomach.

'It's all right. She'll be all right.' Violet had followed. She rubbed a hand across Lily's back as Lily straightened up and pressed a hand over her mouth.

'She won't be all right, though, will she? She's lost er and.'

31

CATHERINE PEARCE

Catherine's eyelids flickered open. The room was lit by only a small amount of electric light. The uncomfortable mattress she lay on was not the one on the bed in the room in the Faradays' cottage nor the one on the bed in her room at her parents' home. She had no idea where she was.

Nausea twisted through her stomach and a sickly feeling pressed at the back of her throat with a bitter taste. She remembered waking before now, and a man in a white coat, a doctor, pushing a needle into her arm. He'd depressed a syringe. After that she couldn't remember anything until this moment.

Her eyes became more accustomed to the dark. Black spaces developed shape and depth. She saw other beds. The outlines of other people asleep in those beds. She was in some sort of dormitory. Why on earth was she in a dormitory?

Wide awake now, she moved her hands to press down and shuffle back a—

Bile rose in her throat and she cried out as if she'd had a nightmare.

A nurse in a white uniform rushed along the centre of the

room. Catherine hadn't seen where she came from. She stared at the crêpe bandage, stained with blood and iodine, wrapped around... *She didn't have a hand.*

'Miss Pearce,' the nurse whispered. 'How are you?'

'I have no hand.' Her voice was quiet and weak as she raised the bandage-covered forearm that just ended.

'I know, dear,' the nurse whispered, answering as if it was a very simple fact.

'I have no hand,' Catherine said more strongly, speaking as though this woman had taken it away, carelessly clearing it up by accident, like a packet of cigarettes moved from a coffee table onto a mantelpiece, as though the woman might look for it and bring it back.

'Do not distress yourself.' The nurse patted Catherine's shoulder.

'I have lost my hand,' Catherine said more forcefully. *Of course I am distressed.* She closed her eyes, praying that when she opened them again she'd wake up from this nightmare.

'Is it painful? I can give you something for the pain,' the nurse whispered. 'I don't want to disturb the other patients.'

Patients... Catherine's thoughts spun.

She opened her eyes. The nurse was still here. She squeezed her eyelids closed as tightly as she could and swallowed repeatedly, fighting a desire to cry, as a dismal feeling told her this was real.

She opened her eyes again, the nurse remained.

'Do you want something for the pain, dear? I can call for the doctor to give you another injection.'

'What was the injection?'

'Pethidine. It will help—'

'I feel as though it knocked me out. I don't remember what happened. What happened?'

'You had an accident in a workshop, Miss Pearce.'

'Call me Cath. Everyone calls me Cath now.' *Pearce... Not Clifford.* The nurse knew her real name. 'Does my father know?'

'Yes, Cath. He's sat here beside your bed every afternoon. Shall I call the doctor to come and help you with the pain?'

'Every afternoon... How long have I been here?'

'For eight days.'

Catherine closed her eyes again. She had lost eight days. The only thing she could remember was the doctor injecting her. The numbness of shock became absorbed by the throb of pain from her... right... hand... Her mind told her it was her hand, but it couldn't be pain in her hand; she didn't have a hand.

'I will call the doctor and I'll fetch you a cup of mint tea. We don't have any more of the tea from India, but mint is plentiful.'

'No.' Catherine reached to touch the nurse to stop her turning away, only to see the bandaged blunt end of her arm. She couldn't hold the nurse's arm. She wouldn't be able to hold anything any more. 'No more injections,' she told the nurse. 'But I would love some mint tea, thank you.'

'And aspirin, can I bring you some aspirin at least?'

'Yes. Please.'

The pain began to thump in her arm with the pulse of her heartbeat. She had no memory of how she lost her hand. She searched her mind. She remembered the funeral. Maggie's father... Mr Abbot was dead.

Last night – not last night now – the nurse had said she'd been here a week. But Catherine remembered it as if it was last night when she'd sat around the coffin with Maggie's family.

Catherine had been tired. She remembered that. She remembered the burial. She was going back to work... She did not remember working.

After she'd taken the aspirin and drunk the tea, Catherine

laid still and quiet, staring about the room as it gradually light-ened by degrees. As much as electric light couldn't escape through the blinds, the rising sun struggled to penetrate the blackout fabric.

Catherine discovered that she had fallen asleep at some point when three nurses came to raise the blinds, calling, 'Good morn-ing, everybody! Rise and shine!' Bringing the little Railway Village hospital to life. Catherine was given more aspirin at seven, mint tea at seven thirty and buttered toast with honey at eight. A bowl of cold water, a small flannel and a towel were placed beside her bed at eight thirty and curtains were drawn around her bed, providing her with enough privacy to wash her body with her one good hand. The hospital ran like a precise clock mechanism.

As she struggled to use her left hand alone, she stared at the blood and browny-yellow iodine stains on the stubby end of the bandage, her heart and mind not able to truly believe what she could see.

The doctor arrived at ten. He felt Catherine's forehead as she remained upright, leaning back against a couple of pillows, in the bed. He held her left wrist, pressing on her artery with his fingers and looking at a pocket watch to count how many times her heart beat. She stared at the ring on her finger, the solitaire diamond that held so many memories and so much love. The ring she touched with her right hand a dozen times a day. The doctor moved to the other side of the bed and pressed his fingers into the pit underneath her right arm, then looked again at his pocket watch and counted.

'If you would open the neck of your nightdress, Miss Pearce, I will just listen to your heart.'

She released a couple of buttons with a shaking left hand. He breathed on the metal end of his stethoscope and rubbed it with the heel of his palm, warming it, then pressed it against Catherine's skin, over her heart. He listened for a minute or two, then moved it to the other side and listened to her lungs.

'Lean forward please?' He listened through her nightdress on her back.

'I think you are fit and healthy in all regards other than losing your hand, Miss Pearce. Would you like something for the pain?'

'I can manage with aspirin,' she answered. 'You can save the more significant help for those injured in Europe who will need it more than me.'

'Good lass,' the doctor said. 'That's it, a good British spirit.'

'How did I lose my hand?' she asked. 'I don't remember.'

'In the machinery. It was badly crushed. I couldn't save it. I had to amputate.'

He'd cut it off. 'Can I see my parents?'

'It is not visiting time I'm afraid.'

'Can I go home? If I am well, can I go home?' Her only thought was for the comfort of her childhood home. Somewhere private, with the people she loved. Her father had feared this would happen, though. Would he accept her home now he'd been proven right?

'Certainly. If you think you are ready. I will ask Nurse Smith to call Mr Pearce.'

'Thank you.'

As he walked away, Catherine closed her eyes and a tear escaped. Her right hand rose to wipe it away... More tears escaped as she used her left hand.

* * *

'Hello, darling.'

A man's voice woke her.

Something touched Catherine's left arm, pulling her from a

dream in which Hitler was flying an aeroplane himself and grinning as he dropped bombs on Swindon. There were explosions, flames reaching into the sky licking up towards the stars, making the night bright, though the air tasted hot and acrid—

'Catherine.'

A woman's voice came from her other side. Catherine felt as though she were trapped beneath the rubble of bricks, mortar and roof tiles, a heavy mountain on top of her, crushing her chest and her right arm.

'Catherine.' The woman said her name again.

Catherine knew the voice. She opened her eyes. 'Mama.' She looked into her mother's eyes, but behind her mother she could still see the disaster she'd dreamed, and she could feel the pressure on her arm too, to the point where pain rolled her stomach over and became a desire to be sick.

Her mother stood on one side of the bed. 'We have the car, and your coat and shoes.'

'And blankets, and towels, and a chamber pot in case you feel sick,' her father added.

Catherine's mind left her dream entirely and remembered her reality. She was in the GWR employees' hospital in the Railway Village and a surgeon had cut off her right hand.

Her father's expression was not angry. It did not say that he had told her this would happen. All she saw in his eyes was concern.

'Is this a rescue committee?'

He smiled. 'I suppose it is. Are you ready to come home? Do you feel well enough to walk out to the car?' She had not heard this tone in his voice for many years, not since she was a child.

'I am,' she answered, sitting upright.

That was a mistake. She'd sat up too quickly. The room spun and nausea grasped at the back of her throat. She lifted her right arm to press her right hand over her mouth, and faced the stained bandage. She covered her mouth with her left hand.

The nurse had told her the dizzy spells were because she'd lost a lot of blood.

'Do you need a pot?' her mother asked. 'Are you sure you are well enough—'

'I want to go home,' Catherine answered. The desire was desperate. She wanted to be in her own bed. She felt as though if she was home when she laid in bed, her right hand would rest on the bed covers, and everything would be normal.

'Turn yourself to sit on the edge of your bed, I'll buckle your shoes and we'll help you put your coat on over your nightdress.'

Catherine nodded and turned more slowly to do as her father suggested. As she did so she saw the doctor and nurse walking towards her, passing the other people sitting upright in their beds. The doctor's quick stride held a purpose Catherine did not like the look of. His expression made her think he was going to say she couldn't leave. But he had agreed earlier. She needed to escape this place. With the drugs and dark windows, it felt like a prison, not somewhere that was helping her but torturing her.

'Miss Pearce,' he said. 'You will have to visit a nurse to have your wound rebandaged twice a week.'

'I will organise that,' her mother said.

'And you are to rest your arm, keep it up high on pillows beside you.'

'She will do so,' her father answered.

For the first time in years, Catherine was completely malleable and accepting of them answering for her and directing her. She couldn't think for herself today. She just wanted to be home... Home was everything. To be home in her bed would feel like having reached the peak of Mount Everest.

The coat her father produced was not Catherine's coat, but her mother's satin-lined fur coat.

Her father supported her forearm firmly as she walked out to the car, as though it were her legs that were injured. But it was a cold day. A hoar frost clung to the rooftops and the tree branches as well as coating the pavements. Her mother carried the few possessions Catherine must have arrived with, and the towel and blanket. There had been a layer of snow on the day of the accident.

She had taken more aspirin before leaving the hospital, but as the car bumped across uneven areas of the tarmac road, pain jolted from the wound and raced all the way up her right arm. She gritted her teeth, breathed deeply and stared ahead. Her brothers had told her often that she had a high tolerance for pain. They'd tested it when she was young. She did not give in to pain easily. She would not give in to this.

When the car arrived at the house, her father parked beside the kerb outside the front door. He climbed out, walked around and opened the front passenger door for her, holding it wide as she climbed out, while her mother opened the rear passenger door and raced up the steps to open the front door for her.

She was not really an invalid – she had full use of her legs – but their fussing felt good today. She did not need it physically, but emotionally, yes.

Within half an hour she was tucked up in her own bed. The fire had been lit in the room with a rash use of the family's coal and she was sitting upright, leaning against a stack of soft feather pillows, her damaged arm on another stack of pillows and a warm cup of proper Darjeeling tea, with a curl of steam rising from it, standing on a saucer on the bedside chest beside her left hand. She had spurned these luxuries for weeks, because they made her feel ashamed in front of others who didn't have them, but today she rested back and relished every comfort, tears gathering behind her closed eyelids.

'Don't forget to drink your tea before you nod off,' her father said. 'Don't waste it, darling.'

'Oh, no.' She opened her eyes, turned and lifted the cup to her lips. It felt cack-handed to do so with her left hand. Awkward and clumsy.

Her father stood beside the bed watching as she drank, his eyes swimming.

Catherine knew him well enough to know he must be thinking – *I told her the workshops were dangerous.* But he did not stand in front of her saying, I told you so, as he could be doing. His eyes presented his distress – he was upset over her pain and for her.

'Can you I bring you anything else, Catherine? One of your mother's magazines, or a book to read to distract your thoughts? Or a piece of cake? We have some apple cake.'

'I'm sorry,' she said.

'For what?'

'For putting you through this, Papa. I know it is harder to watch someone in pain than to be the person who is hurt because there is nothing you can do to help. I must learn how to live with this.' She raised her bandaged stump, then let it rest back on the eiderdown. 'And you must be cursing me.'

He shook his head. 'No. I never curse. You should know that.' His eyebrows lifted in the sort of characterful expression he'd used when she was a child to make her laugh.

She smiled.

'May I remain here and sit with you for a minute?'

'Please do.'

He sighed as he sat in the chair that had been placed beside her bed. 'Tell me, Catherine, do you regret working with the heavy machines?'

She did not answer immediately because she had not dared to ask herself that question. She did not want to regret what she'd done. Her gaze fell to the place where her hand should be. In her mind she curled her fingers and formed a fist, then opened her hand again, turned it and looked at her palm. She looked up at her father. 'A hand is very little to give for the sake of beating Hitler and stopping his Nazis in their tracks.'

'That is what I thought you would say,' her father answered. 'So I presumed there was no point at all in returning to the conversation about whether you should have been there in the first place. What has happened, has happened. You knew the risks. You made your choice. But Catherine, I would never be happy to see you hurt. I love you. You know that. Everything I say to you or do is only because I love you. I tried to stop you working there because I love you, and now I am here to help you because I love you.'

It was her turn to sigh. 'I know.'

'Shall I remain here and sit with you for a while longer?' he offered.

'No. But thank you, Papa. I will drink this tea and then sleep.'

'We have some soup for lunch and fresh bread, so you can eat it when you like. I have put a bell beside you so you can call us and don't have to get out of bed unless you want to.'

Catherine looked at the clock on the bedside chest. It was twelve forty-five. 'Don't you have to work?'

'Not today, darling. As I said, I am here for you today.'

'Thank you.' The people her father worked with knew about his angry finger and fist, but they did not know this man – the father only her family knew. When it was right, he could love stubbornly too.

He left the room and she drank the tea, her railway sisters on her mind. *What must they be thinking? Did they know who she was now? Were they concerned for her? They must be...* A memory returned. They had been working on a copper press together. An image of the machine dropping to cut and bend a sheet of copper raced through her mind's eye. But she could still not remember how her hand must have been trapped.

32

Lily Franklin

Lily nervously climbed the broad shallow steps of Mr and Mrs Pearce's stairs, tilting her head back to look up at the extravagant plasterwork on the ceiling two floors above.

'Catherine is navigating quite a bit of pain, so she may become tired,' Mrs Pearce said. She was dressed in a perfectly tailored fern-green skirt and jacket, with a string of pearls draped about her neck. 'And, as you know, she's a trooper so she won't tell you if it becomes too much. You will have to bow out if you notice her flagging.'

Violet and Maggie climbed the staircase in front of Lily, Naomi climbing beside her, as they all followed Mrs Pearce upstairs to see Catherine in her bedroom.

'This house is huge,' Naomi whispered to Lily.

'It's like a palace,' Lily whispered back. She thought Lenny's parents' house was magnificent, this was twice, or perhaps three times, the size of that, with pretty details and furnishings and polished wood everywhere. 'Fancy movin out of this...' Lily gestured with a hand.

The only truth Lily remembered Catherine telling her was that her father worked in the factory. Yes, he did. He ran the factory in Swindon. Lily and Violet had gone to the hospital the day after the accident and asked to see Catherine Clifford, only to be told there was no Catherine Clifford there.

'The woman whose and was crushed,' Lily had said in a panic, fearing she'd died.

'You mean Catherine Pearce?'

Lily had looked at Violet, her mouth dropping open. *Had Catherine married and not told them?*

'But I cannot let you in. Her parents are with her. If they leave before visiting hours are over, then you can come in and see Miss Pearce.'

They'd waited for as long as they could outside in the slushy snow. Lily's fingertips had gone numb inside her woollen gloves, and her feet had become solid blocks of ice.

Violet had looked at her watch in the end and said, 'Our shift starts in fifteen minutes, Lily, we need to go.'

Lily had let herself be torn away, but as they'd left she'd seen two people come out. A man wearing a suit with a black tailcoat and a top hat, and a woman in a brown fur coat. She'd watched them and whispered, 'Violet, do you think they're Catherine's parents? She said er father worked for GWR... Ee must be a chief!'

Violet had shrugged off Lily's words, but she'd found out, by asking Ron, that there was a Mr Pearce among the senior managers in the factory. Mr Pearce the chief clerk. Then, as the rumours spread across the site that there had been an accident and Mr Pearce's daughter was hurt, they knew that Cath, Catherine Clifford, was really Catherine Pearce.

The Faradays had discovered the unravelling lie at the same time Lily had. They hadn't known who Catherine really was either. Lily, struggling to understand why anyone would turn their back on a life like that, had asked Mrs Faraday, 'Why do you think Cath would lie about who she was?'

'She'd said she wanted to help the war effort. That is still true, and I suppose she must have thought we would treat her differently if we knew.'

'I wouldn—'

'But we don't know what she's experienced. I've been told she was working as a clerk previously. She must have had a good reason to use a different name.'

All Lily knew now was that she missed Catherine living in the Faradays' house and missed walking back and forth to work with her. Her friends didn't know why Catherine had reached towards the machine after she'd pressed the button, though they had seen her knock Lily's hand aside. They didn't know Catherine had lost her hand because of Lily. Lily had ruined Catherine's life because she'd been careless. She should have concentrated harder. How was Catherine going to live without her hand?

Lily's heartbeat thumped quicker with each step she climbed.

Would Catherine remember? And if she didn't, should Lily confess? She had confessed to Father Arnold. He'd told her God had forgiven her, but she must ask her friend for forgiveness.

'Just here,' Mrs Pearce said, holding her hand out towards a door that stood ajar.

Lily was last to enter the room. It was wonderfully warm, and everything from the furniture to the carpet and curtains was colourful and pretty – expensive luxuries that Lily could not even have dreamed of. She looked at Catherine. The others surrounded her. She was not in bed, but sitting in a chair near the fire, her damaged arm resting on the arm of the chair. The wound looked freshly bandaged, wrapped in criss-crossed off-white crêpe.

Violet hugged Catherine's shoulders and kissed her cheek, then Maggie, then Naomi. Then Catherine looked at Lily, as if she expected her to step forward. Freed from fear by the kindness in Catherine's eyes, when she was the sick one, Lily did step forward. She bent and wrapped her arms around Catherine's neck.

'I'm so sorry,' she whispered in her ear. 'You know it was my fault, don't you?'

Catherine patted Lily's back with her left hand and pressed a kiss on her cheek, then she whispered back, 'Was it? I don't remember. It was a horrible accident, obviously.'

Lily hugged Catherine tighter for a moment, then released her.

Catherine looked around her friends. 'I am so glad to see you all.' Tears gathered in her eyes.

'I think we are happier to see you,' Maggie said. 'We thought you were a goner at one point. There was a lot of blood, Cath. How do you feel?'

'It hurts.' She raised the bandaged arm. 'But I am getting used to it, and men in the military are suffering much worse, so I have told myself I will not complain.'

'You don't need to be brave,' Lily ventured. 'You can shout at me. The metal pulled my ring off. I reached for it, an you knocked my and aside an trapped yours.'

Catherine looked at Lily. The other girls gasped. Lily lifted her chin, waiting for Catherine to be angry and to tell her to get out of her beautiful house, and for all her friends to turn their backs on her.

'Lily,' Catherine said. 'Don't blame yourself for an accident. I am sure, even though I don't remember it, that you did not deliberately lose your ring.' Catherine shook her head, as though she shook a thought away.

'Accidents happen to all of us, Lily,' Violet said.

'You must have been upset. Why didn't you tell us?' Naomi asked.

'You didn't do it on purpose,' Maggie reassured her. 'No one would have blamed you, if you'd told us.'

Lily breathed and felt the air reach to the bottom of her lungs for the first time in days.

'It's me who owes all of you an apology,' Catherine said. 'I'm sorry I lied about who I am – that was not an accident. You have every right to be angry with me. But I kept it secret to avoid being treated differently because of my father's position in the factory, and then one thing led to another and I became too deeply involved in my fictional self and there was never a right moment to tell you the truth.'

'We certainly don't care about that,' Violet replied, pulling a chair closer to Catherine.

Naomi sat on the edge of the bed. 'We would not have thought of you any differently.'

'We've always known you're posh anyway,' Maggie said, and walked across the room to fetch a stool to sit on, one that stood beneath a dressing table.

'I still think of you like a sister,' Lily said. 'Will that be odd for your father?'

'No. Why? Because you live in a railway cottage?' Catherine answered, as Lily sat on the edge of the bed next to Naomi. 'We are a railway family first and foremost. My ancestors were some of the first to live in those cottages. My father was born in one too, and he was lucky he had the opportunity to go to university and progress.'

'An with me bein *coloured*.' Lily spat out the word that others used to label her as different.

'No. My father is not a bigot, Lily, and since this war began he's become more broadminded still. He didn't want me to work with the machines, that's why I moved out of home – not because he didn't want me to work at all, but because it is dangerous.' She raised her bandaged arm, showing it to them. 'He was right. But instead of cursing me, he is now proud.' She smiled. 'I am a sort of martyr to him, I think.'

'Tea, ladies!'

Lily expected to see a servant at the bedroom door, but it was Mrs Pearce who carried the tray.

Life had changed so much since the war began, but not everything was a change for the worse. Lily looked around at the women who meant more to her than just friends. She had found these women and a new way of life.

She accepted a cup of tea and a slice of apple cake.

Who knew what tomorrow would bring, or the day after that, or the one after that? She thought about the tea leaves in Catherine's cup, which she'd read months ago. Loss... Separation...

But whatever happened on any day in the future, Lily knew one thing – Catherine would have these women as her Great Western Railway family, just as Lily did.

These women were special.

33

Lily Franklin

The birds were busy singing in the trees, with their best spring courting voices, as Lily walked through the park to the lodge. She was still exhausted, but the longer, warmer days were making life feel a little easier.

'Straighten your damn back, boy!'

She glanced over at the group of about a hundred men being drilled by an ex-army major on the lawn in the centre of the park.

'Stiffen up your shoulders and stick out your thumbs. You need to show the Nazis you mean business if you're going to stop them attacking the factory.'

She smiled to herself as she passed them, thinking of Lenny's opinion about the need to stick out a thumb.

These drills took place daily now, when the men in GWR's Volunteer Guard had finished their shifts in the factory. It was a bit of a game really. They used dummy rifles carved from wood, and they had no uniforms; they were dressed in working clothes.

'Their kit is coming,' Mr Faraday had said, when Lily had joked about them over dinner one night.

She'd told Lenny about the tin-pot army, as she'd nicknamed them, in a letter. She knew their games in the park would make him laugh. But he'd not replied yet.

'Left... Right... Left...!' the ex-major shouted.

That meant they were going to parade around the village.

Lily stopped. They'd need to walk in front of her. She waited, hands held in the pockets of her dungarees as the men marched past. A couple of them looked her way, and she nodded to say hello if she knew them.

Then she caught John Finch's eye.

Bastard, she swore in her head, as he grinned.

The grin was a mean threat, not a nice hello. Every time she saw him now, she felt her hackles rise like a cat's. The men's boots paced on the tarmac road, a little out of time. It was a clutter of sound rather than a drumbeat.

The last of them passed and she ran on, rushing to reach the gardener's lodge.

She used the back door as she'd always done, though now she never knocked. She turned the handle, pushed it open and was greeted by the smell of a rabbit stew and the sound of Mrs Faraday singing a popular song, her hips swaying along to the tune as she peeled potatoes.

'...begin the beguine...' she sang, without realising Lily had walked in.

'Ello.' Lily made Mrs Faraday aware of her presence as her eyes spotted letters on the table. She put her lunch tin and flask down beside them.

'Hello, Lily, love,' Mrs Faraday said. 'We've heard from Leonard.'

'I can see. Can I take them upstairs an read them?'

All three letters were addressed to her.

'Yes, of course. Go along. Dinner will be ready in an hour.'

Lily bent double, untied the laces of her boots, took them off and left them beside the back door. She had been so glad of these boots the last couple of months, and Lenny's essential gifts stood proudly beside the back door every night.

The soles of her socks slipping on the floor, she ran out of the kitchen and upstairs, the thin paper letters crumpling in her hand.

Despite her dirty, dusty dungarees, she threw herself onto the bed and tore open the envelopes, then read them in date order.

Like Art, he'd faced fighting. He'd been sent to protect Finland, but now Finland had surrendered to the Soviets. Most of the men and women in the factory thought that was a good thing, that peace might follow. But the last of Lenny's letters was only half a page and it finished bluntly.

We're retreating. I've got to pack everything up as fast as I can. I'm not meant to be writing, but I thought if I scribbled this quickly, I can get all my letters into the mail that's leaving now. Then if I can't send you anything for a while, you'll know why.

The bloody Finns betrayed us. They've given up and signed a treaty. The Soviets have taken some of us prisoners. The army pushed so many soldiers forward to help the Finns. The bastards. We've been promised that Britain and France have agreed they will never surrender.

Now we are fighting with the Norwegians. I'm going to—

The place he must have mentioned had been drawn over with a thick black pen. He'd told her their letters were being read.

I'm not sure when I'll be able to write or send the next letter. We're going to be marching for days, they said. Unless they can find space on a train. There are hundreds of GWR trains that they've shipped over here.

I love you, Lily. I wish I could kiss and cuddle you in bed. Those nights feel like years ago.

I have to go.

I love you,

xxx

Your Lenny

She pressed all his letters, the paper that had been in his hands, against her chest. It was the only way she could be close to him. Her throat tightened with suffocating emotions. She'd hoped the war would be over soon. It didn't sound like it was anywhere near over from his letter. It didn't sound as though he would be coming home, but marching into more danger.

What did 'retreating' mean? Were the allied forces losing?

The other day, the papers had published a story saying that people had been killed in a place right at the top of Scotland called Scapa Flow, in the Orkney Islands. She'd never heard of the place before. But for some reason the Luftwaffe had dropped bombs up there and they'd killed the first British civilians, for no reason that anyone could tell.

Mr Faraday had said he didn't think the war was going to be over soon. He said that everyone was just saying what they hoped for, when there was no likelihood of it.

If the army were retreating on the continent, what would happen next?

ACKNOWLEDGEMENTS

Firstly, thank you to the employees of Swindon Borough Council and the volunteers who manage and support the work of the **Steam Museum.** It was one of the fabulous preserved objects, and one of the stories the museum staff had captured in time, that inspired this series. To find out which ones and discover more real stories you will have to follow my **Jane Lark blog** at https://janelark.blog. It has been lovely getting to know some of the people who manage the museum archives. The GWR monthly magazines have given me some super stories – like the mouse that workers thought was a spy, which was so funny I had to squeeze it in.

Thank you to the volunteers who give their time, knowledge and commitment to support the **Swindon Heritage Preservation Charity.** Especially to those who work in the **Railway Village Museum.** This small museum is a foreman's cottage that has been preserved at a point in time. It's furnished as a Victorian property but even so, being able to see inside a period cottage has been very valuable to enable me to describe scenes set inside the cottages. You can find out more about the cottage at 34 Faringdon Road here: https://mechanics-trust.org.uk/MUSEUM. I also want to thank the volunteers who lead the walking tours around the site, and tell some wonderful stories that bring the history of the area back to life so beautifully.

Another not-for-profit volunteer-led organisation I want to thank is the **Rodbourne Community History Group**, with a particular thank you to Gordon Shaw. The knowledge of this group has supported the development of my understanding of the GWR railway works themselves, and how daily life operated inside the works. I joined Gordon's walking tour a couple of years ago – this was around what is now the Swindon Designer Outlet Village – and he pointed out all the historical architecture and equipment still in place. He shared stories of working life in the factory while we were surrounded by Christmas shoppers oblivious to the deep history in the area, just enjoying a day out and letting that history live on today.

Last but not least, as always, thank you to **you**, my readers, who continue to support my books by telling others about them, posting reviews and encouraging the growth of my readership so I can continue writing for you. I appreciate every new reader you bring to my books. Without you there would be no need for books. So, if you have enjoyed this new step I have taken into historical fiction, please log on to your online bookseller and post a review.

Thank you.

ABOUT THE AUTHOR

Jane Lark is a writer of compelling, passionate and emotionally charged fiction filled with diverse characters. She is an international bestselling author of both historical fiction and psychological thrillers, and a finalist in British Fiction Industry awards.

Sign up to Jane Lark's mailing list for news, competitions and updates on future books.

Visit Jane's website: www.janelark.co.uk

Follow Jane on social media here:

X x.com/JaneLark

facebook.com/Janelarkauthor

instagram.com/jane.lark

youtube.com/@janelark3537

BB bookbub.com/authors/jane-lark

Sixpence Stories

Introducing Sixpence Stories!

Discover page-turning
historical novels from your
favourite authors, meet new
friends and be transported
back in time.

Join our book club
Facebook group

https://bit.ly/SixpenceGroup

Sign up to our
newsletter

https://bit.ly/SixpenceNews

Boldwood

Boldwood Books is an award-winning fiction publishing company seeking out the best stories from around the world.

Find out more at www.boldwoodbooks.com

Join our reader community for brilliant books, competitions and offers!

Follow us
@BoldwoodBooks
@TheBoldBookClub

Sign up to our weekly deals newsletter

https://bit.ly/BoldwoodBNewsletter

Printed in Great Britain
by Amazon